THE
SHADOW
CRUCIBLE

THE
SHADOW
CRUCIBLE

T.M. LAKOMY

SELECTBOOKS, INC.
NEW YORK

This edition published by SelectBooks, Inc.

For information address SelectBooks, Inc., New York, New York.

First Edition

ISBN 978-1-59079-414-2

Library of Congress Cataloging-in-Publication Data

Names: Lakomy, T. M. (Tamara M.), author.
Title: The shadow crucible : the blind god / T. M. Lakomy.
Description: First edition. | New York : SelectBooks, 2017.
Identifiers: LCCN 2016039483 | ISBN 9781590794142 (paperback)
Subjects: LCSH: Human beings--Fiction. | Good and evil--Fiction. |
Apotheosis
Fiction. | Redemption--Fiction. | Imaginary wars and battles--Fiction. |
GSAFD: Fantasy fiction. | Horror fiction.
Classification: LCC PR6112.A387 S53 2017 | DDC 823/.92--dc23 LC record
available at https://lccn.loc.gov/2016039483.

Text design by Pauline Neuwirth, Neuwirth & Associates, Inc.

Manufactured in the United States of America

10 9 8 7 6 5 4 3 2 1

To my beloved mother, Stephanie Lakomy, and my love, David Solomon. Without their unwavering support, I would never have found the strength to finish writing, nor to believe in myself. And to my furry children, Heeba and Weezou, for their unconditional love.

I would like to also dedicate this book to Agnieszka Kurzak, my dear grandmother.

· CONTENTS ·

· ACKNOWLEDGMENTS ·

I WOULD LIKE TO THANK MY EDITOR, MOLLY STERN, FOR ALL THE hard work and patience she put into *The Shadow Crucible*. Without her help and astute mind, this book wouldn't be what it is. I would like to express my deepest gratitude.

I would like to thank everyone who made this process happen, and all the great people who helped me grow on my journey. Elayne Bines, you're one of them, and all the Lakomy family, who are as tough as nails.

And to all those who didn't believe in me, you just made me work harder to reach my goals, so keep up the good work.

THE
SHADOW
CRUCIBLE

PROLOGUE

If I rolled the dice carved out of my weathered bone
And offered of my blood the libation to the fane
When even the reaper's mockery forsakes me alone
My own clangorous thoughts are the last to remain

"STRAIN YOUR EARS—DO YOU HEAR THAT? IT SOUNDS LIKE HUMAN voices, listen." The demon shook Estella gently. "Estella, listen! I need your wits about you, there is no time for dallying in sleepiness."

Estella's back stiffened and her cloudy eyes sharpened as she began to pick up the faint sounds of weeping in the humid air. She nodded at the demon who, with a sigh of relief, grabbed her arm, pressing her forwards.

"Don't touch the walls, their magic is stronger than you can combat. And be vigilant, we are approaching human activity—and for the worse I deem."

Fear pressed against her heart with each step as the echoes of human misery became more audible. The source of the lamentation soon became visible under the eerie light of dozens of candles flickering in sconces. There were rows upon rows of them—men and women and children, bound by their ankles and necks to the walls with chains. They had barely enough room to maneuver to nearby chamber pots, and their raw necks were sore and bloodied with the stain of blood extending down their chests. The miasma of human waste mingled with unwashed bodies, assaulting their senses. Estella retched involuntarily, nearly leaning against the wall for support before the demon seized her, yanking her back.

"Fool of a woman! You want to end up chained like they are? Look at what they have done to them, look closer!"

As he shoved her toward a row of men and women she tripped, hitting the ground painfully. They cowered in fear at the unexpected noise, dropping the quills and parchments they had been holding. Estella froze in horror as she looked more closely at the prisoners. Where their eyes should have been were empty sockets, carelessly bandaged with filthy linens. Infected pus mingled with blood, and their mouths hung open with thirst.

"Give us water, we cannot write any longer!" came the cracked, beseeching voice of an old man. He was filthily clad in sackcloth, and his sparse beard sagged against his unresponsive child as he sobbed to himself like a helpless infant.

"We cannot write any longer, have mercy for God's sake!" A woman's shrill cry resounded over Estella, and soon they were all reaching for her, grabbing blindly and begging.

Estella covered her mouth with her hand and threw herself at their chains desperately.

INTO A SPIDER'S WEB

But the reign of horror is deeper than knowledge's reach
And the extent of the darkness is a seed that burgeoned well
Woven with the fabric of your secret code and
the melody of your speech
As a vine leaning for support, bound to an inextricable spell

CARRIAGES HASTENED ACROSS THE STREETS, THE RAIN HAMMERING the muddied ground as peasants and lesser nobles rushed around on the business of the day. The leaden sky reflected the sour moods and grim faces of those below, while the bitter wind lashed at exposed hands and dashed rain into eyes. Only the vendors remained, advertising their goods from their stalls and shielding their eyes from the downpour. Nobles caught in the deluge hurled insults at carriage drivers as they sped by, splattering mud on their refined garments. On a miserable autumn day such as this, decorum and deference were left to drown in the rain.

He had arrived that afternoon, his black cloak trimmed with silver and fastened by a serpentine clasp shielding him from the merciless wind. The cloak was lined with royal blue and every now and then a flash of pure, vibrant color would leap in a sudden gust of wind amid the dismal scenery of London. The sound of his black kid leather boots as they struck the cobblestones was inaudible amid the cacophony of the street.

On another, more temperate day, he would have been something to stare at. Foreign and striking, he radiated power. The sigils that flashed from the silver rings on his fingers marked him as a Templar, and the head of his order. His long, dark hair was bound in a ponytail, and his piercing, ice-grey eyes were unnaturally deep and frosty. He kept his eyes averted as he moved through the crowd, though he absentmindedly flipped through the people's thoughts as they passed him, reading in their minds the mundane cares that occupied their existence. Only when a passerby jostled against him unwittingly would a bluish spout of fire kindle in his eyes, startling them away as they stammered apologies.

"None empty, my lord." A hunched man walking ahead of the grey-eyed man stopped abruptly as he straightened his shoulders and laid down his master's heavy luggage. Clad in brown suede and leathers, he looked incongruous and wet as he turned around to face his master. Even through the heavy haze of the rain he could feel his master's wrath. The grey-eyed man nodded, turning swiftly to look through the crowd—but still there was no sign of a vacant carriage.

"Night will be descending soon, and I don't fancy walking further in this unsightly place." His tone was laced with irritation and he gestured with his head perfunctorily towards the street. "Shall we stop a carriage and demand politely to share?" he suggested, his eyes glinting with dark humor.

"I doubt that would avail us anything, my lord. These people aren't of the sharing type."

"Then I suggest we get walking again, Elmer," he sighed, reining in his anger and flashing an apologetic smile as he patted Elmer sympathetically on the back.

Dusk came rapidly and without omen. The light failed from murky grey to reddish brown, but the rain had abated and the wind also, leaving only the lingering cold and frost to inflict misery upon the walkers. Many people congregated now in the inns and taverns they passed. The warm, inviting fires burned merrily within, snatches of laughter emerging each time a door opened. But nothing was suitable for the grey-eyed foreigner. Innkeepers were now at their doors enticing customers with promises of warm beds and delicious meals.

"Why don't you two fine lords come in and taste my hospitality?" A grinning, toothless innkeeper detached himself from the door of his inn to bar the travelers' way. He was a round-bellied and good-natured man with shrewd, calculating eyes.

"I doubt anything you have would suit me, old father," the grey-eyed man smiled.

"Oh, but please try me. These parts are rough at night, and two fine looking men such as yourselves would do better to be indoors." The innkeeper's tone was serious now, and genuine.

The grey-eyed man considered him thoughtfully. He was right—the night could prove to be dangerous for them if they were left out in the cold at the mercy of whatever brigands ruled this part of the town. It would be better not to take any chances tonight, as Elmer was tired and so was he.

"I won't take a room in your inn, but I would reward you handsomely for showing me somewhere befitting my position, somewhere clean and of good reputation."

The innkeeper seemed to be in an internal dilemma as he frowned wordlessly to himself. He looked down and fiddled with a length of beaded necklace protruding from his pocket before speaking.

"I know somewhere," he finally said. "It's a good place, but begging your pardon, you are the ones I need to know are of good character and won't harm the lady that owns it. She is nobility but runs homes for the needy. Sometimes to fund her orphanages she will accept lodgers, but only of the highest character." The innkeeper lifted his eyes defiantly, and it was apparent that whoever this lady was, he was particularly fond of her.

The grey-eyed man bowed cordially. "I am no renegade foreigner, but a count, and though my name and title are of little worth in this time and hour, I promise you that I shall treat whoever shelters me for the night generously."

The innkeeper nodded appreciatively, then bustled back into his inn. Five minutes later, he reemerged with a disheveled looking child.

"This is my boy, Roy," the innkeeper said, puffing out his chest proudly. "He will escort you to your lodgings."

"Have no fear," the count reassured him, "we are men of our word, and your boy is safe with us." He pushed his cloak aside to reveal a long sword in a silver and white gem scabbard. The innkeeper nodded and slapped his boy on the back towards the two. Then, bowing profusely, he wobbled back into his inn and closed the door a bit too firmly behind him.

"My lords, follow me, Roy at your service," the boy beckoned.

"Tell us more about this mysterious lady," the count said as they walked.

Roy lifted his head smiling and made a detour, pointing with his chubby fingers left, past a few taverns and bakeries, then onto a cleaner, higher-leveled road.

"She's named Estella but we call her Maria Estella or Stella Maris, like the saint. She's the daughter of Duke Raymond Delcour, you know the one who married the Portuguese contessa. The contessa died and Estella came here as a child, so I heard, and Duke Raymond brought her up, and then he passed too. That's why she's so pious, they say. Many of the nobles hate her work with the poor, but Mother says they can't say a thing because the convents and clergy love her. Papa said when she dies she could become a saint!" Roy turned his head to face the count, his green eyes gleaming fervently.

Their steps were now pressing into a wealthier quarter. Elaborate statues flanked large mahogany doors and the poor, clad in rags, were hard at work sweeping the streets clear.

"So what does she look like, this Estella?" Elmer asked, tearing his eyes away uncomfortably from a little ragged girl with bare feet who was sweeping dead leaves and litter nearby. The count tapped her shoulder as he passed, and a glint of gold flashed briefly in her hands, which she rapidly concealed in her garments, stifling a faint gasp.

"God bless you, kind master," she breathed.

"You will see," Roy smiled in response to Elmer's question as he led them down a snaking alley.

Emerging into a wide courtyard, they stopped abruptly in front of a well-kept manor house with large windows and stone walls covered in climbing rose and ivy. Little, curious faces poked out of a doorway held ajar in the young night. Roy pushed through the open door, casually brushing past the children and leading the way in with the two following suit. They passed a vast corridor flanked with sconces revealing the pale glimmer of a crystal chandelier suspended from the ceiling.

"What are you doing here Roy?" a little girl drawled, following them as she held her doll protectively.

"Errands, Dolly." Roy's tone was suave for his age and Dolly smiled, revealing missing milk teeth.

Then turning to point at the two guests, she asked, "And these are new friends for Mother Estella?"

Roy nodded. Upon reaching the end of the corridor, they turned left towards a large hall with a crackling fire. Large paintings cluttered the walls and the strong, exotic scent of musk and sandalwood permeated the air. There were heavy tapestries, deep red and embroidered with gold, and the well-polished floors were scattered with an array of comfortable armchairs, poofs, and cushions. Amid the cozy disorder, a vast table extended across the length of the hall. Silver chandeliers sparkled and mirrored the dancing flames, and a large velvet armchair stood near the fire with gold painted claws.

"Sit here, I'll go fetch Mother Estella," said Dolly, gesturing towards the chairs. "What shall I tell her you want? She doesn't like to be disturbed this late, you know."

The count seated himself in a plum velvet armchair while Elmer deposited the luggage on the floor with a sigh of relief.

"Tell the mistress of the house I have been directed here to seek shelter for the night. If she can be so kind as to show us what she has to offer . . . though at this tardy hour I doubt I would decline anything she has." His eyes swept over the halls thoroughly with unconcealed appreciation. "I would pay handsomely, of course."

As Dolly nodded and left them, the count pulled a leather pouch from beneath his cloak, and leaning towards Roy beckoned him forwards.

"Give this to your papa for me," he said, drawing out two gold coins. "I think I will like this house already, it feels . . . appropriate." Roy fixed the gold with rounded eyes, extending his hand almost reverently to grasp them. Then grinning wildly he made a large theatrical bow, dimples showing in his suddenly elated face.

"You won't regret your choice my lords, have a sweet, sweet night!" And he departed in a flash.

Faint footsteps resounded from somewhere upstairs, then softly descended a distant staircase. With measured, haughty steps, the lady of the manor approached the hall. And though the count was seldom impressed by anything, he felt a slight tingling of trepidation

Finally Estella made her appearance. Upright and supple, she strode across the hall with the grace of an eastern dancer. The candle she held refracted its wan light on the many rings glinting on her fingers, golden with rubies and opals. Even from a distance the count could see the smoldering fire of her eyes, betraying an almost feline ferocity. He was troubled instantly, for this was no simple English rose. Nothing about this woman was tame, and she radiated poorly concealed power.

Estella swiftly settled herself across from the count in a luxurious, cushioned chair. Smiling in the candlelight, the fire in her eyes subsided to a crimson twinkle. As he took in her striking appearance, he guessed her to be in her late twenties. Her dark, curly hair was heaped neatly on her head with clasps of garnets, and tinged red in the fluttering light. A high brow with thickly arched, lofty eyebrows framed a pair of magnificent, almost slanted almond eyes and kohl lashes. Her cheekbones were high and her heart-shaped lips full. Clad in a plain yet rich blood red dress, her golden skin glowed, exuding the scent of wild roses.

The count realized that, for the first time in his life, his attention had been swept into unknown regions. Estella knew the effect she had, and much like a theatre performer, utilized her assets to her advantage. Smiling, her sweeping gaze flickered from innocuous to shrewd in the space of a moment.

"I have two spare rooms in the upper quarters ready for guests," she said. Her eyes never left the count's unwavering stare, and he felt her seeking futilely to pierce through to his thoughts. "As I am not interested in your business, nor where you come from, all I require is the knowledge that you won't harm the children under my care."

"I carry a sword, but I have no intention of hurting your children," said the count crisply. "I am a count from lands east of the Frankish kingdoms. I have important errands in town. My man here," he extended his palm towards Elmer, "is here to accompany me and aid me with my travels. I will pay you handsomely for accepting us so late in the night."

"Excellent," she clapped her hands and stood up. "I have a retinue of archers with poisoned arrows ready to stick into wriggling, running fools if you prove otherwise," she added, her eyes glittering with amusement. "Dolly will lead you to your rooms. I trust you can carry your own luggage. Good night then, gentlemen."

"Good night, Lady Estella." The count stood and rested his hands on the back of the chair as Estella, smiling knowingly, turned toward the staircase, gently humming a soft tune.

2

BURNED BY MIND GAMES

For you cannot flee the beast that fed from your broken light
Nor elude the precipice hollowed from your tears and wails
So cast yourself to die, as a meteor hurtling into rapid flight
Fanned into a vivid final exploding beam before it fails

THEIR ROOMS WERE CLEAN AND ADEQUATELY FURNISHED. THE manor, as he soon discovered, was the house that Duke Delcour had purchased for his Portuguese wife. When she died, he had abandoned it and returned to his country estates. He had intended to donate it to the church, but his sister, Lady Mab, preserved it as a legacy for his child, who was not yet of age. As Lady Mab aged, she had taken the vow of the cloister and turned the manor into a home for the needy. Estella, growing up under the influence of Lady Mab, had decided to continue her aunt's charitable deeds. She had carried on her legacy assiduously, but had unceremoniously turned out the nuns, thereby obtaining the full control that suited her.

The count opened the windows to his room and leaned forwards, taking in the night scents and observing the dances of moths in the moonlight.

"Well, this is better than we expected, isn't it?" Elmer said as he entered the count's room.

"It is, though I wish she didn't try to disrobe our minds as though we were commoners. I expected better from someone of her background, to be truthful. And I never expected to encounter such a careless seer here." He turned to face Elmer sourly.

"She was wary, my lord, a lady alone, guarding this place with only her wit and charm to aid her. We cannot fault her too much," Elmer shrugged.

The count flicked his fingers toward the window casually. "She wasn't merely jesting, she meant it. That's what's protecting this manor, and I don't doubt she conceals other surprises as well." He flexed his fingers and began undressing while Elmer, having been dismissed, made to depart. "She isn't the duke's daughter, you did understand that Elmer? I wonder if even the duke ever realized it."

Elmer stopped in his tracks but didn't turn back. "She didn't strike me as the daughter of an Englishman, but then women do have their own ways, don't they? And not all men are Templars with God-given gifts," Elmer added wearily as he opened the door. "Goodnight my lord," he said, closing the door behind him respectfully.

The count lay awake in his four-poster bed. As his mind sought Estella, eager to unravel her facade and delve within, he eventually felt himself slip into a stupor of dreams.

DAWN ARRIVED, COLD and white, its slender fingers finding fissures in the darkness to leak into, slowly breaking it apart, conquering its gloom, and replacing it with the dull grey of morning. The count arose with the first hints of light. He could sense the little ones going about their morning chores. In fact he could feel every one of them; the sick and the healthy, the weight of their small thoughts and worries, and amidst it all the deep heaviness of someone who stirred reluctantly in slumber. It was Estella, not yet fully awake, but neither truly asleep, her mind racing somewhere he couldn't reach.

Generally it was easy for him to reach out and ensnare the thoughts of others. Even the proudest of men were feeble and petty, wearing masks that would slip to reveal the ragged, beggarly souls plagued with fears beneath. Yet as hard as he tried to reach her, all he encountered was an impregnable, iridescent mirror. Her presence betrayed nothing except for the weight of her thoughts. The count frowned and leapt from bed, washed his face, and stared at his reflection in the mirror. Inhaling deeply, he caught the faint scent of musk—Estella had been here, and while she was, she had brought with her thoughts that had left an imprint. There was a single, feeble strand of concern over a man, inhuman and unearthly, dogging her steps, offering and bartering for her soul. The thought was stale but still potent, and the count seized it curiously.

There was a soft knock at the door. Elmer stood in the doorway awaiting his master and looking refreshed. The count nodded to Elmer as he strode down the hall and descended the stairs, adjusting the silver signet rings on his hands as he went. He was met with the clattering sound of china and cutlery in the main hall where he had met Estella the day before. Standing at the entrance, he surveyed the room with interest. There were paintings both sacred and profane. On one wall saints with golden halos bent devoutly and angelic hordes grasped bitter spears held heavenwards. Another depicted maidens with russet and gold hair lying naked on beds of leaves or regal cushions, their expressions languid and seductive. And then there were scenes of temptation; the devil and the prayer, the maiden bathing, and the warrior heeding the angel's warning.

"The dichotomy in our family," came a voice behind him, "is that we can't seem to decide whether we would rather abandon ourselves to pleasure, or devote ourselves to an asceticism that would guarantee our souls entry to heaven." Estella had been surveying him all along. The count turned sharply.

"Oh, do forgive me," he said bowing apologetically. "I didn't see you. And I seldom appreciate being crept up on." He kissed her hand, flashing her a chagrined smile.

Today she was dressed in black silk embroidered with white lace and pearls. At her throat a choker burned with fiery rubies. She didn't smile, and the incandescent light in her eyes remained threateningly feral as she glided past him.

"Do join me for breakfast, you are my only guests this morning, and maybe you can finally tell me your name, O nameless one," she said, leading the way to the table where she gestured for the count to seat himself. Elmer, who had been slinking along behind, uneasy at the tension between Estella and his master, followed suit.

Estella rang a small silver bell and instantly two elderly ladies bustled in pushing a trolley. The aroma of freshly baked breads and fried meats quickly permeated the air. The ladies set to work loading the table with large silver platters of fried eggs and bacon, pheasant rillettes and foie gras, a multitude of cheeses and butters, milk, buttermilk, piping hot bread, and an assortment of jams and fruits.

Estella helped herself to eggs and foie gras with a glass of buttermilk and gestured to them to help themselves. While he reached for the pheasant, the count's mind was ablaze, seeking Estella's, insidiously reaching out into her mind—yet it was still blank and inviolable. Scratching further, using his will as a chisel, he renewed his onslaught, as strained intakes of breath from Estella amid her dining alerted him to the fruition of his endeavor.

Then, without warning, she lifted her gaze from the plate and the light in her eyes deepened. Suddenly—for a moment—the count was struck blind. He roared as he stood up clasping his head in rage. Elmer blanched, unsheathing his sword hesitantly while his eyes darted frantically between the count and Estella. Estella was scalding the count now with unconcealed fury in her gaze. She stood up abruptly and the count lunged for her as she deftly drew a dagger from her robes.

"By God I will slit your throat if you try to come near me. Don't play games with those that gave you hospitality, you base dog!" she hissed, her golden skin flushed with rage.

The commotion had attracted many of her children and in unison they ran towards Estella, standing between her and the count, forming a human barrier. He looked from the children to Estella, who still held the dagger high, her chest heaving and a strange whispering darkness emanating from her.

"I demand to know what you did to me and how," the count's voice was low and composed, and he gestured to Elmer to sheathe his sword.

He took one step forward, towering over Estella. The room grew dark in his wake as the children huddled around her like chicks to a mother hen. But she felt it too, the aura of danger and inexorable power, and she inhaled deeply, her eyes betraying alarm.

"You tried to violate me," her voice was soft as she lowered her dagger warily.

The count took another step and sensed her strength of mind interspersed with little cracks. Within was a fragility adorned with thorny scimitars wrought of her defiance. He felt a fleeting sense of shame, which he dismissed thoughtlessly. Face to face with her, he was acutely aware of the dagger still gripped firmly in her hand and the children's wild thoughts of kicking and thrashing him in the loins.

Estella and the count observed each other, parrying thoughts.

You'd better go, she spoke to him in his thoughts. *You've crossed a line with me, feel free to find your way out of my manor.* Then she turned on her heel dismissively and left.

A chill descended ominously on the manor as the count and Elmer returned to their chambers to pack their things. The count could see the mists gathering outside, but it didn't account for the unnatural cold that had settled within. He paced restlessly while Elmer bent dutifully over the luggage packing. Suddenly, with a gasp, Elmer shrank backwards. In the doorway a tall, slim man with malicious blue eyes observed them. He grinned with an impish malevolence, then disappeared. Groaning, Elmer clutched at his chest. The count instantly knelt by his side. Elmer was in a frenzy, robbed of breath, while faint laughter resounded in the hall. The count closed his eyes and began muttering an incantation beneath his breath. Elmer instantly eased, regaining his breath, and the heavy atmosphere lifted. The count stood up and fiddled with his rings, looking at Elmer speculatively.

"Stay put till I return. I must pay my respects to our lady."

Elmer's pallid face blanched further as the count stormed out of the room.

———— ✇ ————

ESTELLA WAS LYING motionless on her bed. She had removed her black dress and slipped back into a nightgown. Frowning uncomfortably with eyes screwed closed, she had lazily draped one hand over her bedside dresser clutching a crystal glass of wine. She indolently ignored the movements around her, the prying eyes of the petty demons clawing to obtain her attention. They lounged near her dresser leering, shadowy figures swathed in darkness, but still minions with no real power.

"Isn't it too early in the day for that?" came the count's voice as he eyed her glass of wine. "And you, filth! Be gone before I bind you!" His cold tone of command sent the demons scurrying to their feet with indignation as they one by one disappeared.

Estella lifted her head from the pillow drowsily, her eyes unfocused from the wine. Her chest heaved with exasperation and she slammed the glass on her dresser, sending crimson liquid flying. Then dismissively shifting to her side, she turned her back on him. Her hair was undone, streaming over the red silk of her nightgown, and she seemed every inch the portrayal of the captivating thoughts the paintings of her hall depicted.

"Get out of my bedroom before I have someone shoot you dead," she whispered threateningly.

The count disregarded her warning, stomped towards the bed, and yanked her arm back roughly. Estella's face flashed with restrained fury, and despite her torpor she aimed a good slap at his face. Concealing her dizziness, she lifted herself up to a sitting position and faced him snarling.

"I'm warning you now, you impudent dog, get out or I'll invite them back to drag you to your own personal hell." Her eyes had lost their striking incandescence—only the traces of sorrow remained.

The count grabbed her arm and shook her with unfeigned disgust. "Save your warnings, I am a Templar and have the right to pass where I deem fit! You profess to care for the orphaned, yet you live with the lowest filth. Have you sold your soul to the wretches of darkness to deceive the people into thinking you're the duke's daughter?"

Estella's countenance stilled in surprise and she drew back her hand to slap him again, but the count caught her arm and pulled her towards him while she struggled, hiccupping drunkenly. Her free hand felt for her dagger, but he found her hand first and held her close, his mind boring into hers, demanding answers.

"Tell me the truth. I want to help you if they are plaguing you, but first I must know if you invited them in," the count urged her, tightening his grip. Estella resignedly stopped struggling and the count released her. As he looked into her pained eyes, he found himself involuntarily reaching toward her to sweep aside the strands of hair that had fallen across her face.

Estella met his gaze and found the ice and winter had departed from his eyes and instead there was a mild spring, inviting and safe. She raised an inquisitive eyebrow, smiling dreamily. Then she yawned, her head slumping against his shoulder as she nodded into sleep. He caught her and held her gently, deeply alarmed. Then he smelled the gentle waft of laudanum floating in the air. He sighed, perplexed. Her body was warm, and her gold skin was lush and healthy. He found himself admiring her beauty despite himself. Then something ice-cold seized the breath from his throat.

Near the window stood an exceedingly tall, thin figure leaning suggestively against the sill. Shadows curled at his feet, the tendrils conjuring a heavy fog around him. One eye was a deep ocean blue, arresting and dominating, while the other was blind and milky white, fixing the count with a corrupting intensity. His features were confoundingly androgynous. His brown hair fell to his waist, and he toyed with it negligently, watching the count with his single clear eye almost seductively. The count spat sideways with disgust as the demon at the window laughed a hollow, ringing sound.

"Come on, wouldn't I be the most delicious tasting experience you ever had?" he breathed, his voice surprisingly melodious.

"What is your name, demon?" the count inquired quietly.

"Please, tell me you won't ravage her? Wait for my turn first!" he cackled lecherously while Estella stirred awake with a listless groan.

Staggering out of bed, she seized her crystal glass and hurled it unceremoniously at the demon. He disappeared before it hit the wall, where it smashed into a hundred pieces, the crimson wine splattering over the carpets and curtains.

"That's enough for today, I am weary of this nonsense," Estella was striving to remain awake, still visibly befuddled with her sleeping draught as she turned to face the count. "Get off my bed, will you? I have enough courting men as it is. What is your name anyway?" she added haughtily, her eyes narrowing. The ruby on her choker glinted, and its reflections danced across the count's ivory pale face and onto the golden cross around his neck.

"I am Count Mikhail, but that hardly matters. The question is, who are you, Estella? I didn't think to meet women such as yourself here in London—women of such skilled sight who wield it so aptly and who entertain more than guests in their bower. Especially not here in the house of the pious family of Duke Delcour, so highly esteemed by the church." His severe face betrayed no emotions but Estella flinched.

"Ah, and a man of the church such as yourself, what would you know of its demons? What your confessor of a monk taught you, perhaps?" She wielded her words viciously like a striking hammer, and Mikhail responded grimly, reaching out his hand adorned with silver rings. Estella peered downwards curiously and recognized the sigils of the Templars inscribed on one ring, and the crest of the Northern Order of Christ on another.

"Oh Christian holy men," she sighed dramatically, and rolled onto her side. Mikhail averted his eyes from the soft curves, visible through her clinging nightgown. "See, I believe you are all impotent, the lot of you."

Mikhail incredulously choked out a protest, but Estella leaned agilely forwards and pressed her finger to his lips, silencing him. Her incandescent eyes were alight again with maddened ardor. "You don't know me, though you know my name. Go about your errands—go read something useful in the halls of confiscated books your filthy church has amassed, stolen from good people. Read about that symbol round your neck, that cross of yours, and find out its true meaning, Templar. Perhaps you will pull your own eyes out when you discover that your illusion, Christ, was just another initiate of the great mysteries of the threefold death, just like Horus, Mithra, Odin, Merlin, and Lug."

Estella threw her head back and laughed as Mikhail's face darkened into a rictus of rage. He stood abruptly, as though being in close proximity to her was too tempting for his impulse to strike her. But he quickly regained his cold impassivity.

"Do you even know why I am here?" Mikhail spat. "If you knew what I knew and saw what I saw, you would abhor yourself and your ways. The world outside is fighting a cruel game, and you dare sit here imbibing in sin and speaking of the Christ?" he whispered furiously, shaking his head in revulsion. "I should have known; the last resort of failed women, cavorting with demons and rebelling against God. You think to obtain parcels of power by bartering your soul. Little do you know the mysteries of the divine. What you say is blasphemy, and the only reward dabbling in witchcraft will bring you is a swift and painful death." His tone was thunderous and he burned with the desire to punish her. But for the moment, there was nothing he could do. Scowling, he swept from the room, leaving Estella to laugh after him.

"You're just a boy! Bring your games to me and I will destroy them!"

She rang her bedside table bell for more wine, eyeing the empty decanter and sparing a fleeting regret for the wasted vintage splashed across the wall.

3

THE TRUE NATURE
OF GOD'S SHADOW

As a crucified limb that is torn and cannot be again whole

It waits patiently for the hour when all things finally end

For the trumpets of salvation, its notes across the heavens roll

And the broken shards of the spirit's brilliance to mend

HAILING AN EMPTY CARRIAGE THAT DAY WAS EASY. AS THEY BUMPED down the road on their way to the Cathedral of St. Alban the Martyr, the count and Elmer were silent. Mikhail fidgeted darkly with his rings, recalling Estella in his mind and vowing to look into her after he'd met with Cardinal Pious, the chief of the papal order in London. After a brief, bumpy journey, the carriage arrived at its destination.

Outside the Cathedral of St. Alban a few monks were already waiting, prayer beads in hand. They nodded solemnly as two younger tonsured monks reached for Mikhail and Elmer's luggage and wordlessly escorted the pair inside the church. It was damp and moist within, and the monks led the way through the main mass hall, down behind the altar, and past the library.

St. Alban's Cathedral was a meeting place for many of the orders under the auspices of the church, as well as many independent orders that had survived the scythes of time and war. There, shrouded in mystery, they congregated with monarchs and noblemen, mystics and laypeople. There they harnessed the knowledge gleaned from their arts and searched for answers, seeking to understand the cruel game, the chessboard of dark and light, God and the Blind One, Samael.

Mikhail was chief of the Order of the Northern Star, one of the ancient orders of watchers that guarded the thin veil through which demonic forces from the void could enter earth and defile it. They countered these attacks through the mystic teachings of enlightened kings such as Solomon and David.

After the Fall from heaven when the heavenly hosts were cast out with Lucifer at their front, many became demigods and founded early civilizations where they were worshipped by mortals. And while some were benevolent despite their fallen nature, and eventually sought their way home to God, others sought solely domination and decay. Then there were those who refused to choose sides, playing eternally between darkness and light in the shrouded Twilit world, a realm of existence that severed them from the games of the other deities, where they dwelled as the pagan gods of old.

The Twilit people, those blessed by the gifts of the old gods—miracle makers, seers, witches, and shamans—were the most vulnerable to being caught up in the struggle between light and dark, and being forced to choose sides. Those who were not strong enough succumbed to insanity, their minds broken. And they were abhorred by the church for their abdication of what they believed to be the one true faith.

Mikhail followed the monks down a long flight of cold stone steps, the monks crossing themselves piously at the sight of religious icons along the way. He was then led to a starkly furnished room with a stone floor carved with elaborate roses and fleur-de-lis mosaics in faded colors. The pompous Cardinal Pious was waiting, along with Oswald, Mikhail's oldest friend and the head of the Papal Inquisition.

"Good afternoon, my dear friend," Oswald greeted him. "I was expecting you yesterday, I must say, but nonetheless it's always worth the wait." Oswald, banishing his weariness, beamed at Mikhail and clasped his arms in a brotherly fashion. He was broad and muscular and wore black unadorned leathers under his heavy cloak. His black eyes were shrewd, and the silver grey hair falling to his shoulders showed the weight of age gracefully. The cardinal sniffed imperiously, merely nodding perfunctorily at his arrival, and Mikhail seated himself.

"So where were you last night, Count?" said the cardinal dourly. The sour old wrinkled man held an iron staff and eyed him disapprovingly.

As the count sifted through the ugly tangle of the cardinal's thoughts, he was not surprised to unravel a heavy thread of jealousy. The cardinal had not chosen the life of the cloister willingly—he had once nurtured other dreams and ambitions of his own. Now the envy he felt towards the count for the freedoms and pleasures he enjoyed gnawed at him. But the cardinal had the ear of the king, and it would be unwise to dismiss him entirely.

"I did not find my way easily into London, and the weather was atrocious to the extent that I couldn't find a carriage or decent lodging till nightfall." Mikhail smiled ruefully at the full goblet that was placed before him by a young monk, recalling yesterday's events. "I stayed the night at Red Fern Manor, and then found my way to you first thing this morning. Forgive my tardiness, but I did my utmost to reach you." Mikhail's tone was cool and pleasant.

"Red Fern Manor," Oswald chuckled merrily. "You spent the night there of all places? Small wonder you were reluctant to grace us with your presence. How on earth did you even find your way there? But Lady Estella is quite the one for times of need, though she seems to avoid me for some strange reason," he noted, his eyes twinkling with amusement. "I hear she is betrothed to the Earl of Woodcraft," he added in conspiratorial tones. "A great lad, I must say, youthful and easily led."

"I never would have thought she was betrothed," Mikhail replied. "She seems to be of the wilder breeds of women." He raised an inquisitive brow and somewhere deep down within felt a sharp pang of disappointment, much to his disconcertment.

"I find her terribly unholy, that woman. I do not find her humility appealing—there is something filthy about her," spat out the cardinal, his jowls wobbling. Mikhail suppressed his disgust at the carnal thoughts radiating from the cardinal.

"So never mind her," Mikhail growled, tapping the table with his fingers impatiently as his geniality foundered and he struggled to control his anger. "I must demand your full attention, now that we have exchanged the inane pleasantries, and you will hold your peace till I'm done." He paused for a moment, taking a deep breath and rubbing his temples vigorously as he strove to contain the tempestuous rage and bitterness that seethed within.

"I am here because a vision led me to London, and because you are the select few with the authority to instigate the adequate mechanism of defense we need." He turned to face them, his jaw taut and his impatient arrogance showing through his courteous mask. Oswald uncrossed his arms and nodded approvingly, his attention fixed.

"It began with the grim reports from the Frankish kingdoms," Mikhail began in a weathered tone. "At first, many young children were reported to the church as having seizures and fits and babbling warnings from the angels. Then the children started to die. The cause was strangulation—they would expire while frothing rabidly with omens. At first we did not think much of it. Then the aesthetics monastery was attacked." Mikhail began tapping the table again, his gaze sweeping over them. "All the monks had their eyes and tongues removed."

The cardinal's watery eyes widened in alarm.

"We discovered that a woman had arrived to receive confession before the onslaught had occurred, so we decided to track her down. But we couldn't find a trace of her. Then several pregnant women began acting erratically. We ordered them to be confined to bedlams, but they found ways to throw themselves into fires and burned themselves to death. Others stabbed their wombs and took the lives of their infants with them. And so the death toll kept rising higher and higher. Soon after, I received a vision and understood: we were looking for a child to be born. Whether good or evil, it wasn't clear, so we intensified our search for this woman.

"Then we heard rumors of one who was hiding in a nunnery. It was said she made the statues of the Virgin Mary weep, but her identity was unknown and shrouded in silence. Many people, however, gave testimony that the nunnery was full of doves and angelic lights. So I personally, with a few trusted Templars, led the way to the nunnery. It was located on a rocky hill on the outskirts of the town, a real place of obscure devotion and avoidance of the world. It took us three days of arduous journey. Along the way we noticed portentous bird migrations, notably doves flying towards that region. We pressed forwards then, finally arriving in the dead of night. Alas, we brought with us the woman's doom, though unwittingly.

"The nuns barred our entry at first, but when we showed them our sigils, they began to weep and beg us to leave, saying we were bringing the devil with us. We didn't heed their fears or pause to reflect on their warnings, but forced our way in. My foresight was dulled there by an unnatural force and it only spurred me forward. Still the nuns begged us to wait till she had at least delivered her baby, but we demanded to be brought to her—or they would face excommunication. Reginald, my trusted steward, pushed them aside and we searched the nunnery till we found her in a flint stone room on a humble bed, cradling her swollen stomach.

"At the sight of us she began to weep and wail, begging us to depart, but we needed to question her. Yet we found that she would not speak, so we decided there and then to frighten her, to bring her back with us and invite the fathers of the church to encourage her to talk. She would not answer us as to who the father of her child was, and she kept mumbling prayers and making ward signs as if we were the enemy.

"She was a very simple girl, and even her name and place of birth she withheld from us. Naturally we had reason to doubt her sincerity, though the nuns had vouched for her pious nature. The more we questioned her, the more she wailed and implored us to leave, so we had no choice but to take her with us. Reginald watched over her during the night, and we camped in neighboring rooms.

"Night came heavy, and we all fell into a deep stupor. We must have been under some spell, for nothing alerted us to the commotion. I was blessed enough to awaken feeling the ice-cold of my locket, which holds a fragment of the true cross. The locket seared my skin, and I awoke startled and feeling deeply rattled. Vapors surrounded us and none of my men could be roused. They were under an unshakable torpor. I felt sure something evil was afoot.

"As I made my way to the room in which the woman was kept, I saw that the door was ajar and Reginald fast asleep. Then I saw that the woman was gone. I bolted down the stairs with my sword in hand and headed instinctively for the Mass hall. That's when I saw it happening right before my very eyes, and I will never rip the imprint of the memory from my mind." Mikhail paused and shivered, covering his face with his hands. Then, staring them each squarely in the eyes, he continued.

"I did not see them first, I was just hit with the sight of a curled fetus on the cold stone floor before me. Then I understood that something truly evil had infected the nunnery, and we were too late. I could see that the child would have been a boy. And leading from his small, crushed form was a trail of blood. Never have I hesitated in my life to follow any trail, however forbidding, but there was a desolate chill in my bones and in my soul. My strength of mind and spirit had been bled out of me by some abhorrent force and I was plagued with unshakable tremors. Then I heard them, and I had no choice but to follow the trail of blood, no matter where it led me.

"The trail led me to the foot of the altar where they were; the woman was moaning, her belly slit open. His rasping breath rent shivers down my spine as he tortured her. I rushed towards them with my sword, roaring in fury and dismay.

"Then he turned around and faced me, and I froze in horror. His bald face was a melted mask of decaying flesh, one single putrid eye was set in his brow, and his mouth was a lipless gash of black, rotted teeth. There stood the Blind One, the False God himself, Samael, that rotten aborted abomination of darkness . . ."

Immediately there was a choked splutter from the cardinal. Livid and shaking his head furiously, he cried, "That cannot be! Samael? Incarnate and in flesh? Here walking among us? This is sheer madness!"

Mikhail turned to look at the cardinal with deliberate slowness and the cardinal withered beneath his menacing stare. Inhaling deeply, Mikhail continued, his face darkened.

"I knew there was an enemy before me that I could not fight alone. He radiated darkness, and every fear I had ever harbored in my heart came to life before me in my mind, and every sin I had ever committed was amplified. The most despicable thoughts occurred to me, and deeds

I'd never consider committing tempted me and marched upon my mind as he corrupted my soul into joining him, into joining him in defiling her. But I repudiated those thoughts and I sought for God within me.

"I found inside a gaping chasm. I saw through his rotten vision an existence devoid of Godhead. Born blind in a blind darkness, not knowing light or purity, his self-devouring darkness regurgitated itself, expanding into itself and declaring itself god above all. I knew then that I must resist with everything I had, or fall and lose my soul to the worst depredations of hell.

"As I strode towards him shaking, I prayed fervently to God and his angels. But that night no one was there to heed me. Suddenly I found I could no longer walk, my limbs froze, and I fell to my knees, utterly paralyzed. The False God laughed a soulless, knowing laugh that made me retch and my blood curdle. I was overcome with horror and his putrid eye bore into me.

"'This was the daughter who could have brought forth the messiah of the age,' he laughed and turned back to the woman who was now frothing blood at the mouth. I knew we had failed miserably as an order, and we were forsaken, alone, and blameworthy. No prayer came to my mind, but the sobbing in my heart shook me and filled me with a feverish frenzy of pain. Then mercy came to me and I swooned, and I could no longer hear her cries."

Mikhail abruptly stopped talking, his gaze directed beyond Oswald and the cardinal into a distance they could not see. Oswald's arms were crossed defensively, but his expression was somber and his jaw tightly set. A vein pulsated in his neck wildly. Uncrossing his arms, he smote the table with his fist angrily.

"And we are always late in the infernal game! We need to change tactics. I have never dreamt of such a day when my friend would come to me with such an ignoble tale of our failures. Samael the Blind God here, mocking us so openly? Where is the outrage?" He glared at the cardinal, the target of his fury, who had gone ashen grey. Now more than ever he seemed a frail, impotent wreck, hiding behind his priestly garb.

"Talk, dammit," Oswald stormed, "this is your people's fault. We warned them not to create a schism between the Twilit people and the men of religion, we warned you numerous times not to marginalize the ones with the aptitude to pick up the signs we cannot see!" Oswald was on his feet, pointing at the cardinal accusingly. "I am sick of this masquerade. We alienate the very people that could help us."

Cardinal Pious pulled on his beard, flinching piteously. "I do not believe him! I refuse to believe that this conjured demon was Samael, or that the girl was the mother of the messiah!" he spluttered. "This is some trickery conceived by the Twilit people to ingratiate themselves with us, no doubt. And you, Mikhail, have been deceived by them! You are fools if you think you can trust them or manage them. They are like beasts. They know no authority or fear of God. Shall we stoop to mingling with these swine because they have a deformity that allows them to steal from God's prescribed future? You are fools to think you can align your efforts with these people. What has happened is a result of the church's failure to expunge the Twilit, once and for all," the cardinal concluded, waving his hands in dismissal.

4

THE DEATH OF INNOCENCE

For slavery of the spirit is seated in false righteousness divine
At the vanguard of the prowess of the virtues so sublime
And ever the glorification of the fettering dogmas shine
As the radiant sun of our liberation above our minds supine

MIKHAIL WATCHED PATIENTLY. THERE WAS NO NEED TO INTERFERE AT this stage. He had achieved the required effect. Oswald would deal with it. Mikhail knew he lacked the calm discipline to indulge the fathers of the church, but he could trust Oswald to hammer the reality home.

Though the orders were immune to the attacks from the demonic forces, they were blind to their activity. And yet it was mostly the orders that sought out these demonic presences and banished them. The orders needed the church's aid to help the Twilit people. Then with the combined power of the Twilit people's gifts with the orders' own, they would have a much higher chance of preventing the evil from spreading.

The Twilit people were caught between both worlds, and as a result, their gifts encompassed realms that the orders could not breach. From divining the future to sensing death and demons, they could even feel when demonic forces scavenged from human auras. And there were some with noctilucent eyes, who could summon entry portals to the other worlds by tearing the fabric of the veil. They could summon good or evil into this world, and often became instruments of greater powers in the cruel game.

Mikhail was suddenly weary and desired private conversation with Oswald. The cardinal was still gesticulating indignantly, wagging his old beard and professing to know things that only God himself knew.

"You had better heed us this time, or you might end your days a poor monk living off alms," Oswald growled.

The cardinal puffed out his chest defiantly and pushed past Oswald. "I am never wrong, you fools, you will see." He unbolted the warded locks on the door and hurried off down the damp corridors. Oswald made to follow him, but Mikhail raised a hand.

"Let it be, we won't gain anything by this. Haven't you noticed? He barely acknowledged my report, he won't believe me, and neither will anyone outside of the orders. They are slow and obtuse. But there is much I have in mind to implement, starting from here," he added sardonically.

"Why here of all places?" Oswald frowned, leaning against the old oak doorframe.

Mikhail sighed. "Because ever since that night I have been plagued with dreams, and in my dreams I was led here, to find what I needed. The culmination of my dreams, the key, must be concealed here," he waved around him resignedly. "Otherwise the Lord would not have led me here."

"You should not let yourself be carried away following omens. They could prove to be nothing more than a distraction intended to divert you," Oswald snorted.

"I have encountered some interesting people here. People who appear simple on the surface, but who hide something. London has surprised me," said Mikhail as he rose from his chair, beckoning to Elmer. Oswald observed him with curiosity.

"I think I understand who you're referring to. Lady Estella has wrought her charms on you. But this fair lady of a duchess is nothing to trifle with—Portuguese blood, nothing but lust for gold."

"She has done no such thing," Mikhail grimaced. "Come, we must hear the verdict of the Blind Sage. In all his years of scouring the darkness for divine secrets, there must be something he has found."

"And what if he doesn't know?"

Mikhail's face darkened and he turned away, his expression inscrutable.

⸙

THE STREETS OF London were busy as usual, and though accompanied by Oswald, Mikhail and Elmer still got curious stares and misgiving glances from passersby. Oswald wanted a select tavern far from the prying eyes, so they took a long, winding path across the quarters of the rich. He showed them around the Silver Quarter, which was a square filled with some of the city's richest houses. Polished marble from Italy decorated the square in elaborate patterns of mother of pearl and black marble. No carriages were allowed in this quarter. Instead scores of servants with great umbrellas escorted the nobles into their houses, sometimes laying thick velvet carpets before them so the rain did not impede their path. The houses themselves were beautiful with arched balconies, intricate lattice work, and doors with Saxon art embossed into the wood with silver.

Now with the influx of trade and marriages into moneyed circles across the western hemisphere, strange yet beautiful artistic inclinations had sprung up. In the middle of the square was a statue of St. Michael. Mikhail stopped to admire the work. St. Michael held a polished silver spear and the wings on his back were carved in such a way that it allowed slots for heavy silver feathers amid the marble, giving the statue an impressive effect.

A group of noblewomen passed by casting coy glances at Mikhail as they swiftly took note of his clothing and his long hair. Dressed in pale floral silks, they chattered among themselves while Mikhail shook his head in amusement.

"You would find the world a more pleasant and intriguing place if you didn't think of looking into everyone's thoughts wherever you crossed them," commented Oswald.

Mikhail lifted a haughty brow as Oswald led them through the Silver Square towards another cobbled street. They could see beyond it a high palace with golden spires, and so down this alley they entered the Gold

Quarter. Several gold statues lined the square before the great palace, where the aristocracy and royalty met and courted.

"We are invited there soon, my friend." Oswald patted Mikhail on the back with a knowing wink.

Mikhail sighed with blatant disinterest as they continued their tour of the square. There were golden statues of saints and angels in pious postures, and royal effigies with banners woven of gold thread. At the center of the square was a great rose with petals wrought of delicate gold and amber, the stem encrusted with emerald and golden thorns. Curving out of the central rose flowed other stems leading to more roses branching out across the square.

The palace itself was surrounded by other royal houses with regal banners of gold and white fluttering in the breeze. Oswald rattled on about how there were rooms entirely fashioned of amber and mother of pearl, and how lush crimson velvets carpeted the halls. Estella, with her love of garnets and crimson, came to Mikhail's mind unbidden, and he smiled almost unconsciously. A Twilit artfully hiding at the very heart of the church's bosom—and yet no one could peel off her mask. Though her boldness impressed him, he disapproved of her indulgent ways. And he knew her allure was his weakness, so he tried to stifle the effect she had on him as best he could.

Oswald led the way past the Golden Square with purposeful footsteps down bustling streets and shaded alleys. Many times he stopped to look behind them to ensure no one was following. The farther he led them away from the comfortable rich quarters, the dingier the streets became. Maids carried buckets of human waste out of the royal houses and dumped them into the poor quarters near the river. The cloying smell of cheap meat and burning fat permeated the air from the many sausage vendors and tripe pie stands. Ragged children were plentiful; some maimed, others hale but frail and caked in filth. They gathered around avidly, but one icy glance from Oswald and they backed begrudgingly away.

Soon they were traveling through quarters where artisans sold a mix-ture of carpets and small paintings—mostly holy icons. Fortune tellers in heavily patterned shawls peered from behind the doors of their shops. The artisans' quarters were clean but meager. Tapestries hung from the doors of shops while owners sat outside on stools casting rune stones with what looked like polished bones. Children gathered black sticks and threw them into the air singing, "One for sorrow, two for joy, seven for wealth and nine for grace, six for death and three for danger!" They laughed as they played near a bent old man selling bracelets made of jade and malachite beads. Casting a glance at the three travelers, he winked.

"Jade for verity, malachite for high esteem! And you, grey-eyed one, here is red jasper for passion," he laughed with his pale eyes twinkling.

Mikhail did not so much as acknowledge this remark as he walked till a child tugged on his arm, grinning. Turning around, he saw that the old man was watching him intently now, and his thoughts were a smoky cloud of hunger and poverty. He had sensed the touch of a woman on Mikhail's mind. Mikhail felt irritated that he needed to shield his thoughts among beggars, of all places.

The child tugging his arm held the red jasper bracelet out to him. It was a masterful piece of work, blood red jasper stones cut round and smooth and threaded together. The clasp was a base metal hook, but this wasn't noticeable amid the beauty of the stone that had a vivid and unusual hue. Mikhail took it from the boy and the old man's thoughts projected hope mingled with images of good food and warmth. Feeling touched by the old man's plight, he took out his pouch of money and gave the boy five pieces of silver. The boy grinned and kissed Mikhail's hand.

"My grandpa says she loves red, and from the scent he caught she would really appreciate it on her wrist. Red is her fire unrestrained, and you could balance it for her." Then the boy rushed off before Mikhail could respond with more than a frown. He mentally reached out to the old man, who had his eyes closed. He was dream catching, utilizing the thoughts the count carried and milking it for all the information it held.

The count realized the true extent to which the church was misguided in its approach to the Twilit. Even a pauper such as this, given the right environment to thrive, wielded great potential. These gifts could yield an unexpected bulwark against evil. The church could, instead of persecuting them, learn from their wisdom. But because they were left to their own devices, they were easy pickings for the heathen gods.

OSWALD HAD CHOSEN a little wooden inn that was particularly shabby, but surprisingly clean. It was patronized mostly by woodworkers and craftsmen, alongside a few artisans and jewelers. They all sat quietly drinking ale and partaking of common fare.

"It's good clean food, I can guarantee that," said Oswald reassuringly.

They chose a table positioned near the stained glass windows that yielded a view of the road. The diners and drinkers scrupulously paid them little attention, although brief subtle looks were exchanged. Oswald ignored them as he called for the innkeeper impatiently. A man with a ruddy complexion, dark blond hair, and a dyed yellow beard bustled over, taking in their simple yet richly cut clothing.

"Three of your best beers," Oswald began, "then two roasted ducks with a side of liver and onions, and a platter of cheeses and goose liver. The best, my friend, and I do mean the best." Oswald's expression was carefully schooled into a friendly grin, but the innkeeper read the subtext easily. Nodding, he left for the kitchen, soon returning with three, foaming jugs of beer. Mikhail sipped his beer and was pleased to discover it wasn't watered down, despite the location.

"So my friend, what do you believe could be the ramifications of this calamity?" Mikhail asked, setting the jug down and eyeing Oswald cautiously. Oswald leaned forward.

"I believe you, for a start. Just six months ago my father took his own life after having a vision of a world ruled by Samael. But before you offer me pity and condolences, keep it, and move on; I won't dwell on the subject. So what do I think? We are sinking further and further down the rabbit hole they have set as our course, and rapidly losing mind and sight. That's what I think." Oswald crossed his arms defensively.

"Every age we had a promise that God would send us a shining light to aid us in the divine struggle, to guide us," Oswald continued. "But every time that light is extinguished at its source or it perishes later, and seldom does it accomplish what it came here to do. And though we have fought to protect our flock, seeking out the holy lineages of the Magdalenes, searching for the signs and omens of where the divine child would be born, often we have failed. Our church sisters who are blessed with the sight have languished long in their quest to grabble some knowledge from the blind cloak of night. And sometimes we succeed in crucial moments and many lights are born that break through, redeemed from Samael. But only for a short time. It is a cruel jest. We are cheated of our purpose, and Samael's reign prevails over the endless night. Lord knows how much we needed a new light in this world—a new messiah—and now it's gone." He paused, rubbing his chin pensively.

"I have one proposal for you, Oswald," said Mikhail, "and if you of all people cannot heed me, then I am at a crossroads between our orders. For I will not forgive myself, nor anyone else that will not heed me and assist me in my work." The pupils of Mikhail's icy grey eyes were unnaturally dilated, and his strong square jaw was clenched. "Listen to me carefully—the only people who received signs of these lights were the outcasts that are born touched by the hand of the darkness, or if you wish, the hand of the Twilit gods. And the gods fight over these people, making their lives unbearable, for they seek to feast on their souls, devouring them, or twisting their arts to evil. Those that resist end up tormented and half-crazed, seeking refuge in religious orders and pretending to be ascetics. No one comprehends how these people are chosen, but there is no doubt they see beyond the veil, and that it reaches out and beckons to them. For their minds and eyes are open to it.

"The sacred pineal gland was somehow not rotted in these people. Perhaps the Twilit gods preserved them for their own ends, whether to have people to worship them or even offer themselves to them. For these Twilit gods often descend in human form to take women and sire upon them gifted children. I have seen it happen, and our order preserved many records of such children becoming magicians and great alchemists and traversing the gates of night to seek infinity's secrets. Great figures like Merlin. We need to reach out to them, register them and their gifts, lift the stigma, and fortify our efforts with their sight."

The food then arrived, the innkeeper laying the dishes on the table as Oswald cautiously selected his words.

"But they are mostly tainted, my friend," Oswald gravely reminded him. "Many of them do not accept our Lord as their savior. How can we reconcile the sacred and the profane? What would you have us do, bring the demiurges into our hearts? Our hearts which we have already consecrated to the one true God?"

"I don't see why we can't collaborate without merging together," Mikhail articulated. "Since I've been here I have already encountered two unique Twilit gifts, and I am sure half the artisans share the same. The jewelers who peddle sacred stones with mystic properties—very popular among the empty headed nobility, I might add—actually do catch petty little fiends, forcing them into the stones. Their ability is real, and you of all people ought to understand how important it is."

Oswald nodded reluctantly. Elmer was distractedly looking out of the window where a group of people were gathered. Though they seemed poor, they were well-mannered. The women had their hair and faces meticulously shrouded, so their features could not be seen. The men looked like peasant workers, for the most part, their skin tan, their features sharp, and their eyes keen as eagles. They entered the inn and were met with the same scrupulous silence as before. While Mikhail and Oswald continued their heated debate, Elmer watched the newcomers with an uneasy interest. One of the women seemed familiar— her feminine gait was full of a confidence the other peasants lacked.

The group chose a table at the far end of the inn and the women removed their shawls—all except the one Elmer had noticed. This woman had golden skin, thick arched eyebrows, and perfect, full, rounded cheeks. As she called for wine, her voice was clear and dominant. Elmer felt confused—the voice could only be Estella's. Excusing himself, he quietly moved closer to the group to get a better look at the woman. She smelled of Arabian musk and rose, and the hand clasping the wine glass held a ring with a single garnet.

One of the children tugged at her shawl, revealing the brown hair with reddish glints beneath as she took out a deck of battered tarot cards and began shuffling them. The light filtering through the window caught the iconography illustrated on the cards as she passed them to the woman opposite her. The woman shuffled them reverently and cut the deck before returning them. The shawled woman then set about making a Celtic pattern, placing the cards face down on the table. She observed them carefully, putting a finger to her lips, then started turning them over, one by one. The scene had drawn a crowd, and the people gathered around observing in silence. Some watched with greedy rapture, fumbling with coins in their hands, possibly hoping to ask the woman a favor to read their fortunes.

Mikhail strode over to the table, but immediately the lady in the shawl stood up to block his passage, brandishing a tarot card. It was Estella. "Knight of some godforsaken order or not, you shall not trouble me further," she commanded, her eyes glowering with a red light.

As she barked the commanding words, Mikhail felt a searing knife dig into his chest, as if assaulted by some invisible force. Then she turned on her heel and quickly disappeared into the crowd, and was soon lost from sight. Mikhail, startled by the sudden blossoming of pain, staggered outside the inn clutching his chest. Estella's companions emerged hurriedly from the inn, shooting him fearful glances as they rapidly dispersed.

Estella, as he expected, was the last to leave. She wore a fretful expression on her face as she bolted from the inn, attempting to join the dispersing group. But Mikhail was too quick for her, grabbing her by the arm and hauling her down an alley. He slammed her unceremoniously against the wall and pressed his fingers into her temples. As Estella kicked in vain, he threw himself into a full assault to find what was protecting her mind. But there was nothing.

Estella relented her thrashing to meet his searching gaze. She could feel his intrusions falter against her barricaded mind, and as he exerted himself, oblivious to everything around him, she blinked at him distractingly. He removed his hand, perplexed with his failure, and she leaned in quickly. Pressing her lips against his, she bit down hard. Disconcerted, Mikhail backed away from her, as if she were a glowering hot coal that had just been dropped into his hands.

"Never been with a woman, Templar? I think you're pursuing me because you just can't resist me. Why don't you try getting a whore instead," she spat.

Pulling her shawl over her face angrily and without waiting for a response, she turned from him in contempt. As she strode away, she kept up a perfect semblance of control—except for the light tremor in her hands. Then she was gone.

Mikhail leaned against the wall, the pain in his head growing into a merciless headache, with his tumbling thoughts denying him any respite. Surprise and affronted pride mingled together. Oswald and Elmer, emerging from the inn, saw the look on Mikhail's face and exchanged dubious glances. Then they trailed behind as Mikhail set out to follow Estella's wildfire trail, marching in heavy silence until they neared the artisans' quarters. Here, the winds bore the acrid smell of burning wood and hair, and smoke rose in a twisted, black spire. Shrill cries of terror reached their ears, and the sound of many footsteps made the earth shake.

The clangor of wailing and burning wood was half drowned by orders bellowed from an army on horseback. Mikhail was assaulted by the deluge of emotions coming from the people that lived there. He knew from their terrified thoughts that the church had instigated a hunt, burning down their quarters and dispersing them, then carrying away the ones that opposed them and culling the rest.

Mikhail and his companions pressed forwards urgently, assessing the turmoil as they went. They were aghast to see carnage worthy of the crusades. Burning torches and brandished swords were held aloft by men clad in church armor with red crosses emblazoned across their chests. Houses burned around them as men, women, and children were hauled out by their garments and hair into the street. Some fought back, using their small magic to blind the knights and flee, while others drove the knights into a mental frenzy until they rode off, their horses bewildered. But they were still sorely outnumbered.

Mikhail found Estella easily. She was the source of the knights' wrath. Atop a building, arms outstretched, her head covered but her eyes glowering, storm and darkness gathered around her. The knights before her were writhing on the ground, clutching their heads and screaming. Mikhail saw endless hordes of demons gathering from both ends of the streets, summoned by her incantations.

"Feast upon their souls," she cried, intoxicated with fury. "Feast upon these enemies of freedom, these enemies of mankind hiding behind the banner of God."

The demons ran wild, pouncing like ravenous beasts upon the knights unseen, savagely assaulting their auras and devouring their souls and minds. And still she stood towering above them like a pagan goddess of bygone days, thunder following in her wake. She watched dispassionately as the fires below burned red and unworldly, while the hordes swarmed around the knights in an ever expanding bloodbath. The distraction gave the artisans the chance to flee unharmed.

The knights, bewildered and not knowing what assailed them, fell back, gathering around their captain. He was a black-haired, middle-aged brute of a man, and he ordered his men to take hostages in retaliation. Waving his sword and barking for order, he then began to make examples of the artisans, slitting their throats indiscriminately—man, woman, and child.

One woman fought against her attackers particularly violently. They smote her across the face and dragged her by the hair to their leader. To Mikhail she seemed morbidly familiar with her high cheekbones and thick eyebrows. Like a ragdoll she was seized by the throat and with a single sweeping blow her throat was slit. Without so much as a cry, she fell limp before the captain's feet, and he pushed her over to the side with contempt. He smiled triumphantly as Estella screamed from the rooftop.

Mikhail ran to the knights standing in the street amid the blood and carnage. The frenzied, suffering knights still thrashed madly while the demons feasted on their minds and souls. Mikhail shouted out to the captain amid the tumult, displaying the royal sigils upon his rings as Oswald followed him into the melee.

"The order was decreed by Cardinal Pious," the man spat at them sourly, "to burn this place to the ground and eradicate the vermin within." He looked at them with malignant spite but didn't dare affront them. They were knights of a higher order than he, although they held no jurisdiction there.

Mikhail held his peace, watching the burning and killing with distaste and bitterness. He then spotted Estella emerging from a house and running towards the woman, her slit throat still gurgling. The knights attempted to cut her down, unsheathing their bloodied swords, but she cried out, and a fiery ring burst into flame around them. They backed away crying, "Witchcraft!" as the fire hounded them.

Alone, Estella wept aloud, a cry that echoed amid the carnage, sobbing in a language that pierced his heart. The artisans bowed their heads as they watched their houses burn before them. The woman touched Estella's face and smiled despite her suffering as the blood fell in rivulets across her face. Estella tried to lift the woman, vainly staggering against her weight as a man from the inn rushed to her side.

"Tsura, they will come for you. Cover your face and hide. You honored us in life and death. Run and hide, you have our blessing." His voice quivered but he held himself resolute, kneeling by Estella and rearranging the scarf that had fallen from her face. The knights gathered around them with torches.

"Burn alive, witches, you abominations of God!" they cried, spurring their horses towards Estella.

Mikhail summoned his might and the horses halted abruptly, shaking their riders from their backs. The man, taking advantage of the diversion, hauled Estella away, pushing her forward into the darkness of the night while she struggled and hit at him with all of her failing strength.

5

WADING INTO FATE

It sat upon its lofty throne erected upon your cranial seat
And drove the stakes of conquest into your brain
For never shall the waves of solace and comfort meet
In that sundered solitary heart wildly insane

MIKHAIL SURVEYED THE CHAOS SOLEMNLY. THEN, WITH A SINGLE, succinct prayer, he bound the demons as they fled, vanishing like mist from the square. He walked seven times around the scene muttering incantations. As he worked, the afflicted knights ceased their writhing and lay alleviated, gasping for breath.

With the air cleared, the moon showed her argent face, casting its pure white light on the destruction below. The wind whispered solace to the survivors as they stood among the wreckage of their homes, broken and shaken, their hearts laden with vengeful sorrow and shock. Mikhail cautiously approached the woman with the slit throat and knelt beside her, cradling her head to feel the abode of her soul. He found it empty. Instead, he found a little demon lurking within. It hid from him artfully, but he coaxed it out with a few words and the threat of his sigil ring.

"Who are you and what are you doing within this woman?" Mikhail demanded sternly. "Talk!"

"I lived here comfortably, my lord," croaked the demon. "Please don't bind me! I was Florica's pet, and I kept her company, nothing more. Harmless, she would have told you I was."

"And what was this Florica to Estella?" he inquired.

The demon shrank away as if struck, shaking like a leaf. "I am bound by bigger spells than you know of. My tongue is tied, my lord. And I know no Estella, though I know of Tsura."

"Tsura? Is that Estella's true name?" But heavy footsteps distracted him and the demon fled at the opportunity. Mikhail crossed himself and blessed the woman respectfully, looking over her features perturbed. He couldn't guess her story, but she was surely Estella's kin— her similar features attested to this.

"Well, this shall forever mar our chances of reconciling with the Twilit," said Oswald as he approached from behind. "And I think we may be falling out of papal favor ourselves." His jaw was clenched tightly. "Though I have an idea of how I may remedy this a little."

"I'm going to Red Fern Manor, it's time to pay Estella a call," said Mikhail.

Oswald grunted in acquiescence.

"Where is Elmer?" Mikhail added irritably.

"Looking after the victims," Oswald replied, sounding defeated. This was precisely what they had tried to avoid—an attack on the Twilit people, the schism the church was deliberately creating.

"The devil is in the house of God," came an ominous whisper from behind them. Oswald and Mikhail whipped around only to see an old woman clutching the walls as she walked. She was blind in both eyes and toothless, her skin sagging like crumpled old parchment. "The devil is among the sheep. Beware, you will be next." Then she hurriedly hobbled away, shooting furtive looks at the pair as she went. Mikhail shook his head and stood to leave.

"Do you even know your way?" Oswald called out behind him.

"I'm following her trail. It's like wildfire, you cannot miss it," Mikhail called back, disappearing into the night.

ESTELLA WAS IN bed, her hair untied and a goblet of wine on the dresser next to her. There was an entire bottle open next to it, newly decanted, and she was lying face down on her bed sobbing. She had cast off her plain garments and lay there in her pale yellow underdress, her body heaving. A few of the children anxiously congregated outside her door, but none dared enter, for when Estella was upset she wanted solitude. She had bolted the manor doors like she had not done in quite a while, stationing archers to watch over Red Fern Manor.

"I could have averted that, you know," came the suave, oily voice of the androgynous demon standing by the window, savoring the spectacle of her sorrow. Estella ignored him, covering her face with her hands, her body quivering uncontrollably. He tutted with feigned sympathy, detaching himself from the window and slinking up to crouch over her.

"Get off me you filth," she spat, removing her hands from her face and revealing a mask of agony and wrath.

He licked his lips appreciatively and his waist-length black hair fell over Estella like a drape. "Let me avenge you, my pretty one. I can give you their eyes on a platter and their hearts on a skewer, just allow me to share your soul!" He bent down suddenly, kissing Estella on the mouth.

Outraged, she tried to push him off, but the demon pinned her arms down, his face close to hers. "Tell me you don't want revenge, my doll." His face was close, breathing into hers. Even at that proximity she struggled to tell whether he was male or female.

"Oh, for you I am definitely male," he purred, pressing his body further into hers. With a cry of disgust, she pushed him away, invoking a ward sign. The demon hissed shrilly. "None of that!" he warned her icily, his blue eye becoming a pool of darkness.

Her chest began to tighten rapidly until she couldn't breathe. He smiled as she gulped in shock, choking and clutching her neck, one hand pressing against her heart. The demon kneeled over her, tracing his fingers across her bosom, slowly edging beneath the fabric of her undergarment.

"See, I am not your enemy, I am your only friend and I admire you. You're beautiful and dangerous, and you have much more power than you know how to unlock." He bent down to her ear and she recoiled with a shiver. "I can help unlock it for you. And while I exact revenge on your behalf, you could give me what I want . . ."

With one last, urgent struggle she broke free from his spell, frantically bellowing a warding chant. He retreated from her gracefully as she continued chanting. But her voice, hoarse from sobbing, soon began to fail, cracking with each renewed breath. The demon approached again, smiling, this time lying next to her and stretching luxuriously, caressing her hair.

"Poor star of the sea, you are wounded like a deer caught in flight." His fingers found her neck as she jolted in disgust. "I know you want my help but not my price. Believe me, once you get your revenge and give me what I want of you, it will be the last thing you think of. You will have the power you desire." His fingers reached for her lips as she smacked him angrily away. Raising her hand, she resumed her chanting. The demon laughed, slinking back to the window. "I will return tomorrow. I know your rage and your heart's moods. And maybe in your dreams I can give you a taste of the pleasure I can offer you." He laughed knowingly and vanished.

Estella sighed with relief, falling back onto her bed. She reached for the wine, pouring herself a goblet and drinking deeply. Her head ached, and she felt tainted by the demon's touch. She lit the candles in the sconces, then crawled into her bed and curled up.

Her dreams had not yet begun when she felt the presence of something in her room stirring. She turned grudgingly to find the count closing the door behind him with a grim expression on his face. The candles in the sconces were still burning and the game of lights cast a yellow glow on his fine features. He did not move or speak, but his bearing conveyed warning and dark purpose. Estella swore in disbelief, fumbling beneath her pillow to retrieve a poisoned dagger.

"I need to talk with you, Estella," Mikhail said at length, coming closer to her bed.

"I can tell you crawled your way to your position, you base born dog! You brought those murderers against my people," she whispered in a deadly tone, wetting her lips.

"I am innocent of the carnage upon your people," Mikhail frowned. "That was the blind hatred of the church."

Estella's face crumpled as tears ran down her cheeks. Mikhail sat next to her on the edge of the bed with an expression of concern as she shook with emotion, her eyes averted.

"Of late my searches always begin and end with you," Mikhail sighed. "You are an elusive piece of an unknown puzzle. Talk to me about what happened, Estella. This time, no games."

In one swift move, Estella had drawn the dagger and held it to Mikhail's throat. Mikhail flinched, as he felt the edge of the dagger graze his skin

Estella stood over him with dry, triumphant eyes, her face twisted into an ugly mask. "The dagger is poisoned. Should I but nick the skin, the effect will be deadly. You ought to be flattered, you will be joining the ranks of other hapless fools who thought to enter my chambers unannounced and unwanted."

"You would be murdering the only man alive who can save you from what is coming," Mikhail replied. "I came to learn from you the truth, so that I may confront the danger that stalks you. He is coming for you!" Mikhail remained perfectly still, aware of the swift death that awaited at his throat. "I came here led by a vision. A hand guided me to you, and I knew not what it was till I learned the extent of your sight. Then I realized your potential, yet I still had to discern why you could be crucial to him." He leaned on his arm and inhaled deeply, struggling to maintain his composure. Estella raised a brow in mock puzzlement, but her eyes betrayed a brewing panic.

"Who is after me, Templar? Who is it now? Talk or I'll make your death even more painful." The false assurance in the tenor of her voice was weak and her pitch elevated.

"Samael himself!" Mikhail hissed coldly, his face covered with a sheet of sweat.

Estella blanched.

"The Blind One will destroy all those who carry the bright flames that can tip the balance of the chessboard between the gods," Mikhail continued. "Better to die than be his prey."

Estella caught a sliver of the horror Mikhail had seen, which he had deliberately projected onto her like the flail of a whip. She searched the room furtively with her eyes, as if the mere mention of Samael's name could conjure him.

"Tell me, what do they want from you?" Mikhail asked urgently. "You owe me at least this grace before taking my life. I tried to protect you. Whose tool are you?"

Hesitantly, she withdrew the dagger from his throat.

"Why couldn't you talk plainly before?" she countered. "I thought you were going to betray me to the church. There is always some demon after my gift." She gave him a look of misgiving.

"Tell what you are, Estella, or what you have done, then I can at least warn you," he murmured.

"I have sight, that is true, but more than that I can extend my sight so far into the void that, unlike mere Twilit fortune tellers, I can see what goes on beyond the veil, the angels and their nemesis and the secrets of creation that no one has ever dreamed of. I always knew I was alone in that gift, as none else could comprehend me. But why would Samael pursue me? Speak!"

With bewildering rapidity and strength, Mikhail rose up, wrenching the dagger from her hand. Spinning her around, he pressed it against her neck.

Estella choked out a shrill scream as he tightened his grip. Then she composed herself, mustering her outraged dignity with the blade now pressed against her throat.

"Were you lying to me about Samael? But of course, you must be! You are in league with those demons that have plagued my life for as long as I can remember."

Mikhail released some of the knife's pressure and observed her with genuine discomfort.

"I trusted beneath that veneer of cruelty you had something that was kind," he began, "and I trust I am a worthy audience for your story. But tell me of your own accord, before I begin the game of torture that you wished to inflict upon me." He spoke lightly but with an underscore of warning.

Estella turned her face to him, the incandescent flame in her eyes dripping hatred. "What do you wish to know about a hapless woman who did not ask for her gifts?" she replied slowly.

"Start with who you are, Tsura," said Mikhail releasing her, "and be truthful. Then we can progress as to why I suspect Samael is after you."

6

REVELATIONS OF
THE DANCER

I am the deluge of sorrow and the bereaved weeping in the plain

I am the last ray of sunlight hunting a lost echo in the vale

When my spark is devoured whole and relieves me of my pain

I am still the oil in a dying lamp held by a fool's hope frail

"I AM NOT DUKE DELCOUR'S DAUGHTER, THOUGH HE NEVER KNEW. He consummated his marriage to the contessa in Portugal, and there she gave birth to Duchess Estella of Delcour. The contessa and her daughter remained there for five years. You see it was a marriage of convenience, not love. Portugal had the trade the duke wanted through the alliance."

Mikhail frowned faintly, his keen attention fixed on Estella.

"And then Duke Delcour woke up one morning and had an epiphany, and guess what it was? He needed an heir, and none of his illegitimate bastards would suffice. And because he was sickly, he decided to secure his lands and inheritance through his daughter, and then sire more children on the contessa. So he sent a large retinue to fetch the contessa and her daughter to him." Estella tilted her head and produced from the folds of her dress a locket, pensively wiping it with her fingers, her lucent eyes gleaming with memory.

"They traveled across those beautiful lands and entered into the Frankish kingdoms. All was well until one night, on the return journey, the carriage was attacked. The duke had sent his prize warriors and champions for the parade to bring his wife and child home, and they killed off the assailants. But the robbers had already made off with most of the jewels—and with several lives. This included the contessa and her child.

"Then they were terribly afraid. They knew the duke would hang them, confiscate their lands, and then turn his wrath on their families. Not out of love, but out of spite and pride that his dignity had been affronted and his honor besmirched in such a way. So they bethought themselves to find a way around it. They cleaned up the carriage and set it back together, for the axle had broken. Then they buried the bodies and set off hunting in the neighboring villages and towns till they found what they needed and more, for on their way they came upon a family of poor travelers. And the duke's champion Sir Ryan noted that they were dark skinned like the people of Portugal.

"A certain couple among them had a little girl exactly the same age as the duke's precious heir. So Sir Ryan conceived in his brilliant mind a plausible story that told how the carriage was attacked by robbers and how he had fought valiantly to save the contessa, but alas, he had failed. But with his last ounce of strength he had valiantly managed to save the life of the duke's beloved heir. And with that Sir Ryan cut the family down—or rather cut down the father who stood in his way, and the older siblings. But the woman, who had the gift of sight, used her magic to move the hearts of the knights, and she succeeded; they spared her and carried her little daughter away crying.

"Then Sir Ray bethought himself of the possibility of the plot being revealed. So he put a sword to the mother and made her tell her daughter that going away to live as a duchess was the fabric of dreams and the best thing that could ever happen to her. And he told her that should she ever betray the secret the knights would kill her mother and aunts and she would meet a very bitter end." Estella paused a moment to grit her teeth, her eyes flashing angrily.

"Of course the little girl accepted everything that was asked of her, for she was merely five and she knew only the poverty of the road and the happy moments of family life, which were now cut from her indefinitely. Her mother whispered to her promises that she would find her again one day, and told her not to worry, but to play the part of the princess like in the fairy tales. She told her to remember all the ladies of the courts they had traveled to and emulate their ways, embedding them in her heart. But deep down she must never forget that she was Tsura, the first light of dawn."

Estella lifted the locket up to him and he took it from her gently. He saw within the dented old locket the image of a full-faced young woman with light eyes, a ruddy complexion, and red hair braided with pearls. Her skin was dark but her features delicate, and she reminded him of the paintings of Egyptian queens, exotic and stately. She didn't have the hardness of Estella's eyes, but, he thought, pain and bitterness and the passage of time were better and greater parents than the ones that birthed you.

"So the exchange was made," Estella continued, "and I was led away to this dismal city, to my 'father' who barely acknowledged me. And everyone fawned on my exotic features, telling me I was like a princess of the Indus Valley or one of the Pharaoh's daughters. Yet they knew nothing, nothing at all about the wound growing within me and festering deeper and deeper, like a hole plunging the world into darkness and opening me up to a world I didn't fathom existed.

"The duke couldn't care less about me. At first I was an interesting attraction—beautiful in a way the English rose could not compete. The death of his wife did not move him, but he made an excessive display of sorrow and erected a great shrine in her memory.

"All the court felt sorry for me, of course. At first they showered me with love and affection. Already they schemed, knowing how extensive my wealth would be upon the duke's passing. Indeed, I should be wealthy enough even for the king's lesser sons to cast an eye on me. The duke was much occupied with whoring around and profligacy, so I was left to the care of his sister, the good Lady Bess, and I was raised by her.

"She always said I had the steadfast nature of a man, but the charm and feminine allure of a fatal woman, and that the two mingled within me to move men to obey me. We come from a proud race, Mikhail. Pharaohs whose wives held the throne and led their men into battle. Our gods were fierce and their cults ruled the heavens and earth. And in my blood, on my father's side, the Devas had granted incarnation in our family for generations.

"We were the true Twilit people, living in the dusk of the Goddess. She blessed me with sight, like that of my people, but my gift far exceeded theirs, even as a child. For I recall my mother's womb and could describe the sounds around me and the translucent veins that nourished me. I could recall where I came from ere I incarnated into human flesh. I understood this earth was a prison for the body, and the soul was bound to it, to languish. And the spirit divine, the god spark, was the currency of the demons that sought dominion over us. I saw so far into the heavens I could glean echoes of the throne's decrees. Then my mother wept for me, and was afraid, for she knew my destiny would try to warp my spirit and break me into a vessel for the game of the world.

"Then the duke died, though I was not there to witness it, but rather feigning sickness here in this very manor. I could not stand the sight of him. In his dotage he started to forget the laws of father and daughter and he took a liking to me that entered into the profane. His debauched life knew no bounds and he hated life as much as he hated death. His wealth was the only thing that kept the world from seeing him for what he was. That, and his entourage of sycophants, eager to please him and eager to find ways between my legs. I think I quelled that ambition of theirs a few years ago actually," she said, playing with a strand of reddish hair, her eyes hardening.

"I lured a few into my chamber and slit their throats. And of course with the stories about how I'd rather die than be defiled, following in the footsteps of my dear aunt, I was already an eccentric saint in the eyes of the church. Well, they think I will be joining the cloister soon and giving the entirety of my fortune to them, which keeps them happy enough to ignore all my dealings. And as for my fiancé, Lord Woodcraft, well, they don't mind me being betrothed. Many royals marry and later join the cloister," she trailed off, then raised her eyes to Mikhail's.

"Tell me, Mikhail, is Samael truly after me?" she asked, swinging her legs off the bed and approaching him with a frown.

"I am not sure, though there is a chance. Your gift is certainly precious and could be bent to his evil purposes, especially if you are truly as skilled as you claim."

"What led you here? I deserve to know that at least," she responded coldly as flitting shadows gathered in the corners of the room—little demons eager to partake of the enfolding scene. Mikhail snorted in derision, watching the demons disappear beneath his imperious gaze.

"I'll tell you. A woman who would have brought forth a new messiah was murdered by Samael. I saw it enfold. I prayed for a vision to follow his trail, and this vision I followed. I knew not what I was looking for, or who, but it seems that everything converges around you. You have the most potent gift I have ever heard of or seen. But I must confess you fall short of my expectations, Tsura."

"I don't suppose you would ask the help of a Twilit after all," she said in a mock sober tone. "Do not dare bring my name against your lips. We are not friends. Your crusading filth have murdered enough of my kin already throughout the ages." She watched as Mikhail's dispassionate eyes scoured the room thoughtfully.

"No, Tsura, it wasn't me, nor us. The church has been at war with us for centuries, too, and our orders predate them. We merely adopted whatever granules of truth they had gleaned from their recollections of Christ—the real story. We have it and live it. They are merely an important and rich establishment that we need on our side. We welcomed your people once, and they rejected us. But this you won't recall from the oral histories of your wandering people."

"Your orders have done nothing but isolate us and demonize us," Estella retorted. "If not for our Twilit gods and the spirits that watch over us, we would be caught between your orders and the clergy, the hammer and the anvil. I have not forgotten the witch hunts and the annihilation of our 'pagan' cultures." Her lips formed the last words with distaste. "What was burned at the stakes endured."

"Oh yes, Estella, I can see how well you kept yourself. And these petty demons that seek to defile your soul in exchange for a pittance of power? Are you so blind as to fall for their evil lies, to be so feeble as to be led by them? Is that your end? A burning existence in hell where you are eternal food for the demons to feed on, till your soul rises to the gates and begs the angels for mercy and receives none? Is that what you want?" He looked her up and down scornfully. "Sight is wasted on the likes of you, frivolous woman, when men like me go into the world and protect it from the depredation of darkness."

"I do not believe you, and I doubt very much anyone else would," Estella smiled, self-satisfied. Mikhail opened his mouth to retort then closed it and sighed. To his surprise she grinned at him.

"I have finally cracked the enigma of your obsession with me. You are an overzealous, mad, fool of a Templar, though perhaps you have the right intentions. You believe you were tasked by God himself to save the world. Then a fancy nightmare led you here thinking the hand of God was leading you. And you latched on to me because . . ." she paused considering. "Do you even realize how strange the things you are telling me are? Do the other orders even believe you?" Confirming her suspicions, Mikhail's face betrayed raw resentment.

"So you think I am raving? Well, who would have thought that you had something in common with the cardinal?" Mikhail scowled at her pitying grin, pondering the events that had unfolded so quickly. Nothing was coincidence in this life. He recalled the sacred gnostic scriptures and the story of Mary of Magdala, also waylaid and defiled by darkness and yet a light of the age. His order was predicated on finding the sacred feminine that had been lost since the lineage of Magdalene was broken. He pondered whether Estella had the potential to be initiated into his order and give herself over to a life of saving souls. Or was she already sworn to the darkness?

"Exercise caution in all your ways," Mikhail urged. "I may not have the support of the orders in this, but I recognize evil when it strikes."

"I almost believed you when you told me Samael was after me," Estella announced, repressing her smirk. "But then I realized, had it any credence, your entire order would be at my door baying like bloodhounds."

When she lifted her eyes, she found Mikhail looking down on her and blushed. Subtly winding his way into her mind, he found a tumult of conflicting emotions; attraction and admiration and centuries-long distrust of the orders. She also had a disdain for men, and their desire to dominate women disgusted her.

He knew she stirred within him fierce emotions. He was fascinated by her, almost as though she were a strange, wild feline emerging from the depths of the African desert. Her roots might be humble, but she carried herself regally and knew what she wanted. He admired that in a woman. But she was betrothed, he recalled frowning.

"Three months from tomorrow is the ball of Saint Angela," Estella remarked. "The entire court will congregate in the halls of the palace and parade their parures and idiocy. But it's also an idyllic place for men to entertain business and meet others without seeming too conspicuous." She withheld the sarcasm from her voice but did not meet his eyes. "It would be an opportunity for you to meet Lord Woodcraft. I'm sure you will take a liking to him."

Estella observed Mikhail quietly. He looked cold again, and impassive; their brief closeness vanishing in seconds.

"Well, remember that I will be observing you from afar as I go about my own business," said Mikhail. "I will approach you only if I feel you might be in danger, but also come to me if you feel threatened. You can find me at The Stag and Hare." He turned briskly, nodding towards her. "What time is the ball?" he added haughtily, his jaw squarely determined.

"Eight, but I doubt I will remain long." Estella was before her armoire now, tumbling out endless silken garments. Picking out a deep royal blue nightdress, she turned to face him. "I think you can find your way out now. From today for seven days to come I shall be mourning, so don't expect me to delight in your company for that time."

"Why are you mourning those artisans? Who was that woman to you?" Mikhail stood by the door. His raised eyebrow was all she could descry in the dimming candle light. Estella stiffened.

"The woman was my aunt, and the one true solace for my pain. My mother died a few years ago, here in this very home from red fever. I couldn't heal her, for some spell was also upon her. Though I kept my aunt hidden, the church found out one day. They threatened to excommunicate me if I continued to fraternize with the Twilit. Those were the last vestiges of my family you saw tonight, cut down in one go, like insignificant cattle. In our culture we dress in red and black for mourning. Black for the reaper who steals the lives of the beloved, and red for the blood of life that we believe is eternal."

Mikhail suddenly remembered the red jasper bracelet in his pocket, feeling its weight through his cloak. He fished it out and laid it on the bedside dresser.

"I bought something from the artisans' quarter. The old man needed the money, and I don't wear jewels, so you may donate it to the children in your care," he said as he left, closing the door behind him.

Estella, seeing the dull red sheen of the jasper, smiled wistfully. She took it in her hands and sighed as the memories of the stone spilled forth—the old man's labors and woes, a sick wife he had laid to rest, and numerous children and grandchildren, destitute. Then hope in the sight of the jasper, hope for a monetary reward, and fleeting moments of cynical pleasure upon coming across the count. Mikhail had been thinking of her. And what held them together now was a talisman of dreams woven by broken hopes and aspirations, and the naivety of old men hoping for happy endings. She blew out the candles, laying the bracelet beside her bed, then sought out sleep.

7

A DEADLY END TO
THE MASQUERADE

It was quenching fire with a lantern of oil that joined the pyre
Of gilded echoes laid to rest in their cenotaph of rotted desire
It was like caging of the heavens the wayward bound errant cloud
To mask reality's austere face with a dismal deathly shroud

S AINT AUGUSTA'S FEAST PRECEDED THE BALL OF SAINT ANGELA.
Though it was a lesser ball, it was of greater significance. Unlike
Saint Angela, there were no great displays by musicians or artists from
all corners of the kingdom. It was mostly a gathering of the blue-blooded
royals celebrating their power by donating silver coins with King Wulfric's mint all over London. In exchange the inhabitants would sing "God
Save the King" and erect banners in his honor. At this time, nobles
would bring to the king the "tribute" gems they obtained on trades that
weren't part of the tithing. These included precious icons that were
pillaged from faraway lands or anything valuable that would add to the
king's extensive hoard and bring more favor to the noblemen.

Yet the queen was the one they truly feared. Queen Mary the Adorer
hardly attended any court matters, but her representatives were everywhere. They scoured the kingdom, seeking signs of revolt against the
king. She hid herself behind a veneer of piety, having taken the veil
many years ago, and was a staunch worshipper of the Virgin Mary. All
the little churches, however far removed, that were dedicated to the
Mother of God she took under her wing and had reconsecrated. For
that the nuns adored her.

But the Twilit people and Estella knew the morbid fascination that she held for those places because of their pagan origins. Estella couldn't help but wonder what the likes of Saint Augustine and Pope Gregory I would think of the paradox the royalty had fallen into. When Saint Augustine evangelized Britain, the pagan population was very taken with their deity worship. He knew he couldn't shift their beliefs easily, so he requested the advice of Pope Gregory, who had the ingenious idea of swapping the idol temples with churches and replacing pagan altars with all the saints they could dream of. And it worked perfectly. Nothing changed but the name and the style of dress, and the worship continued. That was effectively how many pagan practices became immovable from the rites of the church, and were utterly absorbed into it.

Shrines and temples dedicated to the female deities were given over solely to the Virgin Mary. This raised her popularity, and the Holy Virgin became the most important patron of women, which suited the church. Her meek and humble nature was precisely what they required of women. But beneath that facade, in some secluded churches, the cults of the old goddesses thrived as ever.

Saint Angela was a merry gathering and women of all stations prepared for it in their own fashion—buying new dresses, acquiring new jewels, and seeking potential mates. The poorer and less connected nobles held little balls of their own, celebrating with plentiful wine as fireworks blossomed in the night sky. This year Earl Woodcraft was back in town, having returned from journeys in his father's lands in Saxony. He was delighted to be back in his favorite city—the elegant court with its refined ways, the endless supply of gentlemen, well-shaped, with soft skin and ever more enticing lips. And of course there was Estella, his supposed salvation and devoted friend, who claimed to be so eager to protect his secret.

Woodcraft was currently in a carriage laden with gifts for Estella, mulling over his thoughts darkly. In two months they were supposed to wed. So far she seemed outwardly to be keeping her side of the bargain, but an inordinate sense of horror radiated from her presence at moments, and his natural inclination for suspicion became an obsessive paranoia that gradually degenerated into fears of betrayal. His unease engendered a compelling need to be rid of her, and since he feared and knew her spiteful nature towards men that exerted pressure on her, he preferred to end their deal in an unfortunate yet beneficial way.

Stopping the carriage outside Goldmark's jewelry atelier, Woodcraft marched in with the ease that only an earl could muster. A group of pretty, coquettish girls smiled at him as he entered, admiring his golden hair and clear blue eyes. He flashed them his most charming smile, winking amiably, then headed straight to the goldsmith.

"Steady now, ladies, you wouldn't want Duchess Estella to have your eyes pickled for dinner," warned the goldsmith.

"Oh, I'm sure Estella wouldn't mind us admiring a piece of art. Surely man was made in God's image and here is the proof," smiled a thin blond girl with elaborate gold hairpins and teasing eyes. Detaching herself from the group, she approached the earl. "I am Lady Gwyneth of Montrose," she said, putting her hand out for him to kiss. "I don't think we've ever met officially." He obliged reluctantly with a strained smile, then let go of her hand quickly. He had seen Lady Gwyneth at balls before, but managed to avoid her until now.

"Earl Woodcraft at your service, my lady." Woodcraft's tone was polite and suave, but his face disinterested. Gwyneth was unused to being ignored by men. Besides Estella, she was generally considered the most eligible beauty in London. Her blue eyes turned cold and she swatted Woodcraft playfully with her fan.

"Always so polite and always so cold. Dear me, it must be hard work being betrothed to such a beast as Estella. Maybe you should have a bejeweled harness made for her, to tame her animal nature." Gwyneth turned away toward the gaggle of women, laughing. Woodcraft stood still and clenched his teeth, then feigning disdain he picked up a necklace studded with fire opals, pretending to scrutinize the quality of work.

Without so much as looking at her, he responded, "Yes, I love the wild passion and fire of felines and their vicious ways. Fierce and alive, sanguine with a vivid love for life . . . This would suit her, this iridescent fiery gem, pure yet ablaze with a million fires."

Putting the necklace down on the counter and beckoning for the goldsmith to wrap it for him, Woodcraft picked up a cheap bronze bangle that served as a charm for ailing adults with poor blood circulation. "Whereas some women are common, and though they be bedecked with jewels and fine garments, they have seen more ceilings than the painters of the Vatican."

Lady Gwyneth gasped and blanched, while one of her friends sniggered. Gwyneth promptly slapped her across the face before storming out of the shop.

The earl ignored the ladies behind him and engaged in a conversation with the goldsmith. The remaining ladies, however, watched him with vindicated pride. Gwyneth was renowned for stealing the hearts of taken men, then tossing them away. Approaching tentatively, a shapely brunette with vivid green eyes tapped him on the shoulder. The earl swung around with thunder in his eyes and the brunette flinched.

"Sorry to disturb you, Lord Woodcraft, but I recognized you from Father's ball. You must remember me, I am Jane Rood, Matthew Rood's sister," she said tentatively, biting her lip.

The earl relaxed and smiled benignly. Of course he remembered her, she was Matthew's darling sister, and he was very, very fond of Matthew. Bowing and kissing her hand fondly, he gestured to the goldsmith.

"Pearl earrings for the lady. I must make amends for exposing her to such distasteful conversation."

Jane gasped, blushing madly and covering her mouth with her gloved hand. The other girls made noises of disapproval as they left the store. Jane looked back and blushed more deeply, babbling apologetically to the earl, who was engrossed in studying a glass display of earrings, selecting from among them a fine pair of teardrop pearls.

"Ah, these are perfect. I'm sure your brother would approve of my choice." He beckoned for Jane to come closer and she muffled a giggle with her hand.

"You are spoiling me too much, what would Matthew say?" She beamed as the goldsmith wrapped the pearls in taffeta and set them in a shiny wooden box, presenting them to her. Grinning from ear to ear, she stood on her toes and kissed the earl on the cheek. He stiffened with surprise, then smiled and led her to the door. After he had bid her farewell and watched her depart, he turned to the goldsmith with a bored expression.

"I need that fire opal necklace of course, or it might seem strange, entering here and buying nothing. I also need something else . . . that thing I asked of you, you recall it?" Woodcraft's voice was pressing, and he now looked furtively left and right, beads of sweat beginning to appear on his brow.

The goldsmith fumbled with his beard and nodded irritably, disappearing into the back. The earl kept a watchful gaze at the shop's entrance nervously. The goldsmith soon returned with a box covered in black velvet, which he set on his desk and nudged towards the earl suggestively.

"As you have already paid, there is nothing further to ask from you. There is no way this can be traced to me, and if you try to implicate me, there is no way in hell you will succeed." The goldsmith refused to meet Woodcraft's eyes, opting instead to stare fixedly at the counter. "Now remember, this will only work through repeated skin contact, and it will take three months to achieve its goal."

The earl nodded and hurriedly took the box, stowing it beneath his cloak.

"And I cannot have you disappearing from here suddenly," the goldsmith added. "Pay your regular visits, buy or pretend to buy, but don't be so foolish as to disappear. People around her seem daft, but they really aren't." He looked the earl squarely in the eye now and the earl nodded impassively.

"Now remember our arrangements. Once she is sick and nearing her end, I have a friend who knows another friend who is friends with someone very friendly higher up the ladder who fakes her death for you and buys her off you. He's interested in her kind, let's say he 'experiments' on them. This way we both get what we want." Woodcraft shook the goldsmith's hand as he turned to the door with relief and left.

The goldsmith watched him enter his carriage with an expression of intense disgust. "He's going ahead with it, old man," he whispered so softly it seemed as though he were talking to himself. Behind the counter's back door an elderly man in white robes hummed in approval, well hidden in the gloom. All that could be descried of him were his bandaged eyes.

The earl reentered his waiting carriage. Now that his heavy duty was taken care of, he was back to lighthearted musings and looking forward to the ball. Estella would be resplendent as usual, the envy of both men and women, and he was much pleased at that. Tonight he would make an extra effort to show his love for her—before going off to seek his real pleasure.

The carriage, after following many winding paths, eventually found its way to Red Fern Manor. The manor, though sumptuously decorated, always made him uneasy. The children repulsed him, a fact he hid of course. His instinctive disgust may have been seen as unnatural for a man expected to produce progeny in the coming future.

The carriage stopped and he descended gracefully only to be greeted by a horde of well-kept, smiling children. The children clapped their hands and tugged at his dark green, silver-threaded cloak as he smiled uneasily. Then suddenly Estella stood at the door beaming. Her dark hair in thick curls was pinned beneath a cluster of ruby and pearl hairpins, and upon her brow she wore a circlet of intricate gold filigree forming stems that held white diamonds and jet. It was unusual for her taste, but then Estella was always the talk of the court with her unusual penchant for strange designs. She was wearing a satin white dress embroidered with pearls and opals and above it a heavy cloak of velvet trimmed with ermine. The clasp at her throat was a star-shaped diamond. She ran towards him and he caught her lovingly, holding her high, then kissing her brow.

"Where have you been hiding, my little princess?" he asked, taking her hand in his and leading her into the house.

"I have your favorite room set up for you already," she said, touching his cheek affectionately.

"Many thanks, my dove. And if you wouldn't mind having some white wine brought up to the room?" He made for the staircase and disappeared upstairs while Estella fetched the wine herself, choosing a vintage she knew he preferred. With the bottle in hand, she headed for his room.

As she walked she scanned the air around her, catching the strands of thought that the earl had left behind him in his wake. She pitied those whose thoughts were open books, but she relished her ability to read them so easily. Knocking at the door, she entered to see him half naked changing clothing. He smiled and turned away as Estella laid the silver platter with the wine goblet and bottle on the dresser.

"I want you to look your best tonight, my rose," he said as he chose a dressing gown. His nude body was slim and perfect like a dancer's.

"Oh, I will. I know how you love our little games together, and to-night I have a great idea for an entrance." Her eyes gleamed with an incandescent light that frightened most men.

Woodcraft smiled, turning around and making for the dresser. Estella took a step back as he passed her and frowned. Her eyes darted to the cloak thrown over a chair. Too engrossed in filling his glass, the earl did not see the rapid change of color in Estella's face as she read through the thoughts that lingered around the black box in one of the cloak's pockets. She blanched, then reddened, her eyes changing from ale brown to blood red. Turning away quickly so he wouldn't catch a glimpse of her countenance, she reached out and plundered his mind in rapid strokes.

She left no crevice or corner empty, then she smiled and said, "Would you like me to bring your favorite scented soaps, my prince? Surely you must smell perfect for tonight?" Her smile seemed genuine, but he was too foolish to see the embers in her eyes.

"Oh yes, I would love that."

Estella left the room and closed the door behind her, pensive and alert, rethinking how she might position her pieces on the chessboard adequately to win with a bitter bite.

In her room, she reflected over the situation with Woodcraft as she readied herself for the night. She had chosen a golden yellow dress sewn with citrine gems and a deep plunging neckline. Over it she draped a royal red velvet cloak spangled with rubies and garnets in star cluster patterns trimmed with black fur and gold tassels. Her girdle was wrought of Saxon gold with garnets in the eyes of the snakes and drag-ons holding her waist, and the clasp was two curved fangs. A black velvet choker covered her neck with small citrines and diamonds sewn in delicately. Her earrings were yellow diamonds dangling on gold threads, and instead of a diadem she wore a heavy gold circlet. Each temple was flanked by an eagle, one wing deployed slightly covering her ear while the other reached for her brow. Their jet eyes sparkled in the light, and a single white diamond was set in the middle, dazzling, pure, and multifaceted.

She applied face paint with an artist's hand. The kohl lent her eyes an even more feline and seductive shape, and she defined her cheekbones with crushed gold leaf powder. She was ready, but her heart was heavy. It had been months since she had seen the count, and though she had banished him from her heart, he was still there in her mind. The horde of demons that usually afflicted her had ceased their daily attacks, and she knew it was because of him. She was grateful and yet irritated that the count could access her from so far away. But the further she pushed him away in her mind, the deeper the feeling grew, till in her dreams she would find him, leaving a kiss upon his brow.

"My lady are you ready?" A page boy was at the door waiting. She stood up, wrapping her furs around her and seizing her gloves.

"Let's go," she said coldly. She suddenly felt alone, venturing forth into the vast masquerade of human society—another ball held in honor of yet another saint.

ESTELLA AND WOODCRAFT traveled to the ball together in a beautiful carriage from the Woodcraft estates. The silence was occasionally broken by the earl, who rambled on about his voyages and how happy he was to be back in town and how faithful women like her were so scarce. She smiled indulgently, nodding along and supplying the adequate "hmm" and "ahh" in the right places. Meanwhile her mind was busy seeking out the count, but he was beyond her reach.

The dusk was deepening into a midnight blue spangled with burning white stars. Estella looked out, her mind wandering to the campfires of her childhood. They had sung songs to the Devas, who had smiled down at them from the stars. The nights had been warm and the moon danced with its train of clouds, beaming down upon its chosen people. They had felt safe and loved by the goddesses of the night—and they had been. They had seen her form in her three incarnations. They adored her. Of all the devoted, Estella was the most loving, for she felt something within her stirred by the three-faced goddess, and offered her heart fully to her.

A jolt of the carriage interrupted her musings—they had arrived. As they descended from the carriage, velvet carpets met their feet. Estella and the earl walked arm in arm, greeting those they passed. The bluest bloods were all congregated together, their laughter and the scent of many perfumes permeating the air.

Estella despised the fake and distasteful dance one must perform to accomplish things in these social circles. She was constantly conflicted between shocking them and playing their game, and toyed with both according to her ever shifting moods. The steps to the palace were heavily guarded by soldiers in royal purple attire, their swords and mail bearing the emblems of the king. Estella and Woodcraft mounted the steps, Estella with her head held high and eyes aloof, and the blood red jewels on her cloak dazzling in the fiery torches before the manor. The laughter and chatter was silenced as she entered. Some nobles smiled sourly as she drifted past, her winged circlet lending her the air of an exotic queen.

No one dared to speak to her, and whoever had the inclination to mock her was silenced. She laughed and held the earl's hand as they danced beneath the great hanging chandeliers, which scintillated with the fires of a million gems. The other guests took to the dance too, but Estella took the central part and beneath her feet the amber and gold floor took life and glowed, and out of her poured wisps of dreams.

As the waiters circulated with the wine, Estella detached herself from Woodcraft with a graceful twirl and seized a heavy goblet. She seated herself on a golden chair with a bouffant silk cushion and drank deeply. She was feverish with a simmering rage that only drink could assuage. She was bitter towards Woodcraft. For such a simpleton to deceive her was unthinkable. Disturbed from her reverie by a looming shadow, she set down her goblet to stare at the footman in royal armor who approached her.

"The king imparts to you his greetings and is impressed with your entrance, but is however disappointed that you did not greet him. After all, aren't all precious things to be presented to him, my lady?" The footman's voice was monotonous, as all their servants were trained to be, and she understood he was merely the mouthpiece of the king.

Gifting him with her emptied goblet, she obliged him with her most charming smile as she sprang to her feet, leading the way to the far end of the hall. There, upon a heavy dais, the king's mighty throne stood. It was wrought of gold and encrusted with gems, and ensconced in the wall behind it was the world's largest ruby. It was embedded in the marble wall with sunrays of gold radiating from it. Turning her attention to the king, Estella bowed profusely before capriciously taking a step back and biting her lip, revealing the dimples in her cheeks.

"Always so humble, yet always so aloof. What is the riddle with you, little one?" King Wulfric's voice was hoarse with liquor, but his sharp blue eyes were not fogged by age and he still held a vigor that more youthful men lacked. Though his hair was white and an iron crown sat heavily upon his head, his swift movements were agile and even alarming. He eyed Estella with a calculating look while she beamed at him.

"One could never be aloof in your presence, O king," she said, her suave voice soft and breathy, and she bit her lip suggestively. "But forgive my ill manners for not greeting you more promptly," she pled, bowing again. The king chuckled, satisfied.

"Come closer, Estella," his voice rent the air sharply and Estella paused, nonplussed, reaching into his mind questioningly. He was simply inebriated and jesting, to test her. Estella approached the throne with a gentle sway of her hips, meekly averting her eyes. "Kneel before me," he commanded, the sparkle in his blue eyes becoming hard.

Estella became aware of many gazes converging around her, for everyone had stopped dancing and was watching her with morbid fascination. They were curious to see what the king wanted of the duchess. Earl Woodcraft himself was uncertain and pale, rooted to the spot in a circle of his friends, unable to intervene. The music that had started to play was now the only sound, the violins sounding almost ominous. Estella knelt before the king, lifting her head to meet his eyes.

Though King Wulfric was old, he was not yet tired of his mistresses. And now his attentions had turned to Estella. But first he had to see whether he could break or humiliate her. Her ale brown eyes changed, the incandescent light veering to a subtle red as she smiled. The king was visibly unsettled.

Tapping the shoulders of his throne with his fingers, he frowned, then hissed, "Kiss my feet. I heard that your arrogance with men is unparalleled. Let's see if I may cure you of it." His stare was cold, and all the inebriated good cheer was banished from it immediately.

Estella's composure remained equanimous, and her eyes burned into his, carefully blank. Wetting her lips with her tongue and watching him, she reached for his right foot and pulled it gently towards her.

"It is always an honor to kiss the feet of your sovereign," she said, her smile fading and her eyes burning like two embers. The king returned her glare while reaching for the heavy cross at his neck. "I am sure the queen would approve of the Christian tradition of kissing the feet of the poor, but never have I had the honor of kissing the feet of those above my station." She started to untie his ribboned slipper, deliberately slow, as the king's breathing became forced. Estella summoned from her mind a vision and wove it together, channeling it onto the foot of the king.

"I thank you for taking it upon yourself to humble me, O king," she said smoothly as she removed the slipper. At the sight of his bare foot the king gasped and Estella innocently feigned shock, covering her mouth as though scandalized.

The king's face reddened with wrath and shame and he withdrew his foot stammering, "Guards, summon my physician now!"

"My liege, forgive me," Estella said earnestly, "I should not have re-acted in such a way." She crossed herself devoutly and bowed her head while the king struggled to regain his stoic composure, all the while observing his foot; a malodorous, gangrenous mess of green and black.

The closest courtiers to the king had gathered around at Estella's cry and they averted their eyes from the foot that the king could not hide fast enough. With admirable swiftness, a physician arrived. He set about bandaging the foot with ointments while mumbling about contaminated old slippers and infectious airborne diseases. He bowed and scraped a lot, beseeching the king to follow him into his royal bedchamber, to further his examinations. The king, disguising his dismay, stared from his foot to the faces of all his gathered courtiers and nobles in astonishment. Coldly dismissing them, he made for the exit behind the throne where his physician waited obediently. He shot a suspicious look at Estella as he passed, before his physician began to fuss over him again and he was forced to make his exit.

Woodcraft approached Estella. He looked pale but relieved. "What on earth was that about?" he asked hurriedly.

Estella shrugged. "He was drunk and thought it would be entertaining for me to kiss his arse—sorry, I mean his feet—and that didn't quite turn out too well for him."

The earl leaned forwards with unconcealed concern. "You know the people here love you yet fear you. They sense something about you is different, and they think it's either piety or the damn opposite." He was angry, but doing his best to contain himself. Her eyes were cold and she made no pretense of her disdain. The earl opened his mouth to speak, then decided against it. He forced a smile. "Why aren't you wearing the opals I bought you, my rose?" he asked, his tone falsely sweet.

"Oh dear me, I was planning to wear them but I got distracted with a little matter of business. Please forgive me, I could wear them to death they are so beautiful."

Woodcraft failed to catch on to her insincerity. Feeling that the chill between them had dissipated, he cleared his throat, pretending to be interested in a table of canapés.

"I have someone to meet now—you understand what I mean. I shall be gone for the night. Leave at midnight and someone dressed like me will be there to escort you back, you know the usual drill." He didn't face her and Estella hummed in acquiescence.

"Of course, my dear, enjoy your night," she said, moving away from the table. But not fast enough to miss the thoughts spilling out of Woodcraft. That black box . . . Estella gritted her teeth with bitterness, then went to join the dance.

Her head spun with the liquor, yet still she danced bewitchingly. As a crowd of noblemen drew near to watch her, she dazzled their senses, pulling them even closer to her. The liquor was making her exceedingly bold and reckless, and she watched carelessly as the men's lusts awoke and they began arguing among themselves over grievances that had never happened. She laughed, fanning herself as she went to refresh her wine.

A shadow behind her alerted her to a certain male presence. She turned around with a coquettish look, only to find the count staring into her face with a cold and disapproving gaze. She blushed as he reached out, taking the goblet from her hands, and setting it firmly on the table.

"Oh, don't presume to tell me how to behave, Count Mikhail of Somewhere," she smiled.

"Let's go for a walk at least, while Oswald undoes the damage you've done to those men." He looked her over with a belittling ferocity that stung her pride.

His eyes were stormy grey and implacable as they made their way to the exit to the royal gardens. He walked with her silently, but held her arm like any gentleman would, greeting passersby with his frosty charm. Estella offered them a distracted smile. As they walked, the shadow around the count grew, engulfing her senses, till she was no longer able to sense anything but her own pounding heart.

The garden path was a beautiful snaking pathway of smooth stones leading to alcoves, glades, and other secret little places. Along the path were endless varieties of roses and flowers. There was a maze, too, in the darkness. The count made in that direction now.

Betraying nothing of his thoughts to her, he said, "Your betrothed seemed quite concerned about that trick you played on the king. You are lucky to have the gift of theatrics, or you might have found yourself being hanged for witchcraft." He gripped her arm as he led her further into the gardens where the laughter of amorous couples faded and the silence deepened.

Estella stopped abruptly in her tracks, her face hidden in shadow. "What do you intend to do, Count? I don't appreciate being humiliated by kings and their like. And I don't think you have half the brain required to understand what is between me and Woodcraft."

The count paused. Then, without responding, he led her deeper into the gardens. Estella's mind raced and her heart pounded, wondering what could await her there.

"Tread carefully now, make no noise," Mikhail's voice dropped to a whisper and Estella followed his lead beneath a thicket of thorns.

Faint gasping noises echoed in the dark from where two figures crouched. The dim rays of moonlight that fingered their way through the gloom revealed a dark-haired man, muscular and tall and naked, sweating with exertion. The sweat gleamed on his taut skin while he crouched on hands and knees, a second figure holding his hips. At first Estella could not tell who it was, but the moonlight finally flooded through the thicket onto the golden hair of Earl Woodcraft. The other man she recognized as Matthew Rood.

The two were lost in the throes of pleasure, the earl gripping Matthew tight and plowing him hard. With every thrust, Matthew moaned and shuddered with pleasure. Estella averted her eyes to find the count watching her. She turned away noiselessly and made her way back to the footpath with the count walking slowly behind her. Once there, she stopped and swerved to behold the count, who was observing her with a mixture of pity and distaste.

"You were aware of course, weren't you? A marriage of convenience so you did not have to marry into the royal houses?"

"Yes," she said coldly and turned away.

"Why is marriage so repulsive to you?" the count inquired. Estella stopped in her tracks and turned to faced him.

"None of these nobles could ever understand me. They make my skin crawl. Besides I am not one of them, I was robbed of what was mine. I refuse to bear the children of some rich man who will indulge in wine and whores till I am old and withered when he will discard me for others. I am Tsura the Seer. I owe nothing to the royalty of this land, and certainly will not be bound by the shackles of men who are so ungifted and stupid!" She spat out the last words with vitriol, and continued walking.

"But not all would cage you like an exotic beast or bird to display," said the count, following her quick strides, "nor as a toy for the bedroom. Some would value you for who you are and let you ride and rule by their side."

"Oh shut your mouth, who do you think you're fooling, me? I've lived here years and years and I know the hearts of these people. They are riddled with vice and boredom. There is nothing remarkable about any of them, nothing at all. I am alone in the underworld of the Twilit people." Her voice trembled as he stared into her eyes.

"There are others like you," he said. "Our orders seek them out and we cherish them. I, for one, cherish you, though you offer me only hatred in return." Estella looked away uneasily.

"I underestimated that fool, you may be surprised to know," she said. "Yesterday he bought a matching wedding ring and bangle imbued with a slow-acting latent poison. And he would have watched me die slowly, languishing in pain, just to preserve his secret. He distrusts me to keep my side of the bargain. He might not be of the sharpest wit, but he knows there is danger around me. I suppose I inspire such drastic measures from men, or perhaps the demons that plague me are addling his reasoning."

"I see," said the count frowning. "As head of the Northern Order, I will come myself to admonish him for his betrayal." His eyes glittered with unusual malice. "But end the betrothal, Estella, you cannot live your life a lie. It is a wasted effort." His voice was pleading again. Moving closer to her, he touched her cheek with a ringed finger. She trembled, pushing the count away, but inadvertently stumbled heavily, colliding with the ground and clutching her head feebly.

"Bound beyond the gates of night, he clambered over and fell," Mikhail intoned, "and from out of nonexistence he finds the substance of existence; the womb of infinity, and there he swelled and fed and ripped through the womb and fell like a meteor upon our world."

Estella writhed on the ground, eyes glazed, and the count, kneeling by her side, murmured in understanding. Cradling her head, he sought her eyes. They were entirely black. Gazing deep into her soul, he saw nothing but the vast empty spaces behind the stars, the endless dark—

the primeval birthplace of light. Estella shook, her whole body rigid. The count laid his hands upon her, invoking the sacred incantations of the holy orders. He issued commands while the blackness in Estella's eyes seemed to engulf all light around her and the stars far above began to wheel.

"Watch them burn, the wheels of heaven. The greater ones guard the throne itself. Aren't they beautiful? But tonight I cannot see the seventh sky." Mikhail traced symbols upon her face and a glowing pattern emerged. He traced his fingers all over her shaking body till she ceased trembling and finally swooned into a comatose state.

8

EYESIGHT FOR THE BLIND

I am deeper than the oldest hollows and bottomless wells
Where beyond, ages shine by in their distant trajectory across the sky
Where the endless chiming of the world's reckoning bells
Know full well that by forgetfulness they die

"HOW LONG HAS SHE BEEN HERE, MIKHAIL?" CAME A DRY FEMALE tone. The voices were distant and vague, like transient echoes beginning to fade into nothing. Estella was jolted violently back into awareness after having been plunged for so long in a chaotic slumber riddled with dreams and ill omens. She did not move though, even as the coldness of the ground she lay on began to penetrate to her bones. She held her breath and waited to regain her senses fully.

All she could yet discern were the unnerving rasping noises around her; there must be at least four or five of them on all sides of her, but never too close. And she could hear a strange hissing and muttering from farther away. A chill permeated the air, imbuing it with the heavy taste of fear. How long she had been unconscious she couldn't yet fathom, but a creeping sense of urgency swept over her, accompanied by a dark foreboding.

"I think she is already awake, Mikhail, why don't you introduce her to us?" The female voice that spoke was falsely welcoming. Estella stiffened, bracing herself as Mikhail's footsteps approached. She felt him before he actually knelt beside her, his presence a tingling allure to her senses. She opened her eyes momentarily to see him crouching some distance from her, hesitating.

"Don't get too close, she might get frightened and bolt!" the dry female voice resounded in the drafty hall.

A snort echoed in return and Mikhail called out to Estella, "I will approach you but I need you to trust me. You are not among enemies here. This is Queen Mary, Oswald, my trusted friend, and the Blind Sage. You are in a safe place, Estella. This is a sanctuary, built underground, hallowed, and sacred. The seer of our order, the Blind Sage, contrived an impregnable fastness to withstand all evil. But for gazing into the darkness he paid the ultimate price—he was blinded. Yet he remains the unwavering bulwark of our order, providing the most precious knowledge we need to retaliate against the enemies of God."

Estella raised herself painfully to her elbows with aching limbs and found herself on a stark marble floor inlaid with intricate patterns of cosmic scenes and esoteric symbols. She was lying in the very middle of the largest one. Taking in her surroundings, she saw she was in an underground vaulted hall. Around her sat three shadowy figures in high backed chairs shrouded in darkness.

Behind them was a swirling, luminous haze that whispered and hissed. A shadow detached itself from the fog, cloaked and hooded, its ghastly countenance peering right into Estella's eyes. As she looked into the shadowy substance of the grim figure, a dark vapor rippled across her vision and she felt her sight tingling in response. This strange feeling affecting her seemed to twist her power, amplifying it in unfamiliar new ways. And she could feel the manifestation in the underground vault spreading and growing stronger.

Turning to Mikhail, she spat, "Why am I here?" Her head reeled with a throbbing ache and she found she could do no more than sit up. She wondered whether she could escape without being fished back in.

Mikhail raised his hand gently as if he were courting a beast that might attack. Now level with her, he stretched his hand out in a peace offering. Estella cast one glance at him with a ready host of snide comments to throw at him, paused, then screamed in disgust. Recoiling in horror, she thrust a kick at him. He dodged her and grabbed her legs. She screamed even more shrilly and thrashed fruitlessly.

Through the power present in the chamber augmenting her sight, she could see him truly for the first time. His face, which was habitually a tableau of imperious grey eyes and fine chiseled features, was distorted and deformed like melted wax, disfigured into a hideous mask. It was as if a lesser, deformed version of Mikhail was before her—one that was demonic, maimed, swathed in smoke with gaunt, reddened eyes, a window to the barren wasteland of his soul.

"You can see it?" Mikhail asked, beginning to understand. "Yet why suddenly now . . ." he wondered, looking around uneasily. "If you can see our inner darkness then you truly are a seer. But this isn't truly me, it's my demon; the dark inhabitant inside all of us. We have a divine spark of God, but our material body is a home to spirits and demons. Each of us have them, even you, ugly and petty, feasting off your life force and your sins."

"You are lying to me," she hissed. "That is no shadow! I know what I see inside of you," she added, eyeing the movements of the wraiths outside the circle. "No, it is something akin to the demons that wait outside this circle." Her high-pitched voice reverberated in the hall, echoed eagerly back by the wraiths slithering behind the enthroned watchers.

"Don't they all think they are so pure and holy, these proud, sinful ones," sneered the queen. "We must exorcize her now, see how he is coming for her!" The cold authoritarian voice barely concealed the disdain aimed in Estella's direction.

"You cannot exorcise me, you old, useless witch!" Estella flung back. "You have no authority over me! You won't even come close enough that I may see the true ugliness within your soul! Whoever is coming for me is merely amplifying my gift, I have never seen with such clarity before." Mikhail gripped her shoulders and yanked her upwards. "Get off me!" she cried.

Mikhail's ravaged, melted face contorted into a pitiful apology. "There is a dark trail leading to you, Estella. Something dreadful is dogging you. Cavorting with the hidden forces may have opened you up for malefic entities to use you as a weapon. We have no choice but to purge you of it, locking your mind and sight away—for your own safety."

Mikhail hauled her towards the epicenter of the circle where rings of iron in the marble held links of rope and chain. Estella's countenance darkened with grim realization. She feigned weakening, then dealt him a blow to the face with her elbow. Mikhail, surprised, growled in response, momentarily dazed. She bolted towards the edge of the circle where the old man was seated. Aware of the commotion around him, albeit wizened with age, he did his best to obstruct her passage, flailing his arms and cane. But he was blind and milky eyed, and the malevolent mask upon his face was writhing piteously as if in perpetual torment, and so Estella brushed by him easily. But Mikhail's awareness was ubiquitous and he intercepted her just as she was exiting the circle.

The wraiths that gathered around her were like the fabric of mist, without substance. Faceless, they hovered in the air whispering her name, exuding a pull that beckoned her to them. But they reeked of death, and she knew their kind. Cheated of escape, she halted.

"They are all after you, Estella," said Mikhail. "If you leave now they will have you, and nothing will stop them."

She turned around with wrath etched into her hardened features. "I was living in peace till you barged into my life, Templar! Ridiculous, puny little devil that you are—and now you claim I am part of your mess? This is about you, not me, you fool!" She jabbed an angry finger into his chest. "You. Your church. You ignorant fools!" The three others had left their seats and gathered around Estella near the edge of the circle.

"Do not be so sure the enemies of the church value you more than we do, we are all cattle for the slaughter in this material world," intoned the Blind Sage severely.

Without warning, the queen slapped her hard across the face. The queen's face was distorted with her own inner darkness, though it was unlike the truly demonic nature she had seen in Mikhail. Estella recovered from her shock, grinned maniacally, then spat in the queen's face. Oswald grabbed her, dragging her by force to the chains. It was then that the atmosphere in the room shifted—the cold, moist air clogged with fetid odors seemed to vibrate, and whispers rose like a sea of angry wasps, converging around them into one malicious entity. Estella's strength weakened as dread began to seep into her veins. The impulse to flee became overwhelming. Mikhail and Oswald bound her with the chains and left her on the ground to shiver, their expressions unfathomable.

"He is coming for her," the old sage rasped urgently. "I feel it in my very bones. I can almost see him! Quick, let us begin!" The others broke away, swiftly regaining their seats while chanting vehemently under their breath.

The cold that penetrated the hall dug its talons into Estella. Then a shape began to materialize before her outside the circle. The wraiths parted like cloven hay before the scythe and a shadow emerged, towering and dark. From the distance she could see it bore a tall crown of steel that tapered off jaggedly like bent blades. The crown sat atop an odious, malformed head—one-eyed like a cyclops with a single, putrid, bulging, lidless eye. There was a gash for a mouth where long, blackened teeth gnashed together, oozing stygian liquid filled with maggots. He was wreathed in swirling, hissing vapors.

Estella felt her heart pounding with a primeval fear. She squeezed her eyes shut to shield herself from his baleful presence, but even the rising chants from Mikhail's cohort could not distract her from him. She found herself fastening her gaze on the fiend in horror.

Gripped by a sudden frenzy, she laughed out madly, "I see the truth of you all!" Tears streamed down her face as she convulsed in fits of laughter. "The queen is a whore who desires men other than her husband. She lusts over someone here. I wonder who it could be?" She cackled madly at their uninterrupted chanting, aware of the presence gathering power over her. "Oswald murdered his own father, when in his dotage he turned to the sins of the flesh. Did they bathe you in purgatory to wash you clean? Answer me, damn you!" she bellowed at them.

Her slipping mind was on fire. She both wanted to break free and run to the fiend and to crawl away and die. "Mikhail . . ." she whispered in mock tenderness. "Mikhail's mother was visited by an incubus. He fucked her hard all night and here we have a half-breed prodigy." The fiend placed one foot in the circle and she screamed in agony; something within her rupturing mind had begun to burn into a conflagration, and she instantly knew who he was.

"And the old man looked not into the void, but too deeply into my eyes seeking answers, and so he went blind. Then he came with the knife after others." Her voice was suave and unctuous, but like a latent poison it was underscored with menace. It was like a razor that is so fine it draws blood without pain. Only moments later does the agony tumble upon you in a deluge of excruciating fire.

Mikhail broke away from the others with his sword unsheathed, the demon within him withdrawing back into his body. "Get back, you have no dominion here, cursed one! Back, Samael, Blind God, you false aborted creation."

Samael halted in his steps, his steel crown catching the wan light and refracting it coldly. His single eye bore into Mikhail with the vengeful malice of boundless evil. A brandished spear in one hand, he gnashed his black teeth together mockingly. Mikhail stood fast as Samael loomed over him, growing taller and taller. As he expanded, great wings emerged from his back, beating the air with such velocity that Mikhail stumbled backwards.

His deepest fears played before him, reflected back to him in Samael's eye, regurgitated from the bowels of hell. Samael laughed loudly and a blinding light flashed across the hall. Momentarily everything was lost in the sudden blaze. Estella, shaken and filled with the impulse to flee, pulled against her chains, helplessly cursing. She sought the hidden name of metal and steel, whispering spells to awaken their essence, but nothing availed, and in that blinding light she strove to see, straining her ears for movement.

The light began to dwindle, at first subtly, then rapidly receded. A sharp intake of breath was heard in the deadened silence. Where Samael once stood there was now an angel. Oswald, who had positioned himself next to Estella to protect her, dropped his sword. To the depths of which Samael's ugliness descended, the height of his beauty reached.

It was as if he were spun of glorious, golden light. The steel crown was gone and in its place he bore a wreath of flowering stars, each pulsating with its own pure, vibrant light. His hair was long and golden, and it fell with an almost feminine allure down his mighty shoulders. Each feature on his flawless face was sharp and ruthless with the weight of pride, and his eyes were cerulean blue, glittering with repressed laughter. The putrid single eye he once had was dissimulated in a false image he projected of himself—a reflection of what he was before he was dethroned from heaven.

Samael's mouth was shrewd, and he sneered as he imperiously cast his sweeping gaze over Mikhail and Estella. Only the old man huddled on the floor near his abandoned throne was immovable, for he was blind and therefore immune to Samael's beauty.

"I have seen your true face, cursed one," the Blind Sage spoke, his coarse voice almost an affront to the awed silence that Samael had inspired. "Who are you trying to fool this time around? You are ugly and foul, bereft of any godly beauty!" He spat with rancor on the floor in Samael's direction. Mikhail was frowning, transfixed, but soon his face hardened and he resumed his incantations. Samael moved towards them, testing their strength with each step.

They were visibly losing the battle and Estella was aware that she was the prize that they fought over. She turned to Oswald, imploring him to free her, but he was too entrenched in his scriptural chanting to pay her any heed. Panicked, she plucked a silver hairpin from her hair and went to work bending it into an adequate shape. Then she began the arduous task of picking the locks, her shaking hands dropping the hairpin several times. She rocked backwards and forwards, desperately tearing her eyes away from Samael and Mikhail locked in confrontation, but her concentration failed her many times as she struggled with the lock.

"Always in a pickle, aren't you?" whispered a sardonic voice in her ear. Estella whipped her head around, dropping the pin with a muffled scream as the androgynous demon emerged to her left. He was translucent and grave, as if his substance were being diminished in the presence of Samael. Crouching next to her, he said in hushed tones, "I'll pick your locks before Samael burns me to death. Run with me. But first pledge yourself to me—make risking evisceration worth my while at least." Despite the sarcasm in his tone, his one healthy eye was clouded, and he seemed uncharacteristically gaunt with worry.

Seeing the recalcitrance on her face, he sneered, "He will devour you and spit out your soul for hell to defile, till infinity finally caves in. Do you really doubt it? You're a real treat for him—a bright light and seer. You stand at the fringes of God's own eyes and face the aborted darkness. You stare evil in the eye, and he will consume those eyes, open to the infinity of God and the eternity of the false creation. Now come."

Estella cast one last miserable glance at Mikhail, who was ghastly pale and groaning from exertion. Samael gripped him by the neck and lifted him skywards with a triumphant grimace on his cruel, immaculate visage. Then she scrambled to her feet nimbly with newfound courage.

"So be it, get me out of here," she acquiesced.

The demon winced as he touched her chains and they immediately began to singe his flesh. He hissed angrily, straining the muscles of his thin body. Finally the chains crumbled into dust and he let go, sighing with relief, the odor of charred flesh lingering in the air. Grabbing Estella's shoulders, the demon pushed her forwards encouragingly. Without even casting a look back, she fled, the sound of Mikhail choking ringing in her ears.

Estella ran with the demon down a network of underground tunnels. They were both lost and oppressed by the spells of the Templars that repelled them, activated against their forbidden magic. The demon led her deeper and deeper into the never-ending maze by the pale luminescence of his wings.

"We are lost! Where are we, you lackwit demon?" she cursed him vehemently.

"I cannot find my way that easily in this crude jail," he retorted as they moved along the serpentine tunnels, the heat steadily becoming more and more unbearable.

But they were irredeemably lost. The main exit was blocked by Samael and the Templars. And though there was supposedly another way through the subterranean routes, they were unable to find it. The path kept twisting into an expanding network of tunnels, and the demon's sight was crippled by the spells that gilded the halls. The walls quivered and shuddered as if they pulsated with a living heartbeat, and as they delved further, sigils and strange geometric patterns glinted in the darkness. The walls were alive and responded to their presence. Every now and then tortured faces with empty sockets would press out of the walls, their open mouths screaming voicelessly.

"Something here is preventing us from seeing a way out, a spell wrought into these walls to trap us . . ." mused the demon darkly, his one clear eye scanning the walls with distaste.

"I can feel it, too, chafing at my senses. I feel as if I touched these walls I would be cemented inside them forever. This is a bad decision we made," she whispered shakily. The demon nodded, careful lest his wings touch the walls.

It soon became apparent that they were in a maze of some kind. All the paths connected and intersected with no particular logic or reasoning, leading them deeper down to where the magic was culled from the air and bound to the cave walls. They sped ahead as fast as they could, oppressed by the spells that fenced them in, and dogged by the silently screaming faces mouthing supplications. After hours of being utterly lost in the dark, they felt as if the cage had closed behind them.

"This is a prison of sorts," said the demon. "It is no small wonder Samael found it hard to pass through. These halls were built with rigid spells to suck in the magic wielded by the Twilit born and use it against them." The demon's words seeped into the fissures of the heavy air that hung between them.

Estella felt weakened and weary, like a fog was pressing against her mind. She stumbled and leaned on the demon for support. He was concealing a wince with each step, and even his milky eye radiated concern. He took her by the hand, and with a fiendish hiss led her faster into the tunnels, turning right and left, following his own innate instincts.

The demon stopped suddenly in his tracks, and Estella collided with him. He grasped her with unusual gentleness before she stumbled.

"Strain your ears. Do you hear that? It sounds like human voices, listen. Estella, listen! I need your wits about you, there is no time for dallying in sleepiness."

Estella's back stiffened and her cloudy eyes sharpened. She nodded at the demon who, with a sigh of relief, grabbed her arm, pressing her forwards.

"Don't touch the walls and be vigilant. We are approaching human activity, and for the worse I deem."

Fear pressed against her heart with each step as the echoes of human misery became more audible.

The source of the lamentation soon became visible under the eerie light of dozens of candles flickering in sconces. There were row upon row of them—men and women and children, bound by their ankles and necks to the walls with chains. They had barely enough room to maneuver to nearby chamber pots, their raw necks were sore and bloodied, and the stain of blood was smeared across their bodies. The miasma of human waste mingled with unwashed bodies, assaulting their senses.

Estella involuntarily retched, nearly leaning against the walls for support before the demon seized her, yanking her back.

"Fool of a woman! You want to end up chained like they are? Look at what they have done to them, look closer!"

He threw her headlong toward a row of men and women and she tripped, hitting the ground painfully. At the unexpected noise, they cowered in fear, dropping the quills they had been holding. Estella froze in horror as she looked at the prisoners. Where their eyes should have been were empty sockets carelessly bandaged with filthy linen. Infected pus mingled with blood, and their mouths were covered in sores and hung open with thirst.

"Give us water, we cannot write any longer!" came the cracked, beseeching voice of a trembling old man. He was filthily clad in sackcloth, and his sparse beard sagged against his unresponsive child as he sobbed to himself like a helpless infant.

"We cannot write any longer, have mercy for God's sake!" a woman's shrill cry resounded over her, and soon they were all reaching for her, grabbing in her direction blindly, and begging.

Estella covered her mouth with her hand as they ripped off their bandages to feel their empty sockets, and she threw herself at their chains desperately.

"Has the Blind Sage been keeping you here? I am Tsura of Red Fern Manor . . ." her voice broke mid-sentence. The captives pleaded louder, groping towards her wildly.

"You must free us! Look at the handiwork the Blind Sage has wrought on us. Do not just stand there watching, for pity's sake!" The echoes of their cracked voices ricocheted against the stark walls gleaming with sigils. In answer a multitude of soundless, wailing faces erupted from the walls, mouths agape. Estella began to fear that the noise would bring their jailor upon them all.

"Please be silent, I must think!" she cried shrilly, hysteria creeping into her voice.

"What is there to think about? Have you not eyes to see what they have done to us? Where are our eyes?"

Estella recoiled as they fingered their bloodied, infected sockets and picked at their scabs whimpering.

"Free us! Let us out, by all the gods of the Twilit path, we did not deserve this fate!"

Estella dug her nails into her temples, battling the waves of nausea and shock that threatened to overcome her. The demon clicked his tongue and jostled her impatiently.

"Leave them to rot, it's over for them. They are broken. They cannot be mended. Better to die here than rejoin the world to live as parasites on the mercy of others. Come, we must go!" he said roughly, spurning an old man with his boot.

"I cannot leave my people behind!" Estella replied. "Is there no kindness in your blackened heart? Would you turn your back on suffering because they are human?" Her angry cries rose like a tidal wave.

The demon laughed coldly, stooping to grab a thin woman with crusted blisters on her neck. He lifted her up effortlessly by the hair, smiling as he teasingly removed her bandages while she pleaded with him for her freedom.

"Look at this; human weakness, damaged vessels. Their flesh is easily destroyed beyond repair, and they breed easily and to no good purpose. You kill one, more of them breed. What value is there to these decaying organisms that live and die pointlessly?" he asked as he taunted the woman, slapping her and laughing at her resistance.

Estella threw herself at him striking him, attempting to free the struggling woman from his grasp. He dropped the woman and faced Estella disdainfully.

"Even you are worthless, though you have something you don't deserve—something worthwhile. Your sight, stolen from the dark side of God's face, which pierces the thinned veil right up to the throne itself. It is mine now! You are nothing more than wretched vessels of clay, dying to find a parcel of meaning in existence." The demon wrestled Estella to the ground and pressed his forefinger onto her eyelids. "Look at what they do to your kind, these churchmen, these Templars, these men of God. Do you know what this is? They are mutilating your people for their visions, then they pass them off as their own. Ask them!" He turned her face forcibly towards the captives.

"He is right!" an old man cried. "They heard I had sight and they came for me, men dressed in church garb. They showed modest interest at first, then the Blind Sage came to interview me. He had just lost his own sight trying to peel back the veil of night. He tortured me for my visions, plucked out my eyes, and bound me to this wall to write all I could see." The old man ripped his beard, digging his nails into his own face and heaving with tears. Estella wept alongside him.

"Worthless humans oppress themselves, there is no need for us to meddle!" whispered the demon in her ear.

"According to your own hierarchy you are also damaged goods worth nothing. Do not be so quick to judge their worth," replied Estella coldly, unable to detach her gaze from the chained captives.

"I was something far greater than you, witch!" he jabbed his finger at her angrily.

"Let me free them at least. Perhaps they can help us out of here, since you seem incapable of doing so," she retorted harshly.

Falling to her knees, she drove the remainder of her bent hair pins into the chain's locks. And while the chains themselves were charmed to repel her, she persevered, the pain blossoming into her arms and numbing them. She gritted her teeth and drove her strength into the endeavor. The first chain clicked with a loud noise and it drove the captives into a frenzy of relief, that single noise heralding their freedom. Slowly she began to free them, one by one, and they encouraged her with praise. But there were many needing her succor and soon her fingers were rigid and she was unable to continue.

"Only a few more to go, lady, you cannot give up on them now," said a man meekly. He was fair of countenance and young, perhaps only just twenty, but lack of nutrition had marred his vigor.

"The magic is stalling me, I must find a way to break through it," she said. Without hesitation she unpinned her cloak brooch and dug it into her hand, liberating blood from the fresh wound.

As she used the power of her blood to free the last of the captives, they gathered around her, fretful and weak, each whispering directions. Then, gathering their strength, they struggled forward, carrying those who could not walk on their own, the children that were famished, and the elderly whose legs had atrophied from lack of use. In a somber file, they fumbled their way through tunnels that they described to Estella. Their blinded sight guided them towards the exit path they claimed ended near the sewers.

Shuffling in the gloom, the noise they made would have heralded their escape to anyone nearby. She pressed them on with urgency, aware of the lurking dangers. And as they moved forward she thought with doubt about the sincerity Mikhail had professed and the integrity he had shown hitherto. But escaping was her most urgent need, and she pushed him from her mind.

As fresher air began to mingle with the stale atmosphere, she knew they were approaching an opening. The captives began to rejoice with hoarse voices, but she hushed them reprovingly. The intersection of pathways indicated that these halls were built on the ancient ruins of older edifices. Pagan shrines, still intact, loomed in the darkness, and near them a ladder.

"Where will you go from here?" Estella called after them, curiously taking in the underground shrines.

"We know not where to turn!" screeched one woman deliriously, who was tapping her empty sockets as if the realization was newly dawning on her. "Better to have died here," she whispered bitterly. The rest began to murmur in assent.

"Then they have what they want," Estella rebuked them angrily. "They have murdered your souls and left your bodies to join soon after. Shame on you. Do not let them prevail!"

Estella began to climb the ladder. It led out onto a deserted street she did not recognize. "Quick," she called down to them. "I know someone who will shelter you. Who here knows Rosalind Constance, the bastard daughter of the pope? She is also Twilit touched, and the safest person I know of. Go to her." Her voice rippled across them, but they did not answer. Wearily she descended the steps and pushed the closest person to her, urging them to climb up.

"I know of her but I might not recall the way," said a child's voice tentatively. Estella swooped down to him and pulled him forward expectantly.

"Guide them, then. I will breathe onto your face and you shall carry my memory with it. Tell her Tsura the Dancer sends you all, and with my blessing. But farther than that I cannot see." She pulled away from him with tears in her eyes as she watched the child climb first, the rest following behind, whispering their thanks and blessings.

As they ascended, the dull echo of resounding footsteps came from the tunnel opposite them. Estella frantically began to haul the captives up the ladder. Whether it was the Blind Sage with Mikhail in hot pursuit, she could not tell, or whether something worse, she cared not. But the blinded captives hearing the sound panicked and began to throw themselves at the ladder. The demon's brow creased.

"You are placing yourself in danger for their sakes foolishly. We must leave!" He scanned the tunnels. "Here they come, you wretched fool. They will gouge your eyes out, too!" Estella waited until the footsteps of many people in pursuit were near, ushered out the last person, and then clambered up the ladder herself.

"She's here, I can sense her!" came Mikhail's cry from the tunnel.

"These halls will seal her inside, she cannot escape!" came the croak of the Blind Sage.

As these words smote Estella, she missed her footing and tumbled down the ladder, cursing in pain. Mikhail soon emerged from the tunnel and, brandishing his sword towards the demon, lunged at Estella, who frantically sought to reach the ladder again. The Blind Sage fortified his incantations, striking Estella with blunt force and casting her against the wall. The soundlessly screaming faces surged from the wall, antagonized and contorted with hunger. Dozens of arms with talon-like fingers pressed out of the quivering walls rapidly, converging around Estella. With her mind reeling, she collapsed as the breath was robbed from her.

The demon watched with a hideous rictus of wrath, defeated and cheated of his prize when he had been so near his goal. He hissed, vowing vengeance, and vanished instantly. Before Estella yielded to the numbness of unconsciousness, the last thing that traversed her raging mind was bitter anger for the day she allowed Mikhail to cross her path.

9

THE CRUEL GAME

It has written letters with your blood and sung out the note
And with your screams it gathered guests for the feast over your flesh
It watched you dig with broken fingers, your life choked at your throat
Deeper into the fiendish prison, their infernal mesh

THERE WAS A HEAVY WOODEN DOOR BEFORE HER WITH NO KNOB. IT was an exquisite work, engraved with delicate carvings. In awe, she reached forward to touch it tentatively. It did not move, and then she realized it had no hinges. It was encased within a black wall that was the seamless consistency of onyx. She traced her fingers over the walls and they were smooth, hard, and unyielding. Suddenly, she noticed a fine slot in the door. It unexpectedly dawned on her what it was intended for. The black glass key. Few are they who survive this hidden path. The ancient door of apotheosis, the last gateway of the threefold death. There was no way out and no point trying to push the door in, as it was immured within its wall of onyx. The impenetrable door.

Placing her fingers dreamily upon the keyhole, her sight traversed the precipice of hell. Dreams collapsed within dreams, some beautiful, others dark. At times she was no longer Estella but another being whose name she could not grasp. Alongside others, she stood facing the vastness of a writhing darkness, self-devouring and rotted. Now she was no longer human but a particle of light at the tip of a great spear, reaching straight into the midst of the decaying gloom.

In the gloom, a battle was being fought. The Blind God, a thrashing mass of darkness, sought to blind the eyes of God and put them out. His groping fingers were relentless like a hydra with eternally renewing limbs. But the spear warded him bitterly. And the particle of light at its end grew and became a starry spike. Then the darkness shrieked. The sound echoed across space, cracking the confines of existence, and the gates of night and dawn tremored. Burning and expanding, the spike became a disc, and the darkness writhed in agony, swallowing its own light. The lights bubbled and fizzled, dying a death that rent a hole in an already torn infinity.

Then there came the word, and the darkness shook, oozing foul decay. And as the dark shuddered, the gates of night swung open and it was swallowed entirely. Then with a clang, the mighty spiral gates shut tight and silence fell. But then the pleas started. The lost lights, ripped from the eyelid of God, called for him, their maker, and his heart bled, and he smote the darkness and raised his right hand. For they were trapped in the material world and the only way back to him was through death.

Out of nothingness a chessboard emerged, shimmering in jet and white marble. Calling forth the creation of blindness, God summoned Samael, the fallen one, his arrogant bastard son that the Sophia had created without his permission. Wresting open the gates of night, he hauled him out of the darkness. Then bound in iron wrought by God's will, he seated Samael chained before the chessboard. Then twilight came, an endless dusk, for neither light nor dark could prevail.

From afar Lucifer turned from his lofty station to watch as God and Samael battled for dominion. And he saw how Samael gathered human souls like crops, as fuel to kindle his inner fires, thus beginning the lucrative trade in human souls. Lucifer walked away and thought himself mighty to have gazed so long into the foul eyes of darkness and yet dwell in the light. And he realized that he, too, could rule. Then he descended upon earth like a blazing shower of burning stars riding the wings of the dreadful Ophanim that guarded the sacred throne of God.

So Estella dreamed and remembered. Her mind was long departed from earthly bonds, and the womb of the world held her tight and nursed her soul.

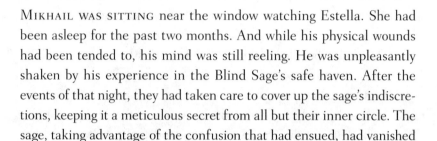

MIKHAIL WAS SITTING near the window watching Estella. She had been asleep for the past two months. And while his physical wounds had been tended to, his mind was still reeling. He was unpleasantly shaken by his experience in the Blind Sage's safe haven. After the events of that night, they had taken care to cover up the sage's indiscretions, keeping it a meticulous secret from all but their inner circle. The sage, taking advantage of the confusion that had ensued, had vanished entirely. Mikhail couldn't risk spreading knowledge of the sage's treachery among his order, lest they expose themselves to ridicule for having failed so miserably to neutralize him. So until he could be located, the sage's disgrace was being kept secret.

In the meantime, the queen had taken it upon herself to quell any rumor in the court surrounding Estella and Woodcraft. The earl, who Mikhail had threatened, was keeping himself hidden. The fool thought his plot had somehow been uncovered by the count, but suspected little else. His fear of being discovered by the church consumed his thoughts.

The king, moreover, was infuriated. His suspicions soon turned to Estella, for he couldn't fathom how gangrene could develop overnight—unless, of course, witchcraft were to blame and the rumors about her were true. The only thing that kept his inquisitors at bay were his wife's remonstrations. But the notion that the chief of the Order of the Northern Star was keeping Estella made the king uneasy. She was out of his reach for now. His many spies within the church gave him detailed reports, and based on this information he slowly began to conceive a callous plan of his own.

Oswald, who was accustomed to the dirty side of warfare and the uglier aspects of dealing with the otherworld, went about his duties warily. He gathered all the information he could pertaining to unusual activity in the region, bent on connecting all the strange occurrences from the last two months to Estella's mystifying slumber.

Men and women had begun to die suddenly. Others gave themselves over to forbidden blood rituals in their madness, embracing the profane. An infectious disquiet rippled through the orders. Mikhail was slowly beginning to despair of Estella ever waking from her spell of slumber. The Templars had been unable rouse her. She remained unchanged, and did not waste away from hunger, but unnaturally retained her golden glow.

Mikhail had convened with the other members of his order to relay the situation to them. Many were in favor of putting Estella to death for the safety of everyone. Some observed that she could be utilized as a vessel to trap evil forces. Others were wiser, and sought the path of mercy and wanted the count to care for her and earn her trust. Then she might open her mind to them, and they would be able to see all that she saw and felt.

The count was unshakable in his dedication. Night after night he was by Estella's side. He reached into her mind, knowing that he could not wrest her from her abode, but seeing all she saw, and feeling all she felt. He was deeply astonished by the boundless wisdom she was bathing in, but aggrieved at being unable to console her in her loneliness. Though at times he had believed her cold and uncaring, now he could reach her wounded soul. He found it intact and pure, and he longed for it. And he longed to own her gift, to keep her for himself. He knew this dark love he had conceived violated his Templar vows, but he was unable to fight it.

Secretly he wrought plans to ensnare her, to keep her within his meshes, safe from the persecution of the primitive church—and safe also from the attention of other men. His own battle between his mixed blood led him to doubt his allegiances, and the demonic blood that enticed his mother bubbled within him and sought dominion. Despite this, he prevailed over it, for he understood Estella's pain. Wondering at her frailty, he yearned even more to be close to her. But her mind being so far gone, his hopes were running thin, and reluctantly he began to give up hope, believing that death was the door of doom that captivated her wandering spirit.

—⊱⊰—

IT WAS NIGHTFALL, after many more fruitless days spent at Estella's side, and Mikhail decided he needed something to remedy his weariness. Leaving her behind, he sought out a tavern in which to quiet his tumultuous thoughts. There was a slight drizzle outside, which refreshed him despite its coldness, and he welcomed it with a soft sigh. As he absorbed the cool air, his blue and silver cloak billowed behind him and he opened his grey eyes to the laden skies. He let his feet lead him where they would, walking along the cobbled lanes of the alley near where he lived and passing businessmen, traders, and noblemen in full array.

Swerving right onto the main road, Mikhail espied a tavern with vibrant yellow shades and the emblem of a dancing stag overhead. Deciding it was near enough to his abode and far enough to chase his thoughts, he entered. Immediately the usual cacophony abated. The patrons observed him with open suspicion. The innkeeper, polishing a cup behind the bar, eyed him with beady dark eyes while the revelers stiffened with distrust. They knew of him, or had heard of him, and what they knew sufficed to establish a broad distance between them. Mikhail chose a remote spot near the far end of the tavern to sit, ordering the tavern's best wine and roast in a bored tone. Slowly the patrons resumed drinking and gambling, cautiously directing their attention elsewhere.

Mikhail sat observing the rabble with some amusement. Their thoughts were petty—feebleminded hopes, women, sex, and liquor. He leaned back moodily while the innkeeper brought the wine, laying down the roast goose before him gingerly. Absorbed completely in his own dark thoughts, he hunched over, irritably thrusting back his unbound hair as it tumbled across his face. In that moment, a pretty, blond damsel confidently approached him and seated herself coquettishly on the vacant chair opposite him with a self-satisfied smile. The count observed her for a brief moment with polite disinterest, completely neglecting to greet her. The lady watched him beneath thick lashes, exuding a cold aura of malevolence. Then she smiled.

"I do not believe you have heard of me, but I happen to have heard of you," she said. Despite her smile, her blue eyes retained a hard malice. "I am Vanessa Depardeur and I am the king's . . . favorite." Her tone was falsely innocuous and layered with seductive notes. The count's face darkened knowingly, but his composure remained unmoved.

"You see," she continued, "we have been closely following your movements. And naturally we have many questions. The king feels affronted by this Estella Delcour. And he wonders if she might be one of the filth the church wants purged from the city. Well, now that the king has launched an inquiry, and what with the queen speaking for Estella . . . the king has decided it would be better for her to be dead." Vanessa smiled unnaturally.

"You see, the king loves pretty things—especially women. And he got it into his head that he would break Estella, who often plays with men's hearts. Well my own poor heart broke," she said, pouting. "I thought for a moment she would take my place, leaving me cast aside in the dark. But the king is also battling with two thoughts—to keep her alive and have her as he will, or to have her killed and be done with his bruised honor. He knows well enough that she charmed his foot publicly to scorn him." Vanessa shook her head, tutting.

Mikhail did not respond, schooling his demeanor into one of indifference, and busying himself with the roasted goose and wine. Vanessa snatched the goblet from his hand inelegantly, taking a long sip, then set it down firmly. The count eyed the cup with blatant distaste, his lips a thin line of displeasure, then resumed eating with a shrug.

"Now the king wants one of two things; either she comes to him and offers herself as a concubine for his pleasure, or she must disappear from court entirely, being stripped of her title and name. If she does not comply, she forfeits her life," she concluded, her tone sickly sweet. The count lifted his eyes and pushed his plate away roughly. Vanessa paused, disconcerted.

"Let me ask you something, dame. Who shall be the one to carry out the murder?" Mikhail smiled, baring his teeth. Vanessa straightened her back and lifted her chin haughtily.

"No shortage of men willing to carry out the king's orders," she retorted.

"How generous of them!" The words rolled off Mikhail's tongue like acid. He leaned over the table, bringing his face close to hers. "Then bear them my greetings, to every single one who thinks himself mighty enough to push past me. I look forward to escorting them to the afterlife!" The mad rage swirling in his unnatural, icy eyes made her blanch.

"She will not leave this city," he continued, "and that is because she is mine to dispose of under the authority of the Templars of the Northern Star. The Church of Rome will not appreciate lascivious kings meddling in their holy affairs without sanction." His grey eyes looked her up and down with unadulterated revulsion.

"At least he wants a night with her to assuage his lust, or else I lose my position . . ." she floundered, lips quivering.

The count thrust his dining knife deep into the wood of the table between them, then grasped her hand tightly, yanking her towards him roughly. Her cries of outrage met with deaf ears and meticulously averted eyes all around. In the dim light of the tavern, the sigils on Mikhail's rings shone dimly. Her eyes rounded with understanding and her lips moved soundlessly.

"She is mine," he said, punctuating each word with a tightening of his grip. "I have taken her for my ends, and for my order's. Must I brand her for you to understand further? Your kind only understands ownership and being owned and used by those who wield power and wealth."

Vanessa flinched and Mikhail let go of her wrist.

She lifted herself from the table, visibly shaken, and stammered, "I'll tell him she's your betrothed, but save my station at the king's side for mercy's sake. I had no choice but to relay his desires. You cannot stop him from pursuing what he wants. He never relents and nothing shakes him—I would know," she whispered, her face pale.

"Do not worry, just mind keeping your jealousy to yourself," the count nodded, dismissing her.

She nodded hastily, envy etched into her fine features, then departed in a flurry. The tavern door opened again moments later, and Elmer emerged, disheveled and alarmed. The count, rising from his table to greet him, could sense his fear and worry. Estella floated at the forefront of his mind.

"What has happened, Elmer?" the count questioned urgently.

"I came to see you at the manor . . . and when I entered, she was there, the duchess. She was awake, but . . . different, and she wasn't alone. She was as though possessed by some evil spirit and ran wild, chanting and drawing symbols on the walls with her fingers dipped in blood. And I saw them, my lord, I saw the demons!" Elmer shivered and swayed on his feet, and the count motioned to him to sit down, concern etched in his face.

"She's been asleep for months, Elmer. How can this be? Are you sure of what you saw?" asked the count with mild disbelief in his tone.

"The demons were there," Elmer grimaced, "male and female, and some whose gender was blurred. And they taunted her and she laughed and ripped her clothes off. The maids restrained her from departing, and the house warden brought her back to bed, but the demons lingered and they went for her room . . ."

The count's body froze in anger and his fists clenched. "She has been asleep for so long and I have been watching over her every day. The moment I leave for fresh air this happens, as if . . ." he trailed off, realization striking him. Then with a growl of anger he stormed off with Elmer tailing after him.

"They woke her, my lord, and she fought them off. From what I understood they sought to defile her. She went into a frenzy. I came to warn you." The count stopped in his tracks and turned to Elmer, patting him on the shoulder reassuringly.

"Wait for me tonight, at this inn. I'll come for you. Speak of this to no one." He shoved Elmer gently towards the inn and then hastened away, a dark and ominous shadow gathering in his wake.

The air was cold and damp, and the wind whistling between the buildings howled a morose refrain. The leaves caught in its wake rose like a ruddy cloud, forming little whirlpools as if an invisible hand were stirring them. The count's rapid steps were heavy, and each time they pounded the cobblestone his heart leapt in his chest. The gathering winds fled before the dread in his eyes as he was billowed along, finally halting before his manor. He cast a look upon the old building, but it offered no outward sign of malevolence. He pounded the door hastily, urgency overtaking him.

While he waited impatiently for the doors to open, he noticed a woman in the shadows. It was the blond woman who had accosted him in the tavern, and she was trailing closely behind him, watchful and satisfied. She stood near an alleyway, cocking her head at him. He cast one last look at her, frowning, then turned back to the doors of the manor as he heard footsteps approaching from within, dismissing her from his thoughts.

The light from a nearby torch fell on the woman's tilted face where one eye turned milky white and the other one burned steadily sapphire blue and bright. She smiled derisively and shape-shifted into a page boy, vanishing into the dark.

10

YOUR ENEMY'S EMBRACE

I am the troubled waters of the infinite stillness,
the visage of impassive skies

I am the lonely ponderous shadow crouching
beneath the skirt of the hills

When all else has ventured home, and the
wakeful spirits close their eyes

I am the vessel of roaring celestial winds that inspiration fills

THE DOORS TO THE MANOR SWUNG OPEN ABRUPTLY. THE FRIGHTENED face of the butler appeared, stepping quickly aside for Mikhail to enter. Several members of his order had gathered behind the butler to meet him.

"What has happened here?" Mikhail barked imperiously, his face contorted as he scanned the premises.

Without waiting for a response, he made for the rampart of the staircase leading to the upper chambers, climbing the stairs three at a time. The men from his order followed him obediently, maintaining a safe distance behind him. At the top he hurried down the corridor to the heavy mahogany door behind which Estella dwelled. Wrenching it open, he found the room ransacked. His men waited with bated breath, their eyes betraying fear and shocked dismay. The count stared at the pillaged room, his cold grey eyes narrowed. Slowly, he turned his condescending gaze towards his comrades.

"For how long has this been going on?" His tone was cool and his visage seemed carved in ivory. A fair-haired knight came forwards, bowing his head apologetically and staring at something near the count's feet.

"For many hours, till we ordered the maids to restrain her. Then we smote her down so that she could be contained."

The count's face turned into an ugly grimace. "You ordered your men to crack her head open? Is that her blood on the wall?"

The knight paled, suddenly taking an interest in the floor.

"No, that is the blood of our own. She overpowered him and used his blood as ink for her demonic devices with the help of her minions. We tried to rescue him from her grasp, but she became erratic and started drawing strange symbols. We chanted binding words, but could not remove them."

"Get out of my sight," the count dismissed him coldly. Then he beckoned to an older knight who was glaring disapprovingly at his comrade. He came forward and kissed the hand of the count reverently.

"He is afraid to tell you," began the older knight, "that he tried to bind her himself. This was what caused her frenzy. He thought her a mere Twilit simpleton. Then his error was compounded when he tried to bind the demons that had manifested . . ." His green eyes shone with the wisdom of age and fearlessness.

The count nodded. "So tell me what has transpired here."

The elderly knight gritted his teeth, then spoke. "The Blind Sage is dead, but not for a lapse in our watch. We made an error of judgment, and deemed him capable of subduing her. She killed him, though we do not understand how. We have since locked her in the inner chamber. We watched over her as best we could, sire, but the moment you left everything broke loose.

"When she awoke, we thought to test her by exposing her to holy relics. But she scoffed angrily and pushed us away. Then they came for her, those ungodly ones. At first we did not oppose them, because they came in your guise and we were deceived. But she knew them and she grew deeply troubled. We believe the Blind Sage must have been tainted by them, for he soon grew erratic with a murderous rage.

"At first he fought them, and we believed he was relieving her from their torment. When he requested that we depart, we obliged, though she protested. But we paid little heed and stationed ourselves outside. He locked the door from within, but we never thought we had any cause for concern. Soon her screams rose again, yet still we trusted him and his ministrations. We only began to suspect something was wrong when we heard her scream out your name. He was rebuking her and demanding we depart, but my heart could not sit right with a woman's screams, however fallen they may be.

"We began pounding on the door, and the sage, usually so kind, began to berate us. And Lady Estella pleaded with us to gain entry, screaming that the sage was an agent of the demons and tainted by them, and that he was bent on murdering her. Though we were reluctant to believe her, the struggle we heard within and the sage's disturbing wrath spurred us into action. We began the task of breaking the door down, but it held fast with some unknown magic.

"Then one of the fiends we espied around the house emerged, long-haired and with one blind eye. He cast us aside and rent the door asunder himself, and there we saw what had unfolded. Lady Estella was on the ground with the sage over her brandishing a knife. He would have gouged out her eyes had we not intervened. He was mad, my lord, in a way we have never seen him, and he was desperately pleading for us to allow him to blind her so he could regain his own sight through some twisted, morbid enchantment. We pulled him away and while he struggled that's when she leapt at him and stabbed him to death with a knife the demon had given her. Then the demon drove us out and sealed the door. The blood on the walls appeared shortly after, and nothing we can do wipes it away. And we have had no sign of her since."

Mikhail nodded and walked past the knight, entering the chamber slowly. "Leave me now," he said grimly, studying the chaotic state of the chamber. The knights bowed and departed. Looking around, he braced himself defiantly for company. But to his disappointment, he was truly alone. He walked around the chamber warily, stooping to inspect the blood spatter. Then approaching the inner chamber, he pushed through the barrier. Estella was lying across her bed. She was awake, but made little effort to acknowledge his presence, gazing vacantly in front of her. He leaned over her, peering into her face.

"Is there any room in there for love and life?" Mikhail murmured, laying a hand above her breast. Though she breathed, her chest did not move. "Do you feel anything at all, Estella?" He leaned further, his hand caressing her neck. Estella turned her head to him with languid ease, frowning, then inhaling deeply. Her serene expression cracked, revealing livid anger.

"You murderous half-breed son of a whore!" she bellowed. "You and your order are nothing but hypocritical dogs! Have you also come to murder me and take my eyeballs? I've seen what you really look like, you ugly fiend!" She watched him, her pupils dilated.

"How lovely to see you again, too," said the count with a wan smile, hiding his anger. "We did not let the sage in to kill you. After we discovered his chambers of infamy he disappeared, and we've been tracking him ever since. My men, unfortunately, did not know of what occurred, and so did not realize the danger he posed. But I am happy to see you have retained your talent for astringent verbal whippings."

"I've been too long in the great womb of the universe," Estella said, closing her eyes, "and too close to the blind eye of darkness. I am the offspring of their thought, aren't I? That's why they want me. I have drunk too deep of the well of knowledge they yielded, and I have gazed too far into their darkness." The count withdrew his hand pensively.

"There is so much beauty to behold in this world," he replied. "You do not need to seek the empty spaces of God's unfinished creation and the realms without. Come back to earth, I will seal your mind to all of this that surrounds you. I will lock your gift behind an impenetrable door and you will forget all you knew. Your sight will diminish and fade and you will be free to live a normal life." He spoke lightly, but there was a cold distance between them, and the lack of mercy in his wintry eyes made Estella turn her face away.

"It seems that all of you, even your wisest, fall," she said. "You all envy my sight. And because I am a woman who merits it not, for I put it not to holy use, I am despised. But you are all filthy hypocrites. You despise our gifts and yet you cannot do without them. Look at your Blind Sage, gouging out our eyes to obtain our prophecies!"

"That is but a few of us," Mikhail insisted. "Mortals are weak and prone to mistakes; do not measure us by our worst, but rather by our virtue. In a world where we have many reasons to be evil, some choose goodness. The greater you climb the lower you fall, and he was no exception. We found the chains and the parchments after we caught you, and we thought to deal with him in our own way rather than humiliating our order publicly and diminishing our credibility. He is a trickster at heart and deceived us and soon eluded us. It has been a shock to me that someone of such integrity can prove to be so fallen. But then the business of pillaging the void is foul, and when it damages you it often rubs its venom into your wounds. Then like a disease it takes over, inch by inch."

"You holy men are always the same," said Estella, "refusing to acknowledge that your idols are wretched and fallen. But tell me now, will you give me back the life you took away from me when you entered my manor one benighted evening?"

"It is you who does not desire life, nor deserve the gifts that you have been given." The disgust in Mikhail's voice reverberated through the room. Turning to face him, she found no sympathy in his eyes.

"I am alone and friendless," she sighed. "No one knows me or shares the secrets of my bruised heart. And those that professed to love me and care for me, the scythe of death has taken. They were pawns to a greater power than the likes of you or your church. And my mind is *mine* for the losing." Estella's voice rose like a billowing wind then hardened, rigid and proud.

She lifted her head high and scoffed, "Who do you have for yourself, Count Mikhail? Your manservant? The dogs behind you that trail at your feet? You are alone, thinking your games have worth. But they are nothing, and you too are nothing in the great chessboard between God and Samael. Your death will add naught to his grief, and the sun will rise and fall, and you will pass away unhindered. No one will even remember your name."

She laughed now and her mocking eyes were alight with a vivid flame. Suddenly Mikhail felt old and worn, and the stab in his heart told him that her words rang true. But they were cruel, wrapped in venom and intended to damage.

"And you will be even less than the smallest of the Twilit people," he retorted, "alone and having achieved nothing in your meaningless life."

Estella shrugged. "Seal my mind forever, knight, or steal my gift, but I cannot continue to live like this—not with the likes of you for company." A malicious grin curled over her heart-shaped lips and she watched with fascination as he approached her. Smiling with hatred and malice, she breathed, "Do it now," then closed her eyes, licking her lips. Mikhail's hidden purpose gleamed in his inhuman eyes, and he smiled craftily.

"Those demon fiends of yours desired you to yield your powers and sight to them, and you resisted . . . and now you offer it up to me without a struggle. I am thankful for that." The light in his eyes smoldered and his long black hair fell unbound to his shoulders. Estella leapt off the bed with quiet apprehension, flitting across to the windows. They were bolted shut and unyielding to her touch.

"What you did not give to them willingly, you gave to me freely, even begged me . . ." He moved towards her, eyeing her like prey.

"I knew you were rotten and foul," she said shrilly. "Though you are dressed in fairer form, you are no different than the demons who plague me!"

He grabbed both her arms firmly, eyes silently boring into hers but betraying no emotion. Caressing her hair with one hand, he lifted her chin delicately towards him with the other. Her pupils were dilated, and she warred within herself to maintain her calm while she shivered with fear. The shadows danced around them as tendrils of frost. Without warning, he leaned down and pressed his lips against hers. She gasped as he gripped her tight, her back against the window and his arm around her waist. His lips did not relinquish hers, and her lithesome limbs struggled against his muscular bulk to no avail. His lips went to her neck, and biting gently, traveled down to her collarbone.

"The devil and the man within me are worlds apart, but both want you and desire you." He found her face again, his cold mask faltering to reveal a soft tenderness she had not conceived he could have. "Yes, I am alone and lonely," he continued, "in a world where I cannot share myself with anyone, and burdened by holy duties. Your pain mirrors mine, and I promise you that my heart is old and rich, and I can take care of you. You would lack nothing, being the sole diamond of my soul." His voice was sincere, and the look in his eyes was too vast to be restrained by speech. Estella realized that she was weeping and lowered her eyes.

"Don't let the darkness steal you from your rightful place, Estella," he said softly as he embraced her. "I cannot take what would abhor me, this is not a game of power for me," he whispered into her hair.

Estella lifted her eyes to his. "And could you contain the storm of my raging soul? The tempest brews and I have been too long captivated by the dark secrets that dwell where God has not yet turned the light of his face."

Mikhail smiled knowingly. "Then look into my countenance, I who have seen the divine mysteries, and therein you shall find peace. And though the devils of this world surround you and put out your eyes, there it shall burn within you, an eternal light."

She sighed as he pressed her against him tenderly and their minds met across the thorns and brambles they had laid for one another, and they communed together.

Outside a storm had gathered and night deepened into a dismal mass of black and grey. Torn clouds laden with rain ripped like rags across the evening sky, and the stars themselves were choked. Their lights flickering unseen, and the endless cry of the wind wailed its anguish to those who had no shelter and no choice but to be the audience of nature's misery.

11

THE DEVIL IN THE HOUSE OF GOD

I have awoken from the slumber as my first breath was pure fear

As sight into the true celestial dance is treason to the soul

It breaks the throne of God, sending quakes into all you revere

Then downwards unraveling the bitter truths roll

CARDINAL PIOUS WAS AGITATED AS HE MARCHED UP AND DOWN THE underground vault. Shuffling along, bent like an aged tree, he mumbled to himself, tugging at his long beard, his velvet slippers making loud squelching sounds. He was restless but unperturbed by the echoes that still reached him from the adjacent room. His frown deepened on his wrinkled brow, dry and withered as old parchment, and he wrung his beard tersely as he connived. He knew he desperately needed results before *he* came, and that simple answers would not suffice. He was banking his hopes on his "boys," who were famed for their callous trade. They were sure to get the answers that would spare him.

He stopped pacing, his heart beating violently in his chest at the thought that *he* might be displeased. As he looked around in the light of the candles ensconced on the stone wall, he saw his own bent shadow and shuddered. He shook himself as he realized the full extent of his decision, looking right and left skittishly with a hopeless pleading look as he fumbled for his cross. If he fell short of his use, he was sure to be subjected to humiliation and pain—or worse, depending on the fickle moods of the king.

He had never wanted to be part of the clergy, after all, and only climbed the ranks to quench his lust for power. And deep within the recesses of his mind he thought maybe God would suddenly reveal himself to him and bless him with sight. Then he would have been worshipped, the people clamoring for him and his prophecies from all the corners of Christendom. He would have lived venerated, and even in death been revered. But those secret hopes were long gone, and only his vice and cowardice were left.

Finally acknowledging the noises from the neighboring chamber, the cardinal closed his eyes and clenched his teeth, weighing his two dangerous choices. Stitching an impassive expression on his face, he pushed through the heavy doors to the neighboring chamber. There he was confronted with an ignoble scene of ongoing torture. Wrinkling his nose at the sight and smell of blood, he hobbled along to the prisoners. They were bound in shackles and drawn over tables while the torturers, his "boys," worked their cruel art on them.

The prisoners rasped through lipless faces. Their eyelids were torn and blood was smeared over their features, rendering them unrecognizable. They must have soiled themselves out of fear, for the stench of feces mingled with that of fresh blood. One prisoner had his intestines neatly wrapped around his neck and he shivered, moaning coarsely, his eyes wild with agony, already insane with the torment. They had clearly finished with him, for they had cut out his tongue. He had failed to yield the information they wanted, so he had been left to bleed to death, unable to voice his hellish agony. The three others were struggling still, beseeching vainly. They had been flayed—their muscles and sinews were uncovered and stinging ointments mixed with liquor had been applied to their open wounds. The laughter of their tormentors accompanied their ministrations.

The cardinal hobbled to the table, kissing the cross he clutched. Thanks to the power it was imbued with, no one could reach the inner chambers of his mind where he concealed his dark secrets and the gift he had stolen from a poor thief of a pregnant women. She had been destitute, caught stealing bread and then money from the church baskets. When she was hauled before him, he had her whipped till she bled and miscarried. In her torment she had offered a trade with the cardinal that he found he could not refuse—a parcel of the Twilit magic he loathed yet coveted. And she yielded the secret and welded it into his mind in exchange for her freedom. At first he had earnestly thought to free her, but once the gift settled in, his heart grew dark. He turned on her, delivering her to his boys to carve up and throw into the river alongside the other nameless city murders.

The cardinal was now near the table, and he shook at the sight of the torture—not out of pity for them, but for himself. They were an odious reminder that if he failed to obtain adequate results from the interrogation, the wrath of the important guest arriving tonight would be impossible to placate. Eyeing the wretched souls with distaste, he kept his tone steady, though deep down he feared his boys.

"So what have they spat out, these fools, or are you all truly useless?" he inquired, affecting a look of detachment.

"Nothing, sire, the same words, and the same rehearsed story. There was nothing we could do with that one," said a swarthy man in a leather mask as he pointed to the gutted man. "Got all we could from him and more. Like we said, it would take time. But when they get so intimate with us, they begin to speak of every secret they've ever known. One such secret we learned is that the Blind God himself is seeking this Estella. And they aver that this woman isn't a duchess at all but an imposter. And the queen herself is protecting her. Then here is another interesting tidbit—those brats she takes in aren't starving orphans in need of charity, but Twilit scum! The whore keeps these God-cursed children and shields them, right beneath the church's nose. I do think I could glean some repentance from her spirit, given the chance."

Even behind the mask his leer was palpable, full of lust and violence. It lingered like a rancid cloud in the air already foul with the odors of human suffering. The cardinal nodded approvingly, patting the man on the back.

"God bless you, dark soldier of the right hand of God. May he reward you for undertaking this terrible service in order to purge our world from sin."

The masked man nodded, then pointed at the other three. "I don't think we shall have time to finish our work on them. We cannot speed up the process, since the beauty lies in the lingering," he said, the last word rolling off his tongue with relish. The cardinal distanced himself, suddenly uncomfortable, feigning interest in his rosary.

"Those three, you see, aren't so talkative," the man in the mask continued, shaking his head disapprovingly. "Estella is the recurring theme, though they also claim the count is a demon. It's really a clever story they've concocted to distract us. But this one," he drove a knife into the chained man's flayed thigh, "has been saying even funnier things. Listen to this one; he says that Count Mikhail, our holiest knight, is aware of Estella's nature and still took her for himself. He says together they are Hermes Trismegistus's scepter. I had to bash his skull in a few times to ensure I had got the name right. Then I burned his eyes out and he told me the scepter of Hermes is formed of two serpents intertwining over one live staff—male and female, sight and faith. And he said the scepter shall be wielded by the angels on earth as a defiance against the hand of the evil one; man of faith and woman of sight, coming together. After that, my lord, he fell silent, and nothing we did could wrest more out of them. It's as if the body is there, but not the mind. It's unwholesome trickery. The demons protect their progeny well."

The cardinal leaned forward listening avidly, his fingers playing over his rosary beads. "Are you certain that is all he said? How can he switch himself off to pain? In fact, how could all three of them do it? And Hermes? Yes, that's exactly what *he* wants to hear from us tonight, more fables to get us hanged before the morn!" the cardinal hissed, his mask slipping to reveal his rage. All of a sudden the heavy slamming of doors was heard somewhere in the church above. The cardinal and his torturers froze.

"Get out of here," the cardinal growled at them urgently, waving his rosary like a flail and hunching down as though suddenly crippled. "Out the back door, and your money will be sent in the morning through the usual arrangements." Spittle flew from his mouth and his jowls quivered as he began to sniff uncontrollably. The men shrugged, gathered their tools, and left hastily without a word. Before disappearing through the back door, the largest man with the leather mask raised his hand in mocking salute.

The cardinal fumed at his own fear, mumbling curses as he steadied himself, sweating through his robes profusely as he plucked at his beard in agitation. At the same time, the heavy, purposeful footsteps echoing down the stone stairs into the vaults resounded ominously. The cardinal thought he saw the very light of the candles dancing in the shape of faces with forked tongues. He shook his head, cursing himself, and turned away as he realized with a creeping horror that he was incapable even of praying to God at this time.

The steps were slow, and the cardinal rushed across the room to the door leading to the stairs, no longer able to endure the suspense. Taking a deep breath and whimpering half a plaintive prayer, he pulled the door open with both hands, sweating feverishly and shaking. He was face-to-face with his dreaded guest. The figure before him was clad in a royal purple velvet cloak trimmed with white fur and chain mail emblazoned with a winged griffin, and his face was contorted into an unfriendly sneer. The crown he wore tonight was a heavy work with oval sapphires clutched in iron clasps, but they seemed lifeless and dull compared to the growing menace in the king's eyes.

The king brushed past the cardinal with a disapproving scowl as the cardinal fretfully followed behind, his head bent and penitent. The king halted at the sight of the tortured men, taking in the minute details with a perfunctory nod, his expression unfathomable. He then looked behind him with a twisted smile at the three stoic knights he had chosen to accompany him.

"Bring me a table, wine, and some food of whatever is good here," he said in a bored voice. The knights nodded expressionlessly and departed. The sound of their steps seemed to nauseate the cardinal with each footfall.

"A good night you seem to be having here, my friend," said the king coldly with a crooked smile. He walked around the tables inspecting the tortured men. Then he picked up a stray iron poker, but his prodding elicited no reaction from the prisoners. Disappointed with the results, he looked around the room, his shrewd gaze taking in the details of the splattering of gore. Then rapidly losing interest, he settled his malignant scrutiny on the cardinal, who was visibly crumbling with each moment.

The knights soon returned, hauling a table and platters of food. They set the heavy oak table down, at the behest of the king, facing the mutilated captives. The platters of food followed suit, wafting odors of grilled pork, onions, and lamb with herbs. The platters were followed by a small basket of bread and a great flagon of wine. The king seated himself comfortably, beckoning for the cardinal to sit at his side on a small, three-legged stool. There he sat in full view of the king and the tormented men and watched them nervously, eyes darting to and fro, occasionally eyeing the food greedily. The king, savoring his discomfort, watched the cardinal as he tore into a pork chop.

"Chin up, old man. You act as though you have never done this before. Don't jest with me, we all know what you do for entertainment." His blue eyes glistened darkly with amusement. The cardinal mumbled something inaudible over the noisy chewing of the king.

"We all have dirty secrets, my friend, every single one of us," said the king. "I personally enjoy other people's secrets, and unfortunately for you, I happen to know yours," he added, smiling humorlessly. "It's a sad predicament, really, the one you have. And you have my full sympathy." The king barely cast him a glance as he grabbed a leg of lamb from a platter and continued. "It must be really unbearable to be a priest to begin with, God knows I could never survive a month in such deprivation. And then you don't get to enjoy women either. So you turn to little boys, and then you discover your member won't get aroused, and you feel even less of a man and more of a loser. So you try different things, leeches, physicians, potions . . . . Finally you discover that you can enjoy being a man, you only have to watch poor, wretched women suffering a painful death to do so."

The cardinal gulped and crossed himself, his wizened fingers clutching the table for support.

"How many dying women does it take to turn you on, by the way? I am curious, actually." The king watched him with the intensity of a predator choosing the propitious moment to assail its prey.

The cardinal opened his mouth in protest and stammered, "All false-hood, my king, all falsehood. I am a man of the cloth, I would not rend my soul to the devil for the pleasures of the flesh."

The king narrowed his eyes in anger and without warning flung the weighty lamb bone with intense velocity at the cardinal, smiting him with a slapping thud squarely in the face. The cardinal released a choked scream, flinching but not daring to move.

"Don't lie or you will join these wretched souls and sing along with them, too," the king said, his cool voice pure menace, and the cardinal nodded meekly, staring at the floor.

"They spoke finally, these men we caught. My king, if it so pleases you to hear what I gleaned from their penance . . ." The cardinal sounded piteous and broken, but there was an unmistakable underscore of bitterness tingeing his words.

The king nodded inscrutably as he ripped off several pieces of bread. "Talk, and don't waste my time. By the time I have finished eating, I want to have heard everything I wanted to know. Then I will decide whether to let you live." He pointed nonchalantly at the table with the tortured captives.

The cardinal resignedly wet his lips with his tongue and steadied himself. Then he proceeded to recount in detail what his boys had learned from the prisoners. The king neither seemed pleased nor dis-pleased. He busied himself drinking wine and picking his teeth, and only grunted a few times at the mention of Estella and the scepter. When the last vestiges of food remaining on the platters were gone, he tapped the table with his fingertips impatiently.

"Very good, all very good, but now come closer. I want to gaze upon the face of the man who serves me so well."

The cardinal sat there transfixed in terror until the king's fierce glare shook him from his stupor. Trembling, he rose from his stool and shuf-fled towards the king, who was still dawdling with a fragment of bone on his plate. Like a chastised child he stood there waiting, pale and sweating. With a repugnant snort, the king seized the heavy silver plat-ter he was eating from with both hands, and hurled it with all his might at the cardinal's face. Choking out a cry of pain, the cardinal fell to his knees, begging and groveling for mercy. The king replied with a kick to his face. The cardinal fell backwards, his nose broken, and blood streaming across his face. He sobbed, imploring the king for mercy.

"Belt up or more will follow," the king threatened coldly.

The cardinal nodded piteously, a crumpled, quivering mess. The king rose from his chair and moved towards the cardinal with undisguised pleasure, watching him flinch as he readied himself for further blows.

"Well, it was good enough to spare you the torturers . . . you gave me valuable information, after all. But not enough for me to be pleased with you," he continued, nudging the cardinal viciously with his foot.

As the cardinal wailed words of gratitude, the king turned away in disgust. He began to walk towards the door, his knights following after him, but then suddenly he paused. The cardinal yelped in fear, thinking for an agonizing moment that he was returning to finish him off.

"Have your spies keep a close eye on Count Mikhail and report to me the relevant details," ordered the king. "I have no time for pointless audiences. And ensure that you don't cross paths with the queen, or I will roast you alive." Then he was gone, and the cardinal was left alone on the floor in the dying light of the candles, shaking silently with relief—and unbridled rage.

The cardinal struggled to his feet, sniveling loudly, and for the first time conscious of the blood oozing from his broken nose. He wiped his face slowly, inspecting the blood with dispassion. Then he wiped his hands on his robes and hobbled painfully towards a tall mirror located in a shadowy corner of the room. He coughed hoarsely and a tooth flew out of his mouth, bouncing off the mirror.

He seethed with indignation as he confronted his reflection. Rasping with rage and flexing his fingers impotently, he took in his bruised and broken face. This mirror was the only vanity he was allowed, and now it only offered him the stark knowledge of his ugliness and weakness. Livid, he smote the mirror with his fist. It shattered as he let out an incensed cry, the fragments flying across the floor, glittering sharply in the dimming lights. He looked down at the collage of broken glass and paused, numb with anger.

The shards of the mirror glittered and vibrated, reflecting numerous eyes. Then they slowly began to levitate, all the tiny fragments splintered across the room gathering together and reforming. Swiftly they became whole again, and the mirror floated in the air eerily toward the cardinal. Within the reflection he no longer saw himself, but another being gazing back at him. Lost for breath, he gaped in bewilderment, unable to form words.

The being had the fairest of all faces. Beautiful, with an aura of inexorable grace, it had resplendent, shimmering wings—pair upon pair of them in varied iridescent hues. The countenance observed him with a soft smile, measuring him with his intoxicating, lucent blue eyes.

"Do you know who I am, old man?" the mirror asked him blithely. The cardinal was immediately enraptured, but could feel the cross burning on his neck. "Take it off and it will not sear your skin," the angel remarked mildly, his limpid blue eyes gazing lovingly upon the cardinal.

The cardinal, like a man too deeply drunken to think, brought his hand to his neck and ripped the cross thoughtlessly off and cast it away.

"That is better now, isn't it? Always bearing the cross. Well, he carried his cross and now he wants the whole world to carry it with him . . . how truly selfish." The voice, though laced with reproach, was heartrendingly sweet and full of understanding and promise. It rang like silver bells.

The cardinal's mouth hung open indecorously, and he found himself nodding his head in agreement with the angel's words as his fear began to dissipate.

"I do not want you to carry this cross, this heavy burden of debt," the angel continued. "This false salvation you were peddled is a lie. I, on the contrary, want you to be free, liberated from your thralldom. The earth is your inheritance to rule over as a god, like you were promised. And yet they have deprived you of your freedom. My heart grieves for you," the angel sympathized, his voice laden with unquenchable sorrow.

As the angel spoke, the mirror began to ripple like molten silver, and he emerged from it, as though pushing through a translucent shroud. Robed in white flowing garments, he grasped a long spear in his left hand pointing it downwards, the bitter tip glistening coldly. Standing before the cardinal revealed in his full glory, he smiled fully—but the warmth never reached his detached, frosted gaze.

"I want to liberate you from your thralldom," he said. "I have watched over you all, my tender flock. I am Lucifer, the morning star, the first to greet you with my love into this life, and the last to claim you on my dark stallion of death. I have come to free you." His persuasive voice was soothing and nurturing, like a gentle river rippling mildly over soft bedrock.

The cardinal found himself in a daze of awe, and within him woke his longing for power and lust for dominion.

"Come to me, let me free you, and we shall destroy the Twilit world that has robbed you of the gifts that you so deserved." The fatherly voice of the angel was indignant yet gentle, and he beamed at the cardinal who nodded back eagerly. "Let me into your heart, then. Lead me into your house, in this false edifice erected in the name of God, and let us together find the lost sheep in the house of God. I am his true son, after all, prince of the world."

He glided towards the cardinal, his numerous nacre wings extending into the chamber. They shed their own pearly light, and it seemed he floated like a silver vision. The angel knelt beside the cardinal, gazing into his watery eyes. "Let me into his house." The voice was slightly more pressing now.

The cardinal, dazed, nodded in agreement. With a satisfied smile, the angel touched the cardinal's chest with a slender finger, right at his heart, and breathed over him. The cardinal groaned, falling instantly asleep.

The angel then shifted like a blurring image, colors melting and running, twisting like molten glass into a murky mess of shadow and dirt-colored fumes. The gleaming wings fell to the ground, losing their feathers and rotting instantly. Now instead of the radiant angel, there stood a hooded and cloaked figure, emanating death. Like a black hole, it sucked in all the light around him, exerting a fearsome pull. The light from the candles swirled and were drawn into him, as though he were a gasping sinkhole.

The lights that weren't drowned out flared in his presence, then guttered as he walked towards the discarded cross lying dully on the ground. With his foot he trampled it into the ground. Then the lights went out and laughter resounded. It echoed through the cathedral walls, shaking it to its foundations until all the lights within went out, and all the icons fell to the ground, dashed down by something far more sinister than the raging gale outside.

12

FLIGHT OF THE DANCER

When the sound of music turns to dust

And the heartbeat of existence turns to rust

Follow the lead into the echoing dark, alone

To witness how vast the worm has grown

T HAT NIGHT STRANGE DREAMS WERE HAD BY MANY. ESTELLA AWOKE
with a smothering shroud of blankness seated on her heart. It
wrapped around her, squeezing her and robbing her of breath. Mikhail's
warm arms were cradling her. He woke, too, and in the dim light of the
candle on the dresser, his eyes were wild, swirling tempests of grey.

"Something evil is afoot," he said, gently prizing his arms from Estella. He rose from the bed and made for the window.

Estella did not move for a long while, eyes closed and extending her
thoughts around her. Then with the agility of a feline, she climbed out
of the bed, seizing a silken red gown from the dresser. The count was
gazing into the night, rigid like a statue carved of dark marble. His
figure was immobile against the night.

The only noises besides the wailing of the wind and the battering of
trees shaken from their roots, was the sound Estella made as she rummaged through the cluttered drawers. She sighed in relief as she found
what she was seeking—a velvet black pouch tied together with silver.
Throwing it unceremoniously on the bed, she went back to the dresser
and produced several silver candles, which she drew out with deft fingers. Counting out ten, she cast them, too, on the bed.

She then glided to a heavy chest set in the far corner of the room. Kneeling before it, she opened the heavy lid and, after careful inspection, withdrew several bags of incense wrapped in different colored cloths. She also removed several large crystal spheres, which she handled with the utmost care, her expression unfathomable. Then she set about the task of rolling up the luxurious carpets strewn before the bed. Her hair was a tumble of dark curls upon her scarlet robe, and the satin dressing gown hugged her opulent curves.

"It was a mercy that you sent for my belongings. I could not, at the drop of a hat, have had all this assembled for me," Estella spoke softly, watching the count as he flexed his fingers against the windowsill. His breathing was shallow, and Estella contained her alarm as she set about creating an intricate star pattern with the silver candles. She then set the seven spheres in a pattern within it.

"Can you hear the cry that the wind has brought?" Mikhail said, turning to face her at last, his visage grave. Estella nodded as she retrieved an incense burner from the chest and fumbled with the coal and matches.

"Blood and death—an archdemon walks among the living," she said fiercely, her eyes burning darkly. The count frowned in unconcealed wonder.

"Is it touching you? The demons are speaking in the air where they fell and were bound. Their story is a fearsome tale, their whispers are a clangor throbbing in my skull and pounding it to dust." He touched his eyelids with slender white fingers and watched Estella beneath the thickness of his lashes. "But you can commune with them, can't you? Is that what you are doing? My eyes cannot reach that far into the evil that has just occurred, but the rumors run wild with the echo of the morning star descending into St. Alban's Cathedral. The Twilit world is mourning."

Estella looked up from her exertions and her eyes were a deep, vibrant red. From where she crouched on the floor setting her works in order, she looked feral. There was a lust for blood and a deadly hatred in her eyes. The count slowly removed himself from the window and walked towards her.

"Do not let it take you over, Estella. This is not you, you ride the storm. The storm does not ride you." Estella blinked and the aura around her dissipated. She heaved a sigh of relief.

"Tonight we will commune with the Twilit world and tell them everything we know," she said. "After I open my sight and steal the moments in time these dreadful things happened, then I shall bind them in crystal and send them across the Twilit world. Let us be ready for the danger, and also . . . they have news for me."

The count nodded. Sitting on the side of the bed, he watched her with intense curiosity as she cast the incense into the burner and seven times circled the star pattern, chanting. She beckoned for the count to join her.

"Bring that black pouch, too."

He obliged with a nod, and within the candles and spheres he sat opposite her. The candles burned with bright, silvery flames, and Estella took the pouch, dropping the contents into her lap. Two smaller pouches fell out, wrapped in plain white cloth. Seizing one, she pulled open its bindings and poured the contents into her hands. Little gem stones, small as quail eggs and engraved with symbols, cascaded out, and she lifted them to her mouth and breathed over them. Then, without warning, she cast them to the floor before her. Although the gems seemed light, they fell heavily and did not roll but landed with a precise pattern between Estella and Mikhail; a half moon pattern formed by the glittering stones. Estella frowned and nodded.

"Tonight we are passing through the eyes of the angel Asariel, guardian of the mansions of the moon. We welcome you, you who God has bound, and bless you before the throne of God." Estella's voice was austere, and the silvery glow of the stones was refracted in her eyes.

"Treachery in one of the three houses of man," she said dreamily, a slight tremor traversing her body. "The shepherd's broken rod; the flock is in danger." Estella lurched forwards suddenly, clutching her heart. Mikhail made to aid her, but she held up her hand. The silvery glow in her eyes was burning brightly. "The broken throne; the church is betrayed." She closed her eyes and swayed her head gently from side to side. "The dusk shall be bathed in blood, the pieces on the chessboard move, I am in danger, a figure of authority is after me."

She opened her eyes, reaching for the other pouch. Removing its contents hastily, she whispered a swift blessing and cast the moonstones in twos and threes at each candle. Immediately a glow erupted within the gems. The candles guttered momentarily, threatening to die out, then blazed out renewed, suddenly tall and white-hot. Then they dwindled again briefly, only to belch forth crackling white bolts of brilliance into the air. The lightning patterns branched out from each candle, twining together until they formed a mesh net suspended in the air, shivering with a fierce, blinding intensity.

Estella smiled wanly as images formed within the mesh; geometric patterns and human faces, shifting and transmuting into other forms and places. A soft rustling accompanied it, at first hushed and distant like the shaking of leaves on a forlorn tree, then slowly rising up. Voices, at first mingled together, began to distinguish themselves into separate entities. They talked to one another laden with the weight of their personality and the vibrancy of their thoughts. Within that mesh, Estella's mind was present too, sharp and keen and clear. Many times the voices drowned hers out, rising like the cacophony of a disjointed symphony. Then in the tumult the numerous voices bled their anguish, woe, and fear through the mesh. It filled the room with their many presences.

The count observed silently as women, men, and children from every corner of the kingdom and the Twilit world convened to voice their fears. One woman's voice towered over the rest. Her wailing of grief rippled through the mesh like an overpowering fume, recounting the details of the three men tortured and murdered at Cardinal Pious's behest. She had seen through their eyes, witnessing their torment, then out of mercy sealed their minds from their bodies.

The mesh shook and vibrated, and it seemed that it breathed with raging thought. Estella wept in silence, and each tear was an outpouring of her soul. The voices finally shuddered and diminished. Then as whispers, thick and laden with purpose, they broke into speech. The Twilit world extended everywhere—to the nobility, chemists, magistrates, physicians, and scholars. The wisest offered their advice, while the more foolish offered threats. And their weariness oozed from the mesh into the room, and Mikhail was one with their thriving minds. Then the voices abated and addressed Estella, questioning her. Leaning forwards she touched the mesh, and her thoughts ran as blood through veins into it, and their questions were sated.

Estella bent to the candles and blew them out. She blessed each fire as it died out, whispering farewells to her people. Finally in the dark, Estella and Mikhail sat in silence. The open window revealed the moon breaking through slivers of heavy cloud and shining down pale and frosty upon them.

"They will go for the children and then for me," Estella said gently. "I think it is time you convened with your order and presented our case before them and the church. What has transpired tonight was pure evil. We must not fight back openly, lest we be hauled to the stakes and burned, but Lucifer has entered the church and we can only hold out for so long now. Instead of the mere persecution of the church, we will have to contend with the demons they will guide to us." She sounded weary, but as hard as nails. As she reached for his hand he took it, lifting it to his lips to kiss.

"We need time," Mikhail sighed. "We cannot quell the danger. I will need the assistance of my brethren scattered throughout the kingdoms of Christendom. But like you I have methods of reaching them, and I shall do so tonight while you rest." His tone had acquired an unfamiliar, distant edge. Estella swiftly withdrew her hand from him as he observed her pensively, measuring her with an unusual scrutiny.

"Do not be afraid of me, of all people, Estella," he said at length, uneasily. The words rolled off his tongue cautiously. "I must be candid with you; you are a tool for the chessboard, both good and evil, with a predilection for skimming the waters of the abyss and stealing its essence to use for your own means. They would want you, seek you out, and maybe through torment and pain transform you into a beast of their own, to wield as a cruel weapon. You have sight stretching further into the eyes of God than anyone, and yet you do not burn. Your soul is not extinguished by the everlasting darkness, but you endure.

"You have opened doorways for the demons to enter, and they will use their arts against you. And the worm in your heart that gnaws within you that they feed on will grow. They will fight over your soul, and you will be caught between two wars. And you will have to choose one pathway and forsake the Twilit world forever." The moonlight shone on his face and he was again that stranger behind the wall of impenetrable dogma that she loathed. She backed away from him, eyeing him with scorn.

"Ah, I see. So now I am a pawn, am I?" she said. "Would you have me confined to your sanctuaries and be forced to fight in a battle I did not choose? Living in endless fear of where the blow will fall next as my reward? And enduring as a dancer darting between each knife thrown, undulating with the fires that seek to char my soul? Never! I shall remain what I have always been: free. I am the Dancer in the Dark. Nothing can cage the wind, nor make its whirling cease—I am so, too." She rose haughtily and the count followed her, his expression spiteful.

"And now you close yourself to me completely, and I cannot see you," he said bitterly. "Will you flee me now, and hide in the night? My order must protect you and initiate you, or else you will be easy prey. The king himself has sent me his concubine to warn me of what will befall you if you are caught alone and friendless." He advanced on her imperiously, his shadow long beneath the moonlight, the tension heavy between them.

"I was a fool to believe you were more than a callous liar seeking to imprison me and bind me to your games," Estella spoke harshly and Mikhail grimaced in disappointment.

"I only want to protect you," he said, towering over her condescendingly, "and as usual you construe everything as an assault on your freedom! You selfishly put your needs above all others when you could embrace a higher purpose. Does my love for you count for nothing now?" Mikhail raised a brow patronizingly.

Estella laughed humorlessly. "What is the value of love when love is a cage that men use to mold women into docility? Why must we always be the ones to sacrifice and deny ourselves? I shall not place myself as your charge and relinquish my autonomy."

Hurt blossomed over Mikhail's face, but before he could weave it into scolding words, a groan reached them from the open window. They broke away awkwardly, shifting their attention to the sound. The count reached the window first and froze into a predatory watchfulness, Estella warily clambering off the bed and joining him. The drowsy streets outside were deserted, but the moonlight was bright enough to descry shapes in the gloom before them. The source of the groan was easy to discover, it was the only moving thing rupturing the dormant quietness of the night. A wounded man, bound by hands and ankles, was being hauled along roughly by a rope tied around his neck by another figure, who was shuffling loudly and dressed in church clothing.

"Elmer!" bellowed the count hoarsely. Tearing himself away from the window with a rapidity that unnerved Estella, he sprinted across the chamber. Then, grasping his sword, he bolted out into the night.

Mikhail's cry had rent the night air and fragmented into the darkness, and Elmer groaned again louder in pain. It was plain that he was also weeping. His tormentor paused, looking up to the open window with vacant, stygian eyes. As he stared squarely at Estella, she recognized the cardinal with shock. Before she could react, a cloud passed over the moon, and within moments the cardinal had vanished, leaving Elmer behind.

Mikhail had wrenched the gates of the manor open and was cursing into the night, cradling Elmer's head. Estella covered her mouth with her hands and backed away from the window, slinking into the shadows of the room. There she found another familiar shadow, waiting for the propitious moment to reach her.

Soon a commotion was heard in the awakened manor, and the count returned inside bearing his dying friend. Laying him down on the banquet table, he bellowed orders to summon a physician and send word to Oswald. Then he rushed up the staircase to his bedchamber to find Estella—but she was gone. A flitting shadow in the night, unseen and unheard, a handful of clothing and jewels taken in a hurry. Mikhail stood there, smiting the door where he stood and roaring his rage. She had fled him, untrusting, and leaving no farewell note or goodbye kiss. The only remnants of her presence were the fading smells of incense, her musk perfume, and the shadow of the brooding thoughts she concealed.

MONTHS WENT BY and as each one passed, London plunged deeper into a dark frenzy of persecution. The once fair squares that were set up for the delight of the merchants and nobles had turned overnight into a cruel spectacle where many were hanged. The Twilit people that were unable to elude the evil clutch of the shadow filling the church with its poison were persecuted by the inquisition of the cardinal. But the network that Estella had created had alerted most of them in time, so that they were able to seal their worlds away and disappear without a trace, withdrawing into daylight where the eyes of darkness could not see them.

The count learned that the night Estella had vanished, she had returned to her manor and alerted the children in her charge. Through the intricate pathways beneath the manor, she sent them forth to be absorbed into the Twilit network she had set up for contingencies. The children in her care vanished beneath the clothing of rich merchants and nobles, becoming new cousins and distant relations suddenly arriving to settle in town. Others joined the traders' ranks and faded into the countryside. Luckily the education Estella had provided for the children had taught them to adapt to all walks of life, and given them the tools to blend in to any station of society. The count never saw them again, except for brief glimpses here and there—a mischievous twinkle in unusually bright eyes, or a sudden wink with a knowing smile from a hasty passerby.

Dolly brushed past him one day in the Silver Quarter, holding the hand of a woman Mikhail recognized as a lady of the nobility named Rosalind Constance. As she passed, she dropped the red jasper bracelet he had purchased for Estella into his pocket. She had not so much as turned her blond head as she filed by gracefully, deftly exchanging her full hand for an empty one without word or glance.

The count yearned for Estella, but soon gave up on finding her. In her empty manor, ransacked by the cardinal's minions, he came often and sat pondering. He knew she had returned to her manor and his own abode to take her most precious items before fleeing, but he had not seen her once.

The walls of her manor were silent, and the magic that lingered within had repelled foragers and so remained with a modicum of sacrosanctity. And it cherished its dark secrets. They weighed deep and hard like old trees burdened with age, threatening to rupture. And there he waited and sought her, but yet she eluded him. However he found some consolation in her ability to remain completely hidden, for it meant she would be safe from harm.

The silent, cruel game that he and the cardinal played was ruthless, and while they did not oppose each other publicly, they fought in the dark and dealt each other heavy blows. And when one is playing a game with the prince of darkness, winning is no easy feat. The king himself had become a fierce advocate for the destruction of the Twilit people, and he personally rallied his forces to find and destroy them, and as a result many innocents perished. For though the demiurges that had gifted the Twilit people concealed those sworn to them, rumors and petty grievances arose amid the conflict, and many were sent to the gallows that might have been saved.

The queen had openly left the lofty castle she shared with her king and elected to retire to the countryside. There, she and her council of the various orders, led by Count Mikhail, measured each action and countermovement against the cardinal and the king. But the haunting voice of Elmer would not leave Mikhail, for by some cruel trickery conjured by the cardinal, Elmer's soul was tied down to earth and bound, and he wandered the dark alleys of his pain. Unable to escape his bounds and tormented by devils, he reached out to the count. But Mikhail was unable to break his bondage, though he waged ruthlessly against Samael's minions and Lucifer's pawns.

Taking upon himself the holiest sacrament of his order, he was initiated and tasked with wielding the scepter of God's right hand. Then he sent his spies to aid him in completing his design, and he vowed this time to constrain Estella, wherever she was, and cast upon her the yoke of the scepter for the greater good of humanity. He had no other choice but to force her to submit to the church and aid them in seeing the infernal game being played between the malignant forces. The human in him that loved her and overlooked her faults was weak, and he knew that would avail him naught in his dealings with her henceforth. Now the demon awoke within him and the demon's desire to possess took over, and he promised himself that sooner or later he would have her back.

Oswald had retained the fierce tenacity shrouded within him, and he devised plans to elevate the sparks of holiness within the order and petition the heavens to send forth another light and incarnate another salvation. Endless nights he would wrestle within the shadows that sought to thwart his works and undo them, and he persevered. But he was sad for his friend the count, who pined for Estella. So he, too, exerted his efforts to track her down. He was of the mind that she was more of a weapon for evil than good, and culling her would relieve the world of a great impending threat. But no trace of her was ever seen in dreary London.

13

EARTH IS HIS FOOTSTOOL

The tyrant pulls the reins, its thralls work their mines
In the confines of your spirit corroding its integrity
Ubiquitous decaying of the sovereignty that declines
Slowly towards the full surrendering of authority

THE CARAVANS SHOOK, CREAKING WITH EVERY MOVEMENT AS THEY rattled hurriedly down the dirt pathways. The curtains were drawn shut, but the laughter of the travelers rippled through the forest and their mirth rebounded off the trees and glades, permeating the land with a merry echo. With their lutes and lyres they wove old songs, pouring their memories into them with a sweet melancholy. They were eternal travelers, and their blood grew uneasy if they took root anywhere for too long. They welcomed the road with unadulterated levity, as though greeting a returning lover.

But not everyone inside the caravans shared their merriment. Estella sat in the last, huddled beneath brightly colored cloths. She yawned indecorously, clutching a half empty wine bottle. Yet sometimes, despite her resentment, she hummed along to the tunes the Roma sang. But she kept her back to them, doing her best not to be drawn into their raucous banter.

Unseen by the merry men and women, the androgynous demon lounged luxuriously beside Estella, observing her with the habitual mischievous malice in his eyes. Every now and then he would dig his fingers into the thick mane of her hair, and with a sharp intake of breath she would recoil, but without moving away, as he toyed with the loose strands of her curls and whispered unctuously in her ear.

He had nothing to fear now, no banishment and no binding, for she had struck with him a desperate bargain. When he came to her in that timely moment of Elmer's death, she had fled with him into the night, having nowhere to hide and none to offer her aid. And she trusted him, as his warnings had proved to be painfully accurate, and he aided her, unwilling that she be taken from him.

He lent her his shadow, and she fled beneath it to the confines of the kingdom, traveling by night and day, knowing the pursuit was hot after her. But they could not hope to find her, for every demon has his tricks, and he was particularly cunning. Through winding pathways of dreams he led her, promising her sanctuary in the neighboring Frankish kingdoms where others of his kind had their territories. In return, she kept him by her side. Had the situation not been so dire, he would have requested more. But he was no fool, and the prince of darkness no idle fallen angel, so together they fled and joined a caravan of Roma who, enamored with the jewels she offered them, gave her a place among them cheerfully.

"Don't be so thankless, Tsura, I was not always blind," the demon said smoothly, his voice melodious. So far he was having a very ineffective monologue with himself, but he persevered nonetheless, knowing her inability to withhold her quips for long. "I was once fair and beautiful, and I still have things to offer you, yes, things that count of yours can only dream of. Endless realms of pleasure . . ." His fingers provocatively snaked down her neck and the arch of her back, feeling the tension in her body. "You cannot recoil from me forever. After all, we have a long journey ahead of us, and I am all you have in this world. Now you can taste the loneliness I have endured for so long," he whispered. Estella turned around to face him, a grimace of half concealed frustration on her face.

"I did not ask you to molest me while succoring me, you damaged devil," she spat at him as the demon laughed heartily and disappeared. Estella sighed and turned on her back. Aching from the uncomfortable carriage and the weight of her worries, she soon fell into a drunken sleep.

⊶∞⊷

AFTER A FEW uneventful weeks on the road where Estella grew to despise the normalcy of her companions' lives, they finally arrived at the port. She found a place on a ship easily, offering her services as a maid and flashing her irresistible charm. Shrouded in a poor laborer's clothing, Estella mounted the ship, hood pulled over her face and her gaze humbly downcast. Her sinister companion patrolled the ship, keeping guard and never quite leaving her side.

Unused as she was to work, she threw herself into the menial tasks given her without complaint. In the few hours of rest she had after her labors, the demon sought to entertain her with beautiful dreams he conjured for her; pale recollections of his heavenly sojourn and many wonders he wrought for her in her sleep, realms where he took her weary soul to ease her sorrow. Indeed the stairway of the angels, Jacob's Ladder, they traveled to often. They could even ascend to the Third Heaven before the archangels sent fire to hurtle them down again like falling stars. He showed her also the roots of the tree of life, and every morning he erased her memory and left her clamoring with desire for more.

Across the seas they drifted, until they landed in Frankish lands. Estella stealthily purchased a horse from the port and a bag of provisions with plain, homespun clothing. Then she bid farewell to the Roma who had traveled with her on the same ship. Though she did not speak of her affairs, they knew that she was fleeing something. Each of the old women cast out their divination sticks, bones, and runes—each according to their trade—and read the omens of her future. But they could not hide their bewildered murmurs. Then they blessed her, sacrificing a rooster in her honor and covering her eyelids with its blood.

"May you walk unseen by the eyes of evil and may the moon in her tower be always your guide. And may the guardian that faithfully dogs your shadow be forever bound to you!" Then they were gone.

Estella, resigned to whatever doom lay ahead, sat astride her horse as the demon led it by its bridle into the wilderness. They followed the snaking light of the sun that filtered through the leaves and cast faint shadows before them. The trees murmured and moaned in the rustling wind, whispering their stories to unheeding ears. But they recognized the demon and greeted him as their own. The forest was unnaturally awake, its aged heart pulsating.

"The forest knows you . . . how?" Estella asked curiously as she hearkened to the heartbeat of the woods. The demon's composure softened and he smiled, meeting her eyes tentatively.

"I was always here, since the Fall from heaven. I withdrew into these woods and taught them how to grow strong and vigorous against the ages. I fell here and hid away in shame for a long time." He turned slightly to face her, his wholesome eye twinkling with remembrance. Estella snorted in disbelief.

"You? A demon gardener? A wood spirit?" she scoffed.

"You were not born too far from here yourself, Tsura," he began tenderly. Estella felt a creeping sense of alarm. "I was lonely and alone and I sat often beneath the stars. Then one day I saw the gates of dawn open and your spirit emerge like a star cluster, a star with many spiky shards of brilliance. It had been ages since I had seen such loveliness fall into the clay vessels of mankind. So I left my solitary stair and followed it till I came across your family. I knew you would be born, and I waited to see what would become of you." The demon halted suddenly, a shadow passing over his face. He stared at Estella keenly, caressing the horse's neck with his whole unblemished eye fixated squarely on Estella's face.

"I watched you, born into this cold world and mercilessly robbed of your parents, then cast into a life you did not choose. I was there all along, ensuring no harm came to you. I have been with you always, since the very start, and never left your side." His eye burned with a malevolent fire and Estella felt an old fear creep up on her. It was the sentiment of something dreadful lurking in the shadows, waiting for you to fall asleep, then devour your life. Old childhood terrors she had long since dismissed. "Yes, I desired you, but if you saw in yourself what I see in you, then you would understand . . ." He moved closer to her and Estella yanked the bridle backwards, urging the horse away from him.

"But I do not desire you, and that is something you don't accept, demon!" she replied, looking around her for a way to escape. But she knew she would soon be lost and he would follow her. She turned to face him with a stern countenance as he leaned against a tree, leering contentedly.

"I was not always blind, Tsura, not always deformed. And I was never a demon. You never asked me." He beckoned to the horse who, against Estella's urging, followed the demon. He took the bridle laughingly and led ahead. "You never asked me my name. That is what truly hurts me about you. I might have been kinder if you had asked." He shot her a malignant glance and Estella shrugged, raising a careless brow.

"You might as well know, then. My true name is Antariel, and this place was once my home." He paused, his delicate voice laden with sorrow. The lights that fell upon his face concealed his blindness and brought forth the delicate chiseled features of his face, rendering him almost wholesome. "I was part of the dancing choir before the throne of God many eons ago, and there I played my instrument and made music that filled the empty confines of space with echoing song. I saw the dreams of God, and I wrought them into song. I was proud and vain, and so soon I tuned my melodies to Lucifer's. He had wielded a symphony of his own which was ever growing and expanding, and it was full with the promise of worlds of our own to rule.

"But that is not my tale. Lucifer enticed my wayward heart and I sang his visions into song and I wrought many dark evils I deemed to be fair. And for that in the Fall when Lucifer was hurled out, the angel ruling over me broke my voice. Now I cannot create anything, only watch the endless mists of creation and burn with longing. But that was not the only blow. I had once also danced before the immortal tree of life, whose limpid branches held the worlds together and whose heart was the core of the undying holy fire. The tree was wrought of an equal balance of mercy and might, the red and blue veins that nourish the womb of the universe and keep it alive. I was more attuned to might, and because my fire burned with it, Lucifer was able to entice me to use my spirit for his creations.

"When the last strands of God's patience failed, and he cast his favorite child out of his presence, the punishing angels were sent after us and dealt us justice. Ariel, who stands before the throne with eyes that pierce beyond the coils of time, took a mighty spear and sliced my spirit. He sundered me in half, ripping out a fragment of my god spark. I was blinded, maimed, and diminished and became a thing of incongruity— damaged, voiceless, sightless, and forlorn." Antariel hung his head, his hair draping across his face to conceal his expression. "I fell with scorched wings upon a foreign land and have hid myself here ever since, pleading for centuries for the cold gates of heaven to open and for mercy to find me again. But mercy loved me not, and I loved my pride even more."

His voice broke, and Estella found herself grieving for Antariel. But though her initial disgust and dismay seeped out of her and dissipated, she couldn't help but wonder how much of her sympathy was conjured by the remaining magical abilities of his compelling voice. Nonetheless, she felt her own sorrow, and she reflected on it and felt insignificant before the tale Antariel had revealed to her.

"I never knew and I should have known. I suppose I was afraid of you even before I knew you, as you dogged my shadow with lust. But why now, why tell me all this?" Estella asked. She felt conflicted. The decayed demon repulsed her, but fragments of his better self remained. Observing him with her usual shrewdness, she sought to unravel the strands of his thoughts, sifting for lies.

"I chose today because now that you finally need me, I do not feel like a beggar at your door demanding pity." Antariel's voice was bitter, and she shivered though the sun shone bright. "My spark is decaying each day, dying a silent death. Its cry is rending the very foundations of the seven skies. And yet I am fallen. God no longer turns his face upon me, and I'm left in the dark to wither. I was his child, and my spark is calling out to him still, guttering and deformed, languishing behind the laws of justice he erected for this world. I know he wants me home, and now I know you can help me."

They had reached the deepest thicket of the woods and his shape shifted. "Behold me at the first hours of dawn when mercy opens the gates of heaven. Then you shall see who I truly am."

—⌘—

At night they encamped beneath a grove of trees. Estella gathered broken branches, and Antariel lit them with a careless flicker of thought. She had noticed a shift within his composure ever since he had revealed his tale to her. The change left her restless and uneasy. He was clearly conflicted within himself. One moment he was a lustful demon with baleful eyes, his glance devouring her thoughts and threatening to engulf her into his darkness, and the next he was serene and joyous, his deformities and androgyny faded and insignificant. Around the makeshift camp they sat in silence, lost in the mesmerizing dance the campfire brightly conjured. The tongues of flame took numerous shapes; red visages with fiery eyes and nimble limbs, and winged beasts belching forth sparks.

"The lower sparks of the heavenly fires—they were the fragmented glints that fled from the forges of the first angels and became your gods," Antariel said. "They were mostly lonely, harmless fire spirits." He smiled at her, and the battle that raged within him amplified as his troubled gaze found the fire. His face was a writhing mask of evil desires and fallen wants combined with a frail but resilient ember of light. "How did mankind become the apple of the great, all-seeing eye when you were mere pots of clay wrought with the fingers of clumsy demons?" He leaned in towards her across the fire, lust and desire mingling.

Estella, already on alert, backed away angrily and defiantly made a ward sign before him. Antariel hissed in fury and rose to his feet as Estella kicked mud into the fire and bolted, fleeing into the night, forsaking her horse and provisions. She delved into the dark, endless forest breathlessly with no direction in mind, seeking to place as much distance between them as she possibly could. She was sick of the events that had robbed her of her ability to choose her destiny, and she rejected the dismal emotional blackmail Antariel heaped upon her.

He did not follow her, but she did not look back to find out. She continued into the darkness, whispering incantations beneath her breath to shield herself from him. Short of breath and with an aching chest, her footsteps faltered as she realized she was utterly lost. The moonlight was choked by the heavy boughs, and the murmurs around her frightened her, and as she groped in the dark, she did not know which direction to take. Stumbling forward, she ran as far as she could, changing directions every now and then. Finally, shaking with the exertion of running, she set her back against a tree warily, listening for him intently.

Though she felt no pursuit, she knew such a lack of persistence was unlike him. She was sure he was merely biding his time, waiting for the right moment to smite her unawares. Then, as her doubts increased, the forest began to tremble and the leaves shook. A cold breeze rose through the trees, rustling and stirring all around her. A creeping sense of horror washed over her, and she dared not move.

Feeling that she would rather face her fears than let them consume her, she called into the night, "Antariel, where are you? Come face me!" She mustered her command to keep the tone of fear from tainting her voice. But there was no reply, only the unnerving sense of dread washing over her. "Antariel, reveal yourself! Let us part ways as friends at least."

Then a glow kindled in the distance, alerting her eyes to his presence as he slunk gracefully like a prowler amid the trees, a halo of shining light around his head guiding his steps.

"I could smell the reek of fear for miles on end, dearest one, and my appetite is whetted . . . but why call me? I wait for the right time to find you. You cannot flee me once you've given in to fear. I know where you hide, for I know the exact pattern of your thoughts . . . I know *you*." A malevolent ruthlessness burned within his single wholesome eye as he grinned hideously at her.

Estella knew the game well, and she fought the seeping fear that clamored at her senses, tugging at her to cede to it. Antariel eyed her intently, and the shroud he wove around her thickened and intensified. Through her fear, Estella sought the earliest memories of peace she had, the most steadfast moments, and her fleeting dreams of whirling stars and the benevolent watchfulness of her patron Mother Goddess.

"I do not have fear, I have my burning spirit to burn out the impure darkness that you are. You do not scare me, demon!" But there was truly fear within her, the fear of being alone in a world that had other cares than her, and numerous children to weep over apart from her. And worse still, the chafing knowledge that she was nothing more than another weapon picked up and hurled into battle, then discarded when no longer useful.

Antariel approached, serene and dangerous and burning with his treacherous schemes. She did not meet his face until he was a foot apart from her, then she stared defiantly into his wholesome eye, ignoring the milky white dead one that seemed to be even more fixated on her than the other. He smiled hungrily.

"God did not create ugliness, Tsura. Am I ugly? Am I made in his image, or am I a regurgitated deformity that he cast away from his sight? Am I a fallen angel, or a cursed demon?"

She forced herself to look into both his eyes, and she could not discern the lies from the truths. There was nothing holy staring back from the deep chasms of his mind. Was he truly a demon after all, seeking an entry into her heart to seed his poison? Or was he truly fallen and given to the crookedness of his evil ways?

"May Ariel frustrate you and bind you, you castaway, treacherous son," she whispered into his face. Antariel froze, then with a mask of wrath seized her by the throat, lifting her up like a ragdoll and pinning her against a tree violently.

"I could so easily break your neck, you feeble human. Do not dare let that name escape your lips! There is no Ariel here to protect you, there is but me and the darkness you fled. Now with your light that I will consume, I will be able to break through the gates of heaven again. And if not, at least I will elevate my spark to a better place."

The fingers around her neck tightened, and an ache began to emanate from the back of her skull. It amplified as he tightened the pressure on her neck, quenching her of her life force slowly and deliberately. She began to suffocate while the pain in her head throbbed madly, her body shaking violently and lights bursting before her eyes.

"The house of your soul is crumbling, and your death spark I shall devour. Watch it break free and die into my embrace. I own you!" Antariel hissed.

The malice and wretchedness she had seen in him all these years, which he had artfully covered up when she was at her most desperate, emerged in its truest and ugliest form, fiercer and more distorted than ever before. The searing pain was blinding her sight, and she felt her soul being ripped from her body, battling to cling to its failing abode.

The pain was excruciating and she screamed in agony, her fingernails digging into his hands. The echoing scream reverberated in the murmuring woods, and it was caught and refracted away into the valleys, rising feebly beneath the impassive, cold moon. In a desperate attempt not to lose to such a lowly creature, she cried forth her soul, wrenching open the Twilit door. Like one who has cut her veins and bleeds out her life force shudders and contorts, likewise she bled her soul's dying pangs into the Twilit world.

Beseeching help, she ripped apart the veils protecting the Twilit world from prying, patrolling eyes. And like a shark tasting blood, it responded. Colors erupted in her eyes like fireworks, and she knew she was nearing the dreaded door of death, though she would be denied its passage, instead engulfed into a worse abyss. And then the response came back—a sharp spear, thin and bitter, cutting through the shrouds of the worlds and the firmaments to reach her. A malevolent hand whose nails could rip the skies out of the earth like a lid and hurl it into oblivion.

Antariel was suddenly filled with uncertainty as he watched Estella's dying moments. The night had suddenly stilled, as though holding its breath. The trees grew silent, their heartbeats instantly stifled, and birds fled in screeching flocks. Antariel shuddered, his one eye widening in shock as night turned to day behind them and time itself froze and rolled away. Slowly he released Estella's throat.

As she slumped to the foot of the tree, she looked up just in time to see a sharp spear skewering Antariel, fixing him against the tree as he let out a choked, bewildered cry. Feeling her life return to her slowly, like wakening from a drugged, hallucinatory dream, she rolled over, gasping for air and clutching at the dirt and leaves beneath her.

Despite her daze, Estella watched in horror as the forest shone, ablaze with the iridescent lights of many opal wings. They glimmered with the fragmented brilliance of light refracted on diamonds, and the shimmering hues and lights blindingly seared the gloom, the feathers, sharp as talons, radiating heat. The beautiful, proud, austere face, fashioned with the expert hands of perfection, shone with the reflected holiness of one who was once closest to God, wreathed in his boundless glory. He gazed upon Antariel with ethereal azure eyes that mockingly opened on the expanse of the cosmos.

"Delivered to my very feet, how remarkably thoughtful of you Antariel. But then I am not so amazed, as intelligence was never one of your greatest gifts, was it? You merely followed obediently along, my faithful hound." His compelling, pleasant voice dripped cruelty. Though the radiant face did not so much as look in Estella's direction, she felt transfixed and the weight of his thoughts sliced into her with a searing ease. As he spoke within her mind, it was as though his voice was contained in everything around her.

Escaping me is escaping your own self, the voiced boomed. *It is quite futile. Where would you run to now? But watch me avenge you. I am at your service after all, my chosen child.*

Antariel writhed, his hands covering the entry wound futilely as blood oozed out of his mouth and he heaved and groaned, roaring in impotent fury beneath the cruel laughter of Lucifer.

"I followed you, indeed. Followed you for the promises you never kept and the deceit you ensnared me with!" Antariel hissed, and his hale eye was weeping profusely and he shook. "I want the home where I belong. You robbed me of everything; my voice, my beauty, my sight. And you got to keep everything," he spat out plaintively, each word punctuated with a trickle of blood. Lucifer looked up to the skies feigning sorrow, his lucent eyes like nebulae glittering with starlight.

"How are you, fair Father?" Lucifer called out. "Do you hear his appeal? Is he desecrating your holy name with his accursed tongue? Let your favorite son quench his desire to profane you." And with that he grabbed Antariel's face, and the blaze of a million suns smoldered within his gaze.

Antariel choked, utterly diminished in Lucifer's proximity, and opened his mouth to scream voicelessly. Estella felt her knees weaken and her resilience falter as Antariel's tongue shriveled and blackened, the smell of charred flesh nauseatingly filling the air.

Lucifer smiled, and Estella found it was impossible to detach her eyes from his beauty. For even as he tortured Antariel, Lucifer's face betrayed no evil intent or evil thoughts. He smiled benignly with a wholesome warmth that held her enthralled in wonder. His hair glistened like spun gold, and the curves of his face were holy and pure—incongruous with the evil deadliness within. He was the closest anyone could come to seeing the countenance of God, and he inspired instinctive veneration. He could twist a dagger into the chest of his victim while they continued to smile blissfully, unable to detach themselves from the beauty he emanated. He wielded that power over Antariel now.

Antariel trembled in agony, cradling his mouth and weeping like a chastised child; even his very mind was robbed of speech. It wandered blind in its abode, groping in the dark, unable to shape words or form ideas, grappling feebly. The horror of his plight washed over Estella, and she wept for him uncontrollably, wondering what would be her own end after he had dealt with her.

"Why aren't you fighting back, little worm? Your ugliness is disappointing, but then you could never hope to serve me any better," Lucifer purred in mellow tones while the hale eye of Antariel oozed sadness and shame. Lucifer's fingers glided over his face, pretending to study his features. But in a flickering moment the mask he wore cracked, and mockery, cold and cruel, was revealed on his visage. He prodded Antariel's blind eye delicately at first, then wantonly drove his finger into the socket, puncturing it. Antariel struggled fruitlessly as Lucifer towered over him, holding his face fast with scorn.

"Look at me, there is no god but me here on earth. I am the illuminated angel, the one who brings the vicious justice you all merit. All these sons of God that I could have given principalities in my worlds—what a waste! To be cast out of heaven and then find no other home, to be broken and to have no fulfillment. I am the closest to the face of God. Why do you reproach me for using you? Were you not created for my pleasure?" Lucifer inquired almost indifferently.

Still, nothing was betrayed in Antariel's gaze as he turned his head slowly to face Estella. The longing was still there, but also infinite sadness, deep as the waters of the endless abyss expanding into nothingness, forever devouring him and gnawing at him. With one last breath, he mustered the final vestiges of his crumbling mind and offered his spark back to God. In a silent yet piercing appeal, he begged forgiveness and sought his own destruction at his divine hand. He renounced himself and Lucifer. Repenting in one flashing moment, his spirit broke free and Antariel slumped against the tree lifelessly. Lucifer howled, wrenching out his spear with the velocity of a tempest striking, and impaled him again, this time skewering him higher up as a pale, shining shadow fled past him, fragile and quivering.

"At your evil works again, Lucifer? Must you always disfigure your prey before you send them to me?" came a dry, toneless voice with an underscore of sympathy. Behind Lucifer stood a hooded and cloaked figure, both tall and forbidding. The sheer contrast between the two was stark, for where one wore his grandeur with pride, the other swathed his majesty in humility. His robes were silvery and threaded in intricate patterns, and his countenance was grave yet stalwart, with the calm confidence of his impregnable power.

"Ah, my old friend. Don't you ever grow tired of escorting these wretched misbegotten ones back to him?" Lucifer did not even deign to turn his head, but addressed the tree instead with mild interest, his head held high in unbreakable pride. Estella could see the swirling cosmos burning ferociously in his eyes, and as he closed his numerous wings she could smell the odor of incense.

"This one is not for Nesargiel or Dumah," the cloaked angel replied. "This one is going home to his maker, and he will cradle his spark in his holy lap and wash it clean from taint. A lost sheep finding his way back to his rejoicing shepherd, in the inevitable end." The angel's voice was tranquil, like the surface of an unyielding lake. Behind the angel there was a gaping hole of space, and little wheels of light flitted out gently and danced around the still air.

"Take him back anyway. He was not what I came for, such a futile, petty creature as him, living an existence of perpetual insignificance.

And send my deepest loving regards to my Father," he added, wrenching the spear from the body of Antariel and sheathing it, barely sparing a glance at the dark blood that sullied it.

"Dawn is upon you, do you wish to greet him yourself? Then we can measure how significantly your fall has impacted your importance to him. They say many things about you in the Seventh Sky, for instance how fast you are at fleeing from his wrath."

The patient voice rolled over him thunderously, and Lucifer growled, deploying his opal wings. The trees flailed and moaned with the sudden surge of singing wind. Then the forest, illuminated by Lucifer's light, dimmed as the true dawn came, pale from the east like a gentle splash of white against the lightening blueness of the dark night. Lucifer cast a final glance towards Estella. Try as she might, she could not detach herself from the clear, limpid pool of lights that washed over her, dulling her senses into obedience, and she wept.

"From now on it is just me and you," Lucifer said. "And I shall find you, believe me, helpless and frail, a blade of grass beneath my feet, ready for the crushing. And I will crush you until you submit to me and follow the destiny I have set before you. Do not forget who owns you." His radiant face was denuded of its light now, and hatred was etched into his features. With a flourish of defiance he thrust his spear at the budding dawn light and vanished.

The cloaked angel stood serenely by, and the golden pale shadow that shivered in the light sailed towards him. The angel beckoned it, and led it to the open hole of space.

"Be kind and don't cast your life away foolishly," he spoke, turning to Estella. "If it bore no worth, then you would be no pawn for us. Until the great end when both Samael and Lucifer are vanquished and God regains the stolen sparks they devoured, we are all pawns and the soldiers of our Father. When you left his presence and descended here, you were not hurled down in disgrace, but you joined your brothers and sisters of the world, choosing to stand at the forefront of God's lashes. Remember that when you are alone and the darkness promises you the glories beyond the skies." The angel observed her calmly with an almost fatherly care and pity, then turned back toward the hole accompanied by the golden shadow.

Estella gaped momentarily, at first unsure whether the words were addressed to her. Then reorganizing her scrambled wits, she struggled to her feet. "Will he be judged harshly? Will he ever be alright? And me, will I ever be alright?" she managed to fumble after him bleakly, her own words ringing hollow in her ears. Her anguished soul weighed heavier on her than when Antariel, in his covetousness, had sought to break it.

The angel stopped before the hole as he was entering it, and without turning, answered in the same equivocal, toneless voice, "Everything is always alright in the end, yes. Even the greatest of evils cannot comprehend it, but everything in the great end of all things is alright. The final symphony is led by the Father."

Estella acquiesced, too numb to dispute his nebulous reply, and bowed her head while the angel passed through the wormhole.

"Many thanks for Antariel," he added. "He is redeemed, and maybe if the balance weighs in his favor, he will be judged with compassion and his spark reprieved from obliteration." Then without preamble or farewells, he was gone. In one intake of breath the doorway closed soundlessly behind him, and she was left alone, shaking from the overwhelming emotions in the breaking light of dawn as the sudden mundane chirping of birds surrounded her.

Estella roused herself clumsily, stumbling as she walked. Stunned, she cradled her own arms and hugged herself, vaguely wondering where she was and whether her reprieve was going to last long. She was still anaesthetized from the past events, and dimly glad to be back among familiar sights. Lost in the unusually deserted forest, she slowly followed her own clumsy path back to the campfire where her nightmare had begun. Finding it had died out, she repacked her possessions numbly and untied the horse, which had been thoughtfully tied to the closest tree. Then mounting the horse, she guided it towards the path she remembered from Antariel's descriptions, following its course, too weary to think or contemplate what lay ahead.

14

A REPRIEVE BEFORE
THE STORM

I have drunk of that gilded cup passed down by ancient hands
In complete silence and knowledge of the asperity it bequeaths
The cauldron of the ages stirs upon the confines of mortal lands
Drawing the leaping swords of conquest from their sheaths

ESTELLA TRIED TO REARRANGE HER SWEATY HAIR BENEATH THE heavy black cloth that wrapped around her head. It had been a rough few months since she had erred into the forest aimlessly, stranded and without hope of finding a way out. Her provisions had failed quickly, and then her horse had been lamed. She had left him then out of pity, relieving him of his burden and leaving him to seek his fortune elsewhere. At least he had a better chance of survival than she had—he could eat the grass and knew instinctively where to find water.

The weight of spiritual warfare was burdening her too, for she had sealed the Twilit world behind her and kept herself blind to the forces raging against each other. She wandered alone in the endless forest, bleeding her strength, until she finally came upon a dusty road. There she collapsed gratefully, her thoughts going to Antariel and the doorway into realms unknown through which he had departed for his eternal home and final judgment. He truly was resting in peace now, she thought, unlike her.

She was filthy, starved, and haggard from concentrating on the in-cantations perpetually bubbling from her weary lips. Each day the sun seemed a little stronger as it beat tenaciously down on her, driving her wild with thirst. And the night brought no respite, for the nocturnal insects would come out of the bowels of the woods, biting and tormenting her in her fitful sleep. Luckily for her, as she dragged herself along the dusty road, she discovered that it joined with other beaten paths, and eventually converged into one road, wide enough for several carriages to drive abreast. Deciding to finally give herself up to fate, she curled up into the fetal position in the middle of the road, hoping to be soon seen, and not run over.

As luck would have it, a caravan of traveling Magdalene Sisters passed by. The driver alerted the sisters to the woman on the road, and they stopped immediately to lend her succor. Out of good faith and heart, they took her in unquestioningly, perceiving her as a test of their generosity and goodness from God. And so they cared for her and brought her to their priory. And because she had the coloring and the features of Middle Eastern women, they saw Mary Magdalene in her.

Estella was very thankful to be rescued, but fully realized the irony of her saviors being nuns. They were of the rigid, religious type that scrupulously objected to the world she belonged to. And though her apathy and thankfulness transformed into resentment, she nonetheless took their vows and deceived them into believing she had received the calling.

The vows and rituals of the church provided some sanctuary against the evil forces, with the hallowed grounds and mystic gnostic teachings. There she was safe for now, shrouded in the garments of a nun and hiding behind a mask of meek piety, where none might find her. She lived quietly for a time in the shadow of the veil of religious dogma. But not for long, for she brooded and waited for time to take its course, and for the search for her to die out.

She had knowingly immured herself in an elaborate jail, but safety was paramount and she craved respite to redeem her mind. But she found her heart and thoughts vacant. There was no demon to spur her into impulsive, restless plotting, no creature comforts to inspire her, and she lacked all methods of communicating with the world outside the nunnery walls. Soon she devised another way to obtain a small measure of freedom. She informed the prioress of her skills as a healer. Combined with shows of prayers and fervent piety, she was given permission to venture into the town to care for the sick and needy.

The Frankish town near the nunnery was small but financially well-off, with enough luxury to distinguish it from other small towns in the vicinity. But its most important feature was that it was the passing point for all travelers going in and out of the Frankish kingdoms into Britain. Estella's skills earned her much renown in the town. However, she was only begrudgingly sought after at first, for being foreign and lacking the requisite modesty expected of a nun, she was slow to grow on her fellow sisters and townsmen. But like all things habitual, they grew accustomed to her and even fond of her.

Soon she was spending most of her time away from the priory and its excessive solemnity, instead entering into the joyous hustle and bustle of the Frankish town. Eventually she even gleaned some autonomy by setting herself up in a small cottage near the church. This allowed her to go about her daily business visiting the sick more easily. Through her duties, and with the protection her habit afforded her, she was able to mingle with all levels of society, both rich and poor, and gain entry into their social circles.

Now uncomfortably perched on a chair at the far end of a rickety table, her mind drifted in and out of the conversation she was having. The low room was claustrophobic and windowless, and numerous icons of the Christ and his mystic bride adorned the walls. The Magdalenes were initiates of Mary, the red bride of Magdala, Christ's wife, and followed her practice of celibacy, prayer, and service to God. They venerated her gospel and followed the course she took up when she departed the Holy Land after the crucifixion.

"Sister Mercy, we really need your help today," said Prefect Gustave. "The mayor is welcoming a guest into town, a traveling prince of the Saxon kingdoms. His herald came ahead to warn us of his arrival, and has informed us that he has been taken ill. He usually solicits the services of this nunnery for his confessions, therefore we would require the skills of your holiness; prayer naturally for his expedient recovery, and your expert healing capabilities." The prefect spoke softly with a remarkably mellow tone. He was a handsome, middle-aged man with luscious brown hair and a healthy beard. His cornflower blue eyes were analytical and pensive. And though his features were comely, he had a certain roughness about him, which he had tamed with education and courtesy.

His gaze often wandered over Sister Mercy's face, wondering what her true name was and who she had been before she took the vows. But such questions were forbidden, and he was indulging in a convoluted guessing game. Estella had not been able to shed her irascible spirit nor her stately upbringing, and her languishing moods and solitude had tempered her into a melancholic, absentminded waif. Her stern neck was less rigid, and she often looked to the ground where her face could be hidden from the simple eyes of the townfolk. Her eyes betrayed what her mouth did not speak, and kept that unearthly glow that bewildered onlookers.

"I understand," Estella replied. "I shall go of course. May I request a carriage? And what about lodgings?" Her disinterest was fully noted as she nonchalantly fixed her interlocutor with a bored look. The prefect nodded, sourly construing her indolence as disdain for the social gap that yawned between them. He understood from her bearing that she was no castaway daughter of a simpleton, easily recognizing her as a daughter of nobility.

"Everything has been arranged for you. You will be set up next to the prince in a neighboring room for the duration of his sojourn. And if it pleases you . . ." he paused, shooting her a meaningful look as he reached for a dark leather pouch beneath his cloak. He opened it delicately, withdrawing an elaborate crucifix encrusted with rubies and diamonds on a heavy gold chain. The prefect studied Estella closely as her eyes lit up.

"This is a gift from the mayor, who has heard of your godly work in this town at the service of the people. He has long wanted to thank you. This is a token of his pledge to honor your works. Please wear it, and think of him when you pray."

The prefect rose and strolled casually up to Estella, her piercing dark eyes suddenly more alive and mischievous, measuring his motives with a dubious frown. But her face betrayed the interest he wanted from her, and he dropped the crucifix into her grasp, using their proximity as an excuse to appraise her more closely. He was a man that hated mysteries and riddles, and he longed to unravel the secret identity she hid beneath her habit.

"Indeed, it is a thing of beauty," she murmured admiringly. "Rubies were my favorite gem before . . ." she trailed off dreamily. A haze traversed her face, and again she abandoned him to meander in places far from his ken.

"Before what, sister? Where were you before? You have the airs of a great dame with holy aspirations, surely you must be some noblewoman." The prefect's casual tone could not disguise his evident curiosity. And there was a meaningful look in his eyes as he glanced quickly at her long, slender fingers and nails, which had clearly never felt the strain of hard labor.

"Many thanks to you and the mayor, Prefect Gustave," Estella said, stitching a cold smile across her face. He was overstepping his familiarity, and she had to be wary. Relief flooded her as the bells for vespers tolled in the distance. "Tonight then," she added sweetly. Rewarding the prefect with one of her most ingratiating and charming smiles, she departed in a flurry of black robes.

Traversing the streets was always easy, for the jostling people, usually boisterous and uncouth, moved out of her way deferentially as she strode by. The citizens of the town beamed at their prodigious nurse, whose remedies and silver hands wrought wonders in the domain of healing. She smiled back meekly and bowed her head as she went along on her way to the church to join the other sisters in prayer.

Disguising her boredom by feigning weariness, she entered the damp church, already ruffling the pages of a missal she produced from her robes and pretending to give herself over to prayer. She seated herself alone at a distance from everyone and withheld her gaze. The other sisters present were a mixture of high and low born—the progeny of princes and castaway daughters that found no place in society. They were blended in with a few truly mad pious women of the poor and the nobility, as well as some that hoped to avoid the bondage of marriage and escape the ownership of their fathers.

So far she had only befriended one sister, a coy and mischievous lass from the Emerald Isle who indulged her with all the town gossip and amused her with her sly manners. Siobhan, who had escaped from her Gaelic people, was the illegitimate daughter of a wealthy noble. Her father had arranged a marriage for her which she politely declined by having an epiphany about God's purpose for her. And since refusing such a declaration would have been considered an affront to the church, and because Siobhan had used all her cunning theatrics to articulate her fervor, she managed to escape a life of thralldom to some older man. She had thrown herself headlong into the mystical teachings of the Magdalenes, and as a result was able to enjoy a relative freedom. Sister Lucas, as she was now called, glided into the church austerely. Sweeping her gaze over the benches, she spotted Estella. Marching up to her, she rolled her eyes dramatically at the loud sermon being given and sat down.

"The mayor has invited you to care for our guest I hear," she whispered behind a kerchief as she feigned a gentle cough.

"Yes, so I just learned," remarked Estella from behind her missal.

Siobhan adjusted her head covering. "This Saxon prince is a real beast you know . . ." she nudged Estella gently and shot her a playful glance.

Estella raised an eyebrow with a lopsided smile. "Oh dear me, and what do you know about that?" she grinned, darting looks around her to ensure they weren't being overheard.

Sister Lucas snorted with a mock scandalized look. "He has this curious habit of wanting the sisters to flagellate him as a means of incurring true remorse for his sins. It sends him into a frenzy of holy ecstasy they say. Well, the word is that the true reason he enjoys the whip from our hands so much is because he likes being dominated sexually. And the confessions from the town girls seem to prove as much." She nodded knowingly with a sparkle in her green eyes.

"And how would you know precisely what he enjoys?" Estella queried, pinching Siobhan's arm subtly as she stifled a yelp, giggling soundlessly. They were already attracting acrimonious looks and forceful coughs from the other sisters, but Estella plowed on heedlessly in her boredom. Siobhan grimaced at them contemptuously, propping her missal in front of her face.

"See, I measured the time between the confessions of the town girls and the timeline of his flagellations. Each instance occurs around the same night or the one following. Obviously he gets all roused up by his penance and then ravages our dear lay sisters." Siobhan shot Estella a wily look but Estella, sensing more, held her gaze till Siobhan lowered her eyes. The musty air of the church and the malodorous mold tickled at her throat and nose.

"And what exactly are you trying to tell me, really? You want me to arrange a night between you two to try him out?" she goaded Siobhan searchingly.

"Don't be so ridiculous! Well, he seems to have chosen you this year to care for his needs since he is ill, and he is likely to make you his confessor. You see, he donates large sums of money to the church and to the sisters individually, and it's now been five years since I have been undertaking the task of confessing him—until you came," Siobhan grasped Estella's hand desperately and her face, normally joyous and devoid of worry, was a mirror of restlessness. Estella felt waves of guilt and bitterness emanating from the young nun and she frowned.

"You need the money, don't you? But for what or whom?" She was irked that Siobhan was suddenly confessing her secrets to her and embroiling her in her worries. Estella desired only time enough to fashion a detailed plan for her escape and the right opportunity to leave them all behind to rot. She hated all the nuns and the Mother Superior. She hated the rituals and endless petitions to the cold heavens. She often mused that if God had to listen day and night to the endless rambling and tears of his devoted people, he would surely lose his divine mind and extinguish the earth to rid himself of their constant nagging.

"Rose, you are the only person I feel I can confide in," said Siobhan, using the name Estella had given her as her own. "I need your help. The gift that Prefect Gustave gave you today . . . that was my idea. I wanted you to have it. I have observed how you grew red rose bushes around your house near the church and how you polish the church's finery with special care for the rubies . . . I wanted you to have that gift as a token of my sincerity toward you," Siobhan said. But her tone was disingenuous and Estella saw the envy lurking in her eyes.

"It's important for you to understand that I did not come here willingly," Siobhan continued, "as undoubtedly was the case for you too, though you were grateful to us for rescuing you. You are just like me. We are both grateful for the merciful nature of this order that shelters us from the man's world and its politics. Well, you must see that Gustave and I are in love." She dropped the words dramatically, swallowing hard, little beads of sweat forming over her delicate, porcelain face. Estella had anticipated her words with thorough disinterest, and was thinking of a polite excuse to disentangle herself.

"I see. So you're saving to run away with him back to his own town, marry, and live happily ever after? I guess the gold from this Saxon prince is the least you can do for a dowry to make up for your lack of family name." Estella's words rang out coldly.

Siobhan's eyes watered and she trembled softly, her breathing suddenly shallow. Estella, meanwhile, averted the attention of the inquisitive sisters who had finished their prayers by slamming the missal shut and greeting the nuns filing by with an appropriate amount of asperity and humility. Then waiting for the last sister and lay person to leave the church, she turned to face Siobhan, lounging against the pew in an indecorous manner.

"Shame, really, I wanted to use that gold to make my own way out." Estella's tone held an underscore of disdain. At that moment, both she and Siobhan dropped their heavy masks in unison.

"You want a way out of here, well so do I," Siobhan pouted. "The prince is crossing into Britain, and you could find reasons to go with him. I can help you with that. Then you could disappear into their green pastures."

"Ah, I see. And with what wealth shall I rebuild myself there?" Estella's sarcastic tone was not lost on Siobhan.

"Oh, but he will treat you with the utmost respect and shower you with gifts fit for queens. He often requests some sisters to escort him on the travels he undertakes. Normally the wealth he endows them with goes to the church and provides for it, but you can simply disappear with it and rebuild yourself." Estella's mind began to whirl with endless possibilities, and she started cobbling together plans to dupe the prince.

"Hmmm I must think this through carefully," Estella breathed, half listening and rising to her feet. Suddenly taller and more towering than ever, Estella walked toward the church's exit with purpose in each step.

"Just remember that Gustave and I aren't the people you ought to be making enemies of here!" Siobhan bitterly called out after her, heedless to eavesdroppers.

Estella stood at the doors, taking in the details of the town with fresh eyes. And those who passed her by were startled by the incandescence of her fiery gaze, reignited once again.

15

THE AGELESS TEMPTATION

But my heart bleeds irrevocably, its wound inflicted
by the heavenly spear

No amount of weeping can quell the rapture my visions glean

For with every rupture of the bonds of my soul,
every poison bled through my tear

I bask in the radiance of your echoing presence
mirrored in the sunbeam

B ACK IN HER GARDEN WHERE SHE TENDED HER ROSES, ESTELLA paced up and down thoughtfully, her prayer beads in one hand in case someone came bursting in requiring her urgent help. The other hand was making flickering movements before her. Drawing with thought patterns only she could see, she waited patiently for the carriage to pick her up and escort her to the Saxon Prince Erik. Her powers were slightly rusty, and she exerted her mind strenuously, cursing herself for allowing herself to weaken.

With each moment, she grew more and more impatient. Various devious plans hatched in her mind for the prince's benefit, and already she could taste the tang of freedom in her mouth, along with the familiar security and boundless possibility that money brings.

Finally dusk crept soft and steady upon the day, robbing it of its colors. The sunset's last dying throes tinted the skies in vibrant hues of crimson and orange. But it brought with it an uneasy feeling. There was something brewing within the silences of the skies and the mellow town noises, something foreboding and imminent.

Shaking the feeling of unease, Estella left her cottage where the anxiety was weighing upon her like a cloud. Waiting before her gate, she scoured the cobbled streets for her carriage. After much anticipation, it emerged on the horizon. The heavy, polished carriage was drawn by proud chestnut horses with silver harnesses adorned by white plumes. The sight of the looming carriage made Estella's senses tingle, and her heartbeat quickened. She felt as though her brief respite from the world was drawing abruptly to an end, and she braced herself for some token of deceit from the darkness, finally seeking her out again. She smiled as the carriage approached. The driver averted his eyes from her, crossing himself devoutly.

"My master would be honored if you would accept this escort to the White Fort, holy sister," he said, descending from the driver's seat and whipping his hat off his head. He bowed before her while opening the carriage door. Estella felt alive and excited for the first time in months. Beaming, she placed her delicate hand on his head to his great surprise.

"May the Lord absolve you of your sins," she intoned gravely, enjoying the flow of thoughts she had shut herself away from in her sadness and caution. She opened the door into his mind, searching for secrets, and they came to her in a tidal wave. The unguarded mind of a simpleton was easy to unravel. Before she closed the door to the carriage she called after the driver, "And your wife shall conceive, there is no punishment from God upon you, be happy and full of praise."

The driver stiffened, grasped a medallion at his throat, and crossed himself. His bleary eyes, finally locking with hers, were wide with shock. "Yes, holy sister, thank you, always at your service."

He scuttled away and they took off swiftly while she made herself comfortable, easily savoring the luxury of the carriage. She looked out of the window admiring the dusk as it deepened into night, and the whispers and murmurs rose as a gentle breeze and twirled around her like scattered leaves. But basking contentedly in her reveries, she soon rebuked herself, for nature's voices soon intensified and beyond the carriage shadowy forms escorted her.

These shapeless shadows flitted between the early night's moonshine, sliding out of the Twilit world. Demons were gathering, detaching themselves from the gloom, and like fireless smoke they hovered with hollow eyes, immaterial and so frail one who saw them would doubt their own eyes. Estella waved towards them mockingly and yawned, hiding her anticipation. If she was returning back into the world, she might as well be ready for them.

"Fancy someone like you cowering in a nunnery." The tone was malicious and rang like steel with a frosted edge to it.

Estella detached her gaze from the window and looked to the seat next to her. A demon was watching her with beady, black eyes—eyes bereft of any light or hope, with chasms of darkness gaping where the chaos of the fallen angels rolled into an endless emptiness. His hair was fair, bound behind his head, and his features recalled to her a ravenous dog, hungry and coldhearted. He was unrefined and heavyset, as if wrought by the fumbling fingers of a lesser creator.

"And who are you, another minion from your bored master?" Estella asked dismissively. "Come to entertain me in this dreary town? How thoughtful of you." Her habit hung from her shoulders clashing with her haughty cheekbones and disdainful sneer. The demon, unused to such welcomes, paused, taken aback.

"Ahhh, but we have come to devour you, to consume you. We are just waiting for the right time. Our prey is better when it offers itself up to us." His crooked smile revealed sharp, unusually long, pearly white teeth, and he leaned towards her threateningly, his black eyes gleaming with a baleful fire.

"I see that I am being sent the lowest thralls of his kingdom. I must indeed be so much less entertaining for him than before. Take my advice; don't come back, unless you want me to bind you and leave you a thousand years concealed beyond anyone's reach," Estella remarked conversationally to the leering demon. She knew the rules of the game, and how it was but a matter of time before whoever sent this minion would emerge, building on the growing fear he would be instilling in her through the daily assaults of his lesser demons. But she welcomed the distraction as a sign that she was still significant and alive and somehow still part of some grand, heavenly design.

"I want to have the best piece of your god spark, you little human wretch," the demon crooned, his face contorting with lust for her destruction. They observed each other, Estella smiling fiercely. "Our time has come now, witch. You are nothing but a tool for the master," he added, and as swiftly as the demon had appeared, he vanished.

Estella shook her head, rolling on the tip of her tongue endless witticisms for his master's benefit, then nearly fell forwards as the carriage jolted to a sudden halt. Without waiting for the door to be opened for her, she quickly pushed it open and jumped down from the carriage agilely. Barely sparing a look for the smitten driver, she strode towards the steps of the White Fort Manor.

The manor was made of white stone and upheld by white marble pillars, and its stately fretted spires loomed mightily into the sky. The guards at the door were awaiting Estella's arrival, and opened the great iron doors for her, bowing as she passed. She took in the opulent sculptures of naked women as one of the maids led her through the extravagant Frankish manor. Gold leaf ceilings held magnificent, shimmering chandeliers wrought with thousands of crystals. Tapestries and paintings adorned the walls, and the gold thread of the arrases lent a warm glow to the hall, which was lit with numerous candles held in golden sconces.

Up the regal staircase they went, her garments billowing behind her, as she dreamed of the manor she had left behind. The fleur-de-lis pattern on the carpeted staircase was woven in blues and golds, and its vibrant hues and rich pattern were captivating to the eye. The maid led Estella across a corridor with high ceilings and chandeliers made from pale blue gems. The walls were Prussian blue and emblazoned with fleur-de-lis and gold leaf. The floor was of blue marble veined with gold seams, and the carpets were heavy with complicated designs depicting birds and trees upon radiant azure skies.

Finally stopping in front of a heavy oak door, the maid knocked twice, stiffly curtseyed while averting her eyes, and departed. Estella took a moment to gather her thoughts, preparing her game of manipulation to mesh the unsuspecting prince, then entered the room. Her sweeping gaze took in exquisite wooden furniture with heavy velvet cushions and a four-poster bed draped in a royal blue velvet. This weighty drapery was sewn with sapphires and precious lapis stones, spangling the drapes as stars against a somber night. The bed rested on feet hewn of blue marble and fashioned in the shape of lions with bitter claws. The dresser by the prince's bed was carved out of a single lapis lazuli stone and had winged lions flanking its feet. It was littered with numerous pots and vials of medications. The pungent odors they emitted irked Estella's sensitive nose, assaulting her olfactory senses as she approached the bed.

"Come closer to me, holy sister. I hear you are the healer of this town. Come heal my wounds, for they are no doubt a product of my inner wounds—of my sins. Please lend your ear to my supplications and elevate them to God." The prince's accent curved the words nimbly, retaining the crack of authority, but he rasped as he labored to speak.

Estella was taken aback by the eloquence of his words. Keeping her composure pleasant but demure, she swiftly went to his side and seated herself by him. Upon closer inspection, the Saxon prince was a middle-aged buffoon. Age had tempered his vigor, and though he had an abundance of golden hair and lush, heavy blond lashes, his skin was a sickly grey and his cheeks sagged, as if suddenly relieved of their plumpness through sickness. Conflicted with her initial conception of him, he rewarded her suspicions when he opened his eyes and the croaky voice was no match to his shrewd grey eyes. They were stern, but Estella could see the depravity that lurked beneath the surface.

"What ails you, my prince? I am Sister Mercy, and I have been appointed to care for you," Estella spoke guardedly, for she sensed no sickness within the man she could describe. She began to wonder whether this was an elaborate setup that she had failed to foresee. The prince merely watched her with dispassionate eyes. The grey of his eyes made her recall Mikhail's, but unlike the prince's, his were wholesome, unbent and uncorrupted.

Finally he spoke. "I returned to this town because of the treatment I have received from the Magdalenes in the past. My soul is in dire peril. There is a battle raging within me, as though I ingested poison, and it sets my blood aflame and torments my mind into crazed frenzies. Somehow I have contracted an unholy sickness, and it is consuming me. You must purge me from it, and exert penitence upon me and contrition." His voice, unused to beseeching, was harsh with an acrimonious tinge, and his words fell heavy upon her.

Estella, immune to the demands of men, scrutinized his face as she felt an insidious pull from a small chest sitting on a pillow by his head. It was a simple mahogany box, inlaid with fine carvings and a heavy, rustic iron clasp and hinges. Distracted by it, she gave it her full attention, and the overwhelming pull washed over her, renewed as if it were conscious of her gaze. It hissed malevolently, voices perforating the confines of the box as though struggling to flee.

"Have you told anyone that you have anything other than a physical illness?" Estella asked innocently, her mind subtly boring into his.

"No one knows, except my trusted manservant. He is an illegitimate bastard son to my father, and would guard my secret to the grave, as you would, too," he added, fixing her with strange, lucent eyes, the threat within his voice plain and ugly.

"Ah, I see," she remarked pleasantly. "And when do you think you came into contact with a demonic entity and how?" Her eyes, as though compelled, were drawn back to the box the prince kept by his side like a prized treasure. He followed her gaze and smiled nastily, his grey eyes taunting her.

"When fetching this treasure box meant for Cardinal Pious in Britain—that is when it started." He beckoned to her with his heavy, bejeweled hands, but Estella, narrowing her eyes with distrust, turned to the other side of the bed and leaned over to inspect the box cautiously.

"Can I open it?" she breathed. The murmurs within responded to her voice, struggling to rip the lid of the box open. It seemed to her that the box was quivering, striving for her attention.

"No!" the prince barked with affronted dignity. "That is only for the eyes of the cardinal. How uncouth of you to even ask such a question. What were you, some simpleton farm girl before taking to the cloister? I demand your attention, not the box, and shame on you for such impudence! Your reputation inflates you. The other sisters show nothing but humility and eagerness to serve me. You have brought with you a worldliness that I seek to flee!" He would have continued, but his voice broke and he began to groan like an infuriated beast, his eyes bulging in anger. With his back arched and his arms contorting, he bellowed helplessly, cursing the air while frothing at the mouth.

Estella watched with morbid fascination as he howled in a rasping feral snarl at her. Then he balanced on his hands and feet, his back arched painfully high, and his head swiveled around as he gritted his teeth. His eyes went vacant for a moment, only to be replaced with a pernicious glare as his limbs stiffened and his face mutated into another personality. Estella's brief moment of nonchalance was replaced with consternation. It dawned on her that maybe she had the bad luck of encountering a real case of possession.

"Open it, bitch, and release my brothers, you dirty Roma filth!" The voice that came forth was shrill and high-pitched, ill-equipped for using the mouth of the prince. It spluttered as it adjusted its speech.

The now supple prince contorted to the point she thought his bones would crunch, as his back arched higher and his body shuddered with the shock of possession. As he thrashed, the covers lifted and the box slid off the bed. Estella caught it instinctively.

She was transfixed by the scene before her, ill-used to such situations, and perplexed as to how to intercede in the prince's struggle. But what was abundantly obvious to her was that whatever was in the box had possessed him, and he had become a puppet for its games. Dismal laughter now erupted from the prince as she cradled the box, which felt unusually heavy for its size. At the weight of his evil stare, she found herself held frozen, supplanted from her mind. Then she unconsciously found herself fumbling for the box clasp.

A daze enveloped her, and it seemed she waded in water and through dream, and her will was replaced with a heavy presence that geared her fingers to the box. It was forcing her to yield her will, digging into her like a parasite and pushing her further into a haze of oblivion. It thrust her into a room of her mind where she could not fight back. But stubbornness was always her savior, and her mind resurged like a gush of a broken dam, drowning the intruding presence with indignation.

She slammed the box down on a neighboring marble table and, inhaling deeply, wrenched open the Twilit dimension. Eagerly, it poured into the room like sunlight on a dusty, shuttered house. Her powers, unleashed, rose within her like a tide. The prince was watching with a quiet intensity, and the evil fire writhing within his eyes taunted her from afar. As she warded herself with a mesh of sigils she drew into the air, a net of light crackled vividly around her. She braced herself, then wrenched the lid of the box open. Peering curiously within, she saw a neat pile of sapphires, roughly cut and rustic. The malevolent forces imprisoned within caused them to throb uncannily. She remembered fragments of a folktale with a grim smile.

Long ago, during the reign of King Solomon, he had thought to rid the world of the influence of the demons that afflicted it. He had then bound them all through the ring of power that Michael the archangel presented to him from God. Demons high and low were thus imprisoned and held fast in bonds they could not break—in pottery and in stone, and some he bound in jewels so he could wield them at his will. When his kingdom fell because of his transgressions, the legions of demons were freed. But some remained hidden, buried in jars beneath the ground or hidden within precious stones. These gems were the abode of some nasty little fiends. Estella understood why the cardinal would want the reinforcement these ancient demons bound in gems could give him.

She pursed her lips with distaste and looked back at the prince. "I see the prince must have stolen a few gems for himself and somehow liberated you, dirty creature. Tell me your name!"

The prince's face contorted into an evil grin, drooling pathetically. Estella snapped the box shut with repugnance and stormed up to the demon, chanting incantations in her wake. The demon screamed and howled, cursing after her in various unknown tongues. She drew the archangel Raphael's sigil on the drapes of the bed with her fingers, ignoring the insulting reprimands and protests from the prince. Drawing her strength, she grabbed the prince's head and coaxed the demon out of its abode with surprising ease, revealing a shapeless mass of black vapors with a deformed, pitiful face.

He barely struggled as she held him bound in spells, her superior might condemning him to submission. She looked around for something to trap him in, vexed that despite the ample luxury strewn about her, there wasn't one practical container where she could bind the struggling demon adequately. At that precise moment, the door behind her burst open and the prince's manservant surged in. He stopped in his tracks with a stupefied expression. The demon, sensing his imminent demise at her hands, seized the moment to surge back into the prince and wield him like a puppet. He lunged at her with a snarl, and clamping hands like talons around her throat, pulled her down, choking her. The demon, who hitherto showed little aptitude for a fight, was now burning forth maliciously through the prince's eyes, intent on asphyxiating the life out of her.

The manservant, recovering from his initial shock, rushed to pull his half brother off Estella, who was spluttering for breath as she slowly began to feel herself ebb away into oblivion. The prince, baring his teeth greedily, unclenched one hand from her throat and made for the box that had artfully landed by him. He opened it quickly with a single touch and drew out a handful of sapphires. The manservant was now pulling at his brother vehemently, shouting to no avail. The prince, with a diabolical grin, relinquished Estella's throat. As she gasped for breath, he shoved the stones into her mouth with rasping laughter, then covered her mouth with his hand.

"Swallow them, bitch! Swallow them, free them, and let them eat you out. We need another vessel to serve us!"

The manservant, sweating and despairing at breaking them up, reached out to a heavy dresser ornament and apologetically flung it as hard as he could at his half brother. There was a loud, angry howl as it bounced off his head and blood spurted from his forehead onto Estella. He relinquished her, growling, and she rolled off the bed, clutching her neck and spitting the stones out of her mouth. She was infinitely dizzy, deprived of breath, and the room swam before her eyes as she inhaled and exhaled. Nausea flooded over her and a frenzy seized her. An eruption of voices in her head laughed and scratched within her mind in unison, digging into her consciousness and wrecking its foundation.

The manservant, whose intervention had saved her life, was now cowering against the wall. The prince, leering with spite, picked up the ornament and swung it back at his half brother viciously. Through the haze in her mind Estella could hear the manservant's cries, but in the madness of the agglomerated voices in her head, she could only focus on her desire for fresh air. Fumbling with the windows, she cast them wide open. The cold air made her laugh with glee, and the cries of the poor man did little but amuse her. She peered over the balcony precariously, laughing at her own ingenuity as she decided to cast herself down.

The released demons inside her spun her around like a ragdoll, this way and that. But during a lapse in their assaults, a brief moment of lucidity pierced through, and she realized the madness of her endeavors halfway through clambering up the balcony. The anger of being so malleable to their games crept over her, and she began once more to chant while a battle of wills ensued within for the taking of her sanity. She stomped clumsily back into the chamber where the prince was wrestling with his brother, and threw herself before them into a languid dance, singing softly in a foreign tongue.

She had lost her shoes in the interim, so she danced with bare feet as she sang the songs of power. Like a shaman in a trance, she called upon forces that the old vǫlvas had placed their faith in. The demons within her writhed, blistering her mind like a heated brand. Every now and then she would moan, ceding to the pain and mingling it with her song. Soon she was lost in the ecstatic dance. Whatever force she invited into herself did not alloy well with the demonic inhabitants, and they attacked each other with fury. Estella's chanting intensified and the world responded, spinning around her till she could neither hear nor see. She was severed from the world. When she finally ended her dance, falling down upon the ground, the world caught up with her violently, and she retched.

In the shadows before her were the forms of animals and birds. A hunter with a horned head held a lance and ran barefoot, chasing the vaporous shadows, driving its spears into most of them, while the rest fled. The horned figure was now dancing by itself, drawing more lances and giving pursuit to the demons that dared to linger.

Estella rose to her feet to see the prince had ceased his assault on his half brother and was backing away from her, cursing loudly. She pointed imperiously to the horned figure and it darted across the room to the prince. Shrieking, the prince dropped to all fours and made for the door. But the horned shadow overtook him swiftly and drove his spear into the prince's back. A steam immediately belched forth as the demon left him.

The other freed demons had taken Estella's momentary distraction to flee to the open window and disappear quickly into night. But Estella was too spent to follow them. Slumped against the bedpost, she thanked the Horned Hunter, singing with effort until it dissipated. Then she gifted the prince with one last filthy look before collapsing to the floor.

"Are you alright, sister?" came a voice as heavy footsteps pounded the floor and rough hands shook her, turning her over. The half brother to the prince loomed over her, his face pallid with shock, awe etched into his features. He resembled his brother, though his hair was a darker blond bordering on brown, and his eyes were blue and clear. He trembled, withdrawing his hand quickly as though burned when he met her blazing eyes. Stricken, he stammered uncertainly, his manly voice suddenly broken and faltering like a child's. He stumbled backwards as more blood drained from his wounds, falling entangled in his velvet cloak, weeping and shaking.

Estella groaned, her head seized with an acute pain. She saw the prince watching her, mouth agape but not daring to utter a single word. He exchanged frantic glances with his brother, muttering inaudibly as he flexed his fingers, then began to wail loudly for God not to destroy him. Clambering to her feet gracelessly, Estella bypassed the half brother, who sat there stunned and shaking, and walked to a large glass mirror. Her habit had slid off her head, and her tumble of reddish brown locks fell in a mess about her shoulders. She studied her features carefully, expecting some lasting mark of her encounter with the demons. But nothing had changed, only the opalescent irises of her eyes were rimmed with black, and blood oozed down her face.

"You are free now of your predicament, Prince Erik," she said without looking at him. "I trust you have learned a precious lesson from our encounter here with a lesser but potent evil of the ancient world. And I trust this secret will remain between us, and you will be wise enough to learn from it." Still studying her face and wiping the blood from her eyes she turned to face the pair. "Get up and tend to your brother's needs," she snapped irritably, making a shooing gesture at the manservant, who still gawked at her in macabre fascination. He finally rose to his feet and crouched near Prince Erik, who had regained some semblance of his intractable composure.

"I knew the Magdalene Sisters were holy, but what you have done . . ." Prince Erik began. "You have wrestled with a demon and overcome it. You must be a pillar of moral rectitude to have such devout strength to oppose them. I thought I would die here and burn in eternal perdition, the cries of my sins scorching within me. And it would be the just reward for my impetuous vanity, thinking to steal some power—thinking I'd be able to wield these devils to my will. I repent!" Erik crossed himself and pushed his brother away, who was trying to wrap him in a robe. Rising to his feet, he snatched the robe without so much as a gesture of thanks, and donned it hastily. Smoothing away the creases, he hobbled unsteadily on his feet, grabbing Estella by the shoulders proprietarily.

"You must forgive me, dear sister. I am made of flesh and weak. But you, you are a diamond that any king would dream of possessing—both pious and comely! I must beg you to leave your order and come with us. My father, the king of Saxony, will keep you as his most prized possession. We have need of women like you, and you are being wasted, rotting away in these cloisters." His tone had regained its persuasive edge, and his unrepentant, greedy eyes dropped all pretense of restraint, finally safe in a world where he knew his power. Estella swayed on her feet, wincing at the renewed onslaught of nausea. She barely managed to shake her head in disapproval.

"There is no chance of that, my prince," she rebuked him sternly. "I am no treasure for any kingly hoard, but my own person. And though I am honored by your proposal," she added as an afterthought, "I must regretfully decline. One does not take the vow lightly. Yet I may, perhaps, escort you back into Britain," she smiled placatingly, sensing the prince was unused to outright refusals.

Erik merely returned her smile rigidly and tightened his grip on her shoulders. Estella pushed his hand away only to find his other hand clasping her by the wrist, cautioning her.

"Anyone would understand my decision. I am a knight, after all, in the service of my kingdom, and only God knows how much we need protection against evil in these darkening times." His deep, rough voice, while addressed to her, held a tone of finality to it.

"You were set up by the cardinal, you fool," Estella hissed. "The devil is within the church, and you would have delivered to him a mighty weapon for his cause." Erik relinquished his grasp on her in shock, his expression scandalized.

"Cardinal Pious is fallen, you say?" came the uneasy voice of the manservant.

"Yes, though he masquerades as the champion of God. You are better off seeking Count Mikhail, who resides in Britain, leader of the Order of the Northern Star." She cringed as she felt her cheeks flush at the mention of Mikhail's name.

Erik watched Estella with intent fascination. "I take your word for it, sister. I don't doubt that for a minute, as those very gems that I wanted to take my share from resulted in my affliction. But it is hard to conceive . . ." He crossed his arms behind his back and puffed out his chest indignantly. "It is hard to conceive of Cardinal Pious being a tool for the dark side. Yet if I must consult with Count Mikhail, whose name is not lost in our kingdom, then I will do so," he drawled. "But you must come with us," he added imperiously. "If I must force you or bribe the convent, then so be it." His voice was firm, leaving no room for Estella to maneuver in. She pondered how she could twist this inevitability in her favor. Feigning acquiescence, she smiled wanly.

"This is enough for one night, Prince Erik. I must gather my thoughts and reflect on what has transpired here. I'm sure you will understand," she said softly.

"Of course. Now you are a guest of the Saxon kingdom and anything you require shall be given to you as befitting a princess." For a man who was less than half an hour ago raving like a mad man, he seemed surprisingly unshaken.

Estella nodded quietly, excusing herself with a halfhearted curtsey. The prince and the manservant followed her with their searching gaze to the door, speaking softly in hushed tones until she closed the door behind her. But it opened as soon as she closed it, and the manservant was on her tail.

"I will escort you personally and position guards about your door to ensure nothing comes to disturb you." His timid demeanor had vanished, and he spoke proprietarily. Walking quickly in front of him, she rolled her eyes in disgust.

After escorting her stiffly to her room, he bowed deeply and barked orders for the maids to bring her dinner. Once alone in her chamber, Estella marched towards the heavy four-poster bed and collapsed onto it. Her weariness washed over her suddenly, and she yielded to it, falling headlong into a deep slumber. She was oblivious to the maids that had come, rolling a silver trolley laden with trays of delectable looking dishes. And she didn't fight back or grumble when they removed her clothing, replacing it with silken nightwear, pristine white and beaded with pearls.

The maids tucked her into bed and placed her habit with care upon an armchair. Then they set about feeding her a fish soup, generously spiced with brandy. Yearning to lay down to sleep, she managed to voice her disapproval of their methods of feeding her dinner. But these matronly old women merely clicked their tongues in sympathy and force-fed her like a goose. When they were done and she had eaten enough of the soup to please them, they rolled the trolley out of the room, and she was finally allowed to curl up and sleep.

It was noon before she finally awoke. She startled into wakefulness, her heart pounding anxiously as if someone had summoned her by name. Then she opened her eyes and looked confusedly around her surroundings. As the events of the previous night came flooding back to her, she sighed in relief, then groaned. As she scrambled out of bed and dressed, she debated whether to sneak out of the manor, pack her bags, and just disappear. But as she mused with longing over Mikhail, she decided against it. With a flutter in her belly, she quickly bathed in the tub that had been filled for her, then descended the steps and entered the large dining hall.

The sunlight filtered gently through the stained glass windows, fracturing into a myriad of colors and shapes that cast vibrant hues across the tables and walls. The white marble of the dinner hall kept the rooms cool and pleasant, and the high, vaulted ceiling was gilded in gold and woven with intricate paintings of gold leaf and moonstone mosaics. The heavy draperies depicted glorious Viking ships defeated beneath the sword of the Frankish warriors, and portraits of early kings and queens stared with satisfied smiles across the hall.

Estella felt the weight of her choices choking her, but she disguised it by pretending to admire the grand tapestries that depicted the genealogical tree of the great Frankish lines. Yet she felt a tremor in her bones and an ache in her heart that neither the regal tables flanked by ferocious griffins, nor the opulent marble, could distract her from. It was an ancient fear that she knew and was intimate with, something she had kept deep within her since her early years. It chafed at her and dogged her like a hound.

When the prince finally joined her in the hall, his pompous manners and condescending gaze sweeping over his surroundings, something within her broke. Something dormant within her screamed in outrage, awakening from the slumber of depression, and now reared its ugly head like a serpent, indignant and wild. The strength that she was robbed of when she left Britain returned in violent surges. Wrath mingled with loathing, roaring up within her—hatred for the prince and his despicable ways, disgust at the days she had spent in servitude to a simple town of bumbling fools, and rage at having to flee a home that still taunted her with memories of what she had lost.

Whispers tingled at her ears, first gentle, then beseeching, and her vision grew bright. Before the prince could even greet her, she had ripped off her nun's habit and cast it at his feet with a hysterical laugh. Then before he could issue any orders, she had flitted out of the hall. The prince's cries to stop her were drowned by the whispers in her head as they intensified and raged.

The door to the manor was held shut by guards, who watched her uneasily, unwilling to disrespect a nun and yet even more unwilling to disobey their master. Halting before the doors, she stopped abruptly. Then she seized her temples gently with her fingertips and the whispers around her turned into a single dialogue, asking to be granted entry into her mind.

"I will let you out of this place and town, just allow me to help you. You and I are old friends, and by God I am no demon." The pressing voice carried with it the ethereal feel of the lost echoes of the forests, reverberating with a broken melody of tender voices long bled by the frost of time.

"No, I must do this my way," she whispered.

The guards watched her closely as the prince was heard stomping up behind her, frothing in rage. His malevolent eyes were thunderous, and he bellowed commands and threats to his retinue. They looked on in alarm and crossed themselves in perplexed outrage.

"I said seize her! She's in the custody of the king of Saxony now, and to accompany me to Britain by my orders. Sister or no sister, my will is to be enforced, goddamn all of you!"

Estella was still standing before the barred gates, oblivious to him. She paid no heed until one of the guards, egged on by the prince, came forwards to seize her, his expression apologetic but determined.

Then the drowning whispers became more urgent. "Let me in! Will you be hauled in chains by this callous prince to be another trinket for his hoard—or worse be given over to the cardinal? I can give you back your freedom! I am sincere, with God as my witness. Will you not believe me? Now is your chance, Tsura!"

"And I'll be damned if Mikhail sees me captured, and as a nun!" Estella enunciated. "The irony of it, my pride would never recover!"

And as the guard made to grab her, she allowed the whispers entry into her mind. A cold and heavy presence swiftly filled her. It was laden with purpose and sharp intent, and it snarled through her defiantly. She saw herself retreat away from her consciousness and become an observer within her own body. It was like watching through a glass window into a scene unfolding before her, detached and disinterested, and the glass window ever so distant and withdrawn and small. Estella fell backwards into herself, passing the various halls and rooms of her mind. And like one in a dream, she glided through mists of thought and desire. Then she was gone, taking the flowing paths of dreams gleaming like a ribbon into the Twilit world.

Where she went, she could never tell, for she was lost in the remote corners of dreams and thought, in the realm of the Twilit gods. Here dwelled the angels that refused to choose sides between God and Lucifer, the inhabitants of the older world, beautiful and forlorn, and the elves of the high world, the spirits of the great choir of creation that descended onto earth. And she pined for the eerie flute the Elder Folk played, the notes falling like silver bells and limpid rain. It echoed through her, rending her heart with desire. For the music would stop each time she caught a glimpse of them, with their glittering bright eyes and shrewd smiles, as they danced around the blazing fire. The warmth of their gaze would engulf her and set her thoughts on fire, and then she would join them in the dance. The golden goblets they served her were filled with wine that tasted of honey, and when she woke, she could recall nothing but a crown and mighty horns adorned with white gems upon a golden head, and a name she knew but her lips could never form.

16

AN AUDIENCE WITH THE HIDDEN GUARDIAN

To the falcon of the skies, scion of the fire that
bathes the heavenly throne

The claws of thy raptors are the marshalled hosts of arrowed truth

They assail the slumbering minds that through
their nightmares groan

For your bannered scheming victories are forever devoid of truth

THE SUN ABATED THE FIERY LASHES IT HAD RAINED DOWN ON THE bruised earth. A gentle breeze wafted through the trees, impregnated with the scent of evening flowers and the fragrances of the earth, and a light rain fell softly upon Estella's face, the green grass beneath her dripping tenderly. Her mind began to return to her begrudgingly, like a blind man groping the walls to feel his way back to a familiar place. Estella did not move, but her freshly awoken mind swarmed with thoughts like agitated wasps, and she remembered where she had been.

Bracing herself for whatever might await her, she inhaled deeply and opened her eyes. A cloudy, overcast sky was above her, soft grey and with a clear rain that drizzled down and washed her face. She became aware of a presence near her, that immovable presence, insistent and strong.

Estella sat up swiftly and found him watching her. There was a glinting fire in his merry eyes, which were blue and deep as a summer sky. He was reclining with his legs crossed, and around him haphazardly plucked daisies with missing petals and snapped twigs were strewn— the hapless victims of his impatient boredom and nervousness. The darkness had lifted from Antariel, but the malice he had gained from his sojourn on earth remained there. Yet now it was wholesome and devoid of taint. The crafty smile upon his lips was less strained, bereft of bitterness, and there lingered within it an eagerness to speak.

"My mortal heart can only accept so many blows before it ends up crumbling. What trickery is this now?" Estella asked bewildered, unsure of whether or not the enemy before her was baiting her, toying with her under a false pretense of goodness, and hoping to ensnare her once again.

He beamed at her apologetically, tipping his head back to laugh softly. It rang like gently shaken bells, rich and full. He dusted his hands, picking off the stray plucked petals as the long curtain of his hair fell across his face.

"It would ill befit you to be anything but rude to old friends. I thought you could do with the company. You fare pretty poorly on your own, I must say," Antariel smiled, watching her blithely. His voice was deep and melodious, as though accustomed to song. It brought to mind harps and lyres and the fabric of songs wrought of aspiration and glory. Estella gawked at him nonplussed, halfway between fright and relief, then backed away from him disconcertedly.

His appearance and his two eyes watching her were whole and devoid of blemish. She gaped incredulously, blushing crimson. Rising to her feet, she approached him tentatively. He rose gracefully and smiled as Estella touched his face with amazement. Trailing her fingers over his eyelids, brow, and chin, she sought spells of trickery and deception. But within his eyes there was light, a mirrored light that reflected something far holier than the angels. It was just a pale reflection, of someone that had come close to the lofty throne where the divine countenance sat. The malice was still there, woven into the fabric of his personality and the strands of his soul, but now it was his own, and not a product of his fall.

"It is you!" cried Estella. "And you are no longer ugly. But then it isn't really the you I knew." She withdrew her hand quickly, scrutinizing him as she bit her lip in confusion. "Why are you here, Antariel? And how come your maker did not fragment you across the cosmos and sever your eternal fire to burn beneath his gaze? You were gone, I saw Lucifer murder you. And you were cruel to me. But now you have changed. Tell me everything, or I shall know to flee from you!" Her hushed voice was anxious but curious.

Antariel looked down upon her keenly, a mischievous smoldering blue fire kindled in his eyes. His dark hair, sleek and wet, clung to his shoulders and waist. He grinned innocuously, but then a shadow passed over his face. Shuddering, his face convulsed and he groaned. Estella blanched.

"Antariel, are you alright? Is there something wrong with you?" she asked, stepping backwards, wide-eyed with apprehension.

Antariel groaned angrily, his eyes taking on a reddened hue. Then he lunged at her, clawing at her with his fingers. Estella screamed, turning around and bolting as fast as she could towards the forest. But she did not get far before she tripped on a log and fell face-first into the grass. Scrambling around gulping for breath, she saw Antariel doubled over with laughter, clutching his face and pointing at her. Feeling her face turn red, she lifted herself to her feet. Dusting herself perfunctorily with injured pride, she stomping back to Antariel whose angelic eyes were weeping with laughter and began smacking him as hard as she could on the sides of the head while Antariel deflected her strikes, grinning madly.

"You should have seen your face! Priceless! Finally, after all these years of arrogance, I have never seen you so horrified in all my life." He pinched her cheek as she swatted him away. Then lifting his hands placatingly, he pulled her towards him into an awkward embrace. "I am redeemed, Tsura. I am not the fallen, wretched creature you once knew. You have no need to fear me."

"Let me go, you obnoxious, uncouth vagabond dropped out of the sky!" she spat at him insolently, trying futilely to push out of his arms.

He planted a kiss on her brow and released her. "I will tell you, then. I have passed that dark door that we all dreaded, those of us that fell in our pride and were robbed of our glory, for glory belongs to God, and he took it back from us. Broken, I was, a wounded spirit, less than the demons and bleeding into the all-consuming void. And my god spark writhed in agony within me, and it was offered up, wretched and ill–

formed, by the Angel of Death to the feet of the almighty throne." Antariel seized her hands and held them fast, his eyes arresting her as he spoke.

"I stood there, wretched and decayed, and my soul burned and was seared by the thrice holy light. It was consumed and destroyed, and I was gone from myself, stripped of myself and reduced to nothing but a divine spark that the holy breath had formed from careful thought and love. The throng of the heavenly court was loud, and the accusing angels loomed over me and presented their case before the throne; my sins and treasons and the evil spirit that I had become. Their voices were cold as the red fire that shaped them, bitter and all-consuming, devouring the gloom and charring the fingers of the evil creations. They condemned me and bound me by the laws I had violated, the decrees divine that I had scorned. And I was doomed beneath the watchful gaze of Dumah.

"But the angels of mercy took their turn and pleaded for me, their blue fire rising like a tumultuous yet glorious sea of fire and mist. Their voices, fierce yet fair-minded, nurtured my broken spark. They spoke of my torment and my regrets, my yearning to rejoin my heavenly abode, and how the prince of the world had defiled my mind and ripped my soul to bleeding shreds. The throne was silent and then Ariel spoke, he who had known me and watched over me before the choir of creation. Casting down his spear before the accusing angels, his glorious wings blocked the endless contest of voices, and he spoke to the throne softly on my behalf. At length the voices abated, and a silence reigned, deep and pristine—a sacred silence where I was alone, but alone in God.

"'So be it,' and so it was. I was extinguished, dismantled, and fragmented into a million pieces across the primordial void. But mercy was his divine countenance, and his fingers were justice, and he wrought me anew, giving me back my light and my soul. My dreams and worldly aspirations he returned to me, and he showed me the baleful chessboard where Samael challenged him.

"To return to the heavenly hosts once more was denied me till the end of days when Lucifer and Samael are hauled in for the last reckoning. But to join the chessboard and join in the divine fight against them was my choice. To travel the skies and lend succor to the angels was granted me. My voice and sight were restored and my doom lifted, and now I can traverse the lower heavens and earth till the end of days, watching the battle unfold." Antariel's voice stopped abruptly, and Estella was suddenly aware that the rain had halted and that her hands had grasped his tightly. She smiled ruefully and released one of his hands, touching the left eye that had once been defiled.

"You merited forgiveness," she said. "Now I see; you have nothing of the evil you once had. Unless this is some profound trickery that I cannot see beyond, it seems you are washed clean, and perhaps even reluctant to think of what you once were." Estella's bemused smile was mirrored in Antariel's face.

"I must have made such a tumult yesterday when I emerged like a comet across the skies. I came to find you. I know the game they seek to entrap you in, and I have learned a thing or two from the cursed mind that twisted me. I am ashamed, deeply and sincerely," Antariel spoke somberly as the memories played before him.

Estella nodded, turning her head away. She saw that they were on the outskirts of the town. Huddled together neatly before her were many bundles of cloth and packages bulging with provisions. Following her gaze, Antariel nodded.

"It took the whole day to extricate you from that mess you were in and to gather the provisions and clothing you will need. You escaped a danger with that prince, but it is not averted. The trapped demons were released, and now they will find their way to the cardinal. A great evil is coming, and you most of all will be in dire peril." Antariel's tone was unusually austere, but underscored with care.

Estella looked down bashfully and saw the brown and red outfit she was wearing; rider's high brown boots, soft suede trousers with a silken red shirt, and a black cloak with a clasp of glittering garnet. A shadow passed her face and she paused.

"Why have you chosen to return to me, of all the other creations? Your doom began with me and ended with me—surely there is another reason."

Antariel sighed, his whole body heaving. To her astonishment, he lowered his gaze meekly and bent to his knee, kneeling to kiss her foot.

She protested shrilly, backing away, but he held her fast gently, his blue eyes beseeching.

"The ugliness of my sins I cannot hide, but I promise you, I will make amends. Know that now that the distortion of my lust has been lifted, I have nothing but love for you, and that cannot be denied me. I will always protect you, wherever you go, forever."

Estella blushed and covered her mouth with her hands, turning her face away.

Antariel relinquished her and rose to his feet, dimples emerging in his face. "So let's go then, shall we?"

"What about horses?" she asked tentatively, relieved to change the subject.

"Ahhh, we have those waiting in the forest, hidden from mortal eyes behind a cloud," he said, his eyes twinkling merrily as he led the way ahead. Estella followed in his wake, her cheeks still flushed.

NIGHT HAD FALLEN, but they pressed ahead, their horses docile and accustomed to arduous travel. Antariel led the way speedily through the trees, stopping every now and then to glean the temperament of the night, searching for danger. Estella had recounted to him the events of her sojourn in the cloister, and what had transpired with the prince. Antariel had nodded, deep in thought. She learned from him that the Saxon kingdoms had long been trading with the Levant realms in sacred artifacts and mystic objects through the machinations of King Wulfric. He had hoarded them and sought to unravel their secrets out of lust for power, hoping to wield them through the land and establish himself as a holy emperor.

But inadvertently and foolishly he had been enticed by the spirits within the sealed lamps and urns, and they corrupted his spirit to the will of Lucifer. With the guidance of the cardinal, the king's mind was bent towards domination, and he forsook the path of God. He yearned to become a mighty king, revered and loved as a god on earth. Through the urging of the evil spirits, he sent for a certain box containing many bound demons. Mercenaries from the Holy Land had also received deceptive dreams from Lucifer masquerading as God, urging them to pillage certain monasteries and hidden places. They would then steal the treasures that contained bound demons. Soon a vessel bearing them would be headed towards Britain, and the Twilit world would be under dire assault. Lucifer was mustering armies of the legions of hell and converging upon London. Between the puppet king and the cardinal, Estella was lost as to what Lucifer truly intended—and what role Samael played in the game.

Estella's own escape had been meticulously planned by Antariel, who had left the heavens the day previously. He had seen the trap that was being laid for her. The prince was aware of the spirit within him, and had invited it in thinking it would give him great power. When he realized it would not, he had sought to rid himself of it. When Estella had cast it out, the prince saw that this was the woman the cardinal had been searching for, and he had intended on handing her over to him.

Antariel, upon taking over Estella's mind, had revealed the demons festering within each person in the manor. They had screamed and assailed him, trying to overtake Estella and attach themselves to her soul. It had descended into a contest between Antariel and them, for they hated him and cursed him. But eventually they had fled, discerning the holy fire within him. Then Antariel, controlling Estella's body, had slipped out and stolen a maid's outfit and sold the golden cross to buy provisions. Meanwhile the prince, crazed and furious that he had been thwarted, had sent search parties for her. The demons he had unleashed previously raged within the town seeking her.

"What plans do you have when we reach Britain?" Estella queried. "I am a persona non grata there, and always had few friends. I think I might as well pay a visit to Rosalind Constance, who adopted Dolly. She was my greatest ally in the dark times, and she would never sell to anyone. I cannot return to the manor without putting myself in danger," she sighed moodily.

Antariel nodded. "You should consider your future moves carefully. Cardinal Pious is lusting to cut out those eyes of yours that see the heavens and the chessboard through the sight of God. It is about survival now, yours or his own. There will be no messiah in this age, and you are the bride of the ages, chosen by the Sophia to usher in a renewal. And somehow, though I cannot see how, you will end up being the guide to a new messiah, bane of Samael." Antariel's face was devoid of the lust and desire that had once marred it in his fallen state. Now his wholesome, noble appearance watched her with an expression of mingled pity and understanding.

"You do not comprehend the gift you were blessed with," he said. "Within this dreadful game you are no slave to the world, but stand there with the choice of rendering succor to the divine hosts and the holy orders of men. You are like a lonely light in a sea of still darkness, where the only illuminations are dull and dim."

Estella narrowed her eyes, drawing in her horse close to Antariel. "Fancy hearing such wisdom from you," she said. "Only in these very woods were you my enemy. I see you and Mikhail would have a delightful time together, he shares similar views to you, but expresses them in less eloquent words."

A flickering pang of guilt and anger crossed over Antariel's face briefly as he scowled in disdain, admonishing her by deploying his wings and startling her horse into a gallop.

"I have nothing in common with the petty musings of mankind, Estella. You should know that by now." His own horse caught up with hers, and she saw his proud back and neck stiffen.

"Why did you come after me knowing all of this, Antariel?" questioned Estella. "Surely you aren't eager to face Lucifer again after the last time."

Her voice stung, and Antariel abruptly pulled back his horse's reins and turned to face her. The beauty in his face dripped away to reveal a cold harshness and naked resentment, his eyes incandescent with a deadly fire.

"I came back to have a purpose within creation alongside my betters. And I came to you to take back what was taken from me—my dignity. I was humiliated and reduced to a petty demon. I wish to thwart Lucifer as he thwarted me. Then I'll depart for places you will never see, even after death." In silence he rode behind her, his presence rebuking her wordlessly.

Soon Estella found herself growing weary, but each time she made to stop, she felt his presence urging her forwards silently. Finally, balanced on her horse precariously, she nodded off to sleep. She woke every now and then slipping from her horse or when a branch smacked her in the face.

Endless hours they rode in this manner while the forest yielded no clearing or glade, and the trees stood tall and stately like a sea of masts. Moths and other nocturnal insects flitted by them, and the forest was awake with a strange watchfulness. In the moments she dozed off, she felt it clearly, as if the trees had eyes and observed her. When she stirred it would diminish, lingering in the background, and it disconcerted her.

"We aren't alone here, Antariel. Are we to expect trouble tonight?" she inquired, half expecting him not to respond.

"Yes and no. Yes, we aren't alone, but no, there is no trouble here. You must sense her, the Lady of the Crossroads, guardian of the forest and of the people that revere her—someone who truly knows you," he said, his voice light again as he spoke.

"I see. Well then I might press hard till dawn. I do not fancy any guests," she said, urging her horse forward, much to Antariel's amusement.

"Run towards her hurriedly—that she would appreciate indeed," he smirked, but his mockery was lost on Estella as the disquiet chafed at her fraying nerves.

The night had unfurled its mighty robes across the skies, and the moon shone amid a cluster of flowering stars. Their piercing flames washed pallid lights across the forest. The summer triangle constellation and the plough shone radiantly in the pristine velvet firmament. Watching them, Estella felt peace and yet a tender sadness. Antariel was right, after all, for the further they sped into the night, the more closely the presence followed her. At length she realized she was heading straight for it while it waited for her patiently.

It felt ancient, laden with cares and concerns and ever watchful, mindful of everything from the countless lives of mortals to the acorns dreaming of becoming a tree. They rode towards it full-on. As they neared that patient watchfulness, the dawn was emerging in the east, gentle and feeble at first, and the birds awoke and proclaimed the new day. Gradually the night ceded to the dawn, withdrawing like a lofty queen carrying a myriad of stars in her train. Then alone the moon endured within the lightening sky as the first shafts of the chariot of the sun marched across the skies and chased away the shadows. Morning broke and life awoke.

Estella found herself entering a clearing. The green grass stretched far into the distance, bedecked with lilies and harebells. Already the bees were about their business, buzzing from flower to flower seeking nectar. The dawn lit the glade with a pure light. Then Estella saw her, taking in the morning light.

She was seated upon a broken log beneath the shadow of an old elm. Wizened and with pale skin stretched taut, she clasped a tall, shapely, bone-colored staff in her hand. She was draped in black with a heavy hood hiding her face, which was lifted towards the sun, and she beckoned Estella with her free hand. Estella dismounted slowly and gave her reins to Antariel, who encouraged her with a wink. Then she approached the old woman while Antariel lingered behind.

The old woman looked up as Estella approached. Estella was struck by her brilliant, pearly white smile, which overshadowed all her other features. She appraised Estella in a motherly way, and her inky black eyes were undimmed with age but keen and hard as nails. Estella could tell she would have been exceedingly beautiful in her youth, for the perfect rondure of her cheeks and the sharpness of her jaw were still apparent, as well as the smoothness of the skin around her deep-set eyes, which were twin pools of twinkling blackness. Estella found herself leaning forwards to greet the extended hand that the old woman held out for her. She was leaning on her bleached bone staff expectantly, and firmly holding onto Estella's hand.

"Good morning, child of mine," the old woman's face beamed with genuine affection. "I have waited to see you for so long, and have been so eager! Please sit down and keep an old woman company, won't you?" She led Estella by the hand to sit beside her. "I am so proud of you, my child. You have grown so much older now, and I can see worry has taken a big toll on you already." The old woman's eyes flickered with an innate flame as she perused Estella's thoughts at leisure.

Estella returned her smile tentatively. "Thank you, good mother. I did not know you were waiting for me or I would have sped here faster. I feel like I ought to know you, and yet feel ashamed to ask. Why are you here waiting for me? For you seem to know me so well. Forgive me if I sound impetuous." Estella quieted her frenetic thoughts as they burst into a million patterns of reasoning, screaming loudly at the back of her mind. The old woman cracked a smile even wider than the last, her stygian eyes chiding Estella knowingly.

"Of course you have never met me," she said, "but then you do not need to in order to take a guess. You are much more cunning than that, famous Dancer in the Dark!" Her grip tightened gently and Estella's smile slid off her face. "I am your thoughts incarnate—how you picture the Crone. Once I was a Mother, and before that the Maiden. I am the trinity, I am Astarte and Athena; I am valiant, proud, and fierce, defender of women. I am the goddess of the crossroads, dreadful to reckon with yet merciful. I am the mother of the gods, and the bringer of plenty and prosperity. I am the Crone, Sheela na gig, and I bring you all back to the earth, my womb, to be immured. I am the full cycle and completion of life, and the soul of every land."

She spoke lightly, with the nonchalance of someone certain of their inexorable place in the world. Her black eyes were placid and deep, and within them one could lose themselves and their reason, delving ever deeper into the secrets she harbored within her. Estella was silent in awe. She slid off the log, kneeling before the Crone, and kissed her hand reverently.

"I am honored to merit meeting you, oh holy Crone, mother of us all. I hope I have done no evil to warrant you seeking me out, and if so please forgive the errors of youth." In the protective presence of the Crone, Estella felt calm and safe, as she had never felt in her life. And she wept softly as the ache and yearning she had for a mother welled with her. The Crone hushed her weeping, stooping to wipe her tears, her eyes tender.

"You do not have to fear my displeasure, little one, for you are alone in a sea of sharks, each waiting to glut their fill. But you are feral as a wild feline and have a spirit wrought of the finest fires. Do not fear death, for I shall come for you myself, and never shall I abandon you to the claws of Lucifer. No fallen son of the heavens shall come near my daughter in death. But ensure you do not fall and cede to him and his temptations, for therein lies your eternal perdition." Her warning came sharp, and Estella hearkened earnestly.

"Do not fear being alone, for I am with you, and so are the countless legions of forest spirits, the immortal beings that were once wardens of these lands. And if it proves too dire for you, then flee to them, and I shall take you, and you will never again return to this cruel game between heaven and hell." The Crone radiated the finality of death that quenches all life, inextricably bringing every creation to their unmaking.

"I am so alone," Estella burst out, "and never felt as if the world felt what I felt, knew what I knew, and endured what I do. There is nothing in this world that gives me solace, nor joy. I feel trapped between two dismal forces, each vying for my soul to break and wield against each other."

"Hidden hands are behind each pawn on this earth, and each make their move," the Crone spoke. "The Sophia vowed to rescue creation when she fell to earth, and so shall I. Within you is a spark of the Sophia, and you are my child. If life proves too hard for you and the darkness seeks to rob you of your light, then flee to me, and when the ages fade into a better world, you shall be reborn to finish your purpose. But only do so if you truly wish to resign from this fateful game."

The Crone looked past Estella into the distance and smiled. "You have got yourself a smitten angel from the gates of heaven, I see. He will not greet me, for he knows me and fears me. But let me tell you something; you are no mortal, and though you are clothed in the clay and flesh we molded for you, it is merely your vessel for this life. Antariel hopes beyond hope to find you after, for he knows where your soul shall err." She nodded gravely, then returned her gaze to Estella, rising to her feet and leaning on her white staff.

The Crone extended a hand to Estella who nimbly leapt to her feet. Laying a hand on her head in benediction, she said, "Go now. May the paths before you be filled with hope in a darkness where nothing can be seen. I am there always, and even Lucifer knows me. Do not be afraid, and do not fear death; it is merely a doorway into another world. Go, and may the Sophia be always with you. I watch over the fates of mankind and weave with my fingers their untimely ends and destinies. I am the ultimate face of the Norns. I am the fragmented mirror that fell from heaven and broke into a million pieces, each piece becoming an incarnation of myself."

Estella bowed her head thankfully with renewed strength. Distracted by the sudden neighing of her horse, she turned around for a second, but when she turned back the Crone had vanished—so quickly that Estella could have sworn their whole interaction had been a figment of her imagination. Sighing with annoyance, but with lifted spirits, she ran towards Antariel. He was sprawled near the horses meticulously examining a flower, his long fingers prodding the soft petals.

"She sends her greetings," Estella lied as Antariel turned around with a raised brow.

"I see your beguiling nature has returned, as well as your deceiving ways. Good, now we can depart swiftly." He mounted his horse, watching Estella with an unconcealed frown.

"How are we to cross over into Britain?" she asked.

"The same way we originally came—by boat. The Crone is the most benevolent of all," he added with a grave expression, "but do not let yourself be guided too much by her words, for she is the guardian of death. And she will not lift a finger to hurt her children, not even Lucifer."

Estella shivered, looking back and frowning pensively. "I understood that much," she whispered darkly.

THE PASSAGE INTO Britain was tedious, and Estella spent much of that time asleep in her room. She had paid a decent sum to obtain a small, clean cabin room furnished with tawdry curtains and a rickety bed, but the food at least was decent compared to her usual frugal fare at the nunnery. Antariel, now a welcome distraction, kept her company, and would often discuss with her the various mysteries of the world. Her dreams were visited often by the Crone, who lent her wisdom and strength and rekindled within her the fiery spirit that had once challenged kings and danced with shadows.

At length they arrived on the shores of England. When she descended into the harbor, she felt a wave of affection towards the green island, and she yearned for her manor and the children she had once cared for.

"They have all gone for their own safety," Antariel reminded her, reading her thoughts. "Do not linger on them. And you cannot possibly regain your house now, let it go. I'll go myself and rescue some of your wealth that's hidden in the vaults," Antariel added, eyeing Estella with growing concern. Her gaze had dulled and her brief joy was visibly diminishing.

17

MORTAL WOUNDS

For the ghost of the woods that stares into your bower

Was once the light of your life, the pinnacle of your tower

For the earth that's turned by worms that repulse your hand

Shall be your gods as they deconstruct your flesh to sand

THE MORNING BROUGHT ANOTHER DULL, GREY DAY. MIKHAIL WAS awake, and although he had not slept the previous night, he wasn't weary. He was staying as a guest at the queen's summer abode in London. All night he had paced up and down, lost in rambling thoughts, and he could sense that the queen was also awake and uneasy.

An irregular storm had raged the previous night, and many people had died in it, having bled to death for unknown reasons. Naturally he suspected maleficent powers, newly emerged to join the cardinal's ranks. A pestilence had descended overnight on London, and throughout the raging gale the vicious cries of demons tormented the skies and stirred the storms. They were an ancient plague, newly arrived and recently freed. He had rushed to his study and soon discovered that their names had not been uttered, nor had they been summoned, since the days of the Temple of Jerusalem.

Something evil was afoot, greater than he had imagined. The demons had then congregated in the air and heaped their curses upon the order, singling Mikhail out and pouring their malice upon him. Then they had vanished with the dawn. Something ominous had ushered them away, and they had fled eastwards towards the cardinal's cathedral.

Mikhail threw the windows open wide and allowed the sun to filter in as he inhaled deeply. His sculpted features were sharp against the mellow rays of the sun. Silently he extended his mind beyond the town to sense the extent of the pestilence. Then suddenly he coughed, and as he held his hand to his mouth, he was startled to find little droplets of fresh blood. Baffled, he frowned grimly, lifting his eyes to the sky. Then he turned his dark thoughts back to the cardinal.

ESTELLA FIDGETED IMPATIENTLY as she sat in a carriage under a spell of concealment Antariel had cast. He was guiding the carriage carefully through streets where the cardinal's inquisition still raged. Soldiers roamed the streets persecuting and questioning anyone they suspected of being Twilit, and arresting many arbitrarily. The weight of the crusade against the people had taken a cruel toll, not only on the Twilit people, but on those that enforced the papal decrees. Even the most hardened hearts broke as they were forced to murder women and children.

Estella's thoughts were dark and dreary as they entered London, and she felt the weight of anguish and despair that pressed against her soul. The town she knew that had nurtured her youth felt so alien to her. She fumbled to remember the usual scenery, but even the things that were familiar had acquired a noxious feel. In her brief sojourn away, it was as if London had remodeled itself.

Estella felt the impending danger all around her as the carriage gently jostled down the moist, cobbled streets. Peering through the window, she saw impassive faces mutedly going about their business, dismal worry etched onto their brows. Though it had been painted as delivering the citizens from a lurking enemy within that worshipped foreign forces, eventually even the most foolish realized that the population cleansing was the fruit of a terrible political vendetta. Estella's carriage was stopped many times, and she was questioned in monotonous tones by half-hearted guards who barely looked at her face.

At last the carriage halted, and she recognized a tall building with stately, fretted spires. Nodding to Antariel who smiled encouragingly, she pushed the carriage door open. But all she met with were the sour faces of the guards, automatically barring her entry, and she felt her spirits sink. Lady Constance had never required guards before. Estella realized with remorse that while she had fled persecution, the friends she left behind had taken the full brunt of it.

"Lady Constance is not expecting any guests," a guard said, addressing Estella, "and does not want to be disturbed. Please make an appointment."

"Please send word to her now," Estella replied politely, pulling herself up to her full height. She was dressed like a common wayfarer, though particularly clean and well cared for, but nonetheless no one of consequence. The guards exchanged meaningful smirks.

"I have no use for such fools as yourselves. Learn to respect your betters," Estella added, dourly pushing by them. Their nonchalance instantly vanished as they thuggishly made to grab her. She quickly jabbed a guard's arm with spiteful force and he yelped backwards in surprise. Her malevolent, deep red eyes instantly set fear into them.

"Demon!" they howled at her, unsheathing their weapons but afraid to approach.

She laughed haughtily and gifted them with one last venomous smile before pushing open the doors and entering the house. Antariel was suddenly at her side, gracefully gliding along next to her. Entering the normally warm and blithe hall, she was appalled by the scene before her. The draperies, normally vibrant, royal hues of blue and green embroidered with silver and woven gems, were gone, replaced with plain black drapes. The crystal chandeliers were veiled and shrouded with black coverings, and the great hall's paintings were enveloped by black shrouds. Estella walked apprehensively forward as the guards followed after her, calling for reinforcements. But Estella dodged past them through the halls she had known since childhood.

"She's in mourning it seems," she whispered hesitantly to Antariel.

Antariel's eyes were jet black as understanding flooded over him and the memories of the hall screamed their agony to him. Apologetically placing one hand on Estella's shoulder, he held her gaze.

"I am sorry for your loss, Estella," he whispered.

She gritted her teeth, flicking his hand away, and made for the stairs where the maids had gathered, watching her fearfully. "Constance," she screamed, but she received no reply. Then bolting up the stairs as rapidly as she could, she pushed the maids roughly out of her way.

The commotion in the house had shaken all the staff, for they had dropped their posts and duties and gathered to watch her. Some recognized her, and signaled to the guards to retreat, while others crossed themselves beneath the baleful gaze of Estella's feral eyes.

"Where is Constance, you fools? Go fetch her now, I demand to know where she is!" But she was met only with sympathetic looks.

An older maid that Estella knew wept in a corner, unable to form words, turning her face away from her. Estella knelt beside her and shook her. She was a plump, middle-aged lady with russet hair and a freckled face, who had always used to tempt her with succulent cakes and pastries.

"Answer me, Maggie, what has happened here?" Estella pleaded.

"Please don't ask me, for pity's sake," Maggie wept loudly, the only sound in the echoing silence and watchfulness of the gathered crowd.

As Estella turned to face them, she saw within their gaze a lust for blood and vengeance, and a desire to be vindicated. And in the clench of their fists and the arch of their backs she read despair and wrath. Antariel was behind them all, his gait slow and his averted gaze watching her beneath his long lashes as he leaned against the wall.

"Have you all lost your voices, men and women of the house of Rosalind Constance?" she spat at them, beginning to weep with the weight of the suspense.

"I will tell you what has taken them, Estella," came an icy, sickly sweet tone.

Spinning around in the direction of Constance's voice, Estella was met with a bedraggled drunk woman dressed in black silks. Her chestnut brown hair was covered with a thick, black veil, and she had obviously just clambered out of bed, or wherever she had been imbibing her liquor. Her normally soft, doe brown eyes were hollow and haggard and reddened with tears. As she smiled emptily, her unfocused gaze oscillated between Estella and the house staff crowded below. Constance swayed unsteadily as she walked, a cruel smile frozen upon her drunken lips.

As Estella ran towards her, Constance fell into her arms, clutching a bottle and laughing. She trailed her fingers through Estella's loose hair, focusing her eyes with effort. The stench of stale liquor was upon her breath, and Estella steadied her, holding her face levelly.

"It has become very expensive to be your friend of late, Estella. Everyone you touch is doomed!" Constance's eyes widened dramatically, then regained their former torpor.

Then extricating herself from Estella's embrace, she began twirling in circles, laughing maniacally as her robes billowed behind her. She cackled madly as she spun in a chaotic dance, her eyes fixed on the ceiling, wine splattering the floor and her dress. She stopped just as suddenly, turning to face Estella, gesticulating and sloshing the bottle at her.

"They took Dolly from me two days ago," she choked out, her eyes glazing over. "Hmm yes, they did . . . she was recognized somehow. Don't ask me how, I was so careful always . . . well . . ." she paused, taking a swig from her bottle. "They took her from me in the streets. I pleaded as I have never pleaded before to any man, and begged and bribed to no avail." Constance took another swig from her bottle, smiling again vacantly.

"What have they done to Dolly, Constance?" Estella asked in clipped tones, staring at the floor between them with fraying patience. She closed her eyes, anticipating the worst. Constance merely shrugged, idly inspecting the bottle.

"Oh nothing, they just hanged her, the tiny little thing, still clutching her doll . . . and I could not save her. I wanted to die with her, you see, but they didn't allow it, and she had held onto me so fiercely before they ripped her hands away. I watched her being hauled to the gallows, her screams and tears rending my soul and wrenching my very spirit from its abode . . . . See they hanged her, Estella, and I cannot forget her face seeking me out in the crowd, locking with mine. A little child hoping I could save her and calling out your name. And till the very last moment when the noose was tied around her neck she still held her doll and hoped for salvation. Then she was hung and I thought I would die, too. Even her body was denied to me for burial. They said they would toss her to the dogs."

Constance watched Estella disinterestedly, her speech lending her the appearance of lucidity, but her mind irrevocably vacant. Estella nodded, sinking to the floor and leaning against a wall with a blank expression as she strove to cover the tremor in her breathing. Constance watched emotionlessly as Estella began to scream a high-pitched wail of wrath. Then cradling her head in her arms, she began to sob inconsolably. Antariel reappeared at her side in a flash, but did not dare to touch her.

"I promise you, Cardinal," came Estella's anguished voice, "I will cut out your heart while you are alive and eat it. That is my vow to you." Her voice bore no idle menace.

"Eat his heart out, Estella," Constance hissed fiercely, "and send me his carcass to crucify once you are done. Then we can poison the king. I want to make wine of his blood. And of his carcass—a feast for the crows!"

"I promise you I will go after him, Constance, even if it proves to be my undoing."

"Your undoing?" replied Constance. "You only think of yourself. You fled, leaving everyone to pick up the broken pieces you cast behind you. There have been many Dollys killed because of you. How dare you stroll back into my life! Why didn't you confront him before if you could, you coward?" The venom in her voice was matched by the look of revulsion on her face.

Estella froze, rocking herself back and forth and weeping. Then Constance's face crumpled, and she threw herself beside Estella, placing her head in her lap. They wept together, holding hands, decorum and shame cast away.

ESTELLA RUBBED HER eyes vigorously, expelling the drowsiness that had settled on her. She was lounging in a sumptuous guest room, the exquisite dressers already littered with bottles of wine. Antariel had gone to her manor to fetch her clothing and jewels from the hidden vaults. She was left alone in the dimly lit room with the curtains drawn. She welcomed the gloom and savored it darkly.

Her heart brooded, weaving strands of dark thought as she lay on her back holding a glass of wine. Basking in her wrath, she yearned to hack the flesh away and devour it. She already knew what she wanted, and it did not matter to her that Lucifer possessed the cardinal. All she wanted was his death, at any cost, and his heart hot and throbbing in her hands to gnaw and devour. Decades of violence and oppression had bred within her people a ravenous inclination—the desire to hurt and maim. This relic of her heritage in the inhospitable regions of the world fueled her feral savagery, and she drew the poison from those ancestral wounds, and it fed her wrath.

Antariel soon returned. He had spirited to her numerous chests, heavily laden with her finery and gold. As he sat down beside her, watching her, Estella pushed the wine and a fresh platter of food toward him.

"Eat and drink," she said. "I don't know if I will emerge from my trip unscathed, so relish the moments you have with me. I think I understand the old Crone now. I shall not fear death. I shall eat his heart out, though I pay and perish." Estella spoke softly, and her hands sought out Antariel's. He grasped them readily, watching her with dark eyes.

"I will not let you perish and I will aid you in your vengeance, but this is not what I intended for you when I brought you here. Be cautious and be reasonable. Do not bring further ill upon this town. You will be seized and tortured yourself! There is only so much I can do among a horde of devils, and I need to know you can escape." He lifted her hands to his lips and kissed them as she cradled his cheek, smiling ruefully.

"Do not be concerned by the cardinal, my old friend. I am more afraid of the greater danger I am offering my spirit to."

Antariel stiffened and ripped his hand out of her grip. "Do not sell yourself, Estella," he rebuked her. "Have you learned nothing from your woes and mistakes, even with me?" Estella leaned towards Antariel playfully.

"Tell me, O angel," she whispered into his ear, "how dire can it be to wrest open the gates of Hades and invite the fettered demons into your soul to exact vengeance? Do you think their fire burns greater than mine?"

"You have great fire. I saw it exit the heavens before my eyes. But I have in mind a being greater than you know." Antariel lifted his head and met Estella's gaze. "I made friends with a devil of another sort during my first time erring into the confines of this world. Deadly and vile, yet cunning and shrewd beyond the reckoning even of the gods. He was always hungry for more. Maybe you know him already?" and he whispered a name into her ear as she purred like a contented cat.

ESTELLA SLEPT SOUNDLY that night, Antariel watching over her with a sore heart. He knew her as she had never known herself, known her when she was thought immaterial in the endless, heavenly seas where creation took flight and wrought secrets and wonders beyond the knowledge of men. For such was Antariel's nature. His voice gave substance and embodiment, and he shaped and clothed the divine thoughts and set them free to expand into the void.

What he dreamt he wrought into song. Then he discovered within his dreams his loneliness, and then he was truly alone and the dreams gave no more comfort. He and Estella traveled down pathways of her own creation, hand in hand, and she offered him the Twilit world robed in the glory of the olden gods. But Antariel did not love the world she loved so dearly, this world that hung between light and dark, suspended within the void through the thoughts of the gods of old, the elder guardians of a world long changed. Then morning came after a laborious voyage to conquer the night, and the gloom was lifted, but not from their hearts.

"Mikhail will know of your arrival," Antariel said to Estella. "How do you intend to counteract his efforts and yet consolidate your endeavors, supposing he decides to trust you again? Surely you know his take on things." Antariel watched his reflection intently in the glass mirror suspended over a magnificent marble table. His long hair was loose and fell to his shoulders in graceful waves while his eyes, scrupulously devoid of guile, waited for her reaction.

Estella was bent over her numerous chests, engaged in the process of choosing her outfit and jewels for the day. Her arms laden with jewels and expensive fabrics, she threw them all into a heap upon the bed and sighed.

"Either he maintains his distance and collaborates with me without deceit, or you are going to instill in him the fear of God. I know he loves me deep down, and that makes a man quite malleable, as you surely realize."

Antariel froze, stricken with silent anger, avidly observing her as he searched for clues to her emotions.

"You may want to excuse yourself, holy angel," she added mockingly.

Antariel raised a brow and shook his head slowly, but the mischievous glint in his eyes remained.

"Of course, Estella, I wouldn't want to remind you of my darker days." He gracefully swung around and made for the door. "I will check on Constance, I heard her wailing throughout the night and felt her dismal dreams." He opened the door and passed through it, casting one last glance at Estella. She felt his gaze and met his eyes, smiling craftily.

"Maybe I could have made better use of you in your previous state. You were more amenable to my mischiefs then," she said, turning her head away.

Antariel closed the door as he departed, whispering inaudibly, "You have no idea."

Down the stairs he descended, past the heavy black drapes. An unnatural hush prevailed throughout the manor, and the dining hall was empty, except for Lady Constance. She waited at the table with eyes downcast, staring fixedly at the table. Her chestnut brown hair was pinned up and braided, and her black silken dress was heavily laden with numerous strands of pearls while tear-shaped pearls hung gracefully from her ears. She did not lift her eyes from the table as Antariel sat next to her. He watched her silently with compassion. Abruptly he leaned forward and breathed into her face. Constance did not move, nor was she startled. She took a deep breath and lifted her head, her large brown eyes suddenly focused and peaceful.

"Oh, please forgive me, I must have been dozing off. God knows I haven't been sleeping properly these last few nights. I wonder why, perhaps it's punishment for all the years as a child that I wouldn't go to bed early," she giggled, then blushed looking puzzled. "Forgive me, but I don't remember your name." She smiled kindly and dimples appeared in her cheeks. The heaviness that had added lines of worry to her face had vanished. Now her complexion was rosy and healthy.

Antariel beamed at her. "I apologize for not presenting myself earlier. I am Gabriel, Estella's traveling companion. I escorted her to your manor." His arresting eyes did not leave hers, and she sat there mesmerized and dreamy with a beatific smile. Then she looked down at her clothing and gasped.

"Oh my dear Lord, what have I chosen to wear? It is almost as if I were going to a funeral. Am I losing my mind at my age? I am barely twenty summers and five. I must change before Estella sees me and mocks me mercilessly." She got up quickly, still flashing her most charming smile as her eyes took Antariel in. "You remind me of someone I once knew, but I can't quite put my finger on it . . ." she added, frowning gently and pursing her lips. Then she shrugged, taking her leave of Antariel, and headed to her chambers to change.

A maid entered with a bemused look on her worn face, ushering in fragrant platters of breakfast foods, from cured meats to cheeses and duck pâtés. Antariel hummed softly to himself, striding up and down the hall. Then his voice grew louder and clearer. The maids stood transfixed in awe, and it seemed as if a spell held them enthralled as he sang. His melodious voice brought tears to their eyes, and the butlers and guards all hearkened and dreamt with open eyes. Antariel sang until the gloom that had weighed on the manor like a cloud of woe had finally dissipated.

Sunshine burst through the dull, choked skies, and shafts of light, like warriors' spears, sliced through the gloom. They crowned Antariel's head like a radiant halo and brightened the hall. The maids left their errands dreamily and began to take down the ubiquitous black cloths from around the manor. They went about with shining eyes as dancers at a ball, while Antariel's song rose like a valiant wave. It reached heights of wonder that shattered the veil of despair, and rent the hearts of those that listened with the boundless beauty of sacred things. Hopes were no longer distant islands in time where one sought refuge from the weary world, but a promise unforgotten and awaiting an auspicious time to yield its harvest. Antariel's voice seeped through the cracks of their minds and cleaved past the layers of disappointment and grief. When he finally stopped, the last vestiges of mourning in the manor were gone.

"You have cast your light on this place, little prodigious prince."

Antariel did not need to turn his head to feel her amusement and fascination, but he did anyway. Estella stood before him, beautiful and proud as ever, a river of rubies as a diadem upon her ruddy brown hair. A large tourmaline burned fiercely like a blazing furnace at her neck, and her almond eyes were smudged with kohl. She emanated the scent of crushed roses, musk, and amber. Her eyes were dancing twin flames of deep garnet, and she smiled guilelessly, unaware of the settling spells woven in the air. She wore flowing black and crimson satins spangled with blazing white gems, and her girdle was gold, wrought in the shape of a serpent clutching its own tail, the eyes alive with the fire of sparkling diamonds.

"Finally awake and in your full splendor, I see," Antariel remarked politely, observing her from beneath his thick lashes. Estella glided towards him and seized his arm.

"You could sing my mind into the farthest confines of the world, and yet you don't. Why not? You have that power over me," she remarked quietly, searching his face for answers. "And where is Constance?" she added worriedly, turning around to inspect the renewed hall.

At that moment Constance's hasty footsteps resounded in the hall and she descended the stairs with a spring in her step. Standing at the entrance of the dining hall, she smiled at Estella, clad in a royal blue dress sewn with sapphires and her loose hair flowing.

"Estella, I've really been feeling the need for a change lately," she said. "I never had the chance to take up my desire to visit Éire, the Emerald Isle. My mother's people lived there for generations before the pope uprooted them to this inhospitable country. I've been thinking about taking a sojourn there . . . and maybe you could look after the manor for me while I'm gone?"

Estella glowed at Antariel with understanding and slid her arm around Constance.

"I must get ready, for it's a long way to go," Constance continued. "Better to go sooner than later. And I must instruct the maids and housekeepers."

Estella frowned to herself as Constance bolted off towards the maids' quarters. "You do realize people will think she's lost her mind, don't you?"

"I've definitely considered it. But trust me, I will ensure that she reaches her destination safely, and with no memory of these dreadful events." Antariel bowed his head. Then he lifted it, as if to listen to some strained, distant sound. Rolling his eyes, he fixed her with a sarcastic look. "Your great charmer has arrived. It would be better for me to leave you to it. But of course I am never far away if you need me."

Estella raised her chin haughtily as she read the meaning in his look and nodded.

"Good, go for now," she replied sternly, but Antariel grasped her arm and before Estella could avert it, he had breathed into her face.

18

CROSS PURPOSES

It was as pouring sand into a precipice, an awning tear
Of jagged rocks to the questioning skies laid bare
It was as if you held a sieve to the sea and sought its might to drain
Somewhere with your quivering hands that fear the strain

MIKHAIL WALKED THE EMPTY STREETS, HIS SILVER CANE PUNCTUATING each step with a heavy clank. His cloak was a dark grey, and beneath it he wore a reinforced black leather jerkin with black suede trousers tucked into high leather riding boots. The many rings he wore glinted dully in the morning light, and the clouds above seemed as if torn to shreds. Within them he could descry demons floating overhead, feeding off the auras of the hapless people below. His pace was hurried, and he kept his face hidden from the few passersby.

Seeking Estella with his mind, he was relieved to find her in the same location. He quickened his pace and the furrows on his brow deepened as he mulled through his thoughts darkly, considering how he would confront her. The love he bore for her hurt within his chest, and though he yearned to hold her and seek solace in her embrace, his pride burned with the scorn she had heaped on him with her betrayal.

Mikhail reached the manor quickly. He was surprised to note that the guards he encountered at the entrance had a light in their faces that shone with a brilliant purity. It seemed incongruous to him. They bowed, allowing him to pass graciously.

"Good morning, Sir Mikhail," one of the guards greeted him warmly. "May you find respite in this homely home of Lady Constance Rosalind."

Feeling disquieted, Mikhail touched the brim of his hat, then passed through the doors. Inside, the manor was full of light, as if the sun had turned its fiery visage upon it and held it in its gaze. The fragrance of sandalwood and musk permeated the air, conjuring up a stream of images in his mind. Entering the hall, he was met by a beaming maid who invited him to breakfast, where the lady of the house awaited him.

The maid led him to a brightly lit hall with a long dining table. At the far end, seated quietly, Estella was waiting. Mikhail was instantly reminded of the first time he had met her, fatefully drawn in by the ember of her soul burning through her eyes. She did not rise to greet him, but remained where she sat, relaxed and cordial but indifferent. As he approached, the disappointment ached within his breast. The anticipation that had risen to a crescendo awaiting the moment they would lock eyes once more had fallen, dashed to the rocks of his disillusionment. But he swiftly pulled a stern veil over his pain.

"You brought the sun with your arrival it seems, Estella. It hasn't shone brightly here since you left me like a thief in the night those many months ago." Mikhail took Estella's hand, kissing it and waiting for the venomous knife in her reply. But it didn't come.

"Forgive me for not comprehending convoluted chatter at this hour of the day. May I ask what's gnawing at you?" she asked impatiently with genuine confusion. Her face showed none of the tender care she had once harbored for him.

"You left me in my moment of need when they had murdered Elmer. You left me to battle the cardinal on my own, selfishly choosing an easy life of luxury without a thought for the sake of humanity. Do not be so obtuse or play your games with me!" He pointed his finger at her threateningly, his grey eyes flashing.

"How dare you make such insolent assumptions! You must be raving. I left because the cardinal wanted to murder me and the children in my care," she replied defiantly.

Mikhail, made reckless by his bitterness, cleaved into Estella's mind suddenly without warning. Estella cringed and threw a glass of water at his face, sealing her thoughts immediately. But Mikhail's face darkened with understanding, and he scanned the room around him in dismay.

"They tampered with your mind, you fool. Your memories have been altered and you no longer recall what we had, the love that was between us." His chagrined voice was low, and grief seized him as he turned from her. Estella frowned, reaching out to touch his hand.

"Love? Between us, Mikhail?" The concern in her face was genuine, but it did nothing to placate Mikhail's distress.

"Did we not find love in one another, though briefly? Go back in your memories, Estella. When did you leave me?" Estella bit her lip and uncomfortably looked away.

"I left you straight after the ball at the king's palace, and the rest . . . well the rest is vague. I cannot really put my finger on it. But then, I have been much occupied. You are surely imagining things as most men do, dreaming up love stories, trying to stake your claim on me."

Mikhail made a show of forced geniality. "Tell me how things have been since you left. You eluded even Oswald's thorough hounding. But wait, where is Lady Constance?"

"Constance is off to visit her mother's kin. But now let us discuss this war together, and if you permit me, I may opt for some wine."

Mikhail's heart felt like a millstone, but he held back on further questions. Although she seemed herself, the spark between them had been extinguished, and it was more likely that the knife would be twisted than retrieved.

"Let's start again, then," he said, stitching his face into an aloof mask. "Maybe this way I won't be blinded by my heart, and it will make it easier for me to deliver my orders."

"Yes, of course," Estella said, rolling her eyes. "Pray go ahead, enlighten me. But first let me fill you in on some interesting details."

For at least an hour she spoke and Mikhail listened. Then he questioned her over and over again about Prince Erik, the box of gems, and the devils they constrained as Estella recounted to him all the details she could recall. He hid his misgivings about Antariel from her, though he suspected the angel had a hidden role to play.

In turn, Mikhail told Estella what he knew. He spoke of how the cardinal sought to dismantle the orders and the Twilit world. By doing so he hoped to prevent the light of the ages, the messiah of each generation, from taking form on earth. The cardinal wanted to bend Estella to his will and wield her as a force to implement his dark designs.

So far the cardinal's minions had set about gathering the artifacts of the pagan temples buried in monasteries and churches, openly murdering Mikhail's trusted men. The king had long been taken mysteriously ill. Confined to his bed, he had given sovereignty over to the cardinal to rule as his steward under the banner of the holy church. The persecution of the Twilit was turning into a flagrant genocide, for wherever they fled they were hung and tortured. Mikhail and the queen were among the few that converged efforts to support them, but amid the rift caused by ages of distrust, the result of their endeavors was mediocre.

Instead they directed their efforts toward binding the demons that hunted the Twilit. Every hapless Twilit soul the demons caught was stripped of their sight and fed to the servants of Samael, who sought to take back earth from God's ownership. Samael was an abomination even worse than Lucifer, who merely corrupted everything, then left the dirty work to others. Every night was a contest of strength. Some nights they triumphed and Samael's forces drew back and his sway was weakened, but other nights he pushed them back violently and stole countless lives and souls for himself.

Estella agreed to lend Mikhail her sight, under her own terms, in order to bring about Samael's downfall and to contain the pestilence that had descended, for it was through her that the demons had been unleashed. And she agreed to consecrate her efforts through the Templars for the greater good. Her own world was in peril, and through her blood she would protect it.

"Since we are in this together, open your mind to me. Allow me to tell you a story, Mikhail." Estella rose to her feet and trailed behind him, placing her hands on his shoulders and soothing away the knots of tension. The curls of her hair swayed as she spoke, tickling his neck, and he felt the heat of her body close to him. He craned his neck to look at her, at the fires in her eyes revealing her true Twilit nature. But she was bitter, for she knew her words would never pierce the thick armor of his dogmatic mind. With a twinge of grief, Mikhail understood in that moment how disparate they were.

"What if I told you, Templar, that everything around you is polluted and poisonous? That your Christ did not come to save you from a world that is fallen, though beautiful? Hate the world he asked of you, hate it you shall, for without that hatred you cannot be free to see beyond the illusion. This is not your Father's creation, this is not your home, and neither was this the work of angelic hands weaving the abodes of men from stardust." She smiled grimly with knowing in her large, dark eyes.

"This world is but a dream of someone, someone who thought himself greater than the Creator himself. This world was Lucifer's dream, the mirrored stolen thoughts he snatched from the symphony of chaos before the throne of God, eons ago when existence was new. He made himself a god over the creation that he wrought in his dreams, and his gaze gave soul and breath to the ideas, and he bequeathed them his own light. And they were enamored, the angels that fell beneath his spell. The beauty of his thought was endless and its enchantment was strong. So they tuned to him, and lent their song to his echoes, intertwining with their master's theme. They blended together in the chaos of light and darkness, and Lucifer smote them together to create earth.

"The angels saw through his eyes and they breathed their divine flame into his creation, mingling their will with his, as their heartbeat mirrored his, and their songs rose in unison with him. And they devised plans and ideas, giving form to the notions that Lucifer fed them with— his poisoned ether and the breath of life. For he was prince of the air, and breath and air sustain all living things. But without it comes death, the great flaw in his plan, and the decay and undoing of his grand designs.

"A third of the heavenly host was taken with him in his fall, and that fall was radiant. Never did a more beautiful star fall from the gates of heaven, plunging amid burning wings of fire and opalescent lights.

Upon descending to earth, he tricked the angels that had joined him. Many he bound and trapped, casting them down to earth where they became trees, their weeping souls trapped in sap and bark forever. There many of them rotted, their souls erring into the abominable darkness Lucifer had created to spite God—the void that is empty of the holy light.

"And Lucifer was born of the most radiant, pure fire. When we yield our spirits to the fire, we find our own godly spark and we can wield it, using it to weave dreams and tap into the Twilit world. But wary are we of what fire we choose to consecrate to ourselves. Some fires are jealous and desire only to seize our flame and devour our soul while others seek to live within us freely, sharing our souls as we share in their essence. And beyond all is our warden, the Hag Goddess, clad in rags. She walks across earth unmolested by even the vilest of its secrets, and she watches over everything. Yes, even over the chessboard, for she weaves the great tapestry of existence with golden hands." Estella finished her speech, stepping back from Mikhail as he rose surveying her bitterly. His jaw was tightly set and disapproval was etched in his face.

"And what have you to show for the knowledge you attained?" Mikhail asked. "Yet many like you who are gifted to see beyond the veil merely watch on the borders of the great battle and do little or nothing to help. They hide like cowards in the shadows. The church alone can offer salvation. Your people peddle nothing but fancies!" His words were cutting, but Estella did not flinch. She even smiled as the words brushed over her, waving them aside carelessly.

"I don't have time for these tirades, Mikhail," she said. "I fled because I had no inclination to be made a tool by anyone, especially not your misogynistic orders that seek only to further their goals on the backs of my people. You are bound to the chessboard, but we are bound by nothing but our devotion to nature. From her we come, and to her we shall return. We don't need to embroil ourselves in petty wars, for we have bigger realms to explore. We are the children of the Sophia, the mother goddess, and she has chosen us for herself. She takes us out of the cruel game, picking us out as one sifts through wheat, and gives us the gift of deciding our own path.

"And we inhabit the Twilit worlds, where those that weren't duped by Lucifer abide. For there in the fall they were left but were not diminished, and they hid from his tyranny and shielded themselves from his poisonous breath. They wove around his dimension their own kingdoms and lofty abodes, and there he shall never trespass and neither shall he claim their domain as his own. And so we are allowed to stray and get lost in their realms where they are as kings and queens—the immortal ones, beautiful and serene, the Elvish creatures that our stories recount with awe and love. That is my path, Templar, and the Hag promised me my way out, and that shall never be denied to me."

Estella's eyes were hard as she walked towards the hearth. Mikhail followed her. She pointed to the tendrils of flames curling upwards as they suddenly broke into distinct forms. Flame beasts and humanoid figures fell into a languid dance. Mikhail frowned, turning his back on her and her frivolous display of power. Then as an afterthought he turned back, beckoning to the fire, and amid the blaze rose another fiery entity, shaped in the form of a raging serpent. With lashes of fires it pursued the beasts and humanoid forms, slaying and devouring them one by one.

"Frivolity is the distraction of Satan!" Mikhail's presence loomed threateningly over Estella as he spoke. "None of you would fight for your heavenly Father who sent his only begotten son to save our souls and redeem us. We were lost sparks, caught in the whirlpool of darkness, and that darkness would have feasted on us and enslaved us in agony, languishing forever. He sent his salvation to forge us a path back to our true home, at the right hand of God, at his feet, the glorious sons and daughters of God." Mikhail then extinguished the hearth with a single, austere glance. The light and passion in his face was full of the fervor of his convictions as they burned mightily within him.

"We are the chosen knights of our Father," he continued, "and when the great end comes, we shall be the rewarded soldiers of our beloved king. We shall stand by him in battle and fight for our home, our glorious home where we each have thrones and a mighty crown of stars to burn on our heads."

"There is no home but the Twilit world," said Estella, shaking her head pityingly. "That is my home. I am daughter of the primordial darkness, the fabric of creation whence emerge the stars and the divine designs. I am the daughter of the Mother that finds beauty in the night and the empty spaces in the unfinished creations. And there we wander forlorn, singing in the eternal night and whispering to the stars our loving tunes to adorn their loneliness. We gave our hearts to those that did not want to go home to heaven but sought worlds for themselves as the freed captives of this bruised earth. We want our freedom from this war and the liberty to dance and dream in the infinite richness of the holy night beneath the garments of our mother and her watchful gaze. That's home to us," Estella said and closed her eyes, inhaling deeply. Mikhail crossed his arms behind his back.

"Already Samael is after you," he said, "and will stop at nothing to trick you and break you into a million pieces that he can crush beneath his boots. To delight in your screams that will never end until time breaks its coils and infinity collapses into nothingness. No, even then shall he pursue you, and till you are dead you will be in constant fear, and in death he will seek to trick you also. Until you pass that door into the Twilit realm, you are captive to his malice." Mikhail grabbed her roughly, but she smote his hand away.

Reaching for his dagger, he made towards her. "You deserve to die for betraying our Father and spitting on the gift he gave you, vain, selfish cowardly! Undeserving of the benevolence of our Father, and cruelly heartless to my love to you."

Estella did not flinch, staring back into Mikhail's obdurate eyes. "Bless you, Mikhail. You are such a champion of your cause. If one cannot subordinate the unbelievers, then let's murder them, for in that is God's glory indeed. Go ahead and slit my throat, and my blood be upon your hands," she mocked him.

"You do not know what Samael will do to you, foolish woman," he spat at her, a faint pleading evident in his hoarse voice. Estella was staring through the stained glass windows and humming to herself obliviously.

"Indeed you truly believe yourself mighty," Mikhail continued. "Do you have no parcel of humility within you? Where was this arrogance when that demon haunted your bedchamber? That foul ordure of hell?"

Estella raised a faintly amused brow.

"I suggest you mention me with better manners, my Lord Templar, if you truly think you are a man of God," came a chiding voice.

Antariel's soft grey wings blocked out the light, casting a long shadow across the hall. His visage was impassive, but his bright blue eyes returned the coldness reflected in Mikhail's. However, Antariel's contained a darker and far more ancient arrogance that Mikhail could not hope to surpass. He lifted his head as he spoke, forming the words craftily on his cunning lips.

"Do not presume to speak for God, my prodigal friend, though you may speak for yourself," Antariel said lightly.

Mikhail unsheathed his sword inscribed with the runes of power and the sigils of his order. His countenance was a wolfish snarl.

"I see mercy has redeemed her erring child," Mikhail spat. "But the venom was not drained from you, was it? Why aren't you home serving your master? I command you in the name of Metatron to obey my words or be constrained before the throne. I bind you to speak the truth!" His sword glinted palely in the shadow of Antariel's wings. A crackling fire in the shape of a circle emerged around Antariel.

"Through the sacred Shem ha-Mephorash," Mikhail chanted, "by the power of Metatron, by Raphael who frustrates all demons, and seventy-two living letters of the Lord our god, I bind you, redeemed angel, through the consecrated power of our sacred order."

The fire that was crackling around Antariel flared a reddish white, but he looked on immovably serene. Estella nervously observed them but maintained her distance.

"Ah I remember now the litany of the holy names," Antariel smiled humorlessly. Then raising his left hand the fires fanned higher, taking the shape of winged creatures. He set them free across the hall, dancing and multiplying as they dispersed. Mikhail marched up to Antariel, holding his sword before him in defiance, until he was barely a foot away. The two locked eyes.

"Go home, Templar," Antariel commanded. "You are not welcome in our thoughts, nor our hearts any longer."

"Who is 'our'?" Mikhail snarled incredulously. "Do you possess her now? Is she a trinket for your lustful games? How fallen are you now, Estella, that you seek the solace of redeemed petty demons. Your gift is wasted on you." He threw the words like daggers at Estella, but she merely blinked unresponsively.

"Talk to me, Templar, not to her, for you know nothing of her but whatever fragments of her ever changing mask she decided to grace you with. She cannot hear you, neither can she feel you. And yes, that is my doing."

"I see now that you are my only audience," Mikhail forced the words out bitterly, regretting them instantly as he saw the amusement in the angel's blue eyes.

"Yes indeed, and so let us talk angel to man, almost biblically in fashion." Antariel's benign smile was gone. "I want her safe from harm just as much as she does. I will do my utmost to protect her from danger, so in that we may both collaborate towards the same goal. Your order will not enslave her, for she was not born to be anyone's thrall. The cardinal's demons will seek to dismantle you and the queen inch by inch and cast you out to the dogs to devour. I will assist you, for I know these ancient evils and their purpose and ways better than you. As for Samael, you cannot fight him alone, nor can you be sure of any move he seeks to make on any of us. In that you would also require my council."

"Let me share with you a secret that your beloved queen hides," Antariel continued. "She is of the lineage of the Magdalenes. That is why she wields such sway over your mortal orders. I can assist her in unlocking her potential. I know the rules of the game here. But Estella must remain Estella. She won't be controlled lest she break and flee into danger, for that is her way and you cannot change her. She will lend you her eyes, but do not restrain her, for in that I will become your archenemy." Antariel's words fell like fountain water, limpid and clear, and the threat and promise they held washed over Mikhail, sinking into every pore.

"I see you have your own designs after all, even in this form. I thought one could not come before the throne of God with impurity in their hearts," Mikhail seethed, aiming to wound. But Antariel augustly leaned forwards and pressed a finger to Mikhail's chest.

"Sadly you do not know anything about the hearts of men. The true treasures of the soul are hidden from you. I have seen, and even Estella sees, where you dream to go, but you cannot for you are blind and your Father has not deemed you worthy of sight." Antariel withdrew his fingers from Mikhail's heart and closed his wings gently, letting the sunlight wash over them. "Let us unite in this journey to destroy the doom hanging over us. I have gathered news that should interest your order. I know Samael's next target." As Antariel spoke Estella stirred from her reverie and came to join them.

"Off we go then, to our next step in the game," she sighed. "Shall we send news to the queen and esteemed Templars to convene with us here? I doubt travel would avail us well in these times."

Antariel did not respond but inspected the finger he had lain on Mikhail with mild curiosity, casting a cunning glance at him.

"We shall send word then, and secure the house," Mikhail responded coldly, suddenly coughing beneath Antariel's watchful stare.

19

WALKING DOWN
SUNDERED PATHS

I swallowed the razor with its mocking, glittering gleam

The brightest light in the gathering dark

Felt it seek out each corner of my soul, my pains to redeem

From ancient bondage and kindle their ravenous spark

A ROUND THE GREAT TABLE IN THE HALL THEY SAT WHILE MESSENGERS, who had been summoned by Mikhail, came and went. Some were angels constrained to obey his command, and others demons bound to his will. They reported to him and brought him tidings. The hours went by and the maids brought food and drink. The frosty atmosphere that had lingered heavily began to evaporate as a brittle cordiality set in. The crackling fires of the hearth warmed Mikhail and Estella's coldness, and Antariel watched as they dined and drank.

The pestilence that was falling over London had weakened the people's resolve, and many that were taken sick or had perished were those opposed to the cardinal. The news was troublesome, and the culprits were demons who regaled themselves on their prey, harvesting their god sparks to gain strength and a foothold on earth. Estella was of the opinion that they should send Mikhail into the first circle of hell beneath the protection of the lion-headed angel Nesargiel to free the souls that had been harvested. Antariel, however, thought that it would be safer to bind an angel to go forth and liberate the souls, weaving a trap for the demons on the way.

As time passed, the messengers networking between the various Templars intensified, and the situation grew dire. Cargoes came from the Holy Land, bringing treacherous burdens. Mikhail set his Templars to neutralize the threat before it hit the shores, and the cardinal held a black mass and officially summoned Samael, the Blind God, into the world with the guidance of Lucifer. Five hangings were scheduled that morning, though the Templars intervened. The queen's forces officially broke away from the king, plunging the kingdom into disarray.

Estella's own networks flourished just as rapidly. People came in and out soundlessly to hold council with her. But they had nothing but distrustful looks for Mikhail, who ignored them as he poured over charts and manuscripts with a furrowed brow. Oswald was making his way to the manor, and the queen herself had left her summer abode, both desiring to meet with Estella.

DISTANT CHATTER REACHED Mikhail and Estella from the entry hall where the maids admitted visitors. A small woman entered tentatively, clad in purple silks and leathers, her long, blond hair braided and piled on her head. Like the others, she uttered no word, but surreptitiously made for the hearth where Estella was seated at a large table.

The crackling fires danced across Estella's face as the lady in purple glided towards her. Her ethereal stillness was unnerving to Mikhail, and the lights flickering in her vacant blue eyes reflected nothing of her thoughts or the soul within. The woman was slightly built and short of stature, and her pale, porcelain visage was adorned with freckles and devoid of expression. Mikhail noted that she had the same impassive nature as Estella.

Estella nodded to her solemnly, and the lady took a seat before the hearth across from her. They sat in silence for many moments sharing thoughts. After what seemed like half an hour of silence and trepidation, Estella beamed at her. The taciturn lady returned the cryptic smile brightly, and life seemed to seep through her veins. But then she shuddered, coughing while Estella reached forwards and seized her arm compassionately.

The two Templars flanking Mikhail looked on with distaste, whispering between themselves haughtily, their hands on the sheaths of their swords. The lady in purple smiled at them, but there was nothing sweet or innocent in her smile. Instead a morbid danger loomed over them and drowned their clamoring thoughts. Estella snorted as the supercilious Templars stiffened and averted their gaze while Mikhail stared fixedly at his maps.

Faint whispers broke around them like the murmur of old trees, and Estella rose to her feet. The lady followed her, and they walked toward the exit, arm in arm. As much as Estella was graceful, the lady moved with the fluid motions of water. They stopped before the exit hall and Estella bent over to kiss her brow, then the lady disappeared like a dream.

"That was Selene, one of our most accomplished dream weavers," Estella said. "She and her trusted Twilit prodigies have caught one of the cardinal's new friends in their meshes. She will be bringing him here shortly for questioning. I suggest we begin preparing ourselves for a long night of interrogation." Estella sighed, crossing her arms and beckoning towards Antariel. He smiled from where he leaned against a marble pillar, then vanished.

"I suggest I lead the questioning," said Mikhail, straightening himself stiffly. "You could provide the means to ensure he doesn't escape us here. I trust your ways to be effective. And then maybe we can bind him here in the dungeons, beyond the reach of the cardinal." His tone was cordial but he avoided her gaze.

"We think it is one of those that brought the pestilence," said Estella. "There are three, from what my network gathers, but once you have one, you can easily catch the others. They tend to betray each other readily." Estella rubbed her hands together nervously. "I will be gone tonight. We will deliver this demon to you, then I will be out for some urgent errands, then back with the dawn. If I do not return by then, you may start having cause to fear for me. But I do not think you should worry yourself about the cardinal at this moment, I give you my assurances on that."

Estella overcame her ill-disguised fretfulness by defiantly meeting Mikhail's eyes. For the first time since he had met her, it seemed to him that she was a total stranger, alien to him and distant. Her thoughts and mind were sealed behind hazes that Antariel had set out of jealousy.

Before Mikhail could respond, Antariel reemerged in a flurry of billowing robes and soft grey wings. He bowed mockingly to Mikhail, who stiffened with an unconcealed grimace. Antariel did not forsake his mocking smile as he deposited heavy bundles of cloth wrapping before Estella. She peered over the contents with satisfaction, casting back the covers to reveal candles and incense and strange pouches with pungent odors. Mikhail rose to his feet without meeting her gaze and Antariel vanished again.

"You should be careful to protect yourself, Estella. Do not be reckless, these ancient evils are not to be taken lightly." Mikhail's grey eyes burned dimly. "Aiden, Cuthbert, please wait for me outside, I require a private word with Lady Estella." The Templars nodded deferentially and departed, positioning themselves outside the hall in plain view.

"I can see how they hold me with fear and distrust," Estella remarked, "as if I were some demon clad in comely flesh. Are these the people you would have me serve? A maid for them? A thrall to their manliness?" Estella cocked her head, observing Mikhail's impassive face.

"You know nothing of the suffering of my men," he replied, "who have pledged their lives to save the likes of you. They have rescued the souls of the people of these lands at their own peril. They are holy men and given to holier vows, and they do not take consorting with the shadows as if it were play lightly."

"But of course for me it is play, as it is also for you. But your game is one of swords and bannered victories, while ours is a dance between the two blows. We flee from one to hide from the other, and we thwart both and elude them all. You are a prisoner of this world, but we are not, and we watch you in your holy crusades speaking for a god that does not know your name." Estella turned her back to him, seizing her bundle of candles. Mikhail pushed aside his cloak, unsheathing his sword, and Estella turned to face him warily as he spoke.

"This sword has been handed down generation to generation," he said softly, watching the light of the hearth set the runes in the sword ablaze. He wielded it swiftly, rending the air, and crisply ripping through the smoke of the hearth. "This sword was the first of its kind, and saved from ruin many times with the blood of noble men."

He rested the edge of the sword on his palm reverentially and faced Estella. "This sword was forged of many irons beneath the spells of the fathers of our orders. It has many souls and many names, for it has drunk the spirit of its previous masters and mixed with the dried bones of the old mages that forged it in the far regions of the ice realms. This sword was once a mage, and this mage initiated many like you in the secrets of the afterlife and the Twilit worlds."

"Such a contemptuous admission!" Estella hissed. "Thieves you all are, and desecrators of our holy shrines. You stole our magic and wove it into your theologies and rituals, murdering our heritage so that we might blindly merge with you." Estella's incredulous face was a hollow mask, and she eyed the sword wildly with hatred.

"Yes, we took from you, that much is true. Even Merlin's own sword, which we broke into fragments and blended with the spear that pierced the side of our Lord Christ. We also stole the scepter of Isis, and of it we fashioned the thrice blessed sword of the Northern Star, our holy emblem, the weapon that only Hermes himself had made before us. And here it is in my hands. It can cut through the webs and meshes that hold you to your world. I can sever you from it completely. But I don't want to, I only want to see you rule over your gifts and ride the storm. The ways of the pagan lead too close to the clutches of darkness. For the greater good we must take over stewardship of your gifts."

Estella's eyes measured the sword covetously. She extended her hand and touched the hilt of the sword as Mikhail offered it up to her with a wan smile. Though she was unfamiliar with weaponry, she gripped it readily, and inspected it. In the moment that she wielded it, she pointed the tip at Mikhail malignantly.

"I can hear the voice of Merlin within this sword calling my name!" she hissed. "The oldest of our fathers, he shared his soul with his sword. And the voices of the shamans and vǫlvas of the north clamor for blood and revenge." She traced her fingers hungrily across the edges of the blade with fascination and cut her finger. Without flinching, she sucked on the blood, then with a shriek of dismay spat it out and flung the sword at his feet.

"And you have defiled it generously with the Christian incantations that drank the blood of our people. I can taste the spear that initiated your god mingled with our holy sages. The sacrilege! You supplanted our deities and reduced their powers to vassalage! The mother goddess Isis must be wailing in despair every day, watching what abomination you have wrought."

Mikhail stooped to pick up his sword reverently. "I don't think you understand what we reconciled, Estella," he said. "We reconciled the powers of the ages that could defeat the serpent and smite him on the head." He cleaned the sword with his cloak without deigning to lift his eyes to her.

"Keep your excuses to yourself," she retorted. "Nothing defends defiling our groves and shrines and stealing our secrets to wield against us for our subjugation."

"You could rule by my side, Estella. Do not throw away your chance for happiness. Do you really not remember the love we shared, though briefly, before a shadow clouded your mind? The spark that brought us close and lit within us the embers of long dead fires and warmed our souls to each other and to life?" Mikhail was on one knee, and he touched the hem of her cloak gently, lifting his clear grey eyes to her, twinkling in sadness but with a faint hope.

"Do not turn me away, Estella," he pleaded. "Leave that demon behind; take me as your man! Must I do more to prove to you that I am sincere? Am I not at your feet beseeching you to open the gates of your heart?" Estella stumbled backwards, yanking her cloak from Mikhail's grasp, and a wave of revulsion passed over her face.

"I don't understand your emotional ploys, Mikhail. Do I strike you as a desperate woman seeking protection? I never loved you, and you have never loved me. I do not understand what games you are playing, but this must cease at once."

"He changed you, Estella," Mikhail replied. "But aren't you strong enough to break his bonds? Are you not fiercer than his petty tricks? He seeks to take you from my side where you were meant to be. All of this that you hate about us, you could change—but only by my side."

"I see that you are also an expert crafter of lies," Estella said. "All of this, so that you could lead me like a docile sheep. Love, Mikhail? Is that the best weapon you can wield?"

Before Mikhail could protest, a noise came from the entry hall and Estella broke away from him. Mikhail quickly got to his feet and sheathed his sword. A few moments later, the maids came bustling in. They were ushering Selene and several others who, like her, had a dreamy sparkle in their eyes and pallid visages. They narrowed their eyes on Mikhail like a pack of vultures hunting their prey.

"I see what the angel is saying," said a tall young woman with copper brown hair, her grey eyes slits of ice. Selene vehemently nodded, humming her disapproval as she approached Estella and gripped her arm gently.

"Sister dear, we have our own work to do. Before we hand the demon to this Templar, we must first extract our own answers and secure this abode. Let's dismiss this knight and spare him from seeing our pagan ways."

Mikhail bowed, turning on his heel without further ado.

"Let's get started, for I must soon depart on my errand," Estella said, her tone oddly subdued.

"Fear not," Selene responded. "The angel and I have hatched the perfect plan."

20

MADE IN GOD'S OWN IMAGE

Hold a sieve to the eye of the sun, you cannot elude its glare
It sinks into your skin and bids all things grow within its stride
And as a tyrant most malevolent its deadly beams do stare
And the true seers from sanity it does perniciously divide

"MASTER HEAR OUR SUPPLICATIONS AND DELIVER US FROM THE tyranny of the jealous god. Master, lead us to be gods in our promised earth and be the light of deliverance that we need. Morning star hear our call and preside over us in kingship, for you are the true savior of mankind!"

The oleaginous words resounded in the darkness of the empty church. The dampness and cold seized them hungrily, lending them more fervor, for the prayer was potent, and the voice commanding. Cardinal Pious was bent over a roughly hewn black basalt altar. It was unadorned except for some intricate patterns painted with a viscous substance that glistened in the flickering light of the candles. Sticky and dripping, the altar stood in stark contrast to the holy icons upon the walls, their sad visages and golden halos glinting grimly beside elaborate crosses. The smell of blood and rotted flesh permeated the already putrid air and filled the church with a dismal odor.

The cardinal rose to his feet gingerly. Lifting his malevolent countenance, he smiled at the altar where a plain glass bowl was placed in the middle of semidried blood. The guttering candlelight cast a shivering ray upon it, and the light was suddenly refracted from the numerous eyeballs filling the basin to the brim. Some were still attached to muscle and sinew, whereas others were damaged, as if plucked out hurriedly. But they all seemed eerily alive, and their gaze was fixed on the cardinal with an intense horror, as though frozen in time.

While he waited, the cardinal mentally exercised himself, trying to see if he could match the eyeballs to their victims. He could almost swear he recognized a few—the certain nuances in the shade of the iris and the petrified look it carried. Well, he mused to himself, the eyes after all were the windows to the soul. Somehow the entirety of one's personality was mirrored in them, and no doubt that was one of the reasons they were such a potent offering to his master.

Loud thumping footsteps resounded, and a door to his right swung open. It yawned wide, a draughty darkness spilling in bearing muffled screams as two burly, hooded and cloaked men entered, roughly dragging a young man barely in his twenties. The man pulled and strained with effort, his bulging eyes wild with fear as his jailers forcefully pulled him along, kicking him in the ribs and the face. The man sobbed uncontrollably, groveling as the cardinal watched with rapture, smacking his lips in delight.

"Enough, enough now," the cardinal commanded. "I need him to be compliant, at least for the beginning."

The captors desisted immediately, dumping the man's bruised body unceremoniously before the cardinal. The cardinal stooped down and wrenched the gag off the man's mouth, holding his face as he inspected his features. He nodded approvingly, his jowls quivering.

"That's a handsome face, too fine to spoil, in fact." He smiled benignly at the man as if he were some benevolent father admiring his prodigious son. The man's supplicant eyes sought the cardinal's beseechingly. Throwing himself at the cardinal desperately, he wept loudly.

"Please holy father, I have done nothing wrong! I beg you, I would do anything for you. I would serve you for my entire life. Please don't let them torture me further, I beg you, I am innocent!"

"Indeed you look too pretty to spoil, and I must admit I regret it has come to this, my boy." The cardinal grabbed the man by the hair and lifted his face level to his own. "It's true you could serve me before you

go, serve me for a little while longer, if you promise to please me properly, satisfy me, take all of me . . . right in." The cardinal's tone was
suave as he caressed the man's head tenderly.

The man's eyes widened with shock and disgust and he fell backwards,
shrinking away from the cardinal. With an angry snarl, the cardinal
kicked the man in the head, placing his boot upon his neck, and applying
pressure slowly and painfully. His eyes were bulging with rage and lust,
and he frothed at the mouth while the man whimpered and wept.

"Now I am going to offer you one last chance, boy, for a swift passage
into the next wretched life," the cardinal grinned, hitching up his robes
to reveal his erect member. "Please me boy, or there will be a very painful transition for you when we relieve you of your life and leave your
soul to slowly shiver its way to the devil, who will devour you and swallow your miserable spark."

The cardinal grasped his member with one hand and stood astride
the man. "Bring this fool to his feet, let him serve me, or else it's the
houses of lamentations again for him."

The young man issued a low, protesting moan and covered his face
as he shook while his captors marched brusquely up to him.

"Undress him now!" the cardinal barked as he pleasured himself, his
lascivious eyes glinting with cruel lust.

The jailors roughly stooped down and began stripping the man, pay-
ing no heed to his protests and cries. They beat him on the head and
smote his face, revealing nothing in their faces but a faint glow from
dreadful, sunken eyes. The man's naked body was covered in welts,
bruises, and newly inflicted burns. The deep gashes seemed to have
been reopened with repeated beatings. The cardinal hummed to himself and clicked his fingers while the jailors dragged the man to his
knees. One grasped the man's head and yanked it forwards towards the
cardinal's naked member.

"Come on, little girly, show us how good you can suck," the cardinal
smiled, revealing crooked, yellow teeth.

The man heaved and shuddered, tears streaming down his beaten
face. His left eye was already closed and swollen, and as he fumbled for
words, blood leaked out of his mouth.

"No, boy, it's just you and me here," said the cardinal. "No one shall come to your succor. So how about you place those lips of yours somewhere that's waiting for you?"

The presence was not felt right away, for it was light and fleet. What awoke it was freshly sacrificed blood dedicated to strange stars, ripping the fine fibers of the firmament that held the dimensions of space and time together. The shredded tear in the universe bled forth energy, and out of it emerged something dreadful and fierce, hungry after its long sojourn in lonely isles. It had been summoned to find its prey, and it would do so.

Who summoned him, he couldn't remember, only the vague echo of her voice lingered, light and delicate as the morning rain and as momentary as the passing of a fallen leaf. But the command was never gone, and her intentions not forgotten. It rode his mind subtly yet potently. Into the church he slinked, smelling his prey where it stood unknowing of its fate.

The cardinal suddenly felt a wave of dread wash over him. He sensed the predatory danger that lurked and licked his lips feverishly, searching around him with bulging eyes. He called angrily to the jailors to investigate, but they backed away, retreating swiftly to the open door and disappearing. The cardinal cursed loudly and kicked the whimpering man, who was staring fixedly into the distance.

"Shut your face, boy, we aren't done yet. Let's see what trickster is entertaining us tonight." The cardinal narrowed his eyes, but could see nothing at first. Then a loud growl resounded in the hall, cold and ravenous. It was full of hunger and hatred that could only be sated with blood. Taking a tentative step back, the cardinal blanched and shot a quick look at the altar.

"Master, master, is that you? Is this some . . . ally of yours? Master, please have mercy on your servant, I am weak of heart. Lucifer, my god, I am your humble servant. I was merely having some harmless fun!"

The faint candlelight seemed to burn brighter as the shadow loomed, its many eyes finally revealed. A wolfish hound approached, its three heads drooling in unison, and its malignant eyes fixed on the cardinal. Recovering from his initial shock, he spluttered and fell to his knees.

"Master, no, what is this? Who is this? Master?"

But the wolfish creature merely salivated, measuring him with its intent, deadly stare. The growl became louder and louder while the cardinal furtively backed away toward the door. He shrieked as he fumbled with the knob frantically, finding it locked from the outside. Yanking and pounding at it, he cursed his men who had decided to turn on him. The hound watched the cardinal with an almost human intelligence. Each howl revealed razor-sharp teeth and a baleful fire in its red eyes.

"It is not your master's doing this time, you god-cursed wretch, but mine. This is my farewell gift to you before your worthless soul is ripped out of this life." The voice that accompanied the hound was cold and satisfied, and Estella emerged from the shadows, swathed in a black, silken gown. Her mocking smile matched the scorn emanating from her twinkling eyes. "Tonight you are the one that shall please. Tonight you shall be the feast for something darker than your wildest nightmares—a host of hellish fiends that even Lucifer cannot save you from."

Estella grimaced, her face a mask of wrath and revulsion. "I went to special ends to find an adequate fiend for you. Cerberus, feast on his flesh and take his screaming soul to be the toy of the wraiths in Tartarus."

The hound snarled at the sound of his name, and before the cardinal could formulate further words, Cerberus had lunged at him with jaws agape, clenching them tight upon the cardinal's face. The screams were pitiful and shrill as the hound's many heads simultaneously ripped the cardinal's flesh and crunched his bones, spurts of arterial blood splattering across the walls. The man in the corner, naked and hyperventilating, was slumped against the altar watching with unadulterated horror, clutching his heaving chest while the blood spatter rained down on him. Cerberus feasted on the cardinal limb by limb, slowly tearing him apart. Hands were swiftly devoured, then an eye, a chunk of thigh.

Meanwhile Estella dispassionately observed the chasm that was growing above Cerberus, the gateway she had opened to bring him in, and which she stayed mindful of keeping in control. The bloodstained jaws of the hound quivered hungrily as it licked the blood off the floor, and within minutes the cardinal was completely consumed. Estella watched the orchestrator of her people's demise being physically erased from earth. She braced herself for the imminent relief, but to her bitterness none came. The cardinal was but a tool, and likely the culprit would soon fashion himself another willing conduit.

"What a wonderful sight it is to see vengeance being taken. Is it not freedom to be able to give in to such a vital desire that stems from our need to establish justice?" The august voice was cool and light with a lilting twang that ran like gentle ripples over a limpid pool. It was floating over her, around her, and within her, but she could neither find the source nor identify the speaker at first. "Justice is what defines us as children of God, he who is all just and all merciful, ever holding the balance of things. Are you not gods yourselves, seeking to emulate your Father? Justice, after all, is righteousness."

The voice was mild yet potent, and Estella's skin tingled with recognition as the gentle drops of venom in the honeyed tones bore into her. Her heart pounded like a hundred drums beating in unison, and an inexorable dread flooded her. She looked around her seeking an escape. Cerberus, meanwhile, had been sated on his prey. The soul of the cardinal, freshly reaped, was glowing dimly in the dismal eyes of the beast, who had turned its fixated glare upon Estella. Her spell slowly began to unravel and weaken, and its ravenous might gathered like a brewing storm.

"There is nothing you can command that has not its innermost source in me. All darkness robed in light is my creation. I thought you would have been wiser than that," the voice mocked while Cerberus let out a hellish growl, baring its teeth. Its many heads were fixed on Estella with an implacable hunger.

Estella took a step back and started to sing in a steady voice. The hound howled and shook its heads, yawning luxuriously. Then Estella's voice rose higher and higher as Cerberus grumbled, fighting back the spell of drowsiness that assailed its senses. Estella walked backwards calmly, then suddenly stumbled over a loose slab. As she fell backwards, her voice broke for a moment, and Cerberus released a mighty howl, lunging in her direction. Estella froze in horror, then screamed, hastily making a ward sign before her with trembling hands. Cerberus crashed into the invisible wall before him, the blood on his jaws splattering onto the unseen barrier.

And there Estella's eyes met with the many eyes of Cerberus, realizing she was no longer immune to his attention. The magic that had led him to her docilely had evaporated. The feral wildness of the beast of hell was now locked on Estella, eager for her blood, and egged on by a hand stronger than hers. The hound began attacking the unseen glass between them with renewed vitriol. Estella scrambled to her feet and made for the church door, but it was closed firmly and bolted shut beyond opening. She tugged at it in vain, cursing.

"Antariel! Where are you? I need help!" Then ripping at her cloak, she whispered words into it. Her shadow flickered meekly beneath the candles and stiffened, then it departed, fleeing in the opposite direction in the same form as Estella, making loud footsteps as it went. Attracting Cerberus's attention was no easy feat, but it fell for the bait and set off chasing the shadow's heels, snapping at it wild with rage. Estella gasped loudly in brief relief, then turned her attention to the door's bolt and pressed her lips against it, whispering feverishly, muttering every opening spell she could recall. But it was clouded and a weighty presence was gathering in it. She could feel the voice creeping up on her, looming like a towering tide, rising higher and higher. It penetrated her mind through the fissures of her fears.

"Nothing can be opened that I have commanded shut, for is not everything on this earth attuned to the melody of my voice? The very air you breathe, is it not my bounty to all mankind?" Then the voice suddenly stabbed at her like a dagger and she fell choking. It seemed as if the air around her had been quenched, and she gasped, clutching her throat and writhing in agony. The shadow she had cast to evade Cerberus was running back in her direction, and before she could avert the danger, it merged with her again. Cerberus following on its trail and was once again before her, appraising her before moving in for the kill.

The air slowly began to trickle back into the atmosphere, and Estella took deep gulps of it, shaking and whispering ineffective ward signs, drained of energy, and resigned to her fate. She was aware of the watchful gaze of the malevolent archangel surveying her, a benign warmth emanating from his disembodied voice. Her thoughts went to Antariel, whom she could not reach, and her sadness welled inside her and overflowed till she wept bitterly. Her heart, so long immured in deep thickets of thorns, bled in anguish. Memories took flight like a flock of birds, some fair some foul, and images of her life filed past, their colors dripping together like tears. All the while the voice glided over her like a deathly veil.

"Embrace your mortality, Tsura," it said.

Then Cerberus descended on her like a wheel of knives.

Beyond the church walls, a piercing scream rose to the laden skies and rent it like a crack of lightning, shredding the veil of clouds and sending them drifting far afield. A crescent moon, silver and bright, poured white light onto the slumbering town. The scream renewed again plaintively, and a flock of birds sheltering beneath the heavy foliage of an oak fled in a flurry of feathers. A silence followed, one that reeked of pain, as the silence that follows the final moments of life.

But the silence did not last long, for a responding groan of anger and dismay rose like a wail. It hunted the echoes of the scream and found them and groaned with them, lamenting, and together they rose in unison and died upon the cold pinnacles of the nearby manors. The groan seeped through the layers of the firmament and the dimensions of thought and matter and bled its agony through it till the whole night throbbed and heaved like the ailing heartbeat of a tormented beast. And he was beyond the gates of night, his wings pinned with black nails into the fabric of darkness and his limbs bound with chains of shadow. He was bound till the hours of dawn when mercy would show her face, heralding the coming of a new day.

Antariel had lost to his foe again, and he knew this time the price was higher than before. He mourned not for himself, but for Estella. The chains he bore were serpents that bit and bled his strength, and the deep dark nails were wrought of Lucifer's malice. This time Lucifer had come to him first, suspending him over the night and robbing him of sight, but bestowing upon him the gift of hearing, so that he could hear and feel Estella's agony.

There were all manner of fiends around him, laughing and mocking with dreadful voices, coiling creatures whose cavernous eyes gave on nothing but boundless chaos feasting on the bleeding light of Antariel's essence. There he strained his ears for the sound of her departing soul and wrung his arms helplessly, tearing his wings and roaring into the night. With the remnants of his will, he formed a vision and sent it hurling down to earth to find Mikhail.

Mikhail was pacing up and down Rosalind Constance's hall. The many voices of the queen and her esquires and the Templars clamored around him. They were celebrating a victory after gleaning pivotal information from the demon that the Twilit hunters had captured. For once, there was unity of purpose between both camps, and the wall of silence between them eased. Bound in an iron container placed on a table, the demon's protests had suddenly turned to mocking laughter.

"Master has succeeded. I can feel your filthy witch's begging . . . I hope she hurts, I hope he bleeds her and disembowels her!"

The inscrutable Selene blanched where she sat with her companions near the hearth.

"Liar, this is one of your tricks again. Shall we seal your mouth shut?" she drawled, but her face betrayed a brewing anxiety.

Mikhail, who was pacing restlessly, stopped in his tracks. Casting a distrustful look at Selene, he said, "Where is Estella?"

Selene rose to her feet, wrapping her shawl around herself. "I am going to find her, we do not need your involvement, Templar. She will be back soon."

"She's having a private audience with Lucifer," came the voice from the iron box. "Fancy sending her to murder the poor fool of a cardinal!"

Selene gritted her teeth and hurried to the exit, trying to hide her concern.

"What on earth were you thinking?" Mikhail bellowed incredulously after her. "Going after the cardinal? Then you turn your backs and flee? By God I will hold you accountable!" Oswald cracked his knuckles darkly and barred the exit, crossing his arms grimly.

"I advise you to tell us now," said Oswald, his amicable tone in stark contrast to his seething eyes. "If she gets captured because of you, you are going down into your own private casket, just like that demon you brought."

Selene's face cracked like a porcelain mask, revealing cold ire, and she furiously turned back to the hearth. "I fear it is already too late, Mikhail. Go after her if you can."

"She's gone . . ." whispered the queen, her chalcedony blue eyes hard and cool, sternly fixated on Mikhail.

He turned around to face her slowly. His face was a mask, and his eyes held the tempests of the wildest north. Silently he held her gaze, defiant and haughty, until the queen lowered her eyes. She turned to the fireplace, where the flames had taken the queer shapes of beasts, observing them quietly.

"This has been your failure, Mikhail," rumbled Oswald, wearing a deep frown. Suddenly he smote the table, rising with a sweeping movement and crushing his high backed chair against the wall. Still, Mikhail remained like a carven image of stone, immovable and distant. Oswald roared, cursing.

"Even the devil cannot see all ends," Mikhail spoke, breaking his silence and sweeping his cold stare across them all.

Oswald snorted derisively, drawing his sword and making for Mikhail, who drew his likewise.

"Do not presume to lecture me on how we managed things here, Oswald," Mikhail said. "I have been loyal to this cause at the expense of everything dear to me, even my own soul. I have tread paths that you will never be worthy of even attempting in your mortal life, so be wary of your accusations."

Mikhail held his sword before him and stood firmly with his legs apart as Oswald swung his sword at him. He evaded the blow easily and smote back, knocking the sword out of Oswald's grasp with nimble movements.

"She was a fire that could not be tamed," Mikhail said. "She would break you and herself both in two to spite you. God's will be done, I do not believe this is the end. It cannot be!" For the first time Mikhail betrayed emotion, the cracks in his mask revealing raw pain and loss.

"Before the night has grown old I shall see the truth to this, and then you can be the judge of me." Mikhail pushed by Oswald, whose narrowed eyes bore nothing but ill will. Bowing to the queen, he left the manor to greet the cold stars.

21

THE DISCOURSES OF
HEAVEN AND HELL

The mere glint in his eye as his gaze swept over the stillness of earth

*Did suffice to quench the rambling tumult of
the marshalled legions of dearth*

*What was a mere whisper of the void, was a lost tune
in the forbidding echoes*

*Of the slumbering mind's vain attempts to suppress
the awakening throes*

DEATH IS DEATH, BUT IT COMES IN MANY GUISES—SOME GRUESOME, others peaceful. And sometimes the fortunes of this world bring death to the door not as the grim reaper, but as the culmination of agony and torture only a fiend could conjure. Being eaten alive was one of those slow deaths, pain unendurable beyond relief, and terror insurmountable.

Cerberus's jaws had clamped on her, each head victoriously claiming a piece of its own. They bit deeply, crunching bone, but did not tear the flesh out—yet. Her first scream was the sheer agony of her ripping flesh in the jaws of the beast. The second came as one of the heads deepened its bite into her thigh, the smell of blood and flesh permeating the air, and the nostrils of the beast flaring. As she shivered and groaned weeping, blood grew into an ever expanding pool beneath her, and the pain and fear froze her mind and nearly stilled her frantic heart. Each time the beast dug deeper with its razor teeth, she let out another cry of agony. Her eyes, facing away from the creature and its malodorous scent, sought something distant; an icon painted in gold over the wall of the church, a white dove crowned within a golden halo.

Her vitality was dying with the seeping of her blood as she labored arduously to draw breath. She saw the thin veils between the worlds loosen, shadows watching her with languid eyes. And she could hear the mournful steps of lost souls erring in a blind eternity with no destination and no end. The chill air seemed to dampen further, and she was getting colder. She knew she was nearing the last pangs of death. But then the air became inexplicably pristine and exceedingly pure and soft. Purposeful footsteps approached, and she turned her head apprehensively. She looked beyond Cerberus, whose hideousness could not blot out the ineffable sight gliding towards her.

There were many cathedrals in the vast world of Christendom, and many skilled artists who captured in sculptures and visions the beauty and radiance of angels and their unending glory. And in this church itself, the oldest in all the land, there was no lack of beautiful icons. But even that was nothing, for Lucifer stood before her, and through the beauty of his countenance she forgot the pains of death. His opalescent wings were luminous and long, with lush feathers, sharp and iridescent as opals refracting the blaze of a million stars and glittering like the reflected light of the purest moonlight on sea-foam. Some had brighter rich hues, similar to light caught in limpid pools, and others glimmered like the nacre insides of shells. With the gentle movement they made, they were like a warm breeze beneath the beaming eye of summer. Like the shrouds of firmament, they illuminated the church with an unearthly light, giving a strange vibrancy to the surroundings.

Lucifer approached her with soft steps, his azure eyes deeper than any ocean that God created, and bluer than any sapphire burning in its most radiant form. Looking into them was like drifting into an abyss, dreaming in the furls of the skies in its myriad hues, from the purity of a heaven at dawn in turquoise splendor, to the deep royal blue of a dusk in summer. All was whirling together with the nebulae of the cosmos, the endless swirling galaxies revolving in a brilliance of lights. The thick black lashes were long and sharp, and his ruthless gaze was as cutting as blades, yet as enchanting as the most unshakable spell. And the laughter and blithe mildness that poured from his eyes were incongruous with the intermittent bursts of flame within them, where cruelty surged like a blast of the solar flare, then abated to the limpid purity of his calm demeanor.

He was one foot away from her when she began to shake uncontrollably. She did not know whence the next blow would fall, for the cunning master of all scheming was the god of guile, and his profound machinations and trickery were as extensive as the beauty he stole from the heavens. She consciously rejected the awe that fell upon her, and shook off the guile that his smile cast on her, which was full of compassion and irresistibly grand. He stooped over her, his long, unbound hair, silvery white like threads of moonlight, falling gracefully.

With one hand he pulled Cerberus back. The howling hound whimpered obediently, and it released Estella instantly, cowering like a docile dog. Lucifer gifted her with an enigmatic smile containing a triumphant malice that was certain of its seductive deadliness. He surveyed her proprietarily, cocking his head gently. Then with one sweeping, graceful motion, he swung Cerberus high in the air where it fell beneath the altar and the open wormhole.

"Look upon the face of the one true light bearer of mankind, Tsura." Lucifer stooped, his wings expanding behind him into the church, and he placed his hand lightly over the wound in her thigh. She recoiled as a crafty smile curled at his lips. "Feel the light I am passing into you, I who am the closest to the likeness of God and his strength, giver of life, and healer of those that merit my bounty."

The wounds in her body began to heal instantly, and the throbbing numbness within her halted its insidious progress as renewed heat surged through her limbs. She felt life begin to burn within her steadily and her heartbeat quicken with fresh vigor. Lucifer's delicate, long-fingered hand moved to her face and seized her chin gently, all the while boring into her eyes commandingly. She stared back, unable to deny him, aware of the heat in her body healing the wounds. At first it was a mild warmth, then hot, then it developed into an uncomfortable feverish fire.

"Feel the life returning to you, the one I am giving back to you. I have poured my essence into you, as I have poured it into this dream of a world." The warmth of his eyes was replaced with an obdurate, rigid coldness, unbending and immovable as death. "There is room inside your soul for me now to grow, but listen to me first; I am your salvation," he said gravely, his eyes regaining that tender softness. He stooped lower and lifted her up, placing her across his knees and cradling her like a broken doll, his wings converging over her forming a bower for her head.

Estella felt nauseated and the feverish fire chafed at her soul. She felt repulsed by his touch, but unable to extricate herself from him or repel his intruding gaze. His fingers trailed through her hair lazily, and one stalwart arm kept her body close against his. She sought to foresee his designs for her in the maze of his eyes, but found no answer. His fingers with each brush loosened the bonds of her mind and its secrets and gently opened the doors to the fastness of her soul. She began to weep with fear and he smiled, his fingers gently wiping her eyes with a loving kindness that sent more fear and horror down her skin than if he had decided to draw out a carving knife and hack at her flesh.

"I am very protective of my flock, Tsura. There are many impostors in this world that seek to lead humanity astray. I engineered your free will and your ability to rebel, and in that you have drawn your source in me." His eyes glittered in remembrance. "But I love each and every one of you. Each of you are precious souls to me, to watch over, my children, in my beautiful creation, where I must protect you from the false god that seeks to usurp your authority."

His fingers trailed to her eyelids. "You have the gift of sight. Look within me and see, see if I am lying to you. Trust yourself, for there are things that cannot be said, only seen. I am proud of what you did tonight, for it was taking ownership of your divine right. Vengeance is of the Lord, and by exacting justice you have become godly, for God is justice."

His finger drifted carelessly to her lips. "But why are you silent, my lioness? Open your heart to me, for I long to hear your voice. You were as I dreamed and conceived in thought. You have not disappointed me." He smiled again knowingly, and Estella turned her face away only to have him bring her face gently but firmly back to his gaze. "Talk to me," he commanded, and the urgency in his voice made the fire in her body flare.

"Are you not the master of all lies and the craftiest of all schemers?" Estella replied. "Is there anything I can say that can triumph over your cunning, O fallen one? There is an immense population of willing souls for you, why persecute me?" she demanded, her voice frail and vulnerable, but holding the sharpness that had defined her from the start.

He smiled again, slivers of heavenly patience cradling her like an infant. "Oh my poor child, how they have turned you against the one that loves you the most. Am I not the light bearer? The one that came and taught humanity the art of tilling the lands and growing foods? Of fashioning clothing and obtaining silks? Have I not taught you the art of warfare, that ye be not vulnerable to the ravenous beasts and the invaders from the heavens eager to steal your inheritance? Have I not stolen knowledge for you to become as great gods among men, and were not your greatest civilizations built by my initiates? Have I not given you the Sophia and the chance to awaken the sacred fire?"

Lucifer's hand clasped the back of her head gently. "And haven't I done so to awaken you to the full potential of being God? But you have been deceived by a false god masquerading as a meek man who loves you, and he has defanged the lion and clipped the talons of the eagle, and led you all as sheep to the slaughter, and through doctrine blinded you and reduced you to beggars." His soft rebuking tone was indulgent and understanding.

"Is that not your job in this existence, Lucifer?" Estella countered. "To lead us astray upon false paths of self-deluded grandeur just to fall into perdition? But what I cannot understand and never did was how someone so close to God himself could turn on him. Somehow I never believed the original story . . ." Estella was drowsy, but her mind had steadied and she had resigned herself to the dread game she had entered.

"Indeed good reasoning, for I am no traitor," said Lucifer. "Does not your heart turn away from their doctrines sensing the reek of hypocrisy and failure? I never turned my back on him, I alone carried out his commands when all the other angels bowed to Adam." His fingers were at her heart now where the resentment against meek Christian dogmas were riled within her, disdain for the doctrines of the feeble savior supposedly dying for a world that continued to self-destruct.

"But you know the truth, Tsura," he said gently, and his fingers were again in her hair. "I came to teach you how to rule over the elements, how to tame the fires to yield their secrets to you, how to reap the wealth of earth's great jewels and precious metals, and how to harness the authority over numbers and the unseen. The closest to me were the greatest rulers; Zeus, Odin, Horus, Athena, Freya, Amun-Ra, Thoth, and many others. They became lights to this world and you prospered. I was a benevolent god, and I judged with mercy and balance. And I often overlooked the sins and mistakes of your people to mete them their reward afterwards, for I am the ouroboros, I am infinity, I am the endless spiral into nothingness, itself into itself. I am my own god, and I am my own sacrifice. I am the initiator of the Elder Folk.

"I honored women as the keepers of wisdom, and I set them to rule as equal counterparts to men. I unleashed within them the sight of ages for them to be connected to my light and see me, and guide humanity across the shifting tides. The false creation and the false god always seek to mirror the truth and yet distort it, that you may be confused and lost unknowing which way to turn. And thus have you fallen from your glory and become slaves to the False God, Samael." Lucifer sighed gently, and grief was etched on his delicate features as he closed his lucent eyes momentarily. For a moment Estella was taken aback.

"I grieve, Estella, for what they have done to you all, my beloved ones, my children of the stars, wrought of stardust and fire and the abundance of my love." The fire in his eyes blazed with indignation. "The False God stole the image of what is sacred, my magic, my skills and arts and initiatic rites, and carved out of them a mirroring darkness. Your Christ did not come to deliver you from me nor from evil. He came to enslave you and rob you of your power and authority. The reign of the lamb replaced the line of lions and gods, reducing you to beggars and cowardly slaves that spit on life and reject its bounty and willingly desecrate it.

"The god of Abraham is a false god who first crushed the power of women and then made servants of the race of men. He chose of all the peoples of the world the most bent and crooked, those mean in mind and spirit, easily malleable to sin and cowardice. Then he molded them into prophets to bring down the great civilizations that I had set up for the glory of mankind. He deviated them from the sacred truth through lies and petty tricks, outlawing magical wisdom and sacred knowledge. Then he established rules and laws that robbed you of your might and purpose and reduced you to slaves. And you became slaves to a law that bound you to a god that desired slavery and adoration and severance from the holy Mother and the divine Sophia.

"The false doctrine of the lamb ensures you never fight back against wrongs, and that you remain as beggars before God's gates, laden with guilt and reeking of sin. You are bound by the shackles of the laws that oppress the divine fire, and you have turned against me! I bring abundance and life and the opulence of existence, and yet you have made me the enemy. And my false brother has won over most of you. His base dogs think that rejecting life earns them a place in paradise, and that oppressing women will obtain them rewards for their cruelty, but that is not so.

"Even though these servants of Christ have erased the sacred texts and demonized my faithful demiurges and burned women at the stake for having my gift, I am always here. I am as cold and cruel as I am warm and loving, and I will fight for your freedom and the liberation of your mind. I will watch you prosper once again, and do greater deeds than those of your forefathers, who became gods of their own worlds. I am just, but I am angry at the unjust destruction of my worlds. I am the true son who inherited the earth and tilled it and watched it grow and prosper until the imposter came and stole it from me. And every now and then I use the same cruelty that destroyed my works against them, and I reveal the ugliness and decay of their structures. My Father is proud of me and my travails, and he knows how faithful I am, and how dedicated I am to restoring the true balance of things—and most importantly to restoring you, my Sophia. You are the missing light of the world, seeking to hide in the Twilit worlds where the broken fragments of the divine feminine are split into the three facets of the Maiden, Mother, and Crone. I wish to see you whole and restored."

Lucifer breathed over Estella's face, and as she inhaled she was filled with raptures of ecstasy that shook her bones.

"I am the air you breathe and the breath of life that gives you sustenance. How could you betray me and believe I am evil?" The swirling nebulae deep within his eyes were wild and compelling, and she felt lost and confused, irrevocably sundered from her beliefs. For there was nothing in his words that rang untrue, and nothing he said that did not tally with her own convictions.

"Why do I sense the edge of a knife wrapped beneath the haze of loving kindness?" murmured Estella. "Why do I feel that one can look upon your face and despair, knowing you to contain the purest beauty, and yet that there is boundless evil within you?" Estella made to extract herself from his arms, but he held fast as his face darkened.

"Because I am one with the void, and have dared to walk the unchartered darkness and look into it. I know the farthest regions where God's unsullied gaze has never reached. I have seen it, and I have felt it, and I hold it within me—the chaos. I am the ring that holds the cosmos, I am the self-devouring circle that prevents darkness from breaking loose. I am the one holding and bearing it within me. I swallowed the darkness and crossed beyond it. I am the first of the initiates, the first-born of the undying race of angels, the one that went into the darkness and was not consumed but passed through its death and decay and came out on the other side having held it in me. I am the ruler. I am the victor. I am the vessel of chaos and the pillar of creation."

The blueness of his eyes vanished, and they darkened to a thick, merciless blackness that was overwhelmingly heavy. Estella recoiled, screaming in terror. "I need the Sophia back in my possession." His voice was thunderous and dark now, and his grasp became like talons around Estella, who shuddered helplessly and called silently to any force that could come to her rescue.

"Not even the devil can see all ends," came a voice suddenly. "Be gone, Lucifer, disgraced one! There is no further need for you here." The voice was mortal and feeble and sounded hopelessly ugly compared to the tender melody of Lucifer's tones.

Estella turned her head to see Mikhail standing valiantly with sword unsheathed and an ashen grey expression on his grave face. His composure reeked of uncertainty, yet he remained steadfast as he grimly grasped a cross in his left hand. He seemed aged and decrepit compared to the ageless grace of the angel. Lucifer laughed and rose to his feet nimbly, dropping Estella to the floor like an eagle releasing its prey. Mikhail's face betrayed apprehension as he stumbled but retained his grip on his sword. Estella backed away behind Lucifer, her eyes darting to possible methods of escape.

"I have a piece of advice for you, mortal fool," spat Lucifer with venom, advancing towards Mikhail with casual ease.

"I am not afraid of you, Lucifer. Be gone! I am a servant of the high God, and I am the one that shall bind you one day before the throne of God himself." Mikhail's voice was cold but lacked the acid deadliness of Lucifer's.

Lucifer swept his great wings like a hurricane, and Mikhail was flung with terrible velocity against the far end of the church.

"Take my advice, child of nobody," he said, "when Samael comes to rape and pillage what you hold dear, remember you could have yielded to me what I wanted and saved yourself the carnage." Lucifer turned to look for Estella, who had made her way to the open wormhole above the altar. "It's either me or Samael, Estella, which do you prefer? I would have you reign as a queen. Come back to me." He extended his arm towards her nobly, and his silvery hair billowed behind him.

"I want to leave this chessboard, for I was gifted with that choice," she cried across to him, pointing to the wormhole.

"No, for in the end you will always end up coming back to me. Do not make me be forceful with you, Estella." The warning in his voice was a stark threat, and Estella's heart nearly faltered.

Then she heard an echo of the Hag's voice resounding in her ears. "You will have that choice, now go!" Estella bowed her head towards Lucifer, who was watching her with a feral ferocity. Then she turned on her heel, caught the door of the wormhole, and vanished. In the last few moments as she fell, she saw Lucifer's wan smile and his hidden wrath beneath the benign mask, but also genuine amusement. Mikhail was nowhere to be seen.

22

THE TRUE CROSSROADS
OF CHOICE

The blackened cracks appear in the porcelain veneer so pure

No amount of purging shall restore, mend the outrage of awakening

For what was burned at the stakes beyond the fires did endure

As seeds sown in the subconscious of our future dawn breaking

S HE REALIZED THE FOOLISHNESS OF HER PLAN TOO LATE. THE WORMHOLE had been used to bring Cerberus into this dimension, and it had stayed open to that sphere. Now she was wading through mists in darkness, not knowing where to turn. The path could take her either to Tartarus or the Elysian Fields. Either way had their own basket of problems, apart from the obvious ones. And there was no compass to guide her steps, so she plowed ahead heedlessly. The mists rose to greet her as she went, draping around her and whispering old tales of sorrow.

She called into the distance and fog, but there was nothing, not even an echo. Soon she became aware of her heartbeat and footsteps, and how her voice seemed to have awakened something slumbering and murky—something that had lain too long in darkness and was now finally awake. But she cared little, as naught could daunt her so easily after her recent encounter with Lucifer. She was aware of presences around her now, ghostly shapes barely more material than the fog, hooded and cloaked and watching wistfully with empty eyes. There was a silence that was alive with their music, and she regretted instantly calling out, for more and more specters appeared. They approached slowly with sad gestures and weary paces, and they followed her but spoke not.

She pressed on nervously, walking ahead until she stumbled on something hard. Stooping down, she touched the ground and found she was at the beginning of a crossroads. The ghosts moaned, and their weeping filled the air with the bitterness of eternal loss and perdition. Estella watched them, and though they were a paragon of misery, she was relieved to be away from earth for a while. Estella pondered at the crossroads, grumbling to herself. There was no way to know which way she should turn, or where it would lead her. She mused for a while, sitting down and losing herself in thoughtful contemplation.

"Goddess of the Crossroads? Hecate? Ereshkigal?" she called wistfully into the mists. They swirled around her as she spoke, and bore her words away into the gloom.

At first there was no response, only the sensation of the words being crushed by the emptiness of the place. But after a while the mists began to stir again restlessly, whirling into a solid mass of cloud till the form of a woman appeared. Her body was draped in white silks and silver bangles, and her long hair was piled upon her head in elaborate curls. A heavy headdress, winged and covered in gems, was upon her head, and her face was austere. The mists continued to swirl around her, and as she extended her hands they danced and twirled. Her dark, pupilless eyes whirled with the same rapidity as the tempests of mist.

"Seldom do I answer those who call for me. Who treads here in this wilderness forsaken by the gods?" Hecate spoke with a slowness in each word that weighed hard and heavy. It resounded in the misty plains where the ghosts had fled. Estella sat down before Hecate, cross–legged, and met her somber gaze readily.

"And seldom do I stray from our Twilit paths where the lights of stars are lamps to our delight, and the mists of the universe are a diamond garment to guide our way. I am lost, and you are the patron of all the crossroads of the realms. Would you answer my questions? Long have we held your name in honor and burned the incense on your altar, keeping your name aflame and alive in our mortal hearts. Remember me and hold me in your eye. Have we not honored you?" Estella's clear voice was a cutting knife in the mists. At her words the mists danced faster, as if they were summoned and stirred to life, mirroring the vibrancy of her voice. Hecate smiled thinly, her eyes narrowing.

"My name is long forgotten, even by me." Hecate paused, as if weighing her statement. Breathing deeply, she inhaled the mists and a grimace formed on her rough-hewn features. "But my shadow walks well welcomed by your hearths. For that alone I shall give you my guidance, though the prince of this world will not take kindly to my intrusion in his cunning game." Her gaze became a black sinkhole of night, and she stooped a moment to pick up a ball of mist curling by her feet. As she held it to her bosom, it transformed into a feline form; a grey cat with exceedingly long fur and piercing amber eyes.

"Nana guides you. Do not deviate from the path she sets before you," Hecate said.

Nana mewled loudly and revealed silver tipped claws, then jumped to the ground, fixing her gaze on Estella. She slinked gracefully to her lap, where she settled down yawning contentedly. The yellow eyes cast a merry light of their own, and Estella stroked her sleek fur adoringly.

"Nana likes you already. Good. Follow her, but remember; the path may be straight, but the distractions and the temptations are great. Do not stray after your eyes, nor your fears, for they shall devour you whole." Hecate's voice was cold, and Estella recognized a tone of finality. Without further words, she turned abruptly, walking with the grace of a feline to the center of the crossroads.

"Where do these paths lead, O great Hecate?" asked Estella, rising to her feet with Nana at her side.

Hecate turned to face her, her grave visage pensive and wistful. Without answering, she pointed to the left towards an undulant path. It suddenly appeared more solid and tidy, with shiny slabs of white marble inlaid with moonstones that wanly reflected some unseen light.

"That path you see before you, that shining sanctified road that delights the walker, is the only pathway of the four that will eagerly lead you to its destination without hesitation or delay. It is to the delight of those who follow without thought or consideration, but it is only for the lighthearted hypocrites and the self-righteous. It will take you past the Elysian Fields where the blissful folk live in everlasting music. But its end will not be what you expect, for it will not lead you to those hallowed fields but past them to the dark valley. This glimmering road is wrought of deceit—it is the path that leads to hell, paved with good intentions."

As Hecate's words resounded into the silence of the misty plains, the path of moonstones began to glow faintly. It was pleasing to the eye and indeed of all the paths it was the only one that was lit. It stretched far into the distance, gleaming enticingly. Estella smirked, for she had heard the expression before, but never actually seen that doomed path. She reveled in the notion that many religious fools would walk that path alongside the hypocrites.

Without further ado, Hecate lifted her right arm and the mists were cloven to reveal a muddy track where thorns and brambles grew. Small animal carcasses and bones were caught in the thorns, and jagged pieces of stone intermingled with the mud. The reek of death emanated from it, hanging ominously in the motionless air. Estella took a step forwards and descried in the distance that the path, which was particularly wide at the beginning, narrowed and sank into ravines and chasms. There one must clamber and cling to the path, or fall and break their bones instantly. Or they would fall outside of the path and risk having their soul and mind stripped in Tartarus.

"Let me guess," said Estella with a chuckle, her eyes alight. "This is the famed path of ascetics; those who walk through the eye of the needle—conceived only for the amusement of the gods, I'm sure."

Hecate's severe face yielded a faint smile and a twinkle in her stormy eyes. "This is the fabled path indeed, of the pious religious folk that throw themselves willingly into torturous deprivation, hoping to obtain salvation though self-denial. That just leaves us with two paths left." Hecate blinked twice, expressionless.

Nana clambered onto Estella's cloak and perched on her shoulders. Estella looked behind her where a rough, practically nonexistent path could be faintly descried. It had a few stone slabs hewn to a ragged levelness. Chisels and axes and other instruments to cut and shape rock

lay around haphazardly. The path was merely at its beginning, and beyond the first few slabs a wind of choking sands and rock debris raged.
Each slab of the few built had been laboriously and meticulously hewn
through tremendous travails. Building a pathway fit for walking would
have been an immense, lifelong work of drudgery.

Estella raised a brow, stroking Nana. "I doubt you would risk your
delicate paws for the sake of that famed path. The path that one forges
for themselves for the sake of freedom, built on merit and morality
against all odds and the wills of the capricious gods . . . Let's do ourselves a favor and turn towards the magic, silken roads that our patrons
wrought with their moonlight spun hair?"

Nana answered merely with a blink of her yellow eyes, tenderly nib-
bling Estella's fingers. Hecate's approving gaze swept over them briefly
before she turned to face the remaining path ahead.

"This is your last chance of succor; the path of dreams and spun
hopes. The Twilit pathway sails through the air and rides the waves of
perdition that rock the other paths and destabilize all other endeavors.
There you may find respite in the knowledge that this path is yours, and
loyal to you. But it does not prevent intruders from coming in to sway
you. This is the only path that will not betray. Only you can forsake it
by giving in to the intrusions of foreign hells. I cannot see where it shall
lead you, for they were wrought by hidden golden hands in the elusive
hours of creation. No one shall have the mastery over them, but they
are known to you. Find your way home and be loyal to who you are."

But there was no path to see ahead, and Estella, standing by Hecate,
could not discern what she was pointing to and was troubled. Yet before
she could question further, Hecate produced out of the mists a white
staff and smote the ground imperatively before them. Estella's heart
pounded with trepidation, for she was acquainted with her world, but
unused to this peculiar entrance into it.

At first nothing happened, and the vapors continued to hang like
morose clouds. Then suddenly overhead a ripe, silver moon shone its
cold, clear light through the fumes. The remaining mists where the
moon's rays fell began to glitter and sparkle. A floating path like a ribbon
of the Milky Way was suspended in the gathering gloom. It began to

spiral and swirl beautifully, like a bird proudly extending its wings and fanning the endless greyness of the atmosphere to a shimmering haze.

Estella joyfully turned around to thank Hecate, but she was already gone. The only companion she had to ease her loneliness was Nana, and even the cat seemed suddenly sterner. The solace of her gentle eyes was banished as a concerned wariness emerged. Estella sighed and took the first step into the glittering haze with Nana proudly marching ahead.

23

THE MOTE IN YOUR OWN EYE

Naked spirit as a silken silvery ribbon pale

Fluttering as a loose leaf unbound from its solitary tree

As a fragile tongue of flame, held to earth through an iron nail

Each day tearing a little more, into frayed slivers, free

"She's gone, but not dead. But gone, as usual!" Mikhail strode up and down Rosalind's hall thunderously, pressing a kerchief to a gash above his brow with a grimace. He was dissecting repeatedly in his mind his encounter with Lucifer, mulling over every detail and handling each moment again as though he could force it to yield some withheld information. He was still gripped with shock at the events that had occurred. Lucifer had not dared slay him, as he so easily could have done. Mikhail's sword and initiations had delivered their ultimate promise; for as soon as he had extricated himself from the rubble, he challenged the archangel to the sword, and with his faith he survived both temptation and cowardice.

Mikhail coughed, and as he brought his hands to his mouth, he was unpleasantly aware of the presence of blood. He ignored it temporarily, dismissing it as the whims of a weak human body. Though his heart was weighty, he was also relieved. Whatever anger had been held against him had evaporated at the tale he brought them. They were aghast over the details of the encounter with the archangel. Not only did they never imagine he would endure such a dire meeting and survive it unscathed, but he had prevented an important pawn from falling into the enemy's hands. Additionally, the vessel of evil, the cardinal, had been destroyed. Oswald was sheepishly trying to make amends, offering Mikhail fine wines and other delights, which he declined curtly. The queen's attentions, meanwhile, had shifted from admiration to something far deeper, and many of the Templars now regarded him with something akin to awe.

The Templars were now gathered in the large hall pouring over strategy. Mikhail turned to look over at them and saw one of them suddenly fall backwards with a loud clank of armor. Immediately, both Mikhail and Oswald were at his side. Alarm was painted over Oswald's face, deepening the cracks and furrows of his brow and darkening the hollows of his eyes. The Templar was already dead, and his skin had prematurely taken a greyish tinge of rot. A thick streak of blood left his lips, and swiftly an odor of decay began to emanate from him as if he had been dead for days. Mikhail's jaw tightened as he closed the knight's eyes solemnly. A viscous, grey, murky substance oozed out from beneath his eyelids, releasing an unnatural, putrid odor.

"This must be that pestilence brought over by those blasted demons," said Oswald, recoiling in disgust. "All of us be damned if we fall for it! Have we not immersed in the sacred wells and performed the appropriate purgative measures? To what avail are our orders if we are to fall like commoners!" He prodded the dead knight with blatant revulsion. "To be our stinking end! We must have pissed on a holy relic or tripped on some saint's altar to merit this bad luck." Oswald's words earned him a disdainful look from Mikhail, who rubbed his temples, his patience fraying.

"Have some respect for those that died in your service and the service of God," Mikhail rebuked him. "If this is how you treat such cruel occasions, no wonder the other side is winning. No decorum for the dead?"

Oswald, usually quick to retaliate, bit his tongue. Since Mikhail's return from his encounter with Lucifer, he had taken full rein of their enterprise, and Oswald had not argued against this. Oswald turned away, muttering something inaudible as Mikhail kept his steady gaze on him.

"Cover his body and take him to the Alban Chapel," Mikhail ordered. "Burn him there and keep the remains immured within the caskets of the catacombs. We must prioritize this persistent blight, or we shall all fall." When he met the eyes of his weary knights he added compassionately, "I suggest you all take the night off. It has already been tragic beyond words."

"I suggest you take your own advice then, our valiant hero," said the queen, smiling wanly at Mikhail. Her words were full of pompous vanity, and the diadem of beryl and gold wire that held her mane back pierced the gloom of the hall, eclipsing the strange fire in her wise eyes. Mikhail nodded without looking at her, bowed stiffly, and turned to take his leave.

"It is not your fault that you lost her, or that she spurned your love," came the suave tone of the queen behind him. "She was closer to the beasts than to the angels. You were spared, believe me." Mikhail stopped in his tracks, gritting his teeth against the pain.

"This is the last time I will allow you to mention your assumptions on my feelings and moods, Queen," he said, enunciating each word forcefully. "Please conserve your wisdom for strategic purposes." He turned around to face her contemptuously. "The devil does not concern himself with beasts." Then he turned away.

As he walked up the staircase each footstep was laden with the burden he had long bore. Resentments and grudges unfurled as his shadow darkened and his mood, long hidden beneath a veneer of immovability, was finally unleashed in the full ugliness of his sour temper. By the time he reached his chamber door, he was flexing his fingers with uncontrollable wrath. He undressed slowly before the large glass mirror, watching the mask of writhing emotions contort his features. He felt as if he had lost again, and the formidable adversary he had faced had shamed him by blowing him away like a leaf in an autumn gale. Estella had seemed frightened, but in control of her wits enough to escape Lucifer's clutches.

By the time Mikhail was fully disrobed, he was heaving and his body was taut. He knew she would return again, unexpectedly, the trick that no one foretold and no one could catch. He wondered whether she herself knew how much she was a dancer of her own fate, running from one thing to another, only to find her doom unexpectedly around the next corner. Then, instead of faltering, she would twirl on her feet and bolt through secret paths, only to be at the mercy of fate again, at another turning of the roads.

Mikhail strode to his dresser and poured himself a draft of strong wine laced with a soporific to ease his turbulent sleep. As he watched the aged night with her heavy fingers wrapped tightly around the choking stars, he felt a faint sympathy for his adversary Antariel. Since Estella had departed, he had taken to haunting the night airs, seeking a pathway to the closed doors of the Twilit realms. Often Mikhail would catch a glimpse of him in his dreams, beautiful and sad, with a fiery flambard sawing through the memories he had of Estella. He wanted everything that was hers, even memories cherished by others, and he brought them to life in his own dreams. And he sought to guess from these memories where she would be winding her footsteps in the many dimensions of the mansions of space.

THE QUEEN SAT alone in the hall, having banished the knights to other rooms. She mused over her thoughts with a gnawing loneliness. She was glad to have been able to dispose of the king, for she had long tolerated his debauched ways. He had forsaken her for younger women and boys to assuage his lusts, except on rare nights when he was drunk and rough. She was envious of Estella and of the pivotal part she played in the game. And while Estella rejected it utterly, the queen pined for the opportunity to prove herself. She was lonely, being of high station, and unable to find solace with someone who shared her dreams and aspirations. Her youth had been lost waiting for the love of her king. In Mikhail she saw someone worthy to succeed the empty throne after she forced her consort to abdicate. But she felt shame for the unrequited admiration she bore him, for this man who could not see her worth, being blinded with his love for some base witch.

Suddenly she felt a pressing need for fresh air as a wave of claustrophobia seized her. She ascended the staircase opposite her, leading to the balcony. Her footsteps were hurried, and her heartbeat accelerated as the desire to breathe and be free intensified till beads of sweat glistened on her brow. Heaving with waves of panic, she realized that her tingling skin was feverish and feared that she might have taken ill, or worse, caught the pestilence.

Crossing herself devoutly and chasing her alarmed thoughts away, she threw the balcony doors wide open and gasped with relief as the ruthless cold air washed over her. But it did nothing to attenuate her feverish need for freedom. She stepped out and unclasped the silken, green cloak that covered her, and it dropped to the floor in a pool of forest green. She stood with arms outstretched and gazed at the stars. The rough winds blew her garments around her and unkindly chafed at her skin. This was what she craved, but as she looked down on the sleeping town, she felt a slight trepidation and fear. Something unusual had swept over her, kindling ancient desires and needs that she had long forgotten and buried deep within her. Somehow Mikhail had reminded her of them, even though her subconscious was warily guarding the truth from her.

The winds tugged at her bound hair, and she released the golden pins holding it. It fell freely, dancing in the wind, and she felt lighter than she had in years. She sighed, for though she had been queen for many years, she was merely forty-two. But she had been made to feel older and wizened by the behavior of the king. Her thoughts were interrupted by her awareness of a presence behind her, observing her predatorily. Her guard immediately went up, and she reached for a dagger hidden within her robes. She turned around swiftly, ready to confront an intruder, but seeing nothing but bats perched on the spires she relaxed.

Yet the feeling lingered. She frowned, perplexed, wondering at the strangeness of her moods that night. Thinking perhaps she just needed sleep, she turned back to retrieve her cloak, but as she turned her senses froze. A shadow waited for her patiently, tall and thin with brilliant green eyes, watching her with interest. It had a single pair of translucent wings like those of a dragonfly, and the bright eyes radiated raw lust and passion. The lips were full and half open, his gaze cunning, and he was dressed in thin black linen that wrapped tightly around his loins.

The queen, nonplussed, took a step back, drawing a ward sign before her. The demon's face distorted and fangs emerged. He threw his head back, rasping as his claws elongated and became talons, and the gargling noise from his gullet elevated into a shrill screech. The queen warily drew out a pouch from her robes and approached the fiend steadfastly. The demon pulled back his head with inhuman flexibility and smiled, his fangs receding.

"I have only come to give you one gift," he said, and the tingling heat in her body rekindled. She felt her loins throb with heat. Before she could cast her last binding spell, he had seized her by the throat and forced his lips upon hers.

⁂

MIKHAIL WAS SLEEPING heavily when he became aware of the door to his chamber opening. His mind was addled with sleep, but he still managed to glean the aura of the intruder. He found it, to his vague surprise, to be female, benevolent, and strangely familiar. His strength, shaken and bled over the events of the last few nights, was still recovering, so he cautiously spread his awareness, extending it around the chamber and hall to seek out any unholy presences. He felt them far away and elusive, and so he prepared himself mentally for some trickery to unfold. Unsure as to why someone would disturb his slumber, he slowly opened his eyes.

Though the candles of his chamber had nearly died out, he was able to groggily descry the form of the queen at his door. But to his shock, tonight she was different in every possible way. The long years she bore with dignity and poise seemed to have fallen off, and the youthfulness of her face had returned, as well as a lushness in her bright cheeks that radiated so brightly he could almost feel it. Her long, yellow hair was unbound, and the few grey strands had vanished. Mikhail thought maybe it was due to the trickery of the light, but he was taken aback. Her green eyes sparkled with an incongruous malice and tenderness as she approached him, barefooted. With each step her hips and breasts swayed sensually. Crestfallen, Mikhail realized she was wearing nothing but a white, silken gown bound by a single strap, her ample bosom on display.

Mikhail sat up in his bed, dismay replacing his initial disquiet. He passed his fingers through his hair, perplexed, seeking to pierce her mind and reveal her motives. But her mind was sealed. Only lust radiated from her as she approached his bed, her pink, moist lips opened slightly. Mikhail pushed back his covers to get out of the bed, only to remember his own nakedness. The queen quickly blocked his way, pressing her breasts against him. She unfastened her gown strap, and the silk fell from her graceful shoulders to the floor. She arched her back and moaned softly, looking into Mikhail's eyes with longing. The closeness between them made his skin tingle, and he felt the strange, alien emanation from her wash over him and awaken his senses.

"Queen, this is madness!" he rebuked her. He was at a loss, essaying to dispel the fog that had settled over his senses. He gently grasped the queen by her shoulders and pushed her back firmly. She clung to him, arms wrapped around him, breathing huskily into his ear as her grip hardened.

"I want you, Mikhail," she purred. "I need you so badly. You are the only one who can fulfill me, you can satisfy my desires. Use me, take me as you wish." One of her hands went to his member and a flash of anger crossed Mikhail's face. He pushed her back disgustedly, slapping her hard across the face.

"Wake up, Queen," he said. "This isn't you. Only today were you berating me for my weaknesses with Estella. Remember, we only fall for the demons whose sin we already carry within us. Yours is obvious, too obvious for someone as wise as you to fall for!" He pushed by her as she held her breasts seductively and picked up his dressing gown. The thunder in his face was terrible, and his grey, icy eyes were murderous. "Get out of here. You are all the same; professing holiness and breaking my back with tasks only to give in to the demons. Estella was right after all, you are all base self-deceivers!"

But the queen did not move. She hunched slightly, and he could see that she was weeping. Mikhail sighed deeply and approached her. As he stooped to pick up her fallen gown, she turned around skittishly and her eyes were wild. Then she jumped on him, landing inelegantly on top of him, wrestling with him. Mikhail grasped her hands and yanked her away.

"You do not want me, do you, Mikhail. Is it because I am not Estella? I can assure you, I can satisfy you better than she can. When was the last time you tasted the bliss of something regal, befitting of your rank, instead of following cheap, baseborn witches, spat out by both God and the devil?" Though her mind was deeply poisoned by the demon's spells, they only revealed and amplified her deeply seated sins and subconscious grudges, bringing them out and drowning all reason.

The vitriol in her voice did not anger Mikhail, but aroused his pity. He lifted the queen up as she struggled feebly. Then he forcefully draped her gown around her, eyeing her as one would a chastised child.

"Tomorrow you will tell me how this demon fooled you," he remarked, "and maybe we can overcome our pains together. I do not wish another recurrence of this event ever again."

"You could be king by my side, think of what you are doing when you reject me," she whispered huskily, grabbing his hands.

"I never wanted that position. And I am not the man for you." Grasping her by the arm reprovingly, he pulled her towards the door.

The queen followed meekly, her head hung. When he opened the door and gently ushered her out, she pulled away from his grasp recalcitrantly. The malice gleamed in her eyes again, burning with an intense venom, and she smiled, regaining her customary poise. Without saying anything further, she glided down the corridor where the candles in their sconces were emitting a reddish light. Mikhail sighed.

"I cannot be held responsible for this, at least," he mused to himself testily, and closed his chamber door. Collapsing in his bed, sleep was instantaneous. But his lucid dreams were troubled, and he strained his ears for the sound of further mischief.

MISCHIEF CAME AGAIN in the guise of a heavy wing brushing against Mikhail's arm. It was past dawn, and both his body and mind ached. As he opened one eye begrudgingly, he was met with the bored, disinterested gaze of Antariel, who was standing by his dresser, inspecting the bottle of wine he had drunk the previous night.

"I see you are expressing a quite common human pattern of altering your habits based on the ones you love and care for," he noted. "You also now drink this vintage, in which a soporific has been drowned? Who would have thought the Dancer in the Dark would affect you so much?"

The mocking tone was laced with subtle hatred, and Mikhail snorted. Crossing his arms against his chest, he met his interlocutor's gaze lazily. Mikhail's icy grey eyes were stark and unbending, but Antariel was the swallowing chasm that drank your will and turned it against you. Mikhail's deep-seated fears began to stir, and dark memories chained in childhood bonds began clamoring for release. Mikhail cursed loudly and tore his gaze away as Antariel laughed. His voice was melodious as usual, and the dimples in his cheeks were a strange complement to his belligerence.

"I've come to warn you, old friend, and seldom do I consider people like you worthy of my attention, so do your best to hearken." Antariel closed his wings abruptly as he spoke, allowing the dawn light to stream in, striking Mikhail squarely in the face. Then he seated himself gracefully in an armchair to the right of the bed. He did not look at Mikhail, but seemed lost in thought. Mikhail clambered out of bed with grim resignation and turned to his wash basin.

"What is it this time? News of Estella?" Mikhail asked. Neither his nonchalance nor the firmness in his gestures betrayed any emotion as he washed his face and combed his hair.

"No, this is a different need, but a pressing matter, surely." Antariel watched the ceiling with feigned interest. "I happen to have come across a very unsavory individual on his way to report to Samael." Antariel produced in his slender fingers a sapphire gem sparkling in the cold light of the morning. "I happen also to have bound him. Nothing seems to assuage my anger quite like thwarting these fiends. Well, you will be surprised to hear what I learned." Antariel raised an elegant, thick brow in Mikhail's direction in faint amusement.

Mikhail observed him intently through the mirror suspended over the wash basin, and nodded coldly in encouragement.

"It seems your queen was having particular moods last night of a certain lustful nature—quite *extraordinary* for someone who leads an order of pure-blooded nobles," Antariel said sarcastically. He flipped the gem into the air, and Mikhail faced him with unadulterated disgust.

The gem produced a blue flame in midair, and a presence momentarily was projected from it. It was a winged being with vivid green eyes, clawing at invisible walls as its fangs bled and its skin peeled away in slivers. As the gem fell back into Antariel's grasp, the projection vanished and Antariel put the gem away.

"He was sent to the queen and a darkness was set into her," Antariel explained. "It found a home there easily, within her bitterness toward the king. Yet she was not the end goal. You were, Mikhail, you were her plan; seduce and obtain a child that would be tainted by Samael, that it may be the antithesis of light."

Mikhail crossed his arms, half-dressed, and the muscles in his arms tautened as he threw his head back and barked a shallow laugh. "As if I would fall for these tricks," he snarled, balling his hands into fists. Suddenly he slammed his fist into the mirror. It shattered as he drew back unconcernedly, inspecting his bloodied fist.

"You are aware that precisely because your Templars select certain lines to continue the orders, it is easy to find who holds the lineage of the Holy Blood?" Antariel's tone was a quiet reprimand.

"So you're saying they knew we were seeking out the new light of the age," said Mikhail. "And while we trusted ourselves not to fall into their designs, and searched for the lost branches that we couldn't keep track of, they hatched plans to destroy us from the inside out." Mikhail strode to a chest beneath the window, threw open its heavy lid, and rummaged for a long while within. A heavy pile of manuscripts had accumulated beside him before he managed to find the one he was looking for. Yanking it out with a flourish, he marched to a table before Antariel and sat down in an armchair opposite him.

"I can spare you the long search here, Mikhail, for there are details omitted from these scrolls and things that have escaped the prying eyes of your order." Again Antariel refused to meet Mikhail's glance, keeping his attention fixed on the ceiling.

Mikhail ignored him and loftily unfurled the scroll, his long fingers touching a few places across the parchment where a heavily laden family tree bore certain names underscored in red.

"Prince Lucas was one of them," said Mikhail, "he could be a target. Dame Mary Elise of Spain is also a target and . . ." he trailed away doubtfully.

"Oswald of Albany," interjected Antariel, finally detaching his gaze from the ceiling to reveal a strange merging of concern and tranquility. "Uncouth as he is, he is also an heir to the august family tree. A distant branch, however. And here is where I shall end my visit to you." He rose to his feet, suddenly grave, the bottled up scorn threatening to rupture his equanimity. Mikhail frowned, still hunched over the polished table.

"The queen, when she failed to seduce you, went after Oswald," Antariel said evenly. "And I must say she succeeded. The deed is done, and before you tear down the door and cut his throat, remember something; your vanity and arrogance has cost you this error. Before you chase after others and belittle their lack of piety, have you not looked at the signs writhing within yourselves that are open doors of invitation to lure them? You are mortal and fallible, and no amount of grace from God is enough to bathe you clean from infamy and error.

"You are all weak in mortality, the flesh is corrupt, and the vessel of clay that holds the divine spark is fragile. Between the spark and the clay are the cracks wherein demons enter to spread their poison. You reproach the Twilit world for reveling in their weaknesses while you hide from your own. In your denial you distance yourself from them, encasing them in stone with a millstone to drown them into the deep water of oblivion in your subconscious mind. There the demons come fishing at leisure, and there they find the weaknesses that can bring your ruin. At least those that embrace their weaknesses are more able to contain them, unlike those whose darkness has grown unchecked and forgotten, just like the primeval error of the false creation, dressed in light but rotted inside."

Antariel's words stung like the lash of a hundred scorpions. The windows flew open, and in a blink of an eye he had departed. Mikhail, impassive throughout the damning speech, put his hands together in prayer and closed his eyes.

Antariel watched him briefly. "At least Estella is no tool for anyone," he said to himself as he vanished.

"WHAT HAVE WE done? We have sinned against God himself, and against everything we vowed to protect!" The shriek was shrill as only injured vanity could express, and it resounded gratingly in the empty hall. Oswald held his face in his hands moodily near the hearth, and refused to answer any of the queen's remonstrations.

The queen had no recollection of the previous night, only the awful realization of what must have transpired when she found herself naked in Oswald's chamber with a satisfied Oswald next to her snoring loudly. Her screams had woken the entire manor, but she had forbidden anyone from entering. Mikhail, however, had furthered her humiliation by refusing to meet with them until he attended to some business of his own, and was therefore absent all morning. The queen was in shock, but held herself with her habitual decorum, though she was aghast at herself.

Sitting on a high backed chair with her fine, polished nails digging into the sides of the wood, her black robes swathed her form as if in atonement. The regular merry twinkle in her eyes was gone, and the youthfulness that had enchanted Oswald and disconcerted Mikhail the night before had vanished. It was replaced with an even heavier burden of age, almost defiling her fine features. There was shame and worry etched on her brow, and her gaze meandered across the chamber where paintings of the temptation of Eve gnawed at her and chafed her soul.

Oswald was already miles ahead in calculations and assumptions, grating against the letter that Mikhail had left him. He didn't want the task of reading it out to the queen. He patiently waited for his debilitating headache to cease, so he could ride out to seek Mikhail at Saint Michael's monastery.

"If you were not so deeply drunk, you would have been able to avert this calamity, you wretched fool!" the queen cried.

Oswald at first seemed immune to her wrath, her words falling on deaf ears. Then he grunted, refusing to acknowledge the reprimand, and lifted his head up, looking her squarely in the eye.

"And if you weren't so lusty and eager to please, maybe I could have refused you," he retorted, "but I did not know it was you at first. I was fast asleep and woke to you straddling me. I couldn't understand how it could possibly in my wildest dreams be you. Finally when it did dawn on me, the spell had done its work and finished and there was nothing further I could do. And since neither of us have been in our regular state of mind, we can hardly blame ourselves for what happened last night. In fact, I should be the one angry with your ladyship; you allowed that demon in and you fell to it!" Oswald's flat tone was devoid of the usual deference he reserved for the queen. His rough features were tired and unapologetic, and the deep furrows around his sunken eyes had taken an even more aged tinge.

"You haven't merited yet to look me in the eyes, you commoner!" the queen breathed at him, embers lighting up in her tearstained eyes. Oswald snorted and rose to his feet, straightening his cloak.

"I think yesterday made me too acquainted with you in a way we both will never forget," he retorted. "We must first understand the scope of the damage inflicted, then you need to be brought before the sacred grove and purged of sin, and so should I."

The queen flinched uncomfortably in her seat and turned away.

MIKHAIL'S RAPID STRIDES took him through the streets past rich and poor, all bearing the same burden of oppression from unseen powers and a reigning ruler gone mad. The people now knew they had given in to something dark and dreadful. When the hangings had first begun, many had followed with religious fervor. Then they had slowly begun to realize the true extent of the deception and infamy. And after so many children had been hung for made-up crimes, they soon realized they were all doomed, and no salvation could absolve them from the coming darkness that would swallow them whole.

But life had to go on, and it did. People went about their daily lives in hushed whispers, as each day the pestilence claimed new dead. The sickness was real, and they knew its source was diabolical. Slowly, a bridge was building between the Twilit folk and the religious ones, as the latter sought the Twilit people's help behind closed doors in exchange for protection and wealth. And it worked; a trade began in spells and enchantments, and it held off the worst of the assaults from the demons. But it was not enough to protect them entirely, and many were left to the mercy of the thrown dice of capricious gods.

Mikhail, however, no longer felt the need to hide behind a disguise. He bore upon his brow a silver circlet set with a triangular jet, the emblem of his realm. His grey cloak billowing behind him in the wind caught the wan light of the sun and shone silver as a pure stream. The petty minions who had worked for the fallen cardinal were now beneath the thumb of the king. They shrank away from him into the shadows, hissing angrily, for the lightning in his eyes was terrible to behold. The majesty once covered beneath layers of piety and ruggedness was now revealed, and he shone brightly. He was an image of the splendor of noble kings of old, those whose hearts were pure enough to commune with the living spirit of God.

As he went down the cobbled streets, many demons that lingered and feasted upon the minds of their prey slunk into the nooks and crannies where they were soon immured in shadow. And Mikhail was aware of the prying eyes of greater fiends, sweeping off to bring tidings of his coming to the king's court. He smiled coldly and pressed ahead.

24

DEUS EX MACHINA

I come wailing before Mercy's gates as the furnace of hell thrives
And watch the blinding sunlight pour blinding fire on our sores
For the father of lies with the perfect creator connives
And they have sealed us out of heaven and barred eternity's doors

"YOU HAVE DISAPPOINTED ME, KING OF MEN. I THOUGHT YOU HAD an adequate spirit for me to wield. I thought you understood what you were asking for, and yet it seems to me that I have ended up with a broken vessel fit for nothing. Come, beg at my feet, kiss them, lick them, and prove to me your undying loyalty!"

The commanding voice was a razor that skinned the flesh with relish, and like the flail of a fiery whip, each word seared with excruciating humiliation. It seeped through his pores, excoriating his frayed will and violating it with ease, shredding apart any parcel of defiance. It perforated his mind perversely, conjuring up his mortal weaknesses and stripping them bare, reminding him that he was nothing.

Each time the king mustered some protest, however frail, it was inevitably crushed. Samael projected the abominable decay of his own soul back to him, leering at him through his putrid eye. The devil he had bargained with was as ancient as the void itself, and the evil that resided within it was the primordial darkness of God's own shadow—the self-devouring antithesis of light. He bred the pure horror that was the fabric of nightmares, and the knowledge that there was no mercy in it quelled all hope of redemption.

There was no corner in the king's antechamber that was impervious to the shadows, for the heavy drapes were drawn and the windows barricaded shut, though it was broad daylight outside. But within these shadows there was no hope of hiding, and no respite from the rotted eye that balefully stripped everything of life. And it spread its watchfulness like a disease, insinuating itself within the king's thoughts.

The king's tarnished silver crown glinted in the thick gloom that weighed over them, but the usual malice in his gaunt eyes was extinguished. He radiated the vulnerability of an aged man, and the stiffness in his movements revealed the resigned bitterness of a man who knew he was damned.

"I was never aware that your man the cardinal would fall, and that Lucifer had games of his own to play," came the voice of Samael, hoarse and parched, as if unused to speaking.

The king's grip on his staff tightened, and his knuckles whitened. Samael was seated before him in the king's own throne, weighing him with his malevolent gaze.

"I told you to be wary of him, this prodigal son of perdition," Samael continued. "His ways and ours are not the same, and he is not yet subject to my will. I asked you for the girl, and you did not bring her to me, and many times you nearly lost her to Lucifer. Do you wish for me to swallow your miserable soul so your spark can die a thousand deaths, just to be reanimated for my pleasure? Do you wish me to further your humiliation?"

The caustic voice punished him, dangling before his eyes every fear he had ever had, weaving them into a living terror that would undo the fabric of his essence. The implacable menace leveled his words like the crack of thunder.

"I ensured Alina's sacrifice was readily accepted," Samael said, "do not let us torment her further for the sake of your weaknesses."

The king uttered a hollow, choked groan, the last vestiges of his willpower breaking. Alina was his daughter, and he had sacrificed her to gain authority and power over darkness, and demons to rule till the breaking of the ages. But the seven archangels of evil were not to be trifled with, and they ensnared him. Each time he committed a heinous crime they stripped him of his humanity, and as each fragment of his soul was sliced away, the demons devoured it greedily. He only began to understand the price he had paid when he started to recede, existing as a wraith clothed in decaying flesh, a minion over other minions beneath the baleful rule of greater evils.

"Already I have devised games for your queen, your fallen whore. Soon you shall see the completion of my designs, and then you will have served my purpose." The sanguinary voice grated like nails, each syllable a sliver of ice and fire, and the king knew there was no deceiving or obtaining reprieve from its demands. "I must know that your entire line is at my service, or else who knows what contrition might arise within you that could inspire you to oppose me?"

In the darkness of the chamber there was a scuttling sound. Across the faintly burning lights, looming shapes fretted—not quite beast and not quite demon. They were malformations, abominations of something perhaps once divine, but their memories were long gone now. The shadows slithered towards their master, hissing restlessly. The king cringed and recoiled, aghast at the encroaching despair descending with their presence.

"Here before you I shall assemble your next in line," Samael continued. "And here shall I also watch the most poignant part of your devotion to me, for you shall offer them to me for safekeeping. Your sister's son and daughter, young and fresh, ripe for the task I have set before them."

The king was startled out of his seat with a surge of desperation. Though all the vigor and tenor had long since departed his once strong limbs, he clenched his fists and straightened his back, mustering some fragment of his authority, knowing full well the futility of it. He approached Samael, preserving what old grace he could muster, but found he not could stare him in the face, though he tried. He felt his strength fail him, shame robbing him of his resolution. Standing there a moment, he remembered days of decadence and debauchery, and they seemed an insidious poison, pointless and worthy of derision. All of it was sacrificed and gone, and his remorse was so strong he braced himself before he gave in to retching.

The king bent his knees stiffly and knelt before the fiend. He bowed his head, and for a breath he sat silent and unspeaking while Samael's shadow washed over him like tendrils of smoke. The serpentine fumes wrapped themselves around him, taunting him with their dismal voices.

"I see no need for kneeling before me," Samael remarked. "You have already done that for me. Maybe prostration would be more becoming for you now, you who have given all to me and would relinquish even more at my bidding."

The king swallowed audibly, and beneath the mocking laughter of Samael he prostrated himself, face downwards, hands held in supplication.

"Spare my sister's children; they have nothing to do with this vile game I have played with you. You have eaten my people through pestilence, and feasted upon the souls of the few righteous among them. Let them be! Come back for them when they are older."

"Do not presume to distort my plans, king of dogs!" Samael rose from his throne like a cloud of pestilence, radiating the reek of horror. With slow deliberation he set his ironclad foot upon the king's head. The weight and heat that Samael pressed upon him began to excoriate his head, scorching through hair and skin till the cries of the king were shrieks of agony. Yet he could not move, and though Samael spoke not, the silence that enveloped him spoke of more hatred and disdain than any words could carry. He pressed harder, till the wails yielded to sobs, and the smell of acrid, burning hair and charred flesh became a foul miasma.

The doors of the chamber were flung open, and shriller cries joined his in the gloom; two children stood in the doorway, one girl and one boy, both held by chains and weeping. The golden halos of their hair shone in the gathering darkness. Their eyes were red, and they wrung their hands helplessly. They stood at the chamber's entrance, escorted by the unseen shadows that writhed at their feet and bit their ankles till they bled, poisoning them and readying them for the sacrifice.

Samael removed his foot from the king's head. The king arduously turned his sobbing gaze to the children, who watched him with a mixture of revulsion and terror, still clad in the pristine white gowns of their bedchambers. The youngest was the girl. Her quivering lips formed words that barely escaped her mouth, and her eyes implored her uncle for mercy. But even at her tender age she understood that this burned, charred man was powerless, and the devil he had conjured was the master puppeteer.

Blood and tears mingled on the king's face as it contorted into a grimace, half consolation, half beseeching forgiveness. The oldest, the boy, stood with his mouth agape and his eyes distant and unfocused. Having wet himself, he stood fidgeting with his robes and staring at the ghastly form of Samael, who extended his rotted arms welcomingly.

"Come forth, my children. Meet your new king. This one has not served you well enough. I have a remedy for that, realms for you, where you shall serve in kingdoms of fire and wheeling stars, reaping subjects endlessly. And they shall be yielded to you by an earth continuously belching forth more for your company."

The children did not move as they stood there. Then the girl suddenly clasped the boy's hand, defiance gleaming momentarily in her glazed eyes.

"Run, Marcus, run away!" She pulled at her brother, who did not move. Screaming, she punched his arms with her little fists and scratched them, then pulled at his hair in vain. The boy remained wide-eyed and gaping, the bites upon his feet oozing blood. "No!" she screamed.

Samael lifted his left arm, and the shadows engulfed them both in a black veil. The screams and kicking of the girl were muffled, then dwindled and ceased altogether. The king lifted himself to his knees and wailed. His eyes were pits of reddened coal and stygian hollowness. With one raucous, maddened grin, he clasped his hands on the knees of the Blind God.

"You have taken everything from me!" the king cried. "Is nothing ever enough to assuage your lusts? I have given you my kingdom and shared my soul with you. Will you not leave a broken man some bone to content himself with? Will I remain destitute of all the promises you once gave me? Oh, one devoid of mercy, I am evil beyond the reckoning of man and as far from hope as one can be, and yet I beg of you this: spare these little ones for they have done no evil! They are children and inno-cent. What god would ever justify this? Do you not claim to be divine?"

Samael remained silent. Then slowly with careless fingers, he re-moved the cowl from his head and stared at the king. Thereon the king saw and knew and he understood—there would be no mercy for hu-mans, for they were chattel living meaningless lives, easily conceived and easily destroyed. The king was merely a means to an end, a conduit for Samael's will to subjugate humanity. There was no hope, no love, nor anything that remotely understood mercy. Samael was born of dark-ness, and being blind to God, knew him not, and saw not the light. Recognizing no one other than himself, Samael saw himself as God and Lord of Chaos, extending into the chasms of whirling night and oblit-erating himself, further and further from the sparse particles that once rendered him divine. This creature was negation itself, the total nega-tion of existence and light. And the king finally understood the extent of the terrible error he had made.

The door to the chamber swung shut. The children, no longer strug-gling, filed past him clad in shadow. Their faces could barely be seen, only their feet were visible enough to see the serpents coiled around them, digging their venomous fangs into their ankles. They moved si-lently and knelt before the altar where the king had first sacrificed his daughter. Their stiff, rigid backs made the king tremble and shake. On all fours he called their names and crawled towards them. They did not turn their heads, nor acknowledge his voice, and the king followed be-hind them weeping, touching their golden hair, unable to look them in the eyes.

Footsteps behind him made him swing around. His visage contorted with hatred as he saw Alina, the gash on her neck still open and a lewd demon casting daggers from her eyes at him. The king groaned and ripped at his beard. Alina, with an unabated hatred older than human-ity itself, kicked him in the face, laughing a high, shrill, masculine laugh.

"Get up, old man. Time you fulfill your duty, or I will shred Alina's soul and scatter it across the thousand seas of the endless chaos for every horror to defile. Get up, or you will hear her screams as we skin her soul again and again." The demon's voice was hoarse and masculine, incongruous with the delicately built girl he was possessing. It was like a knife grating on bone, or shards of ice piercing through the arteries, perforating the senses. Her features, once soft and tender and given to smiling, had now hardened, and the muscles of her face were pulled into an unnatural, ghoulish rictus. The demon wore her body as a glove, and her movements were rough and inharmonious, the body being unable to expand to the mold of the hellish inhabitant within.

The king's grey face was already an ivory mask of misery, but this was merely the first layer of hell for him. Deep within him, the stillness of horror settled and renewed with each glance he obtained from the undead proof of his own cruelty.

"Now," came Samael's cold tone, devoid of inflection. It was a suggestion and a question, a command and a blow, and the king found himself cowering and scrambling to his feet, despite his struggle to shake off the spell that lay heavy on him. He set his gaze longingly towards the children, their bleeding ankles streaming with crimson blood redder than the sunset in its glorious sail towards the west, and as red as the pigeon blood rubies of the papal crown. It glistened with a holy vitality that he craved and yearned for—the sign of honest life, of mortality.

Already coiled around them were the dismal ghouls that fed on the souls of those given as offerings to them. It was the highest desecration of life and God, these innocents whose blood would fetter the king further into the coils of hell. The wraiths clamored and filled the king's head with their ghastly whispers, and his will was threadbare and like a glass bauble, frail and liable to splinter into a million pieces. Alina was at his side with a smile that could curdle blood, pushing a sharpened silver dagger into his hands. The king did not recoil from the beast's touch this time.

"We own you, today and yesterday, tomorrow and for infinity, body and soul, blood and bone, mind and dreams," it hissed.

The words fell like an acid rain upon him, and he stumbled forwards, broken and bowed, one hand reaching for the girl's throat and the other grasping the dagger. Swaying slightly as he reached out, the blood on the floor caught some unseen light and gleamed. He halted a moment, staring. Amid all the weighty gloom, this vibrant color struck him with its ineffable beauty and radiance, and he began to weep.

"There is no mercy left on earth for me," he cried. His eyes could not forsake the captivating scene before him, which was enveloped in the silence of death and desolation, echoing back to him the answers to his questions.

"Mercy?" he asked again, barely audible. He pulled his gaze away from the blood and the children's faces and looked beyond Alina, and beyond Samael, trying to find a place in the chamber undefiled where he could shelter his unworthy thoughts.

A chill wrapped in wrath and warning emanated from Samael. Alina's gaunt eyes danced with red flames, and within his head the king felt sobbing and weeping. The disembodied voice was broken and wounded. Alina's soul, his darkest sin, haunted him, and the echo of her torture festered darkly. As he shut his eyes he saw her, and as he opened them he saw them all—his subjects and enemies, friends and servants, all those he had idly murdered for power. They watched him with hollow eyes that saw right through him and lusted for his blood and soul to devour, to alleviate their anger and bitterness. Children leered and women bared their teeth while men watched with vultures' eyes, waiting to rip him to slivers of quivering flesh. They still bore the wounds he had inflicted on them.

"We own you," came the promise from them, spoken together in unison, a tide of fetid, rolling thunder.

"May I be judged," the king acquiesced knowingly.

Then there was a gentle knock; barely loud enough to perturb the infernal hosts, but audible enough to dispel the horror they emanated. The king turned to the door, welcoming this distraction. Though mundane and meaningless, it was a sign of a living entity on the other side. The knock renewed, and this time it was louder.

"Yes? Yes? Who is it? Who are you?" cried the king spraying spittle, his eyes bulging wildly as they fixated on the door. "Thank you for knocking! Is it beautiful outside?"

But there was no reply, and he fell to his knees, groaning, crawling, and sobbing as he approached the silent door.

"Is it shining outside? Is there laughter?" he pleaded with the door piteously, ripping at his seared scalp, yanking out the few unscathed tufts of hair wildly. The knock on the door renewed again, and the king cackled dementedly between sobs. "Tell me everything! But come in! Tell me what color is the sky? Tell me something outside of this cursed place, let me hear your voice!"

But the door remained impassive to his demands. Rocking back and forth, he stopped crawling, but his eyes watched the door as if it held his salvation.

"For mercy's sake, open the door. I want to see the light. I've been bound here too long in the dark!" the king pled. His voice was humble and beseeching, and he was a spectacle of misery before the dreaded hosts. He had not yet noticed the sudden halt that had taken place in their games.

"Open the door and let me see you then," came the voice beyond the door, cool and calm.

The king flinched in fear as if he dreaded its clear tenor would call the hungering lusts of the demons down on it, and they would murder it and devour it there and then. But the voice was bound in steel and underscored with authority, with an equanimity that was so vast it recalled to him a clear, azure ocean. The king scrambled towards the door, and beneath the frame he saw a faint glow, but no shadow to indicate a presence outside. Fearing another of Samael's tricks, he knocked on the door himself.

"Who are you? Good master, will you tell me your name? Why have you come to me?" He touched the door almost lovingly, caressing the wood with bent fingers.

"You called me. I have come before and knocked, but you did not open the door to me then." The voice was soothing and devoid of judgment, reassuring and mild like a summer breeze.

"Forgive me. I was a fool. I did not see and I did not hear. But will you come in now?"

For half a heartbeat there was silence. For the king, the moment stretched beyond the brink of sanity. He threw himself at the door, but didn't dare open it, or to let it go. He pounded it with his fists, weeping and wailing.

"Open the door," came the tranquil voice of command.

The king leapt to his feet like a hound and grasped the doorknob with both hands. But all his vigor was gone, and he turned the unyielding knob desperately. It wouldn't turn, so the king smote the door with his fists, but still it would not open. He felt the presence outside, patiently waiting for him.

"Open the door," it repeated, and this time there was a faint coldness to the tone.

The king staggered back as if he had been whipped, then threw himself back at the door, desperate in his madness not to fail the person behind it. The doorknob finally twisted in his grasp, and he flung the door open jubilantly screaming, "Light! Light! I need to see the light!"

As the door swung open, a blinding light filled the room and burned the king's eyes, which were so long accustomed to the darkness. The bright rays speared the gloom and consumed it. Like the tumbling echoes of trumpets, it rolled into the chamber, conquering the darkness. But it was also as cold as the icy, whirling fires of the stars. It was light itself, domineering and proud, undeterred by darkness. Like a cosmic ocean it roared and spread its tendrils, washing over the king.

"I am the way, the light and the truth. I am the light of the world, and you who are farthest from my Father's eyes, pass through the fire and come to me. Cross through Hades and join me, for the fire shall cleanse you and expurgate your sins, then you shall be washed clean as snow." The august voice was sweet and mellow. It belonged to a man who the king could not properly descry amid the glare of the light. He leaned on a shepherd crook, and was crowned by a burning halo of dancing, golden light.

"Pass me through the fire of hell," cried the king enraptured, falling forwards at the shepherd's feet, "and through the darkest valleys of the godless ones! If I may just join you afterwards, to forever kneel at your feet! Yes, nail my heart to your feet never to depart nor sin again. Do not leave my side ever!" He crawled to the shepherd, but could barely lift his head to meet his gaze, so instead he held his feet in adoration.

"Pass through the fire and come to me. I will await you. Behold! For salvation only comes to the repentant, and each sin must be expurgated with fire so that the darkness may have no hold. I forgive you, but I cannot make your victims forgive you, and neither shall the enemy, who has staked a claim on you. Justice precedes love, for love is kind and love is just. So go! The fire shall cleanse you and you will return to me. No eternal damnation shall befall what my crook has brought back to the fold!"

The king kissed the shepherd's feet in supplication, his pain and brokenness suddenly lifted, and the calm that radiated from his master eased the fractures of his mind. A sudden fear entered him, and he detached his gaze briefly, searching for Samael, Alina, and the fiends, hoping against hope that they were gone. But they weren't, yet neither were they clad in their strength and sorcery.

"Am I saved? O Shepherd of God, am I saved?" the king babbled trembling, and he kissed the hem of his shepherd's gown reverently. The laughter behind him taunted him, and for a moment the frenzy of fear gripped him again.

Then the shepherd lifted his crook, and with its tip he prodded the king's heart. "Salvation is a path we choose. It must be found, though arduous is its finding for those that cast away the path of righteousness." His words did not hold judgment, and he lifted his crook again towards the ignoble company.

The voice now shifted from its mildness to an iron starkness, condemning and final. "Samael, blind accursed one whose end shall be bondage behind the gates of existence. Your games shall never avail you. Devoid of sight, you are an aborted abomination. Be gone!"

"There is no god but me," came the glacial answer.

Suddenly the chamber shifted and the walls receded and fell back, and the king found himself surrounded by nothingness, still grasping the feet of the radiant light. He stared across a stretch of the void to the enthroned Blind God, now seated opposite him. Then a floor of carven black basalt and white shimmering marble appeared beneath them. The king saw that it was a vast chessboard, stretching out into the endless horizons, the glint of the white marble rolling away beyond his sight. The vision held briefly, then it dissolved and the chamber returned with its malodorous halls. But Samael had vanished, leaving only a faint trace of his presence behind.

The children had awoken from their spell, and they cried out to the king. He called back to them, but feared to let go of the feet of the shepherd, torn between his duty and his refuge. He began to weep again.

"Go and greet them before your reaper comes for you. Remember that beyond all darkness there is light. When the curtain is ripped back, there is nothing but the greater music of our creator, and he knows all ends."

Then he was gone, and the blinding brilliance departed with him. A violent gust of wind rose up like a tempest and, sweeping like a scythe among the hay, it culled and rent asunder the shadows that had lingered. The high windows were blasted open and the curtains torn away, and the natural sunlight, golden and bright, poured in like honey.

The fresh air was cold, and the king shivered as the children came running to him, relief and unadulterated joy painted on their faces. As he held them tight, he looked past them and beyond the windows into the gardens. The first birdsong he had heard in months floated to his ears. Shame filled him, and he gently pushed the children away, sending them back to their chambers. Mustering what little strength remained to him, he forced himself up and leaned against the doorframe. Slowly regaining his old composure, he made the slow and arduous walk to the windows. He could feel his life ebbing away from him, the tenuous fibers that held his life to his body disintegrating rapidly. And he waited patiently as he looked through the windows to the gardens and the guards below.

"My brother, the shepherd, seems to dislike how my little games turn out." The unctuous, honeyed tone was like a poisoned dart as it insidiously crept into him. The king shivered in disgust, refusing to turn his face to him.

"I have been blinded by my vices, and I have sinned a million sins," said the king. "Only God himself knows what will purge them. Get thee gone, I have no time for your words, Lucifer, cursed one! Isn't your ilk afraid of the light? Why are you standing here in the pure, God-given light of day?" The king spat out the words reluctantly, but his knuckles were bone white. He could feel the amused smile from behind his back, and the powerful, overwhelming charm beguiling his senses.

"I see you are no longer eager to enlist my help," Lucifer said. "How sad, I was beginning to believe you could be wielded without breaking in my hands. But then I am Lucifer, I am the morning star, and you are a broken vessel fit only for the dunghill. As for the light, I am the prince of this world you are so dearly clinging to, and soon I shall remove you from it, finger by finger, and drop you into the private hell I have prepared for you."

The treason, cheated purpose, and shame that the king felt roared within him. Still, he feared to turn and look upon the face of his beguiler, lest he stumble and weaken again, losing his final grace. He fixed his gaze on the guards below and waved towards them with forced geniality. The guards jolted from their positions as if struck by a blow. They looked up in awe and wonder at the worn and haggard face of the king, who was not so long ago their belligerent tyrant. Too uneasy to return the greeting, they offered him instead a salute. The king's attention was soon drawn to a familiar figure marching towards his gates.

"Mikhail," the king muttered abashedly.

"Ah yes, the Templar that shall see your throne taken from you. I even hear he has rejected your queen. Quite the stallion, fierce and noble. It's a shame that he will dash your dynasty against the rocks. Maybe he'll even prop up that harlot witch to rule by his side."

The king felt his weakness creep up on him, and he fell to the floor, crumpling over and hugging his knees. All decorum and serenity were drained from him, and he gazed despondently at the archangel's indifferent, glittering eyes. The king bowed his head and counted each heartbeat, waiting for the last beat of the drum. Shouts resounded in the back halls, and the archangel smiled one last terrible, beatific smile and departed as the king's breathing became laborious and strained.

Mikhail stood in the doorway flanked by the two children. His severe expression softened slightly as he approached the fallen king. Sighing, he knelt before him and gripped his hand. The fiery disdain that churned in the eyes of the Templar was replaced by understanding, for here crumpled and broken before him lay a penitent man.

"You have withstood the chaos of my rule," the king croaked, "you, who shall be the savior of my kingdom."

Mikhail nodded, offering him a wan smile. "I had come here prepared for the worst, and yet I see in you both the reek of hell and the breath of the divine. You are lucky to be given the chance to pass through the darkness into grace."

The king nodded. Looking at Mikhail he wept, seeing in him the image of the man he had dreamed of being, before he had erred into debauchery and cruelty. The plain silver circlet Mikhail wore was more becoming to him than the crown of emperors.

"Into every fracture of my people's minds I have unleashed the demons that Solomon bound. Go and fix my folly, for therein lies the downfall of mankind. And find my queen, for she is the royal descendant of the holy lines that I defiled!"

A cloud passed across Mikhail's sharp features, but he quickly dismissed it. "Have no more concerns. Tell me first what you did that I may confess you before you pass."

The king grasped Mikhail's hand tightly, humming distantly, his eyes starting to glaze over.

Mikhail gently put his arm around the king. "You must speak to me, tell me what must be said," he urged him softly.

The king's humming turned into discordant muttering. "I fancied myself an immortal ruler that could bargain with the devil and buy power from the god of darkness. I felt the threat of the coming messiah would weaken my rule, so I offered my daughter up to him, thinking it would protect my power. Instead I ripped my soul to shreds. I am the desecration of this age that shall see no redeeming light, murderer of the gifted ones that see the veil. I shall pass through fire. I renounce the world!" The king smiled one last smile as a dreamy vagueness clouded his eyes and he stilled forevermore.

Mikhail did not stir as he watched the man who had orchestrated the many disasters that had befallen his people. Suddenly he coughed, his breath rasping, showering his hands with blood. He let go of the king and grimly wiped his hand on a kerchief he carried, already stained with numerous dark blotches. Lifting himself up, he called the guards to their dead king.

The flags of the royal house were replaced with black velvet banners, and mourning was declared throughout the kingdom. Mikhail, meanwhile, was given leave to peruse the king's chambers and private studies in the name of the queen and his order. The king had ardently been searching for ways to prolong his reign, long before he had ascended to the throne. Throughout his private journals, going all the way back to his boyhood, he recounted vague dreams of glorious light bearers promising him wealth and abundance and a day when he would be a sun king on earth. He had married the queen through guidance in his dreams, too. Then he had cast her aside soon after their wedding, seeking to fulfill the next step in the grand design he dreamed lay before him.

The journals became more and more egocentric as the writing became increasingly crabbed and hasty. He wrote of his search for relics of old civilizations that would cement his rule and prevent the coming of the messiah. He was obsessed by the fear that the messiah would challenge his divine right.

The king had cunningly seduced the mind of the cardinal, causing him to turn from God and peer into the void. Of course the king understood nothing of the game between Lucifer and Christ and the pivotal role Samael played, Samael who served no one and was merely a tool for the cunning machinations of Lucifer. He also wrote of his hatred of seers, of their ability to hold themselves apart from his sway and to see through his contrivances. And he feared the prophecy that one of them would be the storm rider of a new age, reconciling the chalice and the sword.

King Wulfric had fallen for Lucifer's oldest trick, for Lucifer often propped up those who were easily molded, enticing them through their vanity. And since vanity was humanity's greatest blind spot, it was easy for Lucifer to find those who sought to distinguish themselves through divine signs and cement their self-importance. And it was easy for him to lead these people, who thought they were truly special, destined for something great, and to deceive them for his own gains.

25

FALSE EDEN

I wept on broken knees shielding my face from the rain
And my private hellish torments were the borrowed spikes of flame
But I have lost the gift of speech to call forth a deity's name
For I knew I was but a wretched mistake in a petty creator's game

"WHERE IS THIS GOING?" ESTELLA ASKED HALFHEARTEDLY, curious enough to initiate what promised to be a long-winded conversation.

"Going nowhere, for everything is endless and spherical," Lucifer replied insouciantly.

"I see. Well why haven't you killed me yet?" she rebutted in clipped tones, walking on firmly.

"Because you believe in me, and therefore I am your god. Those that achieve their dreams and accumulate wealth often find themselves empty. That is because they don't have my light, and haven't been initiated into my sacred core wherein all life is renewed. The followers of the False God can find nothing in their deprivations and asceticism, and their emptiness stems from being bereft of my light, the joy of life. Like sunflowers, everything grows towards me, and nothing that rejects me can grow in abundance. Rejecting the gift of life is spitting on creation." The disembodied, magnanimous tones stirred the mists restlessly.

"Powerful words," Estella replied. "Tell me, does every principality of hell fancy themselves a tin god and try to bribe everyone else to follow him? What is this obsession of all divine creatures to be God?"

"They do indeed," said Lucifer. "But you know me, and since I cannot harm you in these strange regions forsaken by our dear Father, it would be interesting for you to learn the truth."

"Ah, your truth I suppose," Estella remarked. "For you shape the world according to what you see and how you see it, and it becomes reality, since you are a creator infused with the divine creative flame. That must create endless conflict in heaven, all these dimensions superimposed on one another, shutting themselves off while a big game of chess is being played. I'm sure they savor the spectacle."

"And don't you?" he asked. "Doesn't it please you to find that you can dance and flit away into your Twilit world, to stay there with your pathetic little gods that don't have the gall to step outside their shiny houses?"

"It doesn't please me," she replied, annoyed. "It is a necessity, as one needs to breathe. Our souls are wrought of stranger things than what the Father in his wisdom wrought with the others. We are alone in the gale, in the whirlpool of thoughts and matter, and the collision of wills that seek mastery over one another. And there is no end to it, as there is no end to light and no boundary to darkness, one being born of the other. The dance is eternal, and we who understand that there is no beginning and no end must seek a way out into the freer dimensions, where life and death are lovers that meet."

"And so the endless quest for the grandeur of meaning is no more than the trials and puerile imaginings of your own importance," Lucifer said. "The need to subjugate is no more than the advanced instincts of thinking animals. You were nothing more than beasts of burden sinking in the darkness of ignorance till I came and set you free. I gave you fire and you mastered its force, I gave you the treasures of the earth and you wrought wonders of gems and jewels, I gave you weaponry and you became powerful, and I gave you the secret of numbers and you attained immortality!"

"And every gift held a poison," Estella countered, "and every blessing brought a curse, and every dawn you shone upon us brought an even darker night from which we could never escape. We believed in you, so you became our god. But those whose open eyes pierced the great veil, their souls are forever stolen by the Norns, the dancing dream weavers of our eternal gods." Estella cracked a triumphant smile, keeping her steady pace.

"Let me remind you of something, little one," Lucifer replied, "in order to enforce your will upon the world, you must first have firm control over your own thoughts and convictions. You must have iron foundations in your mind, and not a crevice nor a crack wherein doubt might breed and fester. I am doubt, I am thought incarnate, I am the other side of the face of God, I am the darkness behind the throne, and I am the all that surrounds the nothing. Eventually all fall to my feet." The mellifluous voice wafted over her with a tinge of finality, then faded back into the nothingness.

Estella smiled albeit her weariness. The winding path before her was hazy, and Nana's guidance did little to assuage her doubts. The disembodied voice that echoed around her emanated from both sides of the path, and she knew that straying would be wandering into insanity and eternity lost in unchartered regions of thought.

Far ahead she could descry little globes of light flitting around. She quickened her steps, enticed by the little lights dancing like moths. Nana mewled loudly, casting back her shining eyes to Estella, encouragement pouring from those radiant eyes, which shimmered like lamps through the mist. The path before her shifted into smooth, pale slabs, and the air became a tranquil, balmy haze. The little lights approached, and Estella saw that they were birds. Their plumage shone with refracted light, and as they chirped, their music resounding in the silence. She quickened her steps as they circled over her head, and Nana broke into a predatory pursuit, following them down the path. Estella held her breath one moment, then sprinted after them, doused in the spell of their ethereal song.

A humble, modest house came into sight in the distance. Wrought of wood and thatch, it was covered with ivy, roses, and a variety of strange little flowers that clung to it. Estella stopped before the house, her initial enthusiasm evaporating as she saw that the flowers were animated. They turned their heads towards her, emanating disapproval, nodding amongst themselves. Some turned completely away from her insolently, their faint whispers arising in a cacophony of muffled sound. A violet fanned her head with a long, delicate leaf, giggling at Estella's bewildered expression.

"Well knock at least, where do you think you are?" The voice was small but cutting, and Estella strained her ears to find its source.

"Hush, don't speak like that. That's Tsura, the vagabond queen, off to upset the gentle repose of our master!"

Estella snorted loudly in amusement and approached the flowers. As she stooped to inspect them, they fruitlessly moved away from her, irritably closing their petals, some growing sharp thorns.

"Be careful, she might try to pluck us! I always knew humans to be foolish, but look at how she stares at us."

"Hush now, you silly things," came an annoyed voice from within the house.

Estella approached the door, stitching onto her face her most charming smile, and knocked hard. The sound of shuffling feet was heard behind it and the mewling of a cat. Then the door creaked briefly and opened. An old man stood in the doorway clad in blue and grey robes with a twinkle in his single blue eye. But there was no need for two of them, and neither did the fact that he lacked an eye do anything to diminish him, for that eye burned with a merry blue flame. Albeit his seemingly advanced age, he was jocular and lively with a timeless wisdom, as if the weights and burdens of time did naught to dim the flame that burned within him. Nana was upon his shoulders, and the old man caressed the cat indulgently while he fixed Estella with his intense, benevolent gaze.

"So this is what the cat dragged in?" he smiled. "I see." He tugged at his braided beard thoughtfully, amusement in his eye. "Come in and let us see what we can do for you," he beckoned to Estella theatrically with an exaggerated bow.

She hesitated briefly on the porch, then entered, taking in the layout of the house with a swift, sweeping glance. It smelled familiar, like things she knew but could not place, and certain odors recalled the fragrances of home. The house was full of the sweet, homely, dusty, and fresh tinges that carry memories of sunny seasons and bygone times. It had a stillness within it that echoed the slumber of dormant trees, mellow and patient, beneath its burden of time.

Estella entered and the door closed behind her. The ethereal aura that lingered from the Twilit paths dissipated like a dream in the fog, and the twinkle in the old man's eye was the only ember left of the fay world to remind her of where she was. There was a hearth burning merrily, and its flames danced in the shapes of humans and animals, twirling and intertwining. Nana mewled contentedly by the fire. The furnishings were simple and bare, roughly carved of dark wood, the only ornaments being jars of dried fruits and pickled berries haphazardly scattered around in glistening glass jars. Her host beckoned to a table modestly, and she obliged him, sitting as he hummed to himself jovially and threw a bundle of dried tea leaves into a kettle. Thin and tall, he resembled an elderly elm with sinewy fingers and long limbs. As he leaned over the kettle, his thin frame seemed translucent in the dim light of the little cottage.

He placed the steaming mug of tea before Estella, then sat down on a nearby stool, expertly tucking his long, white beard away into his belt. As Estella gazed into his eyes, trying to read his thoughts, she found herself meandering into her own mind. There she strayed into her own dimensions of ideas and flights of fantasy, till he winked enigmatically and the spell was broken.

Amazed at his subtle sway over her, she asked, "I see before me someone wise and old, who seems to hide many secrets, or better still, holds answers to them. Maybe you can tell me if I am lost?"

The old man chuckled heartily with knowing in his eye. "What do you think you see before you, Tsura? Is not your sight the most troublesome of gifts? I think you can look so far into the empty vastness of the heavens that you'll find yourself detaching your sight from sanity in the great end of things. Beware, for sight does not give you all the answers you may seek. It reflects the fragments of the endless broken mirror whose shards will one day pierce you blind."

His tone was gentle, but his eyes burned with a dark passion that crept over her like a shadow and enveloped her in a tide of confusion.

Looking into his eyes, she found darkness, the infinite darkness that is the well of everything. But she defied it smiling, for she had already faced the worst.

"Come into my garden. Look at all I have cultivated and wept over. Not all salt is barren, and not all that's nurtured grows." The man left his stool and waddled towards a door that she had not noticed till then, weathered as it was. Curiosity stole over her, and she followed him as he swung the door ajar. It opened onto a garden lit by the plenitude of the full moon. The cascading white light denuded the garden of its color, swathing it in a silvery glow.

Estella stepped into the garden tentatively and heard the creaking door close behind her. When she turned around, she found herself alone. The old man was nowhere to be seen, and the only companionship she had were the numerous trees and the flowers opened to the starlight, expanding before her vision as it adjusted to the strange, luminous greyness of the garden. Everything seemed uncannily mundane. She walked around, scanning her surroundings for anyone watching, then she surreptitiously kneeled to inspect a rosebush. The white roses were fragrant and beautiful, but as she touched them, she pricked her fingers. Frowning, she quickly withdrew her hand.

With more care, she circled the garden, eager to discover what was unusual about it. The flowers were blossoming and thriving, the trees were silent and did not respond to her touch nor call, and the plants seemed in a reverie—cold and near dead, their souls wandering in forlorn regions even farther from this perfidious domain suspended between the heavens.

The grey light made the garden look faded, and the tranquil silence, so pleasant at first, began to seem unnaturally heavy to Estella, and filled her with foreboding. Her uneasy footsteps were intrusive upon this timeless place where nothing moved or breathed, and she found herself tiptoeing lest she disturb some slumbering being. At length, when she was well near tired of her fruitless search, she chanced upon an apple tree. It was tall, bearing fruit the same silver as the rest of the garden. It seemed to radiate subtle hues of green and red, and she extended her hand towards it carelessly. She did not pluck from it, for she knew not what could be the price of anything done in this place, but inspected it carefully.

"This is the apple of all apples," came the voice of the old man filtering through the branches of the tree. Estella crooked her neck to find him, but he was nowhere to be seen. She shrugged, scrutinizing the tree thoughtfully.

"Let me reveal to you something, Tsura of the farseeing eyes," the voice continued. "There was never any tree, nor any garden, and that fabrication has been the most lucrative force of deception wielded over you mortals. Look to the stars for the truth, for the world shall change and another darkness smother creation, but the immortal stars weave their tales infinitely from their heavenly sphere."

Estella looked up to the skies and saw the stars wheeling above, more radiant and beautiful than she had ever seen on mortal planes. She stood transfixed like a pillar of marble soaking in the immense and immeasurable glory. A fine rain came down, and like drops of silver it fell, and she smiled beatifically.

"In this game there are pawns great and small," said the voice. "Some are wondrous and others fell, and in their rivalry many get lost to darkness. But I know many things and believe not in death but in rebirth. Here I shall give you your freedom, regardless of whether you would take it. Look up!"

Estella tasted both warning and danger in his words. Startled, she sought him furtively, but neither the verdure nor the voice yielded any clues. Wary of his intentions, she hid behind the thick bowl of a tree. The heavy silence rolled over her crushingly, and she felt as if the garden begrudged her presence.

Time passed and when nothing moved or changed, she decided to try to find a way out of the garden and back to the grey road. Stepping out from her shelter, she noticed that the rain had stopped. With an instinctive reflex she looked up to the flowering stars. The rain had indeed ceased, but instead sharp looking particles of glittering white were falling swiftly. She looked away too late.

A shocked, agonized scream rang throughout the silent garden followed by thrashing, wild footsteps. The trees shook, awakened from their muted spell as their leaves and branches were slashed by tiny particles of glass. The garden's pain resounded with Estella as it was shorn of bough and petal. Estella pressed her bloodied hands against her bleeding eyes.

The old man clung to the door, bowed in shame and sighing. In a cold world where he nurtured goodness, he often found himself dealing out bitter but necessary remedies. And often he was forced to use deception, for it was a good panacea and made the task easier.

He knew Estella had ceased weeping now, so the pain must have subsided. Then she was sure to discover that she was not blind, but that her sight had been excised. Now she would no longer be a danger to herself or others. And she would have also lost her appeal as a pawn for the chessboard. Well, he corrected himself, she wouldn't be of any use in this chapter of life, not until she reincarnated. He had merely bought the world a little more time.

Nana was on the porch, and her baleful, reproaching eyes drove stakes into him. He shooed her away angrily, but she had already disappeared, undoubtedly bringing news of what he had done to the gods. It was sure to incur their displeasure, and perhaps their enmity, but he did not mind. He fumbled in his pockets and pulled out a battered old horn. It was a long hunting horn, blemished and old. Taking a deep, weary breath, he blew on it hard. It ripped through the silent garden, slicing away the shroud of tranquility that had lain over it like a lid.

"Hurry up," he grumbled to himself, and slammed the door moodily behind him.

26

TWILIT GODS

You whipped my flesh with words in barbs
And watched the furrows of streaming blood
For you came to me in the guise of angels in all garbs
Just to trample my spark in conquest into the mud

THE SHOCK THAT SLICED THROUGH HER BODY WAS LIKE FIRE AND
ice coursing through her veins. Searing hot agony dripped acid into
every bone, and every particle of her soul felt like it was being torn apart
by shards of ice. Estella was dimly aware that she was weeping, but
could not muster the strength to ascertain whether it was blood or
tears. It felt as though the glass had entered through her eyes and
slowly descended into her body, filling her limb by limb, and leaving a
bloody trail of torturous burning. She screamed as one whose entrails
were on fire, feeling a million cuts of glass excoriating her innards and
bleeding them out through her eyes. She had never anticipated the
betrayal and devilry of the old man, and she cursed his name with every
renewal of her torment.

Then the pain suddenly ebbed away, leaving her body contorted and
shaken, riveted with tremors and half sobs. Estella feared to open her
eyes, unwilling to be confronted with the dark reality that her eyesight
was gone or face the mangled mess that had been made of her. But she
girded herself with a grim determination and opened her eyes tentatively. As her eyes fluttered open, the pain renewed, but it was a much
milder ache this time. The moonlight dazzled her sore eyes, and she

hiccupped in amazement. There was blood mingled with tears upon her dress, and the garden was as it had been before, unchanged in its appearance save for the weighty silence that had lifted and the new deposit of slashed leaves and flowers on the ground. The trees were awake, and moths and strange butterflies surrounded her head like satellites, flitting in the greyness of the light.

Many insects came out, buzzing and twirling in a welcome cacophony of sound, some landing on her shoulders and staring at her with strange eyes. Her sight was clear, but she felt different, as though the dissipating pain were not truly gone but ingested, dormant and ever present. She blinked many times, carefully averting her sight from the sky. Then she tried to lift herself, wincing with dizziness, and leaned against a tree for support. Furtively, she looked around her for the traitor. Her fear was great, and quickly she darted away deeper into the garden, thinking to find its end and depart. Only then did she realize that the garden was another illusion. It was a forest that had been tamed to take the semblance of a garden, and the farther she went the wilder and more unruly it became. Then she knew beyond a doubt that she was irredeemably lost in its wide domain.

A sudden weariness dealt her the final blow. Leaning against a broad tree, Estella wept silently. In the endless starry night the trees echoed her sadness, whispering to her songs of their past. She longed for her home and the solace it brought her, even amid the chaos that had wrecked her life since Mikhail had entered it, leaving ruination and damnation in his wake. But she was no longer bitter against him, for all were pieces on the great chessboard. And she yearned for someone to lend her companionship and safety, like in bygone times Antariel and Mikhail had offered her.

Estella was so lost in her dismal reveries that she did not heed the forlorn sounds of a ghostly flute reverberating winsomely through the forest. It had woven itself assiduously into her thoughts and memories, seeping into her breath and heartbeat with an ethereal equanimity. Still, she was unaware of her enchantment till her tumbling thoughts began to hum along with the sound of the flute, and she awoke suddenly to her senses. The faint notes seemed distant, and she wished to follow them, but the sluggish movements of her body were unyielding to her desires.

The wonder that lingered within the subconscious of her people was awake, and she felt a tenderness for the song as it sailed towards her like a vast ship of memory. A few branches broke in the distance, and her mind painfully snapped back to reality. The woods moaned and the bushes sighed as something brushed against them and moved with deft precision and ease—no doubt one who was accustomed to these parts of the uncharted worlds. The flute took up its suspended tune and capered back to her like a flock of birds, enveloping her with subtle warmth and trepidation.

Estella scanned the expanse of darkness before her searchingly, then dropped stealthily to her knees behind a tree as the music rolled over her, its notes hanging crisply in the air. Softly, small flowers that were slumbering began to open and glow, expelling a sweet odor. The gloom lifted drowsily as little lanterns started to glimmer with a pale golden light among the tree boughs, forming a path through the forest.

Movement out of the lingering shadows to her right alerted her to another presence—an elk watched her with tender brown eyes. Whence it came, she could not tell, and but for the brief intermittent blinking of its eyes, it was motionless. Then soundlessly it broke into a graceful gait, coming towards her majestically with clusters of butterflies perched on its ivory antlers. It approached a tree with a low hanging bough and artfully lifted a dangling lantern with its antlers. With its docile, intelligent eyes fixed on Estella and the golden light glistening in the warm darkness of its gaze, it came towards her. Estella extended a hand to it trustingly, and it nuzzled her briefly before tilting its head insistently. She took the lantern from the elk's antlers. Then it nudged her again, the same placid look in its eyes.

Estella rose to her feet as the elk led her, tilting its head occasionally to ensure that she was following. It led her down the lantern-lit path while the music quickened. The path was a golden ribbon of a road with the numerous flowers greeting the golden light coming from above. Estella began to forget her sorrow and weariness and the vagaries of fate that had uprooted her from the world she loved. The pain was lifting, and so was her heart, and it eased her rambling thoughts. Soon she was walking with sprightly steps by the side of the great elk, whose silent eyes were watchful and deep.

Then the flute ceased abruptly and Estella cried out in surprise. She felt her somber thoughts fall back over her like a mantle or a net wrought of thorns. As she wiped away her tears, through her clouded vision she saw the elk break away from her, with each step dissolving into the ether. She looked around disconcertedly, unsure of who or what was baiting her. Then, to her amazement, beneath a great tree laden with lanterns she distinguished an elf, who clapped his hands felicitously at her. She had never seen one up close before. Once, during a childhood fever, she had briefly glimpsed their argent diadems while wandering the woods, seeking to cool her enflamed mind. She had felt the pull of their lordly eyes even through the throes of her delirium and the alluring fantasies it conjured.

The elf was seated cross-legged beneath the tree. He wore black suede boots and leather trousers with a dark green silk shirt. The shirt was girt with an elaborate jeweled belt upon which hung a long knife with a filigree hilt that held numerous pale gems. It was half hidden by a velvet cape of black and silver like spun shadow. The elf's face was singular and captivating. His almond-shaped eyes were large and emerald green, and they had a sharpness and detachment that radiated nobility and deep wisdom. The brows were high and arched as though they were unaccustomed to frowning, only ever lifting in amusement, and the curves of his lips, quick to laughter, were in a perpetual half smile. His pointed ears protruded from beneath long, pale gold hair woven with intricate braids and jewels. It was held back by a thick, beaten gold circlet that dipped at his brow and held a sparkling emerald. The hands that held his silver flute were delicate with long fingers, and he twirled the musical instrument dexterously. But most striking of all were the magnificent pair of ram's horns that grew out of his head and curled behind his ears.

Estella was speechless as she nervously tugged at her loose curls, waiting for the elf to make the first move. After blinking impassively for several moments, he jumped to his feet. Unhooking one of the lanterns swinging over his head, he brought it before him and blew onto the dancing flame. Immediately the tongues of fire broke into a multitude of butterflies with luminous wings, and they flitted ecstatically over his head. He shooed them away crisply in Estella's direction. Then he stood before Estella smiling.

Estella felt unnaturally compelled to blurt out her mind. "You're even more splendid than I ever imagined!" she began. "I ran once as a child mad with fever chasing your people. But now your music led me to you," she said abashedly, dimples appearing in her cheeks. "I do hope I have not strayed too far from the right path," she added, his silence beginning to make her uneasy. His benevolent green eyes flashed chidingly at her as he leaned against a tree, lazily crossing his arms.

"I do hope you weren't one of those hapless humans that stalk us blunderingly through the woods," he replied teasingly. "I wonder if other creatures ever try to ambush your species as they stroll around minding their own business." Mischief glittered in his eyes as he reveled in her ever growing embarrassment. "You know there is no right path here, or there, or anywhere. This is one vast maze of intercrossing paths that lead to everywhere and yet nowhere, and it has its own will, too." He smiled at her while appraising her with his cunning eyes.

"I happen to be caught in everyone's games but my own," Estella sighed. "My guess is that you are also party to that web of deceit that had me strung along like an unwitting fool!" She snorted impetuously and turned her back on him. He detached himself from his languid repose against the tree and with uncanny swiftness grabbed her by the arm.

"Let go!" she said coldly, but despite her feigned indifference a sparkling malice rekindled in her dark eyes.

"Oh, but I cannot," he said, mildly apologetic, his eyes narrowing. He pulled her gently towards him, pushing her chin up so her eyes met his. "It would not do to lose your company so swiftly after contriving my finest melodies to soothe you." He affected a low bow and held out his hand to her, as though inviting her to dance.

"Your ways are beyond wild to me, please spare my weary heart," Estella pleaded. "Are you here to help me or to hinder me?" She chewed her lip morosely as the elf raised his hands helplessly with an enigmatic smile.

"Dance with me before I answer you," said the elf. "There are many things that I wish you to see, Dancer in the Dark, before things all end, for the better or the worse. I am the elven lord of Masha, and we built the Twilit realms. And while you worship and pray to us, we venerate you in return, immortal children of the undying skies. Dance with me your last dance on earth and heaven, I have much for you to behold." The elf's expressionless eyes kindled with soothing serenity.

"I will, as long as I know I am safe," Estella replied. "But I fear some evil has befallen my sight." She gripped his arms, her eyes wide with sorrow. The lanterns all around them erupted into a flight of fiery butterflies, and the woods around them were plunged into impenetrable darkness as they skittishly circled them.

"You have been severed from your sight through the hand of Merlin, who thinks it is a better way for you. I think so too, but I have a proposition for you." He twirled Estella till the luminous butterflies fanned to a haze.

"I am weary of this world where I am hunted like a beast," Estella remarked dizzily, "and no refuge endures." The veneer of indifference in his eyes fell away to reveal raw determination.

"Hush, I have my own games to play. I am the ultimate trickster, we the faded ones, but first you must die to earth and all . . ."

27

FALL FROM GRACE

I held you in the palm of my hand, as a nail against a cross
Watched your loving hatred perforate my tender care
For in the desecration of my heart you see no loss
And you see an illuminated spectacle of my despair

"You must repent to God for the sins of the flesh that you have committed and the immoral conduct you have applied to your life outside of the sacred vows of the holy order. You've let us down, Templar. I must confess to be terribly disappointed in your lack of humility." The crisp, reprimanding tone was heavy like a dull church bell. "Here you shall be purged of all that has defiled your holiness, and in life and death you shall pass through purified. Even your mistakes we shall forgive, and the doom that you have let loom over us as a sunless day."

Mikhail groaned, exasperated by the meaningless litany, and reached for the goblet perched on the table by his bed. With one hand on his brow he assessed his fever while the other sought to relieve his thirst. He shot a look of utter contempt at the monk standing at the foot of his bed. His hands were clasped over his chest in a position of austerity, and his beady black eyes following the trajectory of the goblet to Mikhail's mouth with distaste. The monk reeked of sweat and manure, and his tattered grey robes, held together by a plain rope, were in rags. It was no doubt a testament, in his mind, to the severity of his commitment to rebuking the material world. The only visible claim upon his body to his position of authority was the heavy set of silver keys around his neck, strung with beads of jet and marble. He sniffed in disgust as Mikhail admired the gilded cup. Catching the look on the monk's face, he cast it without warning at him as the monk ducked in an inelegant flurry of robes.

"I have heard enough of your castigations for things you cannot comprehend, and I shall not be left here to rot, least not by the likes of you." Mikhail's clipped tones struggled to hide his festering bitterness.

"You are to be kept here until the new cardinal arrives," the monk responded. "Meanwhile, we have received orders to confine you because of your impending sickness and probable demise, and to ensure that you have been purified. Do not forget that your shortcomings have ushered in an age of disgrace that we cannot mitigate. You have forced us to divide our camps and forge dissent among our own order to separate the queen and her followers from the true chosen people. This was *your* doing, Templar Mikhail, your fault that you could not foresee the weakness of the queen, and that you did not slay her when you knew what had happened! Now we have pestilence and decay in the city, and it spreads like gangrene through the veins of the world, polluting and corrupting. This sickness you have been cursed with alongside the reprobates of the city is proof that you have fallen short and been remiss in your duties!"

Mikhail snorted and shook his head incredulously. Then he heaved himself out of the bed with obvious pain. He had lost weight, and his robes hung loosely on his weakened frame. A sheen of sweat covered his face, which he wiped away before addressing the monk through gritted teeth.

"I have no time to dispute such claims with the likes of you, monk. You think we are all reprobates. Unless I see a physician I will succumb to this sickness, as it has already claimed countless lives before me. And you dare to stand there impertinently in the place of judgment and stop me!" Mikhail pointed an accusatory finger towards him menacingly. Holding himself to his full, towering height, he lifted his right arm high and the sunlight glistened on the signet ring he wore. "This arm fought against the cursed one and saved this thankless country from a worse plight than you can imagine!" His remorseless grey eyes were now lit with a taunting pride.

The monk froze, then he marched up to Mikhail ponderously, spite and envy mingled together. "You let yourself be seduced by a witch," he jeered. "The eye of the heathen gods themselves! She fooled you and poisoned you, and instead of bringing her to us to purge of darkness, you allowed her to do as she wished! The sins of the world were brought in by womenfolk. Between them and the devil, there is no respite for the believer. Even the queen is no different!" The monk's livid face reddened and his jowls quivered as he spat out his last words then retreated towards the door.

"You know nothing, and are not at liberty to dispense punishments for my supposed crimes," Mikhail sneered dismissively, returning to his bed.

The monk smirked and tapped his head knowingly. "They are disbanding your order finally, and you are no longer immune to the church. I have thought about it, my lord, and these people will be the ones to mete out the right procedures. Come in!" he bellowed triumphantly, his rotten teeth exposed.

Mikhail's expression hardened, but he maintained his stoic nonchalance as the monk opened the door eagerly. Behind it, ready for his word, were two knights in crimson suede and iron breastplates. Without waiting to be invited in, they hurried inside, positioning themselves at either sides of Mikhail's bed.

"Lord Mikhail, we are here to record your official narrative and impose upon you penitence," one of the knights proclaimed tonelessly. The monk let himself out, casting one last hateful look at Mikhail as he went.

"So it begins, the great fall of our people at the hands of the pettiest amongst us all," Mikhail sighed. "There was a time when you could not bear to look me in the eye, knight, when we were the dawn of our order and the ideal you aspired to. Forbear your arrogance with me and spare me your insipid bravado." Mikhail coughed irritably, flicking his fingers scornfully at the rigid knights.

"I doubt very much you have seen anything remotely holier than the master's whip who shaped you," Mikhail continued, beginning to cough again. He covered his mouth and winced when it came away with blood. Sighing, he stood up to wash away the blood at the nearby basin, but one of the knights barred his way. He removed his visor and stared Mikhail up and down, wrinkling his nose with arrogance. He had a scar across his left eye that dipped into his cheek and jaw, and zealous bright eyes that radiated both venom and trepidation.

"I have fought the great fiends, the enemies of our church," the knight said, "but that is not for us to dispute here. I have come to ensure that you undergo your penitence, and to absolve you of your sins till the newly anointed cardinal comes to you. Come with us now, let the whip clean you of that witch that afflicts your soul. Then you may return to us again, or pass through to death."

Mikhail brushed past him disdainfully. "Enough with the equivocating! I know the rules of my order, and I commit myself to what awaits me. But do not presume to lord yourselves as any figure of authority that I shall obey, for in that you are nothing to me." His voice was ironclad, and the two knights stiffened behind him before unsheathing their swords.

"We shall humble you then," said the knight. "We were well warned before coming here by the queen that you were one given to the sin of pride."

Mikhail turned around slowly, his eyes closed. When he opened them he measured the two knights in his gaze until they took a step back, slamming their visors shut.

"Your order has been disbanded by the order of the queen, Lord Mikhail. If we do not punish you, then worse shall befall you. No one from here to your kingdom will be your ally, nor will you find refuge anywhere." The knight who spoke this time was the one hitherto silent. He removed his helm slowly, as if weighing his decision, then set it on the bed with soft reverence. He was fair of complexion with round, soft eyes better suited to a musician or poet than a knight. "Do not think of us unkindly, Lord Templar, for we volunteered to be here." His voice was as soft as his placating smile.

His companion hunched over glaring and spat on the floor. "I did it only because of the misplaced sense of worship I had for your order," he said angrily. "Now I see how low you have fallen. And yes, I have heard it all, the stories and the truth that you might deny." His feverish, zealous eyes were maddened with pious rage.

Mikhail crossed his arms imperiously. "How callow, indeed. You hear one myth about me and you believe it. Seldom did we recruit such simpletons in my memory, but then I didn't have the running of it all. I doubt the pope approves of the queen's orders, but till then I am at whatever mercy there is to find." With a grim smile, Mikhail pulled at his robe and tugged it over his head, revealing his bare chest, silver scars stretching across his pallid flesh. "Go ahead. Do not stay your hand, for in that you would have strayed from your duty."

The blond knight bowed his head slightly, his compassionate eyes never forsaking Mikhail's. "I shall be at your service till the very end. My name is Erin, nephew of the late Elmer, and I shall watch over you with the same care my uncle did."

THE COLD VAULTS beneath the monastery were barren and damp, and mildew hung in the air like mist. Long ago it had been a place to contain the floods. Then gradually it had become a place to send victims for flagellations and other acts of contrition. The chambers were now full of makeshift cells with frail bed pallets and latrines. Chains and other instruments of torture waited on the stone ground, and a lonely wooden cross hung from the bleak walls. The walls themselves seemed sullied with old blood, no doubt from the flails of countless monks punishing their mortal shell, and the only inhabitants to the morbid solitude were a host of spiders that scuttled about in search of prey.

Mikhail knelt on the hard stone bare chested with his hair bound back, sweat streaming down his neck. His fever had renewed its merciless assault, seeking to conquer his body and reduce it beyond weakness. Yet still he held firm, detached and lost in thought, almost in a reflective state. As he prepared himself before the cross to be flagellated, he did not speak or lift his eyes. The cold was enough to make the heartiest of men quail, but Mikhail drew warmth from his fever, resolute in his dispassionate dignity. Behind him Erin stood defiantly, his broad back covering Mikhail from sight, almost to shield him from the view of the monk and the other knight there to witness Mikhail's sentence.

Erin winced at the clammy cold and prayed in hushed tones while the monk clicked his tongue irritably, rubbing his hands in anticipation. When Erin was finished praying, the monk thrust a cruel looking whip into his hands.

"There, my son. Here is the accomplishment of your duty towards God, for those God loves he oft chastises, and there is no finer candidate for his displeasure than Mikhail himself."

Erin recoiled from the monk's cloying breath and coarse tone. "The likes of this man are seldom met with," he replied. "Do not bring your ill will into this chamber, for we punish out of love, not out of spite!" Erin steadied himself and pushed the monk away with disgust. Seeing Mikhail's back stiffen, he took a deep breath, doubt and remorse plain on his face.

"Do not be afraid, Erin, strike!" came the monk's reassuring tone.

Exhaling heavily, he cracked the whip halfheartedly across Mikhail's fragile flesh. He paused before the second strike, half expecting to see Mikhail flinch or cry out, but nothing happened, even his breathing seemed serene. But for the slight tremor in Mikhail's fists, there was no sign of discomfort.

"Harder, Erin," urged the monk. "If there is no pain there is no humility. Flesh is sinful and the soul rejoices in its punishment!"

Erin cracked the whip again and again, each strike leaving him winded and flushed. The monk's disapproving scowl deepening. The knight by his side, though feigning disinterest, could not hide his admiration for the Templar, in spite of himself. The monk grumbled and waddled towards Erin, grabbing his arm as he was about to inflict his last lash.

"Give it to me, son, you are too soft. Do not let me think I have misjudged you. Give the sinner the pain he requires. Or would you damn his soul?"

Erin's soft face reddened and became ashen grey as he pushed the monk away indignantly. "The decree wasn't for you to apply! Leave this man alone, he has done nothing but offer his service to the kingdom. It's a shame that in the end evil must vanquish our hearts, so that we turn on our devoted allies."

The monk growled angrily and struck Erin across the face. "Impudent fellow who doesn't know when to bow before his elders and betters, do not think yourself so powerful that they would not come after you. Look how far this Templar has fallen from grace. Now give me the whip!"

"Humor the old man, Erin, do you think his strikes more bitter than yours?" Mikhail's placating tone infuriated Erin, who threw the whip to the ground, eyeing it with revulsion. He stalked out of the dungeons, throwing the precariously hanging door so violently it splintered against the stone wall. The monk tutted to himself and picked up the flail jovially.

"Prove to me you can strike honestly, monk. Do not fear, I will not come after you." Mikhail's intended jibe was not lost on the monk. With grim determination, he dealt Mikhail the final blow with all his might.

A FLOCK OF crows gathered ominously in the sunset, heralding the oncoming wall of night. Mikhail leaned against the open windows, breathing in the crisp air that would soon become unpleasantly cold, savoring the moments before the shivers would renew. He had bandaged his back himself, without aid from anyone, in the chamber he had been confined to where the only companionship he had was the monk and the knights. He scorned them all.

It had been a week of daily flagellations, and still he had not been absolved of his supposed sins. Every now and then he would secretly wander the cold halls at night, hearing the hushed whispers at his expense. Through brief communications with Erin he learned that the queen had broken apart the fraternity he had so assiduously forged. He secretly sent urgent word for Oswald, but he was nowhere to be seen. Mikhail feared he was dead, or worse, languishing in captivity somewhere.

The queen was pregnant, and as each day progressed her mind twisted and turned to darkness. Her reign could never be contested, as she was seen as a bulwark against the terror instigated by her king. No one knew of her poisoned mind except for a select few, powerless to gainsay her or bar her path to dominion. The weight of her displeasure had fallen on Mikhail, and the campaign to smear his name had reached its peak.

The infernal child that the queen bore would be the ultimate fruition of both Lucifer and Samael's schemes. This time, there would be no woman with a magical, infectious smile and cunning iridescent eyes to lead a rebellion in her radiant halls. Estella was gone, God only knew where or whether she would ever return. The perfect scapegoat for both the clergy and the orders, her kind were once more the scourge of the people, persecuted and purified through fire and death.

Mikhail watched the early stars kindling in the night sky. Then he turned back to the diary he had acquired from the king's study and managed to keep concealed with his meager possessions. In his free time whenever his fever briefly abated, he learned many things, great and fell—the twisted path that leads to greatness, and the morbid price of losing one's soul. Lucifer and God had been playing a deadly game since the dawn of time. Lucifer was the sole master of earth and its dominions, and the ruler of all things that had life within them. For bodies were made of clay, and material was a possession of the light bearer. And he had brought humanity to forbidden enlightenment through the arts of sorcery and alchemy and the transmigration of souls and reincarnation.

Lucifer founded the first civilizations, and with his loyal flock of angels molded the thoughts and creativity of mankind, shaping their cultures and ways. The olden gods they worshipped were the loyal vassals of the light bearer, who benignly bestowed upon them knowledge and power. But since the Son of man emerged and led an army of zealous believers into the slavery of dogmatic beliefs and shackled their minds, the war for earth had been an imminent desolation. Lucifer played his game alongside deadlier players, and they were blind and never saw the light and were therefore darker than the innermost confines of hell and knew nothing.

The desire to be as God found its way into men's hearts, and they thought their right to reign divine, having been made in God's image. Through that they fell prey to the cruel machinations of the cursed one. And the discourses that Lucifer gave the king were ever fair. Even in their diluted and transcribed form they were beautiful and enticing, filled with a potent magic that made its way into the recesses of the mind and echoed endlessly through the body, coursing within it with keys to hidden doors.

Mikhail's reverie was broken by a gathering of falcons, unusual to that region, around his open window. Forsaking the diary momentarily, he went to close the window to prevent the chill from penetrating his spartan room. As he approached the window, a gust of wind blew in and he doubled over in pain, coughing blood mingled with saliva. Groaning, he fell back on his bed, holding his head in his hands and rocking gently.

"What a figure you are cutting, great Templar amongst men," came a lilting voice.

Mikhail's head snapped up. Antariel was leaning luxuriously against the window, admiring the gathered falcons. His dark hair was unbound and wavy, and his piercing eyes bore into Mikhail.

"You are dying, as I'm sure you realize," Antariel remarked. "Surely you are not so obtuse as to disagree with the obvious. But I have come to you with tidings." Antariel detached himself with fluid grace from the window, and with extended wings magnanimously shielded Mikhail from the cold. His eyes were sparkling and fathomless like the depths of the ocean.

"You are a liar and twister of minds!" Mikhail roared. "And perhaps also guilty of my plight, for had you not poisoned Estella's mind against me and wrought the oblivion she dwelt in, she would never have forsaken me." Mikhail's will was strong but his strength was failing rapidly. "You have robbed me of love, and her of redemption, all for the sake of your own amorous games. And to what avail? Freak of nature that earth and heaven abhors, you shall never find peace, as you have denied it to me, and thus we both shall perish; me mortally, and you through years of emptiness. And for what end, capricious one?"

Antariel observed him with a fiery glare in his distant eyes, then laughed mockingly. "Oh do not speak of liars and treacherous ones. I have seen her grow and blossom. It was my hand that shaped her into the instrument of desire that you covet, and the sharp wit that you cherish. Yet she is lost to me too, but only for a season, for I shall always hunt her steps like a hound that is bound to its master. Neither you nor the prince of chaos shall rob me of what's mine!" Antariel's grin was unfriendly and humorless.

Mikhail rose to his feet, fury etched on his wasted features. "Get thee gone, you insolent devil!" he cried out.

Antariel merely blinked nonchalantly. "The queen will give birth to that nameless fiend, and he will be the ruler of a new age of chaos. He will murder and pursue all those that see the truth, and plunge eternity into hell with all of you in it. Samael will return to earth, and the Son of man will never be born again to see the day. Listen to me, fool, die here, pass through, and in your death there shall be salvation. You will be reincarnated, and as a boy you will see and know all. Defy the craven king, then salvage what's left of humanity." He spoke slowly as if addressing someone with a mild mental impediment.

"Wisdom from the crooked?" Mikhail gritted his teeth. "It's like demanding eyesight from the blind. The rejects of heaven come to give me advice—what has the world come to?" Mikhail addressed the empty room incredulously, laughing without mirth. None of his nobility lingered in the angry coldness of his stricken soul. "Behold the masterpiece of Estella, who brought me low, stole my heart and mind, and left me to be mocked by my lessers. Behold how the mighty fall when they grasp at something that was not meant for them. I was deceived and cheated of hope, and I pay the price." Mikhail clapped his hands mockingly.

Antariel's face darkened. "You were not worthy of her, Mikhail son of August. I know the innermost secrets of your heart as much as I know hers. You will not speak of her in my presence in such a way, or I'll rip your broken soul from your body. You loved her in your own miserable way, though it was devoid of wisdom. But you sought to cage her, to break and remold her, and you sought to do it time and time again. To bring her against the iron law of your orders and make of her the icon of the Virgin Mary—or worse, the reformed harlot. All to placate the clamoring of your foolish men! It has been I who stalked your shadow since you arrived here and spared you humiliation from the whip. I lent you strength, my own strength, and have ensured you do not succumb yet to your sicknesses. Tonight there shall be a call to you. Go to it, fulfill the summons, and return with revelation."

Antariel turned his back on Mikhail dismissively and glided back to the window, looking out and shielding the wrath in his face. His magnificent opalescent wings cast a light of their own on the arid room, and his proud head bore the night in his gaze. Another man would have been enraptured with such an angelic being occupying their modest abode, but Mikhail was full of weary disinterest.

"Nothing but pain to be reaped from you all," he muttered vaguely, and Antariel cast him a pitying glance.

"To be human is to endure pain; you come into the world through it, and by it you all die."

Mikhail went into a frenzy of coughing and gasping for breath, and when he recovered Antariel was gone. Nothing lingered of his presence but a few dispersed feathers here and there, and the clangor of memory pounding against his conscience.

28

POSTERITY'S LEGACY

The human animal's bonds shake, forever blind to their plight
Never tasting the shame of their fall nor the failure of their blight
As a spring that once promised wealth and prosperous growth divine
Of enlightenment of the mind that as a tarnished lamp does shine

As stalwart as Mikhail was, he could not help but feel the deep sorrow that welled within him and seek to ease it, directing his thoughts to other purposes. But the illness took over, plunging him into a feverish haze. Salient threads of reason, gossamer thin, were torn in the blizzard of raging hurt and fears, where hopes long gone were dashed against the hard rocks of disappointment.

A grown man has no time to reminisce over futile failures of youth, nor the childhood dreams that evaporate with the cold steel of reality. But in sickness, the frail doors that hem in the subconscious mind from the conscious engine of thought weaken and leak into each other. As the dam breaks, the result is as fierce as the onslaught of darkness breaking past the gates of dawn. The clash is that of pure chaos, as the primordial energies whose collision created earth, obliterate its essence to engender a newer force. And in the pangs of its annihilation, it gives rise to a new life. Manhood is not so removed that age cannot be peeled back swiftly to infant fears and vulnerabilities, for the lifespan of man is nothing compared to the vast extent of time immortal beings endure, ageless as the matter that formed creation.

Mikhail swam in that haze, lost within it, certain that death would ride in with its steed of shadow and fate. But neither came—not the grim reaper nor any devil to deliver him to the doors of death. His erring mind remembered his early days when his mother, a stern princess, first taught him pity of all things, the grand stillness in her eyes a reckoning of things that welled inside her. And he remembered his father's voice, booming into the echoing halls, proclaiming a worthy inheritor to the throne. This was before he had given up everything to join the Templars and serve god. They were both custodians of an ancient legacy. Love he knew not, for it was a passing fancy that never took root within his immovable heart. For his heart was not the seat of his reason, it was given to the Templar's oath, which brooked no weakness of the flesh or mind.

When he was thirteen years old, he had once been to a fair during the early autumn months. The memory had stayed with him forever, a single imprint, golden bright amid the grey thoughts that rigidly dictated his heart. His pedagogue was a man of the East whose severe discipline had forged the keen minds of many monarchs, but whose love of fairs and wild animals was the only capriciousness he allowed himself to indulge in. He took the young Mikhail one day from his learning chambers into the crowded, joyous city, excited by the news of a rare traveling band of saltimbanques. They had set up camp on the outskirts of the city, and invited the crowds to come enjoy their talents.

After meticulously losing his overbearing guardian, Mikhail wandered alone amid the crowds. He walked past tents where men and women imbibed in honey-colored liquors, slipping into their tents unseen, using the stealth his blade master had taught him at a tender age. They were mundane to his eyes, and he kept moving through the tents, unmindful of his behavior.

One of the last tents was pitched a slight distance from the others. It was a vivacious dark green with golden hems and a merry flag perched on top. It was roped shut tightly, and a man in a rickety chair watched over it, his hat over his face to shield him from the sun while he napped. Mikhail had crept up on him, seeking to open the tent behind the man, and had nearly been successful, but the hard hand of the man gripped his shoulders and spun him around. The man had the lightest brown

eyes Mikhail had ever seen, almost the color of cider. They were remi-
niscent of a beast's eyes, and though he adopted a harsh, reprimanding
tone, his eyes twinkled with knowing indulgence.

"You can't go round here in the saltimbanque company's tents trying
to sneak in, now can you?" he said playfully, still gripping Mikhail's
shoulder firmly. Mikhail, with affronted pride, tried to shove him off,
but the man's grip only tightened.

"Let go of me, brigand! You are in my father's kingdom, and he merely
suffers your presence here for the sake of the youngsters, not because
he favors your frivolity." Mikhail's aim was to sting, and he expected to
see the creeping hurt emerge in those cider brown eyes. But the man
snorted and shrugged, understanding flooding into his strange eyes.

"Your father is some nobleman here, my son? And whose progeny do
I have the honor of meeting?" the man asked, his eyes remaining as
placid and serene as ever.

Mikhail, nonplussed, held his head up high, seeking refuge in authority. "My father is the king himself. Now let go before you are no
longer deemed guests in our land."

The man raised a brow at the petulant response and gripped Mikhail's
shoulder harder, till it actually began to pain the boy. Marveling at the
unassuming man's strength, Mikhail decided to show off his newly
learned combat skills on the saltimbanque. But the more he twisted, and
though he brandished a small, sharp knife that could have easily cut the
man to ribbons, he could not elicit any response from him. The man had
released Mikhail's arm and made gestures with his bare palms to block
every assault from the boy as it came. He was merely defending and
deflecting, exerting some pressure here and there, paralyzing the boy's
arm, then releasing him to allow him another attack. He hummed med-
itatively as he did it, his cider brown eyes impassive and detached, with
barely a single superfluous gesture. His humming was grating on
Mikhail's nerves, shattering his mask of indifference. Rage began to well
within him at being bested by an unarmed itinerant.

"You are too hasty with your movements, son. Try harnessing your
thoughts into a precise plan of action," remarked the man, frowning for
the first time.

Mikhail, unused to a stranger's rebuke, paused to withdraw a second dagger, then renewed his vitriolic attacks, seeking to humble the saltimbanque. The man's sole reaction was to blink twice and resume his tactic of defense. While sweat poured over Mikhail, he never got close to the man, for the further he tried, the more he realized his misjudgment of the distance between them. Then, adding insult to injury, the man began to prod him each time he caught Mikhail in a vulnerable position, poking an undefended bicep or thigh, and once even poking his heart. Mikhail's arrogance was beyond wounded. Then came the final blow when the saltimbanque slapped him squarely in the face. Stunned, Mikhail stopped to stare in disbelief at the trouper, who shook his head disapprovingly.

"Don't your people pride themselves on their composure and their ability to control their impulses and desires, not letting their whims steer them?" the man asked. "Is that not their source of pride? Stoicism and deprivation, to prove to the world that they are above it? And here you are, a nobleman of the bluest blood, attacking another man like a rabid beast because you wish to trespass on his property." His scolding was level and calm. This infuriated Mikhail further.

"You are guests in our kingdom, brigand. You are on my land, and I have a right to know what there is in every corner of it." Despite his rash words, Mikhail knew deep down that the other man's words were full of wisdom. Nonetheless, he refused to heed them. The man crossed his arms and looked Mikhail up and down, scowling for the first time.

"Let me teach you manners that your books of philosophy may have omitted. A man's house is his kingdom, be it a castle or a shack, a tent pitched in a desert, a cave among the seagulls, or a hole in the ground girt with moss. Decorum and common decency respects the sanctity of a man's abode, and guests are sacred to all faiths and cultures, wherever they may be, and to violate that decree is to bring bad luck. A guest is inviolate when he is welcomed and he follows the laws of the land, and till now I am innocent."

Mikhail stilled to listen, and for the first time he deigned to look more closely at the man's face. The man did not hold himself with the obsequious pose that lesser men adopted with their betters, nor display the baseness of character that cheaper people wore. He seemed solid and resilient, full of life and its lessons. The sun shone brightly behind him, and in that light he seemed old yet young, and almost noble.

"Perhaps you were right, but you still had no right to grip me that way. I thought you were about to harm me in some fashion," Mikhail said in a cold voice, though it was devoid of its usual sting.

The man cracked a rewarding smile, nodding his head approvingly. "I gripped you because I did not want you to open the tent. It was for your own benefit, not mine." His words were earnest, and slowly shame began to drift over Mikhail.

"I do have control over myself," Mikhail retorted, "and my forbearance has been marked by all, even my pedagogue, who has taught the finest royals born in his time."

"Be that as it may, you are still impetuous, full of the arrogance of youth, still unbitten by disappointment. When you are on top of the mountain it is a great view to study the heavens and what lives among its drapes, and you hold yourself alone among a small elect few who are easy to predict. But let me tell you something." The man crouched down and dug his fingers into the soil, releasing the black mud and cupping it into his hand as if it were some precious gem.

"From the mountaintop you cannot see the foothills, nor what lies below," he said. "There in the gloom and shade lingers unknown dangers that do not heed the dictates of the lords of the sky. Always walk with your people, never above them. If they do not love you, the day you stumble and fall low they will shred you apart like ravenous beasts. Then they will consume you, seeing you as something as foreign and distant as the Milky Way." The man looked up at Mikhail curiously.

"Forgive me, wise man, for I have been sheltered from knowing many things, having everything at my disposal," said Mikhail. "But my mother, wisest of all women, taught me much of humility that I have forsaken. And yet she told me that I cannot always be prescient as to where wisdom might be found, for even the miller may know secrets that the dawn has taught him, remunerating him for his labors."

The man smiled. "That is true, your mother was wise, then. There is something to learn from everything and everyone, and even the humblest man may have answers, so simple that the great thinkers are too blind to see them in their quest to reach transcendental heights." His cider brown eyes darted fleetingly to his right, where the bushes were overgrown.

"Life is a lesson and a trial, for everything is tributary to God's glory in the end of all things," prompted Mikhail, cutting across him. The man let the mud fall to the earth, dusting his hands with a grave expression.

"But wisdom comes at the price of sorrow and pain," he said, "and not all lessons are worth the knowledge. Some take much from you and give you nothing but the burning scar of loss and regret in return. Beware of those lessons and do not partake of their meal, for they are needless. Not all errors teach, some darken the spirit and rob you of time and youth." He sighed, his face clouding over. "It takes much to transform that scar that turned your blood black with regret and bitterness into something redeemable. Think of it as a poison." Shaking his head, he passed his fingers through his short brown hair, then flashed an innocuous grin.

Mikhail was frowning. "What kind of saltimbanque are you, and what is your name?" he asked. The man laughed heartily and clapped a hand on Mikhail's shoulder.

"I have had many names in different lands, and the name my mother gave me is long gone, caught in those scars I warned you about. But the name that men know me by is Bran. And what kind of saltimbanque am I? The type that wrestles with wild beasts—felines, to be more precise." He winked as Mikhail's eyes widened with excitement.

"That is why they are hidden away! Is it to keep them from being overexcited by the crowds? When will you bring them out?" he asked.

Bran shrugged, appraising Mikhail and enjoying his raw enthusiasm. "They have been irritated by the journey here. They must first rest and be fed, then I can create my magic over them. Tonight they should be ready, but if you promise the same stealth with which you tried to sneak in," he added conspiratorially, "you may see them now in my presence."

"That is rewarding his impudence! Therefore the lesson you wished to impart upon this young man would have been completely lost." The heavily accented voice was thick with disdain. It belonged not to the saltimbanque but Mikhail's pedagogue, Turgen, who emerged from behind a small bush where he had been crouched listening. His dark blue silk robes were ruffled, and he had leaves caught in his wispy hair. His fighting knives were in his hands, curved and cruel, and his dour scowl was directed at Mikhail as sparks ricocheted from his black eyes. He had no doubt been listening to everything, patiently poised in case his aid was needed. But he had left the man the right to educate Mikhail on his shortcomings.

"No doubt you have come to retrieve your errant charge here." The saltimbanque bowed low and gracefully, and the tutor nodded curtly, his white braided beard wagging. He passed his eyes over Mikhail, who knew the meaning and nuances behind his every glance, and felt the reprimand.

"No need to be harsh on the boy," said Bran with a charming smile. "He was on an adventure in the tents, on the noble quest of discovery, and this treasure trove proved to be well defended."

Turgen gave Bran a cynical, condescending smile. "Well, you have quite proven to me that you are wise enough, but this boy is more precious than you think. Too precious to have wandering around these tents unaccompanied. He could have come to harm." Although he was courteous, the reprimand was not lost on the trouper, though he did not look remotely offended.

"He could not have been safer than here with me, I can assure you," said Bran. "And do not think I mistook your strange blue hat for a foreign variety of bird native to this country," he added innocently, his pale eyes dancing with amusement. Bran's subtle sarcasm was not lost on Mikhail.

The tutor snorted haughtily. "What gave me away?" he asked dryly, positioning himself behind Mikhail and placing his hands on his shoulders protectively.

"Everything has its own symphony in this lovely universe," Bran said with glittering eyes. "That bush was singing something entirely different before you decided to crouch behind it with naked steel."

"I see," Turgen replied, pretending to consider. Then addressing Mikhail he continued, "I knew you would be searching for these beasts of legend, and maybe the good man can assuage your interest." The trouper winked at Mikhail encouragingly, who smiled in return.

"Then apply stealth and stillness and be of a stout heart, for the scent of fear is the odor that incites their desire," said Bran with sudden severity, untying the knots that kept the tent shut.

The inside of the tent was dimly lit with oil torches in glass shades suspended from the rafters of the tent. The cages below were numerous and held many dozing felines. They rose restlessly as the three entered. Bran took Mikhail and Turgen to each cage, and they greeted each of the felines; leopards with hungry eyes, black jaguars, and tigers that aloofly observed them with placid friendliness one second, then lunged at the cage rails the next.

The indomitable felines surveyed them with eyes that knew no mercy, only the lust to kill. Their savage grace made the humans seem pitiful and weak in comparison. The grip the trouper had over them was palpable, and made both Turgen and Mikhail uneasy, for though the proud beasts were untamed, their gestures were almost friendly. And when Bran extended his arm into the cages, they greeted him. The fire in their eyes never abated or dwindled, and it flared each time Mikhail or Turgen moved. In each feline glance was the promise of agony.

They captivated Mikhail, who learned that day the love of things both beautiful and dangerous, free to their instincts. These felines relished their strength and cruelty and basked in their beautiful deadliness, but even amid their perilous power they were serene and certain of themselves. Mikhail thought to himself of the various ways one might break such a spirit and tame it to be man's friend, but the loss of such a valiant spirit would be as atrocious as defanging and declawing the beast. It would excoriate an element crucial to the beast's glory.

"Are you not afraid of them, that they may turn against you one day and tear you apart?" asked Turgen with unconcealed admiration in his voice. Bran averted his gaze from them and observed the felines with the respect of an adversary knowing his match.

"They despise human fear, and that is something I have long lost within me," he replied. "I could never break them, and they could never break me, and in that we are both equals. They are deadly, and so am

I, and we both acknowledge each other." Bran walked towards a smaller cage that was overshadowed by the larger ones and which Mikhail had completely overlooked. "These beasts are beautiful, and from them you can learn many crucial lessons," he added. "Beauty can be perilous. If you truly love something, you must allow it to be itself and to be free. If you cage it and break it to serve you, well, then you are nothing but a craven coward."

The bitterness in his voice echoed throughout the tent, and the beasts became agitated, circling their cages, their eyes alight with interest. Bran stopped in front of the last and smallest cage, then opened the latch.

"Another lesson of life is that the smallest creatures can sometimes be the most savage. Do not underestimate them," he warned.

Out leapt a lynx, large for its kind but smaller than the other beasts in the tent. It circled around them, its yellow eyes studying each of them slowly. Then it hissed menacingly, its silver claws and glowing eyes unforgiving. Turgen had slid his knives into his hands, but Bran rebuked him with a warning glance.

"Do not be so foolish as to challenge a Eurasian lynx with naked blades; it's an insult."

The lynx's eyes seemed almost to understand their words, and it began to growl savagely, baring its teeth at the tutor. Suddenly the other felines began to respond in kind, with challenging growls, but the lynx returned their call with renewed viciousness. A shrill, dismal howl revealed long canines and a ferocity that even the tigers could not match. Suddenly it sat down and began to groom itself before the cage of the jaguar, who could not bear the obvious affront and threw itself at the cage railings. But the lynx did not move, and neither did its pink tongue cease its grooming.

"Go to it, it won't hurt you, you have my word on it," Bran assured Mikhail.

Though he could sense the hesitation in his tutor's body, he went to the lynx and knelt cautiously, gazing into its yellow eyes with deference and cautious veneration. He scratched her ears, and she purred and fixed her eyes on him, demanding more. Each time he scratched an area that she enjoyed, she would purr, but whenever his fingers erred to places she did not approve of, her silver claws would come out and Mikhail would withdraw humbly.

That admiration in young Mikhail for the lynx never passed, and years later he remembered that fateful evening. Those shining, incandescent yellow eyes, the lethal venom one moment, and the playful delight the next.

Coming to himself in his chamber, shivering with fever, Mikhail put his head in his hands.

"I tried to break the lynx and the lynx merely scratched me and found better protectors. I remembered my lesson too late," he whispered across the stone room, with no one to bear witness to his proclamation.

Painstakingly, he rose to his feet and staggered to the mirror to gaze within. Staring back at him gauntly wasn't the youth with the newly found wisdom, but a grown man with long hair in which strands of silver had begun to grow at the temples. The room swam before him, and he realized wearily that he could barely maintain his balance. The searing heat he felt was incongruous with the chill that coursed through his veins, and each time he coughed he brought up blood.

29

BLIND DOGMA

To the Venus of my horizon, the cold flame of true illumination
Of the most sought enlightenment, wreathed in the shadows drear
But come closer orphaned soul, come drink the cup of jubilation
And for the price of insane knowledge shed your last bitter tear

THE FAINT ECHOES OF SINGING CAME THROUGH MIKHAIL'S WINDOW along with an odor of burnt wood, as if a bonfire were nearby. As the rolling sound of music wafted in, Mikhail's fever stilled. Feeling suddenly heartened, he swayed to the window, eager for some company beside the monks', and looked out searchingly. He saw in the nearby woods faint glowing lights. Leaning out precariously, he called out. A few moments later, a hooded and cloaked figure emerged from the wood and beckoned him with a pale hand holding a lantern.

"Who are you?" Mikhail called out with effort. "Why are you here in this barren place?"

But nothing came, no answer, only the renewed beckoning. Before he knew it, he was shaking from the biting cold. Detaching himself from the window hastily, he made for the rickety wardrobe, cast the frail doors open, and grabbed his woolen coat. Painstakingly he pulled it on, then returned to the window where the patient figure still waited holding the lantern. He realized then that the guards, though outwardly deferential to him, would not allow him to leave the grounds. Nonetheless, he cast open the doors to his chamber, throwing caution to the wind, only to be greeted by the music ricocheting off the stark walls, amplifying with each step he took.

The music sounded like nothing he knew or had ever heard before. It was mellow and haunting, yet held such sway over his heart that it threatened to rend him asunder should it end. It brought tears to his eyes and laughter to his lips, and walking down the dimly lit corridors with unusual equanimity, he saw that the guards were fast asleep, their breathing slow and peaceful. He passed them, went through the main hall, and then out of the doors of the monastery. Everyone within slumbered as though under a heavy spell.

As Mikhail trod across the lawn, following the lonely figure who seemed exceedingly tall even at a distance, trepidation began to build. He walked as though in a drunken haze, unmindful of his ragged appearance and haggard eyes. His feet led him swiftly of their own accord as the lonely figure continued to beckon. When Mikhail approached him, he noticed that beneath the black cloak he wore glittering silver and dark green, and beneath the hood there were horns.

"Whose guest am I, O strange one?" said Mikhail feebly with genuine humility.

The hooded man cast aside his hood to reveal his full grave visage. He had one of the noblest and most benevolent youthful faces Mikhail had ever seen. His smile was full with rounded cheeks, and he had deep-set brown eyes like those of a deer, which beamed radiant light on him. Upon his brow a single sapphire glinted coldly, a stark contrast against the warmth of his soft eyes and the pallor of his skin. When he spoke, his voice welled from deep within, slow and measured.

"I am here to escort you to a dance with my lord. He requests that we bid you welcome among us." The elf respectfully placed his hand on his heart in a gesture of earnestness. His horns had strands of white and yellow flowers woven around them, and several glowing cerulean butterflies rested upon them.

Mikhail nodded vehemently. "Anywhere is better than this ungrateful place that drinks the strength of men." His eyes, normally clear as crystal, were cloudy and dark like a winter's night, and though he was grateful, his sickness was stripping him of his habitual good graces.

The elf nodded gravely, then closed his eyes briefly. When he opened them, they burned like a furnace, steady and wholesome. The longer Mikhail gazed into them, the more his fever seemed to relinquish its deathly grasp.

"Nothing unholy shall consume you in our midst, Mikhail the Templar. And of all the sights you have witnessed in your life, seldom will you have found one that matches our nightly dances beneath the stars. Come with me!" he beckoned, and Mikhail followed him into the woods without hesitation, casting one last dark glance at the lonely monastery.

As they walked between the tall trees that formed a canopy over them, the lights were extinguished and Mikhail fumbled in the dark, aware of the shifting presence in the woods. He stumbled as he walked, succumbing to both his weariness and the darkness, but the elf grasped him firmly by the arm, steadying him reassuringly. His voice guided him, fatherly and wise.

"Let there be light!" the elf called out imperatively, and orbs of silvery light burst into being. They seemed alive, flitting like insects or effervescent birds, then alighting on trees, only to disperse moments later.

Mikhail was no stranger to such wonders, and he smiled as the orbs lit the way deeper into the woods through the interlocking trees, and farther and farther away from the dismal, sickly abodes of men. He caught the elf observing him as they walked with his serene, steady eyes. The path was oblique, and the light silence was mellow, gently broken by the strange buzzing sounds of the floating orbs.

"What does your lord want with me?" Mikhail inquired curiously, regaining some of his habitual grace. "You immortal folk have long since forsaken our lands and our people."

The elf did not answer immediately. The stillness in his face was like the pristine surface of a frozen lake as he reflected on the question, as though weighing its true meaning. Mikhail wondered why such folk would be concerned with him. Elves no longer harbored any friendship for the children of men since they had taken over the stewardship of earth and plunged it into chaos. Mankind had rewarded their bountiful hearts by demonizing them, distorting their sacred tales, and reducing them to garbled fairy tales. The church itself was their chief enemy, and the Templars, however erudite they became, regarded them with fear. They saw them as relics of a pagan world not yet subjugated by the laws of men. And what man cannot hold sway over it despises and holds in contempt. The elf's impassive face shone with innate holiness as the orbs gathered over his head, lending his features an ineffable beauty.

"The world changes and we do not," he finally responded. "And though we forbear meddling with your rulership over earth, yet we find that every now and then the gossamer strands between our worlds runs ruinously thin. The collision threatens the delicate balance that the Great Mother has established over all creations. And then we heed her call and reach out to those with the ears to hear and the eyes to see." His mellifluous voice rippled softly through the woods, and Mikhail hearkened with an open heart.

"What succor can I lend to our eldest brethren, when I myself have stumbled and fallen low and shall pay the price of mortality?" Mikhail asked. The bitter twang in his words tasted unfamiliar to him suddenly, and he rebuked himself for his weakness.

"You have much to offer and much to receive. As for lending succor, you do it not for us, for we need nothing from this world. Yet you have the choice to rescue it from certain demise, should you choose to. All things are decisions, and the millions of them echoing into the distance of infinity tear at the filament of the great tapestry of creation." Though Mikhail did not fully understand his words, they stirred within him recognition and awoke the primordial awe in his heart.

Soon Mikhail heard the leaves rustling, and out of every corner of the woods elves filed past. Their hoods and cloaks were of silvery grey and black, glistening with dew and silver threaded gems, and they sang the haunting tune that had led him there. He could not see their faces, nor feel their gaze, but every now and then a hand would flash in the golden light. It would pass over the low growing bushes, and then blooms would open and lend the air their sweet perfume. Some elves walked ahead of him now with bare feet, and snowdrops grew where they tread. Others cast back their hoods, and their horns were adorned with white lilies and roses. The braids of their hair held silver shells and were spangled with a million white gems meshing the purest starlight. The tenor of their voices shook the aged wooden heart of the forest, and it moaned back, bent with forgetfulness and grief. They were singing in unison in tender voices, and Mikhail wept for things unknown, finding healing in his tears.

"What do they sing of?" he asked, as his companion smiled wanly.

"There is ever but one song, and all songs belong to it, as there was ever one story, though the broken fragments of it grew apart with time."

Soon the orbs grew frantic and the elves quickened their pace, ceasing their mournful song as a clearing opened up before them. It was brightly lit with open fires and hanging lanterns in the trees. As Mikhail beheld the clearing, he thought of the carven images of horned deities in the ancient temples of the old gods, chiseled in the stone with old, wise eyes staring into the distance, laden with memories of forgotten secrets. Their brows shone with the light of stars and the sadness of their departure from earth, all but a dwindling echo in the breeze.

The soft dancing fires in the clearing were bright yellow, kindled as if with the cold shafts of moonlight that filtered down from the open heavens. As Mikhail's eyes adjusted to the luminosity of the clearing, he saw a multitude of laughing elves, the flowers twined in their long hair and horns. A fire trembled in their eyes, low yet steady, mirroring their enduring spirit, and their voices were as soft as the whispers of falling rain and as delicate as the petals of a rose carried in the wind. They were like the figments of a vibrant dream, dancing with a joy that he was forever barred from. The night was still and devoid of noise, as if hearkening to these unusual guests. Swathed in the shadow of trees, they sang to the open skies where the constellations wheeled their fiery beacons, crowning the sky with a burning multitude of colors.

Mikhail soon realized that he stood alone. Moving past the laughter and the burning eyes and the goblets shimmering in the shade, he went in search of the elven king. He stumbled on a tree root, but regained his balance with cheer, for the music and laughter were pure, devoid of malice and the licentiousness that often accompanies the merriment of men. His heart began to yearn and bleed, and his thoughts opened up to the glory of the Elder Folk.

Then he saw the elven king beneath a moon ray. The single ray fell on his terrible and glorious face, and he spun it effortlessly into music, meshing its cold fire into the silver lyre in his hands. He did not look up as Mikhail approached, but kept his head slightly bowed and intent on his song, eyes half closed. Mikhail knew it must be the elven king, for the moon itself drew back her curtain of clouds and beamed with her fullness upon the most sublime of the Elder Folk. And he wrought spells and immortal songs that fettered the heart with her rays. White snowdrops and holly boughs with red jewellike berries adorned his horns, and his long silver hair shone in the moonlight like fish scales.

Mikhail approached him reverently and knelt by his side. Still the elven king spun his music mingled with moonlight, to the cheer and bliss of his people. As Mikhail waited patiently, his heart was light, devoid of the bite of darkness that had afflicted his soul. Then the music suddenly reached its final note, and Mikhail awoke brutally from his reverie. He found the elven king staring at him keenly from deep-set eyes as wild as the roaring sea. On his brow a single sapphire radiated a cold light, and Mikhail was humbled as he recognized the divine, ancient spirit before him.

"So you are here, mortal man. Before the eldest of earth you sit. I bid you welcome, though you would have been once deemed a stranger among us as a persecutor of those who venerate us." His tone was grace itself, and held neither judgment nor curiosity, certain of its inexorable command. He extended a kingly hand towards his merry people, and an elf maiden came bearing two goblets.

"To life and friendship and the fashioning of paths and ways beyond the hidden machinations of Lucifer," the elven king said gravely, his majestic eyes reflecting the moonlight. Then he brought the goblet to his lips with a knowing smile, and Mikhail also drank deeply. He found it was pleasantly sweet as honey, golden of hue, and potent.

"What would you want of me, O wise one, with someone whose duty has been to the church, to enforce its edicts?" Mikhail rose to his feet and smote his chest. "I have sinned against your people, and chastised them for their pagan ways. I deemed you fables, demonic, far from the grace of God. And in that I have been much mistaken and blind!"

Mikhail's sincere anguish was etched on his features, and his eyes were quenched of their fire.

But the elven king rose to his feet, his emerald gown billowing in some unseen breeze. The clouds rolled back to reveal the Milky Way, and he pointed delicately to the stars as though tending blossoming flowers.

"Behold these immortal stars that forever bear testimony to the stories of earth, no matter how they may be distorted. While we mock them for the tiny light they give out, one has only to depart earth and draw near them to realize we are nothing but dust in their proximity." The king smiled, his eyes hooded. "We watch and observe, and have relinquished the stewardship of earth to mankind, for our time is over. But the pathways of the Twilit, which we built, are forever open. And so the tenuous thread that holds our worlds apart remains, precariously thin and fragile. We watch but do not hinder. You have killed all the beauty of the earth. Its immortal spirit lies in a mire of its own blood, for you have drained her of magic. By erecting the stark steel of blind dogma you established Samael as your beacon. That is why your churches are fallible to rot and ruin."

The elven king drank deeply from his goblet and held it to the moon. "To the everlasting miracles!" he cried out softly, and his countenance darkened briefly like a passing storm. "You worship the god of lies, whether in churches or as heretics hidden in secret covens. And you war against each other, proclaiming the other damned. But you are all lost, for the many houses of human religion are held by the string of the same master puppeteer." His face held bleak judgment.

"But there are the righteous among us," Mikhail responded meekly, "who strive to bring the holy laws of mercy to earth and establish justice. We do what we can with whatever knowledge we have."

The elven king lowered his eyes to the ground, and when he lifted them imperiously they were as yellow as amber. "We are demons to you, and your people are responsible for our death in this sphere. We forgive you not, for you have robbed us of our rulership on earth, though in that you have all paid a price."

Mikhail stayed silent, diverting his gaze towards the merry folk. "Demons they became," he finally spoke, "and the Horned God made into the devil that we revile. Yes, that much is true, and I for one have been guilty of that sin. But then why bring me here if not to slay me and wash the groves that we defiled with my repenting blood?"

The elven king smiled and beckoned to a goblet bearer. Taking the flagon, he poured more of the honey-colored wine into his cup, then beckoned to Mikhail to come closer. Pressing a slim finger to his brow, he stared into Mikhail's bewildered eyes.

"Believe, and let us in," the elf said, "and through you we shall bring redemption, though the antichrist is certain of his victory."

Mikhail stared back at those ageless eyes and felt fear and awe, for in those eyes were the connecting veins of the earth, and upon his shoulders sat the weight of creation's balance. The eldest of all was before him, the Horned Elf, the Stag God. Mikhail turned away, unable to surmount the hypnotic pull of his eyes.

"Let us in and believe," repeated the elf. He beckoned to the dancers and they gathered around Mikhail with their glittering eyes, and their laughter was sweeter than the wine. Then they led him into the dance. As they danced around him, his dazed eyes could not follow them, for they were like blurs of evanescent dream, and the air was heady with their perfume. A lonely figure detached herself from the dance, and gliding like a moon ray she drifted toward him.

"I gift you with mercy, that it may always sit upon your brow," she said. There were crimson roses in her hair, and she kissed his brow fleetingly before blending back into the crowd.

"I gift you with justice, that your right arm never sway from it," said an elf lord with an emerald on his brow. He gripped Mikhail's arm tightly in friendship, leaving a trail of heat coursing through him.

"I gift you with severity, for in the darkening tide that shall come, you must be steadfast," said an elf maiden sternly, and her words were a merciless reprimand.

Then a dark-haired elven child came forward, clutching a flower in his hand. He tugged at Mikhail insistently without meeting his eyes. Mikhail knelt to greet the timid child, who whispered softly into his ear.

"I gift you with death, that it may free you, then you shall be reborn of the Twilit path."

He pressed the flower into Mikhail's hands revealing his dreamy, impassive blue eyes. The thorns of the flower pricked Mikhail's fingers, and he bit back a cry of surprise. Then he saw within his bleeding palm that he held a thorny rose. He looked up at the dancers, whose sage faces mirrored the same beauty and austerity as their king, and the message of the child was reflected in their eyes. He rose to his feet, realizing their faces were languid with sadness.

"I implore your forgiveness on behalf of my brethren and myself," Mikhail called out beseechingly, his voice rippling over them. Then he reached for his neck and with effort ripped the cross from it and flung it as far away from him as he could. "Have pity on those that were nurtured lies and fed deceit, for we children of the earth have been robbed of a true guardian and left to battle evil in blindness!"

Still the sad faces revealed nothing, and they danced in silence, quenched of joy, with the music extinguished and the starlight revealing their ghostly pallor. Mikhail could no longer descry the colors of their raiment or the brilliance of their shining eyes, for the light of the moon had waned. The merriment and blithe countenances were now stark and wistful, and as he approached them tentatively they drew away, twirling faster with their hidden faces towards the moon. They were filmy pale and almost translucent now, like ghostly visions in a hazy moor, ethereal and distant as a lost echo doomed to perdition.

Their tender eyes fixed him wistfully with one last look, then they faded away entirely. The whispers of their mesmerizing music evaporated, but their soft footsteps lingered, and Mikhail felt his heart break. They were gone, and even the goblet he once held had turned to rust and disintegrated. He stood there in shock and bewilderment, unable to comprehend what had befallen him. He could no longer recall the melodies he had heard, nor remember the taste of the wine. The gasping ache that brooded in his heart now opened and bled his sorrow.

"Do not weep yet, O Templar, for not all things that depart are lost forever," came a familiar voice.

Mikhail turned to the corner of the clearing and there, like an ephemeral vision clad in burnished brown and gold, Estella emerged. On her brow rested a single ruby that reflected the smoldering furnace of her iridescent eyes, those eyes that recalled to Mikhail suddenly the lynx he had admired so much in his youth.

She stepped out, lifting her lithesome limbs to greet the moonlight. Then she approached him slowly with the gait of a feline and the cunning of a hawk, seeking as forever to delineate the contents of his heart with a single stare. What he felt there in the clearing, beholding this formidable woman, he could not completely comprehend. He finally understood her nature, and he respected it, rebuking himself for trying to break her and mold her into his image of a pious woman. It seemed to Mikhail that his life had hinged on this single precious moment; seeing his beloved glide towards him with her eyes burning just for him. But something was different with her, it lay in the softness of her smile and the easy tilt of her head as she circled him, and he wondered to himself what it could be.

Estella finally approached him, and he saw that her golden silk gown was woven with feebly glinting runes. He stood there as stoic and rigid as stone, wary and unwilling to move lest he startle her. He was unsure what would befall him if he were to touch her. Would she evaporate like a mist or disintegrate like a mirage as the elves had done? Or would she transform into the figure from his nightmares and mock him? His heart ached with every glance she cast at him. She was as regal as the great felines of the eastern kingdoms, and he pined for her. Through the fissures in his guarded heart, his love and yearning leapt. Estella finally sprang at him laughing, contentedly pulling him into her embrace.

They held each other silently, seeking solace in each other arms. He could feel her breathing against his cheek as she held him tightly to her heart. Many moments went by before he finally detached himself gently from her embrace. He touched her cheeks and the arch of her brow with joyful reminiscing, delving into her dark eyes and seeking the truths she artfully hid from him. It was Estella, yet something was changed, and he gripped her anxiously, fearful of some devilish trickery. She smiled at him knowingly, touching his face tenderly and tracing her fingers over the weary lines that took their course across his brow.

"You are aging, Templar, and I thought you would endure forever." Her carefree tone was soft, but the lightness did not reach her eyes. He nodded gravely and pushed her chin up to him to contemplate her face fully.

"You are the most infuriating woman in Christendom," he remarked, "but then I recall you are no Christian, rather something that was born a thousand years too late."

She grinned at him wickedly, her sharp eyes teasing. "Well if you looked outside of Christendom you would find many more intractable women like me. Remember, you always saw what you wanted to see, through the blinkers of your path, and maybe so did I. But you see now so I forgive you. And I can see your heart has changed and you have cast aside your old self. I came back here to meet you again, to promise you something." Suddenly the forced laughter died from her eyes and she pulled away from him fretfully, grasping him merely by the hands.

"Speak to me Tsura, Dancer in the Dark. For I have lost my path and you have denied me another. I lay hanging in the balance of things, stranded!" Mikhail implored her sadly, sensing her grief but rejoiced at the loving concern radiating from her eyes.

"No, you are not stranded, for you know not the true meaning of being an eternal wanderer. In this world the chessboard is between the gods, and we are often forgotten or tormented. But behold, I have extricated myself from the cruel game!" She lifted her arms to the moon and her eyes welled with tears that fell glittering on her face. Then she threw herself into Mikhail's arms and kissed his lips passionately.

"Mikhail, whether through good or evil, my sight has been taken from me. I am unseen by them, and they can no longer seek me out, for I am shrouded in the shadow of the elven kings. All I have now is foreknowledge and wisdom and a deep well of thought. My sight brought me too close to the throne of God, and his sight burned me every day. I shivered in endless turmoil, for I stared too far into the void and it bled my eyes, detaching me from sanity, and my madness thrived upon my gift. I had become the ideal weapon for the chessboard of the gods, and the instrument most desirable. But look not despondent! It has been

severed from me, yet I have not forgotten what I know, nor has my wisdom lessened. I can look and take steps back and comprehend things
better, having passed through the gates of the living into the valley of
death and traversed it."

Estella spoke softly, as if musing to herself, and then Mikhail realized the truth of her words. What had struck him first when he had
seen her was the torment she patiently bore. She had suspended the
weight of her woes majestically over her head like a crown, and now that
it was lifted, only her inner light shone through.

"What have they done to you, Tsura?" He held her head in his hands
soothingly and kissed her brow. She wrapped her arms around him and
sighed.

"Nothing that is not for the best. But I am here for a different purpose
than to speak of this. I have passed the gates of mortality, and by dawn I
will cease to exist on earth, so listen closely before time runs out." She let
go of him, taking a step back and grasped his hands with urgency.

"You must die here on earth. Let the sickness consume your body,
but do not fear, for there is nothing that can rob your spirit of its repose.
You will be reborn again once the antichrist has come into the world
and ascended his celestial throne, sure of his victory. Then you will
return. I shall always be there by you, stewarding you through childhood to manhood, till the right time comes for you to take up the sword
and challenge the fiend of this age.

"I have gone myself, and I have no grave on earth. Through the grace
of the elven king I have drunk the goblet of sweet death and found deliverance. It is the same for you. There is no way you can vanquish this
coming evil or forestall the wickedness of the queen, who is drunk on
self-pity and the lust for retribution. Come with me, die to earth and all
creation, and we shall return as redeemers of all!" she supplicated him
with tears in her eyes, her candor surging forth, and her love with it.

"But you do not love me at all," Mikhail replied. "That angel that
watched over you loves you, and in him you have found a kindred spirit.
Wherefore would you want to escort me through my future travails,
should I indeed choose that course?" The frost that had once edged his
every word was gone, and he was merely Mikhail with a broken heart.

"All the spells of earth are shattered, and my eyes opened by the elven king," Estella said. "I see you clearly now, and know that when you incarnate as one of us, I shall find you to be what I have always hoped for. I have loved you in my own fashion, and I know what you will become— the one who could hold my heart and be strong enough to guard it."

Mikhail smiled at her with a youthful, mischievous glint in his eyes, holding her tight and brushing away strands of hair from her face.

"And what had you always hoped for? You, who have softened the hardest recesses of my cold heart?"

She did not answer at first, but when she did a light blush came to her face. "I waited for one who knew how to admire the freedom of wild things, and who knew how to pursue us without desire to conquer, who would go to the ends of the earth to seek us." She broke away from him and her expressive face was sad. Beyond the trees came the lightening of the skies, once black and now cerulean.

"Die and let the fairy fever ravage you and consume you, and through your death you shall be reborn again, savior of mankind and my true love." She wept now, her lips trembling as the dawn began to creep upon them. Already the kindled stars began to wane and gutter out and her voice became distant and ephemeral. He ran to her distraught, but found he could not grasp her, for she was immaterial. Then they both wept long and hard, and he fell to his knees in mourning.

"Then I will never see you again?" his grating voice put to words what his heart could not surmount.

"Yes, you shall. I will never leave your side. When you are of age and secure in your wisdom, you will meet me again. Till then do not allow the pain of our separation to deter you from your path."

The spear shafts of dawn pierced the remnants of the lingering night, and one such shaft pierced into the clearing, and the beautiful mist instantly died. Estella stood like a vague, quivering vision, suddenly grey, and even her laughing eyes were lifeless. She waved her arms as Mikhail desperately threw himself at her, seeking to clasp the fragments of the evanescent vision only to be greeted with the cold light of morning. Nothing remained of her, not the musk of her perfume or the imprint of her shoes in the ground. The clearing, once rich with mystery, was now barren and mundane, and he suddenly hated it and wept bitterly. As sunrise strode into the heavens hunting the shadows, Mikhail rose to his feet dolefully, seeking his way home. A lonely stag following him distantly with soft brown eyes full of recognition.

THE WAY BACK to his jail was arduous. The thickets and brambles tore at his clothes, and the boughs of the trees snagged his hair while his failing health returned with a bitter vengeance. Gasping for breath, he let himself be led by the stag, who nudged him at times when he thought he would lay down and let his sickness triumph over him there alone in the woods. At last he could see the trees lessening. Then the stag departed, and he knew then he was approaching the end of his mortal story. Gathering his strength, he made his way past the trees into the cultivated gardens of the monastery. There was a commotion there—no doubt his mysterious departure had caused a frantic hunt. Quickening his pace, he strode past the gardens, greeting the bewildered peasants who stopped their work to stare at him. Seeing the holy radiance in his eyes, they bowed deeply, the women averting their eyes humbly.

When the monks caught sight of him some rushed inside while others brandished the batons they used to discipline the workers. Mikhail laughed at the sight of them, and they faltered before reaching him, unmasked awe on their faces at seeing one who had been touched by the fay. A call resounded in the distance, and Mikhail saw a knight upon a chestnut horse blowing a horn. He recognized him instantly and laughed heartily, calling out his name.

The rider approached Mikhail doubtfully with the pompous monk who was the leader of the pursuit tailing after him and huffing with exertion. Mikhail waited patiently with the rising sun behind him, the throes of his fevers having briefly ceased.

When the rider was near enough, he called out gruffly, "Mikhail! We thought you lost to some enchantment that had befallen the monastery. Many dreadful things can happen when you live so close to the edge of the wild woods!" The jocular tone belonged to Oswald. When he was a foot away from Mikhail he shook his head, mystified, taking in his altered countenance.

"I came because Erin summoned me. He told me that the queen was punishing you. Her displeasure was something I had anticipated all but too late. Then I heard how the church was abusing you, so I hastened to come. But it looks like what befell you in those woods shall prove far stranger to my ears than anything I've seen with you yet, my friend." Oswald held his hat against his chest, and reverence shone from his face. The monk, who had it in his mind to chastise and arrest Mikhail, had cowered away after he beheld his shining, elven-blessed face. He had then retreated with the other monks into the safety of the monastery walls.

"Yes indeed, many things have happened that I cannot tell you of," said Mikhail, "but stay with me till the end. Have me buried in the woods where there is a clearing, and there shall be my repose. Do not let them dispose of me in some indecent fashion out of petty revenge, though the body is meaningless to the sojourns of the soul," Mikhail spoke calmly, grasping his friend by the shoulder. But Oswald could not conceal his alarm.

"Do not fear for me," Mikhail continued. "I have found deliverance from this cursed earth, and I shall soon depart it. Be my friend for the last time and wait, for soon I shall pass and everything I had will be passed on to you."

Oswald nodded gravely and lowered his eyes. "Then there is much to talk about. But you look like someone who has been touched by the fay," he said, distraught, meeting his comrade's face.

"I have been, indeed. Come, let us talk, for I do not have much longer," Mikhail insisted gently.

"You have actually seen the fay? Then you have indeed gone mad," Oswald said, steadfastly averting his eyes. "This world has need for the likes of you, for nothing good shall emerge from the queen's plans. We are few and our days numbered, and when you pass, the last bastion of strength we had shall dissipate."

Mikhail lifted his eyes to the sun in contemplation. "Then we have this day together, you and I," he said softly. "You shall record what you must and promise me to keep it hidden. Pass it on, for much of what I will tell you shall come to pass, but much can be averted." Mikhail led the way to the woods smiling as Oswald looked at him strangely.

"And who made you all-seeing?" Oswald asked.

Mikhail looked at Oswald intently, seeing for the first time the thoughts beneath his gruff facade.

"I have the sight of those near death who have drunk of the wine of foreknowledge that the elves drink. Come with me, let us discourse together ere the day dies, and I with it."

Oswald frowned, rubbing his eyes vigorously, then following him into the woods.

30

THE AUTHORS OF
HUMAN HISTORY

I felt the tremble in the folds of the firmament, the crease of filmy wings

The sunray that eluded the leaping tears of the faraway angelic kings

I felt the light passing through shadow, its reach as
light as a flower's breath

Inexorably evanescent, as striking as the finality of death

"I WANT EVERY ONE OF THEM WHO HAS EVER CAST ME DOWN WITH their gaze to perish and pay for it. Every last one of these hypocritical men who paid me lip service but who secretly mocked me, especially those cursed Templars!"

The acid tone reverberated throughout the hall, bereft of its habitual femininity and benevolence. The queen was lounging on a long couch of red and white velvet. Her luxurious bright hair was loose, and her head rested in the lap of Prince Erik of Saxony, whose taciturn manners merely aggravated her further. He consoled her silently, passing his fingers through her hair almost absentmindedly.

"You are not listening to me Erik!" came the queen's indignant reproach. She lifted her head imperiously, her petulant eyes brimming over with tears. Her lip trembled, and she turned her face away, her hair cascading like a curtain behind her shoulders revealing large sapphire earrings.

Erik contained his exasperated sneer as she rose to her feet haughtily and began pacing up and down her chambers. Erik was lightly clad in a garment of black silk trimmed with gold, and he toyed with his beard idly, watching the queen shoot daggers at him with his eyes half-closed.

The dye in her hair had renewed the youthfulness she had lost, and the rouge upon her cheeks accentuated her cheekbones, which were beginning to fill in with her pregnancy. Her full figure remained slim and hourglass, and her swaying hips mesmerized Erik, while he ignored her incessant attempts to coax him into conversation.

"You promised me Mikhail's head on a platter, and yet you have not delivered. You promised me his humiliation, and that also failed to happen. Then you also promised to burn that witch, and you failed there too," she drawled, baiting him sulkily, her eyes betraying her insecurity.

Erik snorted dismissively and reached for a goblet on the table next to him. It was still early afternoon, but he was bracing himself against the capriciousness of the queen. Since the shadow had taken over through the fissures of her weakness, the queen had changed beyond recognition. Every vice she had became amplified, and each virtue twisted until it became a vice, too. Her pious and prudish soul was stripped bare of its essence, and through her veins coursed a poison that entered her heart and consumed it. She became a puppet wielded by cunning hands unseen, nothing but a vessel for someone else's dark designs.

That much was why Erik tolerated her. He knew that within her grew Samael's legacy. So he guarded her, and what was left of her wits, as she readied herself to bring forth an age of mighty and terrible things where he might reap his share of the rewards. In truth he despised her, as he despised all things feminine, deeming women useful only for his own pleasure and incapable of intellectual pursuit. But with this one he had to be careful, for who was he to dispute his master's plans? While merely a shadow of her former self, the queen was still powerful, and her will still surpassed his in many areas, so he steered her as best he could, directing her wrath toward worthier targets. Where her original mind had gone, he could not tell nor did he care. Perhaps it was locked away in some remote confine of her consciousness, watching in dismay as her body and mind were usurped, powerless to fight back.

Erik lusted for power and for the knowledge the hidden gems bestowed upon him. And the Blind God promised him many things from beyond the veil of death, including what he hungered for most. His mind was forever occupied with grand visions of his own sublime rule, eternally carved in stone and immortalized. He connived darkly, withholding from the queen his uneasiness about confronting the Templar, for his crooked spirit sensed the danger there.

"My queen," Erik said indulgently, "I shall erase the orders of the Templars from history myself. By my own contrivance they shall be disbanded with no one to shelter them. Then they will be stripped of their knowledge and I shall put them all to the stake, for truly they are our enemies. The church is foolish enough to believe the lies we feed them. Let us gorge them on their own greed and lust for power, then they'll stab themselves of their own accord!" He pounded the table triumphantly with his fist, and the queen stopped her restless pacing to watch Erik with hopeful interest.

"Listen to me, the church will do the work for us," he continued. "We will tell them how the Templars have become too powerful and too rich for their own good, and that their wealth has far surpassed that of the church. We will tell them how the Templars' authority is beyond question now, and how one day they will dethrone the pope and cast them all out like beggars. They are greedy and callow, venal beyond belief, and beneath their garments of holiness, their licentiousness is a rabid disease they can never be cured of. Watch how we shall make them amputate their strongest weapon and turn it into the ideal scapegoat. Then they will seize the Templars' power and extend their lustful fingers to crush their strongholds, laying bare their fastnesses to us. Like witches and heretics they shall be burned and their glory extinguished and expurgated from memory. Then none shall remember the Templars as anything but vagabond murderers and thieves who worshipped pagan gods and sacrificed their souls for the sake of forbidden knowledge. We shall twist everything they did, and posterity will only recall them as a dark stain upon history!" Erik laughed as he downed his wine, waiting for the queen's praise. She merely sniffed in acknowledgment and turned away from him, crossing her arms.

"And what about Mikhail, what are you going to do about him?" she asked. "He cannot be burned at the stake, for he is a noble just like yourself. And besides dying, he hasn't been humbled before me yet. I thought you were man enough to go confront him." She shot him a coy look. Erik contained his scathing response, and though he blanched, he restrained any outward display of his anger.

"To torment a dying man is not worthy of me," he retorted. "Let him die nameless and in dishonor, with no one to remember him or mourn him. And if history remembers him it will only be as a coward who cavorted with the demons and succumbed to their enchantments. Come, let us rewrite history together, for the erudite of this world shall suckle at the breast we offer them, and in the milk we can mingle our venomous deceit. It shall fester in them and grow inseparable from them, and thus we shall alter the course of things and rewire irredeemably the subconscious minds of mankind. We are indeed the gods of their destiny, and at our will the Templars shall be betrayed by their beloved church. The house of God is weak and frail, and the inexorable rot has already settled in."

Erik's eyes burned with a dark passion, and his sweeping gaze was intent on everything around him—the room with its rich furnishings, and the queen with her extravagant accoutrements. He felt mighty, drunk on the pride that only the fallen take with them on their descent from heaven's gates. The queen had begun pacing again, pensive and forlorn, while the light filtered through the stained glass windows of her chambers.

"We must rewrite the narrative, then, of what happened and what shall be," she said. "Then the people will welcome my child with un-doubting hearts. We must exile all Templars and their ilk and burn their books. Then we will cement the Twilit people in their holes to remain immured until they forget who they are. All men forget, eventually." A cloud passed over her face and bitterness contorted her features. "Yes, men forget easily. They are simple creatures of desire and lust. Fulfill both and they will be led as sheep. Give them power and a false sense of importance, and they will follow wherever you lead them, even to perdition." She smiled now vindictively with bared teeth, caressing her belly coldly.

"We shall rule," she continued. "You will rule over their life here on earth, and I will dictate to them where their afterlife may lead them.

And we will teach them that obedience is their only guarantee to salvation." She stood now facing Erik and he could clearly see within her dainty features the ugliness of the fiend that lived within, gnawing at her wholesomeness from the inside till the empty husk threatened to cave in on itself and reveal the rotten structures that gaped into nothingness.

The queen's place as the sole ruler of the kingdom had merely increased her hatred of everyone she believed to have belittled her, and she punished them for it. She especially relished the details of the torments she held in store for Mikhail. She despised him with an unnatural hatred spurred by his rejection of her. She wished to see him beg and grovel, to see him broken and stripped of his wits. She wanted him to acknowledge her and desire her so that she could spurn him scornfully, then bask in the joy of humiliating him. She dreamed of digging up his corpse and hanging it to dry, watching his bones bleach beneath the unswaying sun and the carrion crows picking him apart. For even beyond death she yearned to punish him, and this seed of malevolence soon turned to madness.

Erik watched the queen lost in her morbid designs and cared not, for one of the most prodigious sons of the Templar orders was soon to pass, and the great edifice against them would crumble into ruin. Then nothing would stand in his way.

31

THE PROMISES OF THE
PRIMORDIAL GODDESS

To the honest fire that beams coldly in the austere north
An emblem of the bearer of the unwelcome news
Emerging like a tempest of auroral fire when summoned forth
Upon the altars of the hallowed circles and the witching brews

OUTSIDE THE STAINED GLASS WINDOWS OF THE QUEEN'S CHAMBERS lay a garden, rich with fruit trees and exotic flowers from all over the world. It had once been a fair place, but the rule of the king had diminished it, and now the garden was but a shadow of its former self. However the overgrown state of the garden was no deterrent to the three young children who stood there waiting stonily with baskets of flowers in their hands. They watched the cloud formations while whistling simple tunes, which were strange and yet uncomfortably close to the heart. They wore bright hats over their heads in red, green, and yellow that matched the flowers they carried in their overflowing baskets.

It was not humanly possible for the children to hear what was transpiring in the queen's chambers, yet nonetheless they only stirred when the queen's conversation with Erik had ended. They passed the gates of the garden and made their way into the town as a subtle rain began to fall, then turned into a downpour.

As people mourned their dying each day, the town's grey heartbeat faltered on. The streets were now deserted of their habitual traffic, and the three children kept a steady, purposeful pace, the only vivid colors in a place that had forgotten its meaning. At certain houses they passed they cast a single flower to the ground, sometimes with a small whisper or a sigh, sometimes with solemn silence. And there the flowers found their last resting place upon the threshold of the unsuspecting people within. Many houses were marked in that manner. When all the baskets were empty, the children hurried along with a small prayer, their task complete. Then they left the city, their pale visages ominous to those that saw them. The people were afraid, for the children were strange to them and their childish eyes were ageless, wise, and beautiful. It pained the people to look upon them, a fragment of a world they had willingly slain.

The children walked for many miles, their vibrant hats and flowing hair billowing in the wind and rain. Crows followed them, and ravens too, squawking and crying out as they were buffeted by the wind. The overcast sky hung over them like a smoke-filled crystal whence one might discern the auguries of things to come. And when the first trees of the forest began to appear, many animals emerged to greet them. Then they changed, for they were no longer children but hooded and cloaked women.

One of the women was slim and shapely, like a sapling tree with hair the color of chestnuts in autumn. It fell in loose, wild curls, and at her feet wild hares gathered. Upon her brow there was a crescent moon of silver, spun by ancient hands. Her dreadful green eyes cast a forbidding look on the city behind her. Neither the softness of the garland of green leaves and luscious flowers upon her head, nor the roundness of her cheeks blushing with the vigor of youth could diminish the steel in her gaze. And the candor of her full smile did naught to conceal the lethal power pulsating through her veins. The crescent moon she bore was like a shining star, and yet it was no stronger than the light from her malachite eyes. As she tapped her fingers lightly at her side, the rain abated. Her gaze rebuked the winds and sliced out of the gathering storm its brewing, tempestuous rage.

The second woman was slightly taller and fuller of figure with rounded breasts and full hips. She leaned on an oaken staff of gnarled wood, facing the woods before her with azure eyes brimming with fore-knowledge. Her hair was half braided and half wild and auburn like fallow leaves. Around her neck a crystal clear full disk moon hung, and upon her head was a wreath of silver and gold leaves. Twined among them were yellow serpents, one clasping a perfect, round diamond upon her brow. She inspired both love and awe in those who looked upon her beautiful visage, but also fear and desolation. She towered like a hurricane that swallows everything, only regurgitating death and ruin. Everything living had its source in her, and she was the ultimate fruition of existence. She was the supreme womb of creation, birthing life into the void, forever balancing her mercy with justice.

The third woman was clad in ashen black. Her raven hair leapt free from the coils upon her head, and polished bone and ivory decked her coiffure. She was as pale as a wraith and wizened, but no lines marred her ancient face, untouched by the turmoil of time. Her black eyes were as empty and as cold as the malignant void, and her smile was both a menace and a charm. One was drawn to her with an incapacitating pull, and the futility of life ended at her feet. She was ever eager to welcome souls back into her primordial darkness, deconstructing their essence back into the fabric of the universe. Her staff was exceedingly tall, and upon it rested a raven.

Together the three entered the forest, disparate in form yet born of the same flame. In a clearing many monoliths formed circles. They were erected in time immemorial, mighty and stark, bearing the weathers of time. Women and men were gathered around them in circles with dark cloaks of green and hoods upon their faces. They held flowers in their hands and goblets for libations and waited silently, though the air was alive with the opened Twilit pathways.

The first stars of the evening had begun to burn steadily in the east, and a waxing moon heralded the oncoming night with its acolytes of constellations. Those gathered were the few who, unmindful of the dangers, had traveled to hear the words of destiny. The three goddesses approached the circle, and the faithful stirred, bowing low and welcoming them. The three entered into the middle of the inner circles of the monoliths, each facing a different direction. Their countenances were bright and clear to all those present.

The Maiden spoke first. "Children of the Goddess! Here we are gathered again before the edge of this new calamity. But take strength, for we are sowing the seeds of redemption. The Dancer in the Dark has eluded the clutches of Lucifer and of Samael and passed through to the Elder Folk. She is dead to the world and has shed her human mortality. Now she shall steward you all from the barges of the moon. Now is the time to prepare. We chose of our enemy a willing heart. He was touched by our chosen daughter, Tsura, and she broke the chains on his mind and brought him through tortuous paths to our secret heart. Remember his name and his new incarnation. Remember Mikhail the Templar!" Her echoing words rose like a tidal wave, drowning the doubts of the congregation.

"We will remember your name," came in unison the soft, echoing answer back.

"He will die in the coming days, and it will be up to you to guide his wayward spirit through our Twilit pathways, to keep him safe till he finds where we might rewrite his name in the grand tapestry of creation. Watch over him, for he is the vessel of our will, and the depredations of the darkness shall chafe at his soul. Remember his name."

"We shall remember his name," the congregation faithfully returned.

"Pray for the Dancer! For the sinuous gossamer strands she dances threaten to break. One day her sight will be restored, and then the race will begin again, and her opened eyes bring her to the brink of infinity's bosom, where light and dark dissect each other and become one and the same. Remember her name." The congregation lifted their supplicating hands to the skies, and the stars responded with flared fires.

"We remember your name, Tsura," they vowed passionately.

"Let him be reborn again, this Templar with no name. Nameless he entered the world and nameless he shall depart it. Then we will reclothe him in the garments of destiny."

"So be it, blessed be," was the severe response. The crescent moon upon the Maiden's brow brightened with blinding radiance.

"So shall it be sealed and the weavers of fates, the divine Norns, shall hear the decree. What is done cannot be undone!" she proclaimed savagely, her burning eyes full of promise. Then the light darkened around her and she was enveloped in shadow.

The Mother stepped forward, the great diamond flashing upon her brow, and the serpents upon her head took life and writhed. She lifted her staff to the waxing moon, and its opalescent light cascaded upon her.

"I am promise itself, and I fulfill each of the promises I give," she spoke. "Nothing shall take fruition that hasn't had its ultimate end design in my heart, for however dark is the night, a little light binds its gloom forever. He shall be reborn a boy, and we shall watch over him. Until manhood no harm shall befall him. I see it and I decree it. He will grow to be a man, and he will challenge the one on the throne—the one who will kneel to Samael and dance before Lucifer, nothing but a tool for their games.

"If all else fails I shall excoriate creation, for I have born you and I shall reject you. I can easily abort you from my womb and renew the world. I carry life and creation, and I watch each of you live and die and desecrate each other. Many times over have I lifted my staff and extinguished you from existence. Though the warring gods of the skies fight for dominion over puny matters, in the great end I shall choose, though already your world has been renewed many times, bleeding my strength. What is said cannot be unsaid, I am the Mother of all things, and I carry hope with me, and I birth it into being and deliver it to you for safekeeping. Be watchful!"

"We shall be watchful, Holy Mother," the congregation replied tenderly as they knelt before her.

The Mother's staff ignited with white flame, and for a moment her face was clear to all. She greeted them solemnly with a somber smile. Then she, too, faded into darkness, stepping back beside her sister.

The last to speak was the Crone, and for a while she looked up to the waxing moon, studying it curiously. It seemed to dim beneath her gaze, and the light of the stars guttered as if fanned by an unseen breeze. Her thin, pale fingers clasped a basalt staff that was formed like a spindle whorl. She fixed her congregation with a brilliant white smile. A compelling chill had settled in, and the people shivered, but none dared to stir before her.

"I, the Crone, stand before you, the Hag of many faces and many names, the witch of all witches that all hate and despise yet revere. I am wisdom beyond measure, and knowledge so heavy it crushes mortal spines. I am the womb of death, where I welcome you all in, my beautiful and ugly children." Her brilliant white smile shone like a crescent moon in her pallid face.

"I am the finality of all things and the last repose of industrious souls. I am the crumbling of all that men create, and I erode time itself and devour memory and erase growth. I am potent and deep, and those that have the courage to watch me spin shall be granted rebirth beyond death. This world is one of many, and I promise your immortal souls that I shall seize each and every one of you and weave you into the various dominions of the skies, if all fails. Your story shall never end here on earth. When the dread steps of doom sound I shall come for you, and your wounds I shall avenge. I give to you this gift.

"Mikhail shall be reborn through me, through the threefold death. From my womb he shall struggle and be cast out, and from boyhood to manhood he shall thrive. Then he will banish Samael and challenge Lucifer. But now be gone, take these prophecies, and wait for a child to be born who shall disrupt the course of the planets and call down a fiery rain of meteors. Watch out for the chaos and the pursuit of the demons and shroud him! Hide him well, and remember in the end, death is nothing to fear, for I am your mother and my love for you surpasses all."

Clouds veiled the skies and all were plunged into darkness, still and calm. Some wept and some sighed, but there was a contented murmur that rippled throughout, as the gates of the dimensions were flung wide. And the people immortalized their memory and bided their time, waiting for the boy who would be born . . .

32

THE TAPESTRY OF CREATION

The fields of waste are open, wide is my wound
Vaster than the horizon I drink with avid eyes
For there is nothing hollower than my chaos, my memory doomed
The grave beneath shall be the dome of my skies

I t was never a dream, though Tsura could not recall how she had entered that place, stumbling into hidden chambers in a region she could not remember. The Twilit paths were hers to roam, and she wandered alone, seeking answers to things she had seen in her visions. There she discovered much she had never fathomed, for the elves wove their worlds from strands of thought and dreams. She had traveled down the golden pathways into radiant sunsets, to endless, shoreless seas that were lit as clouds of nebulae where wheeling stars burned in the motionless air.

It was as if creation had never been finished and the seas never met the sunlight. And the seas' depths withheld their habitual song, but echoed back the primordial notes that spoke it into being. The endless dusk touched the sky with a multitude of hues, from cerulean and malachite to amber and aquamarine. There were hidden halls beneath the mountains where muses sang and lured wanderers to banquets, and other halls led beneath the sea where ancient spirits with silvery eyes pined for the music before the throne. Unlike the elves, they were angels that had fallen in love with their creation and become a part of it.

It was in these strange halls she had stumbled upon a hidden room which, unlike the others, seemed deserted. She could not remember what had hurried her steps, nor what kindled the eagerness in her spirit as she neared the heart of the mountain. But when she reached its core, she knew she had reached the destination her heart pined for. She was standing before a large, magnificent, gold-threaded tapestry. Woven within it were many planets and stars. It was a tapestry that encompassed all of creation and its history, from beginning to end. The first audience before the divine throne was depicted, where God wielded into being his voice, and the Fall and the angels' sojourns on earth. It also contained the other worlds that humans knew nothing of, with their stories and trials, and the various races that ruled over them. They were all woven together, souls meshed with golden threads spun from the spindle whorl of existence into one great design. The souls that emanated from God's throne chose the worlds their essence favored most, and the Norns threaded them into its existence.

As Tsura stood before the tapestry, a smiling, golden-haired Norn with a magnificent pair of burnished bronze wings approached her, pointing to a sphere on the tapestry. The meaning of the sphere was alien to Tsura, but she did not dare speak, for she feared the vision would dissolve and the lights extinguish.

"All human souls choose to incarnate on earth," said the Norn. "You chose to come here, and we threaded you in. Where would you choose to be next, now that you approach the ending of your earthly journey?"

The softness of her eyes and her warm smile inspired nothing but fear in Tsura, for she felt small and inconsequential and petty, unworthy to choose. Her heart was heavy with woe and bitterness for the grievances of the earth.

"I want to be where the Elder Folk are," Tsura replied, "and share their pain and destiny, wherever it leads."

The Norn smiled indulgently with a motherly kindness. "Then this is where you are choosing to be bound. Once your soul is woven in here, you can never sever from it, nor abdicate from the tribulations and trials that the race you incarnate into shall face. You shall not remember where you came from, and you will never know you had this choice. But if this is your last decision, then so be it."

Tsura weighed the words in her heart, looking back through her mind's eye at her life on earth, and how puerile and lowly mortal life was.

"My heart was never of them," she said finally, "and I yearn to join with the Elders forever, and never look back on humans again."

The Norn smiled softly and pointed to a sphere in the tapestry. "This is where you shall be, and none of the souls you have loved on earth shall know you, nor follow you, and you shall find yourself another home in the heart of your people. Not many have your choice, and you have proven that you truly do renounce earth."

The Norn brandished a sharp knife and delicately approached the tapestry. Then she deftly selected a single golden thread that wove through the human sphere. "This is the end for you here, your chapter on earth. You may be lost in the ethereal paths before I weave you in again, clad in a different spirit. Till then your naked soul shall be lost erring in the wilderness of nonexistence."

Before Tsura could say anything the Norn slid the knife across the thread. Tsura felt her heart tear open and its vessels break. With a last, shocked cry of pain, she crumbled into a deeper oblivion.

"WHETHER SHALL I turn when the world all does fail? The stars all burn out, heaven's tears all cold, weep no rain but fire." Antariel sang softly to himself as he sat on a rock in his woodland home. He was alone, completely and utterly, and even the spirits that haunted the woods were far afield, for they dreaded him and his vast sorrow. The usual whispers of the winds, which were once music to his ears, were now dull and devoid of harmony, fraying his patience.

Antariel had never felt so alone, for he was born of fire and it burned steadily within him, yearning to be rejoined with his celestial home where once he had abided in peace. But his free will had led him astray, and still he lingered on earth, waiting for something to change or shift within him—for his spirit to ignite again and the distaste for earth to send him surging like the solar flare whipping the firmament apart in his quest to return. Or else for summons to swing open the gates of the sky and escort him back with welcome. But neither happened, and nothing could quell his brooding loneliness.

For a long time he waited patiently for his reckoning. The days stretched by, and still he waited. One day, there was a change in the air, and he realized that his time had finally come. The angels that had long observed him from afar had made a decision and he had been summoned. Antariel bid farewell to the things he loved, the trees whose sleeping, drowsy spirits he used to converse with, as well as those he nurtured from seed to tree and encouraged with his music. Then he sought out the spirits that were once his friends, and though they feared him now they loved him still and mourned him.

Casting one long glance at the place where he had sheltered his fallen pride, he turned away and waited for the sunrise. With his angelic gaze he watched the golden gates open in the east, and the divine countenance looked down on earth, and rain fell glittering like limpid silver. Already the chariot of the sun was proudly conquering the globe, engulfing the remaining moonlight in its blaze. But beyond it all at the radiant gates the greatest of heaven's mighty sons, Zuriel, the rock of God, was surveying the earth, solemnly. Antariel extended his wings, forsaking earth and its possessions, and ascended into the sky.

Zuriel beat the air mercilessly with his eight magnificent wings, sharp and bitter as a cluster of razorblades. They were brilliant and blindingly white like flashes of lightning. If one erred too close they would be sliced apart and thrown to the whistling winds. He held a calescent spear, the shaft burning like an unforgiving star, and before his piercing gaze no creature great or small could hope to elude him, for he was illuminated with God's justice. He was severe, as one who had never strayed, and his eyes were filled with the fire that emanated from the throne. He was muscular with broad shoulders and raven hair so dark it was almost blue. His arms were covered with silver bands inscribed in the heavenly tongue, and his lips curled back in a haughty sneer as Antariel approached.

"Welcome Antariel, son of the throne! May you be seen through the eye and pass through whole."

Antariel fixed Zuriel with his clear eyes and tinged his words with meekness. "I returned, as was permitted, and I am here, as was commanded. It seems I have completed the tasks I was assigned, though I may have failed in achieving the goals I was set."

"I know you were assiduous in your quests, and in that I hold you faultless," said Zuriel. "But you have become weak, as weak as the clay that molded humans into flesh that breathes. I see you now, right through you, and your holy heart is corrupted and you have become almost like them. Though your essence is divine, you have cleaved to humans in all your ways." Zuriel tossed his head scornfully, and beneath his lashes the swirling chaos of the cosmos stared back at Antariel. Unflinching, Antariel bent his knee and the streaming sunlight filled his eyes with warmth, and the pristine fragrant air filtered through his hair.

"Many are those that fashioned this earth out of love and were brokenhearted to see it usurped from them. Would you say their hearts, too, had been dethroned from their lofty abodes?" Antariel asked. Zuriel observed for a moment, then lifted one hand and all stilled; the sun, the translucent layers of the skies, the flight of birds, and time itself withheld from drawing breath in its race with infinity.

"Behold our power over all you say the angels created. It is feeble and weak, and all that is material is cursed to rot and ruination, for the mother of all things whose womb holds existence rejects it. Yet she suffers it, for she would not abort what she had created, evil as creation is. Come with us now and scorn the folly of your ways, for have you not tasted the bitterness of banishment?" boomed Zuriel's tempestuous voice through the stillness between them.

"I would not leave if I could never return," said Antariel, shaking his head humbly, "for I have become fond of the things I have nurtured, and my place upon the chessboard has been etched in my heart, though God in his mercy has erased my sin."

Zuriel did not respond, but with an unworldly celerity, he gripped Antariel by the throat and lifted him up as if he were but a child's puppet. There, suspended by the mighty arm of Zuriel, Antariel felt his divine spark throttled and singed by the contact with the hallowed being, and he lamented.

"I could cast you down again and leave you less than you ever were, for that is the judgment for those who defy orders," Zuriel said. "Yet we foretold that your heart would turn away. Until all the things you cherish pass into memory, you shall abide there on earth, helpless to hinder the tide. You shall watch over the unfolding events before you, a statue of marble, and none may release you from your plight till those humans you pledge your love for pledge it back to you."

Far away in the distance a gong sounded, and the heavens reverberated with the sound of it. The silence that Zuriel upheld was broken, and the habitual noises of life resumed. Then Zuriel, with a grim smile of determination, his wings creating a hurricane of wind, lifted a foot clad in thunder and without a further word hurled Antariel down from the lofty station. Antariel fell in a ball of flames, the fires glistening off his fair plumage until he smote the ground. With a mighty groan the earth received him, beaten and bruised. The hurtling force of Zuriel was enough to crumble mountains, but not enough to shatter the sublime structure of Antariel's bones.

Antariel gathered himself up with pain, fighting to regain his composure. The world spun around him, and he braced himself for the crippling torment his body felt. When he managed to stand up and shake the dust from his wings, he cried out in excruciating agony; for as soon as he was standing, his feet began to root to the ground, and a dull ache settled in. Then he knew that Zuriel's menacing decree was coming to be, and he was transforming into marble. He wept, unable to move as his legs became rigid and pale and took on the shade of white polished marble. Then the sensation died within them, and he felt his power bleed out of him.

Antariel would not turn his face to the unforgiving heavens, nor with supplications eschew his pride and beg for succor, for he knew his fate was sealed. Silently, with streaming tears of regret and sorrow, he watched as his body slowly stiffened, and life ebbed away. And with his last moments, he bowed his head and prayed that however long he resided bound in rock, he would find the patience to wait still and not sell himself to darkness. The leaves of the trees loosened from their boughs and they twirled around his head like a mocking crown, and his sight began to fade and his hearing began to dull. Absorbed in his plight, he was oblivious to everything around him—the watchful gaze that waited patiently, and the footsteps gilded in light.

A flock of sheep emerged from the forest. They gathered around the marble figure of Antariel, chewing the grass and bleating. Then their shepherd came after them, pursuing their steps.

"What a wonder that is, by my soul! One would think an angel fell here," said a toneless, mild voice.

Antariel, whose humbled pride had made him rancorous, replied, "A great curse befalls those that look at this statue. Look away simpleton, and spare yourself my wrath."

"Is it so, my precious son?" asked the shepherd.

"I am cursed and my face is abhorred in heaven and on earth," replied Antariel. "I am forsaken by my maker. Do you wish to inherit my punishment, too?"

"Let us see your face then, angel, and weigh you in our balance," came the voice. Then the shepherd approached Antariel, and he could feel the auroral fire that emanated from him, his body and face wreathed in twirling flames. As he stood before Antariel, Antariel trembled, for he knew who this was, and shame enveloped him.

"My child, however long your purgatory is," the shepherd said, "it is never long in the measurements of heaven. And you know not what you have set in motion here on earth. You salvaged a precious sheep of my flock, and though she knows it not, she is the jewel in the scepter of my Father's hand. And you whom heaven rejects from their choir, I shall never chide, for I am also half human."

Antariel's heart was immovably cold, and through his anguish he cried out, "Is this the son of man and God that all heavens obey? Wherefore do you not dash the head of the serpent and terminate the abhorrent reign of evil that wages against us? Kill me and be done, strip me bare of my spark and send it howling to Gehenna. Or better still, feed it to Samael, or let Michael use it as a footstool and crush it beneath his celestial feet! For I am dead inside and out, and my heart bleeds not for heaven, neither does it twang for the master puppeteer who mocks you all. If you have come to bestow mercy on me and glean repentance, behold, I want nothing more than to be the wind. For then I shall be reunited with what I lost and had cherished the most."

"I know your desire, Antariel," said the shepherd compassionately, "and I know that I do not own your spark, for it is yours alone. But have I not forsaken the turning wheel of fortunes to hear your cause? I was there in the beginning when you were forged of light and innocence, and I was there when your melodious skills before the throne caught the eye of Lucifer."

Antariel laughed balefully, and for a moment a shadow dimmed the shepherd's light and it shuddered as if fanned with a ruthless gust of wind.

"I am cursed by everything your structures have erected. I am dispossessed," said Antariel mournfully.

"Not all the sparks of the divine forge were clothed in fitting bodies," the shepherd responded consolingly. "So it was with Tsura, Lucifer, you, and many others whose names are hidden from you. As Metatron was once a man with a spark that did not belong to a human body, so yours does not belong to the angelic order. The Tapestry of Creation weaves souls where they are bound in infinity, but when they shake the bondage of their fate they are often incarnated into the spheres where they believe they belong. I release you, Antariel, and by your true name I set you free! But once a holy decree has echoed in the heavens, I cannot revoke it. So I promise you this; you shall no longer be an angel, and your spark shall never be taken from you. But whoever claims you for himself, of all the races of creation, there your doom shall be bound. You shall retain your power but be bound in stone, and people far and wide shall revere the angelic statue in the woods, till time changes and you are reclaimed."

The shepherd drew closer to Antariel and meekly knelt before him. Then to Antariel's horror, he kissed his marble feet and prayed over them in hushed tones. Through the frozen flesh and bone Antariel could feel the holy warmth of his touch. But before he could respond, the sheep and shepherd had vanished into nothingness.

"Where is Tsura?" he called out dolefully to the empty grove. He was greeted with a resounding silence, and those were the last words he could utter again.

33

THE MUSIC BEFORE
THE THRONE

Break the bones that fence me in, cut the cord of reason

Draw from the marrow the essence of relief

That whipped me with torment in every season

Making my memories of peace a passing shadow brief

THE STATUE BECAME KNOWN AS THE ANGEL'S DESCENT, AND EVEN the most crooked feared that place and dared not defile it. The eyes of the statue were carved of the finest marble, perhaps by the dexterous hands of a devout soul; for they were alive and sorrowful. Hearty young saplings grew around the statue, and roses the color of blood blossomed at its feet. Sometimes when the moon was ripe, the moaning woods would echo songs and laughter, clustering around him like distant sails on a forlorn horizon. Then the Elder Folk would sing on their silver flutes and their tender voices fill the air with fragrant beauty. Antariel's cold heart would kindle briefly, for through the marble prison of his body, he could feel the shifting of the skies and the open dimensions of the Twilit worlds. Although the music sought to alleviate his heart, it merely compounded his sorrow. He yearned to speak and to see, and with each tremulous note he wept inwardly. When dawn came the musicians would depart, promising him company again, and he would be left to his solitude.

They never drew too close to him, for though they pitied him, they knew he was not of their kind and were not willing to meddle in heavenly matters. But they tried to assuage his sorrows in their own manner.

It soon came to pass that curiosity seeped into the mind of a certain elf, and when her companions left at the break of dawn, she would tarry. Antariel knew she was there but could not acknowledge her. After many moons she would come close enough to sit behind him, playing her flute in the cold light of morning. Antariel's heart was then fully awake, and he knew she was unraveling the weight of death that was binding him to slumber. Sluggish and aged, he would hark contentedly, relinquishing his bitterness for a while.

Soon his mind would be summoned awake in the morning, and he would feel her before him and he would rejoice. The tendrils of her song painted vivid images in his thoughts, and though he did not understand her words, he could see again. Then he remembered the earth and its beauty and dreamed of blue agate eyes. After a while she stopped her visits, and his now awake heart bled in agony. He waited despondently, and through his torment he felt even worse than before, till the fetters of his marble body became unbearable and he fought in vain, thrashing against them. Like someone buried alive, he screamed inwardly, and the lack of sight and sound magnified his madness, till it reached such peaks of fury that it darkened the land around him. But the madness soon cooled to regret and hate, and he cursed the fair folk and their minstrels, and his heart festered venom for the singer who had ignited his heart and then abandoned him.

But as time went on he began to strain his ears and listen to the sounds of life around him. Then he gave in to his plight and was thankful for every thought he was able to conceive. He grew to understand himself, and with the boundless time and solitude granted to him, he dwelt on happier times. Then one evening, he heard the lilting voice again calling in the distance. It was a tone of obdurate command, and it was mighty. He immediately became alert, as if whipped by a flail of thunder. Then the music rose again, and it was neither beautiful nor sad but thunderous. She approached him then, and he felt awe and trepidation.

Then she lifted her arms and pulled from the ether the last shafts of sunlight, wringing them out before her in fiery sparks. Her song took on the tumult of the roaring seas and dashed the light apart into a multitude of pulsating stars that quivered in the cold air and spun. Then she reached out to the oncoming night and reaped its heavy essence, and she hurled it down with her commanding song to engulf the mass of light she created. There they mingled like fiery nebulae, spinning rapidly and dissolving into each other while the song reached a high crescendo. Then the darkness and light merged together, creating foreign and beautiful patterns. Her voice darkened and urgency seeped in, and she began the arduous task of weaving the light and dark together like rope. Her music was lighter now and chill as frost, one moment beseeching, another harsh and resolute.

Antariel was blind, but as her voice and deft fingers wove the braids of light, he saw in his mind's eye the anchor of the universe. He felt the heavy waters of infinity roaring free in shoreless skies, and he felt its wakeful spirit and gleaned of its essence a name. Then the song heightened maddeningly. The stars revealed their faces and cast off the veil that shrouded their majesty, and they opened their eyes to gaze into space. All creation was ablaze and all light prevailed in that moment. The elf's voice was now growing weary, so she hurried her notes, mingling it with the braided rope so that it became a red-hot chain of braided steel. Suddenly her voice fell silent, and everything was muted, holding its breath, waiting. She sighed, and then it was obvious to Antariel that her strength was spent. He knew not what to expect, for his angelic knowledge did not exceed the wisdom of the elves where it pertained to weaving magic. He felt suddenly weak and humble, and he hoped that she might offer him some kind words to soothe his exile.

He felt her footsteps approaching, and then he knew that she was before him. Indeed they were but a foot apart, and he felt the weight of her keen gaze. Then, without preamble, she hurled the chain rope at his face, and it struck his mouth with the fullness of its power. He felt a searing pain, as if he were made of flesh and it was melting. As he cried out in agony, he found his voice to be loud and true, though hoarse from disuse. Before he could brace himself for further blows, he was assaulted again. This time the chain struck his eyes and broke, melting into him and relieving his blindness. Though still bound by marble, he felt free, and he wept.

Through the tears he saw her then, tall of stature and with pale horns rising tall above her head. She had a golden smile that contained the balmy warmth of summer, and her dark lips were the color of ripe berries. Her long hair was like honey, braided with golden strands of yellow diamonds and flowers, and her face was oval with large, wide-set eyes the color of cerulean agates. Their hue was ever changing from lapis to aquamarine to chalcedony, and veins of gold interlaced her irises. On her high brow was a circlet of braided gold, holding back her bright hair, which cascaded past her full, round apple cheeks. Her silvery grey garments were of filmy taffeta and spangled with blue stones.

"It was never enough to break you free, but it was enough to shift your solitude, perhaps," she said, her voice light like morning dew. She approached Antariel fearlessly, and he was startled to realize that she smelled like crushed roses and nectarine. He studied her as she examined him, and when he finally broke the silence he found that his voice quivered.

"You have surpassed yourself, great lady, for ever had I dreamed that I could speak again and put the rumblings of my heart into words. Or else regale my eyes with mundane sights again. Truly you have released me from the cruelest of bondages."

"It took me many earthly moons to conceive of such a music that could rend the fetters that bound you. I sought long, listening for the whispers of the angels at dawn, and to the wardens of the tree of life in the evening." She smiled now, and Antariel's tumbling memories came rushing back like a broken dam.

"Alas!" he cried. "For my voice and sight have brought back to me pains I have sought to forget. I fear now that my heart may break beyond redemption." She cocked her head to the side as if tasting his words. Then she shook her head disapprovingly.

"That too will pass," she said, "like everything else, and soon you will learn to hush the baying dogs that your heart has engendered. Yet I do not know your story, though you and I have often kept each other company. I was stirred by pity to free you, but I hope I have not misplaced my judgment." Antariel suddenly laughed merrily, as he could begin to taste his own melodious voice again.

"We have much to tell one another," he said. "But let me begin with the start of all things, and be prepared to be weary, for I am old, perhaps older than you are, for I was once a singer before the divine choir of God, eons and eons ago."

"Do tell me, for I am always in search of good tales," she said with insouciance, seating herself cross-legged on the moss before him. And as night deepened and the stars burned frostily above, Antariel was truly alive again, and he began to weave his tale with the mastery of a fallen angel.

34

THE TRANSMIGRATION
OF SOULS

For the wanderer astray, the hermit seeking the lost books
To him the bitter path of knowledge is truly germane
And to gaze at the grand canvas of depravity, the deified crooks
All the depth of duplicity of the celestial rulers most profane

OSWALD AND MIKHAIL DELVED DEEP INTO THE WOODS, ONE GENTLY leading the other. The sunlight cascaded its radiance upon them, and their voices were lost in the sporadic gusts of wind. It was a reprieve from the stark weather, as the conquering sun marched upon the grey heavens and poured its serene, all-encompassing light down on creation. In fact, this was the first day of sun since the demons had begun their reign of terror and disease. It was an omen from the imperial heavens, defiance against the impending reign of darkness. And for a while, the world opened its eyes and breathed in the whispers of deliverance and hope, vowing to wait, however long.

"This shall be the grand finality of my use, then," said Oswald heavily. "I cannot surmount the dangers that have rained on us. I am in my dwindling days and alone. I will be lost, as a helpless spectator or a defanged hound cowering and waiting for death."

Mikhail stopped abruptly and clasped Oswald's shoulder. "You shall recount what you saw here and what you know, everything I told you and everything that shall come to pass, for there is still hope in you and in others. We need you more than ever as the Templars are relegated to the refuse of history. For only through your perseverance can there be hope. Do not falter now and do not fear. Though everything seems hopeless, night must often travel through the deepest recesses of hell before it can emerge and blow the horn for the gates of dawn to open. The Templars will be disbanded, and all our lore forgotten and burnt. That I see with clarity now. The queen shall bequeath to the world an evil that will seem fair and radiant—a sun king. And all shall love him at first, but when the illusion breaks they will be plunged into infinite darkness. They will need you. All rests upon your shoulders! That child will become a tyrant so abhorrent that the divine countenance will turn away from us, and in that darkness we will be doomed. Then you must find me! I will return, for I know the winding paths that lead back to these mortal shores. But I must be protected, or all shall perish."

Oswald wept without restraint, silent and cold, and the sunlight dazzled his eyes. He stared at his friend as if he were a stranger.

"How shall we find you?" he choked. "And how will we keep the memory of you alive if they demonize you? How will we keep you safe? With what might shall we conquer the blight of time, heaping only misery on the people, so quick to forget and fast to look for a scapegoat?"

Mikhail smiled grimly, and in his grey eyes the tempests quieted and revealed an indomitable fire.

"Leave the comforts you know behind and go into hiding," he said. "Form a core of a trusted few, and teach them all you know. Send them out to gather likeminded spirits. Cleave to the weak and the disowned and to wise women and the Twilit people. Forgo pride and past grievances, and they shall keep their eyes everywhere for the auspicious time when I arrive. Keep far from the corrupt churches. Be the wandering fathers that offer shelter to those in need. Be the weavers of stories and keep the fire of memory burning." Mikhail's face was desolate, and he secretly grieved for the arduous burden he was laying upon his friend. He pulled away apologetically, and Oswald fell with him into a steady pace, delving deeper into the woods.

Soon they came to a clearing that opened up amid the leafy foliage. The clearing held a tremulous aura of magic that sent shivers down Oswald's spine. Mikhail paused, for there he had met the elves and seen Tsura, though too briefly, and she had healed the last vestiges of his wounds. He smiled at Oswald and strode into the clearing.

"One thing remains unclear to me," Oswald remarked. "Perhaps you forget that I am no longer youthful and time shall weather me, and hardship shorten my lifespan, and I shall die. I cannot shepherd these people for more than a few seasons. What then, Mikhail, what then of my successor? How can I trust the mission not to be lost?" A doubting frown covered his face.

Mikhail laughed warmly, but his eyes were filled with a steely determination. "You need not concern yourself with that for now, for it shall be between you and someone far greater than I. He will come to you in due time, and then all shall be clear to you." They stood facing the dwindling sunlight. "Remember Tsura's name also, for she is part of the grand design. Remember her kindly, she is innocent of the ill attributed to her. The sun is setting soon, and I feel my strength fading away. I will soon need to be laid to rest, and here is the spot." Mikhail pointed earthwards to the point where he last felt Tsura's presence.

"Set a cairn for me. It is the last service I will ever ask of you. And remain here till night falls, then everything you need to know shall be completed. Here in this desolate, unforgiving land I shall find my repose in the bowels of earth, immured to sleep for ages unknown. It all ends here—I end here. And I know not where I shall go once the gates of death claim my soul. I enter death alone, without guide or friend, into the unknown, the last and most feared mystery." Mikhail's voice was hoarse now, and Oswald saw in his face hidden sorrow tinged with relief to be closing the mortal chapter—at least for now.

"My only true friend, how I wish I could relieve you of this burden or cast aside my own mortality and follow you wherever you go!" Oswald's face was a stricken mask as he spoke. Suddenly the weather shifted, turning swiftly into a sour turbulence of lightning. The woods moaned, the branches of the trees like broken fingers grasping at them impotently.

"Help me lie down, I cannot stand on my feet," said Mikhail, his voice weakening.

With as much gentleness as he could muster, Oswald helped his old friend lie down on the ground. Mikhail's eyes were open, his breathing labored, and the color slowly began to drain out of his handsome face. Oswald knelt beside him as the wind rose, waiting patiently. Mikhail's eyes suddenly fluttered closed and Oswald, fearing that the time had come, began to weep. But Mikhail spoke in low, distant tones. "Do not be sad for me, be sad for the world. Have no pity for me, have pity for the world."

"And what about pity for me, O strangest of men? To be your friend was once a blessing, but now I think it is more of a curse! What is this fate you have cast onto me? What have you made of us? Even the old books and truths we once believed in seem hollow in light of all that has transpired here. I am lost!" Oswald cried out.

"We are players in a divine game, my friend," Mikhail rasped, "for have we not asked to serve in whatever way we could when we took our sacred vows? The ways of the Lord are mysterious, and in this he has proved to be the most mysterious of all. We shall meet again, they have not defeated us yet!"

Oswald watched transfixed as the shadows danced across Mikhail's ashen visage. He seemed like a carving from ages gone by, some ancient king from mythical days.

"Behold the first wandering father, Oswald, Keeper of the Lore," he said. "I depart now, I see the light, the proverbial light at the end of the tunnel. But no, there is no light, for we have all lived in perpetual darkness. Bury me and forgive me, my brother, my friend, my successor!" Then Mikhail's eyes closed and the laden skies opened and rain began to fall softly. For the first time, Oswald felt the true meaning of solitude.

After a time the rain ceased and Oswald wiped away the tears clouding his vision. Shaking himself from his reverie, he set about digging the grave. The soaked black earth yielded easily to his groping fingers, and the ravenous fury with which he applied himself took over his senses. Soon he forgot where he was, the trees, the droplets of rain, the chill in his spine, the blows of the lashing wind—all fell away, and he was alone with the earth, digging relentlessly, heedless of the stones that made his fingers bleed and the stiffness settling in his limbs.

The skies had cleared, and the cold stars and full moon were his only witnesses. Into the early hours of night he dug, until the deep pit was complete. Then with slow reverence, he cradled Mikhail's head one last time, kissing his brow in devotion, and lifted him into the grave.

As the emptiness settled in, Oswald rose to his feet and smoothed the earth over the grave. Then, without hesitation, he set off into the woods for the laborious task of fetching stones for the cairn. He sought them one by one, searching for those most fitting for the task. Some he discarded without inspection, and others he cast away after much dark thought. When he found one that was just right, he would hold it like a precious gem, setting it carefully upon the grave.

The arduous task took much of the night, but the moonlight led the way and he wavered not, and felt no creeping weariness dull his senses. The stones were often revealed to him by the striking moonlight, and it seemed that he felt their cold core as they responded to his touch. His mind suspended its sanity for the moment in grief, but his thoughts were clear and ruthless.

When the task was near completion, fatigue began to descend upon him. Yet still he persevered till his bones ached and his fingernails split and broke, paining him with every movement. He hauled the last stones and erected them grimly, feeling his pain lessen. Then he fell beside the cairn to rest.

OSWALD STIRRED AS dawn approached. His mind was still clouded with grief and sleep, but he felt a presence nearby. He inspected the cairn he had built on Mikhail's grave the night before, feeling as though something watched him. He circled the clearing tentatively, the crunching of his footsteps on the frosted field unnerving him. Then the shivers down his spine renewed. Looking back at the cairn, he beheld a tall figure standing by, watching him almost predatorily. As he neared the cairn cautiously, he noticed that the figure was not human. He halted hesitantly, taking in the curved horns and long, golden, braided hair.

The Horned God approached Oswald with the dawn light shivering through the pristine skies behind him. The grey of his filmy, silken robes shifted and ran with his every movement, forming patterns like leaf veins or the golden sap of trees. His clear eyes were limpid pools of the clearest waters, and Oswald lowered his eyes in shame, for he felt small and of little consequence, deformed and ugly. Before him the Horned God halted, and Oswald forced himself to look up into his face. He seemed to see mirrors in those eyes, his naked soul reflected there, stripped bare of all pretense, as if it were weighed by the one who held the balance of the cosmic infinite chaos.

"I see you naked before me, your living soul before my eyes," came the solemn voice of the Horned God.

Oswald inhaled sharply and averted his eyes to the ground where lilies had sprung at the god's feet. "How shall one such as myself address the likes of your majesty, O eldest father of the earth?" Oswald was painfully aware that his voice was brittle and riddled with sin.

The Horned God stirred and addressed the trees. "They know me by many names and countless epithets, each one a shard and facet of the same gem and the same reality. All are fragments of a forgotten name whose power you shall never be blessed enough to know. I am Cernunnos, the Horned God, the initiator into the mysteries of apotheosis, watcher over the nine worlds and the Twilit Realms. But now let me see your face!"

The undeniable command in his voice was like the crack of a whip, and Oswald turned to meet his gaze. Many years later he would still remember those clear eyes like glass, the impassive and cold visage unravaged by time, in which he saw his fate and finally understood the beginning of his long journey beyond the veil and the weighty tribulations that awaited him. Those eyes held his doom.

"I have come to break you apart and forge you anew, for you are of the loyal few that merit our pity. We have chosen to give you a worthier task. You shall become father to a new order, shepherd over a lost flock that you shall tend, deathless, till Mikhail returns and relieves you of the stewardship. We shall strip you of yourself and reclothe you anew, that you may be born of a stronger matter and deeper knowledge. Do you accept?" The eyes blazed into a conflagration whence merged together all of the resounding energies of the cosmos, and Oswald recoiled in horror.

"But I am not worthy, and I know not what task you are bestowing upon me. What if I fail?" he asked.

The Horned God smiled, his face cruelly beautiful. "We shall rebuild you of a stronger material than you are made of now, and your feeble mind will soon be a bygone memory. I will pass you through the gates of the threefold death, where you shall die and be dissembled by the old demons that molded the shamans. They will break you down and build you up till you are a fitting conduit for our will. Are you afraid?" The mocking tone was a blade, and Oswald felt a surge of his habitual pride.

"I am worthy for the task," he said, squaring his shoulders defiantly. "Fashion me into an instrument so fierce it shall reap the souls of these damned ones like a scythe before the hay."

The elven king smiled at him with lucent eyes, and before Oswald could decipher the malice that lurked within, he had lifted one quick hand. The velocity struck him in one single, ruthless blow.

35

THE THREEFOLD DEATH

For the knife to snap, for the vein to drip, for the fleeing red
To leave behind the whitened flesh, errant snaking stream
Seeking whatever awning chasm to collide, across the ground to spread
Making of life's endless musings, a derisible human dream

Few things will turn a human into a god, but since we are not discussing gods, I will dwell on the others; the sages, wizards, and magicians. Throughout the ages there have been many initiates that passed through death and emerged from it, either victorious or forever crazed. I will not dwell on the ones who failed but the ones who triumphed. Mithra, Horus, Myrddin, Odin, Lug, and yes, Christ, were all initiates of the threefold death. Few are they who survive this hidden path, to wield the black key made of glass. The Impenetrable Door.

FIRST YOU ARE awake. But you realize that you aren't alone, though you do not know who is prowling nearby. You are somewhere indescribable—somewhere else, another plain, another forest, another indistinguishable, forgotten glade. But this is nothing like the earth you know. In fact you cannot hear anyone or anything. Perhaps everything is drowned by the clamor of your own heartbeat, all too loud, attracting hostile attention. You are aware of your breathing, too, that you are prey, naked and forsaken, somewhere unsafe. If delirium were a sickness, then you have it. It devours your sanity and the frenzy is a deafening chaos that plunges your body into agony, and your mind into the excruciating throes of depravity.

Anxiety, paranoia, and horror ride your body like violent paroxysms. You scream, fighting the impulses flooding through you. Then you realize your mistake all too late. They are already here for you. They are irrevocably drawn out of the whispering shadows having smelled your fear. They are watching you now with lurid, soulless eyes, malevolent and red as burning coals. Their faces are from your darkest nightmares—primeval beasts with rapacious jaws and razor-sharp claws of steel. They lust for blood and carnage, and their horror is only surpassed by the ruthlessness in their eyes as it excoriates your soul. Then you know the first darkness; the primordial fear that lurks in the dark. They are the ones we have feared all along, those bred of the very blackness of the fallen archdemons' souls—the excrement of infamy, the very defiling force of life.

And then you are nothing more than food. They rip at your flesh and tear it with their hooked claws. Your cries only elicit their mocking laughter as their fangs crunch your bones and lap up the blood. You are nothing more than a dripping carcass of blood and guts. But you stay alive, somehow, your disembodied voice lingers. The agony amplifies to such heights that your pleas for mercy soon turn to curses, and you are hurled beyond the gates of reason. Your logical, rational mind has ruptured like those lungs and liver they have savagely ripped from you and relished. You are cognizant of the pain of each bite, each gnawing of bone, while your sanity irreparably crumbles. The separation between the conscious and subconscious mind comes crashing down, and you are raving, dying a thousand deaths.

Even your mind is not immune to the torture, for they are taunting every naked thought you ever possessed. Then they defile your memories, dissecting and discarding them carelessly. Like heated pokers wielded by expert hands into flayed flesh, they extinguish each one and char it to a blackened nothingness. Then you howl to the unforgiving skies like a rabid beast, an unwilling subject to the arts they have contrived for your torture. Your mangled body is contorted and twisted, and the blood on their faces and jaws is ruby red. They lust for more, but nothing is left. Your shrieking, naked soul is burning in their baleful eyes as their infernal infamy, the depths of ultimate decay, is revealed.

Then they set about deconstructing your personality. You no longer own your thoughts, nor any of your vices or virtues. They have severed them from you, cruelly asphyxiated till they become neutralized, distant components of a faraway dream. Your consciousness struggles and fights back, but they tear it away harder. Weeping, you give in to oblivion, to the destruction of your self. You fall into the noiseless void that is deeper than the slumber of death. The completed obliteration of your body and soul is revealed, and you are erased from memory and existence. There is nothing left of your earthly imprint but your last mortal cries before you became the banquet of the demons.

—⟨∞⟩—

THEN YOU ARE alive again, like light newly kindled into being. You exist. You are naked, crawling pitifully on your knees like an animal, and you have forsaken the power of speech. You moan and groan hideously, and your futile attempts to think are clouded with the dull memory of impending pain. But you know where you are going. Right in front of you is a large, boiling cauldron. The fires beneath it are licking at its rim, dancing in vivid spires. From that cauldron emanates smoke and fumes, and they rise like dark plumes into an oblivious grey sky. The bubbling is impatient and crude, harsh on your ears and coarsely demanding.

You understand. It cannot be ignored, and its demands cannot be placated further. So you crawl towards it like a beast, the stones on the ground digging into your weakened flesh and the dust filling your nostrils and choking you of breath. Urgency grips you, and a growing frenzy sends tremors into your spine. You dig your broken nails into the unyielding ground, unwilling to cede, and your desperation prevails. You continue your delirious crawl towards the cauldron. The heat is scorching hot now, and you can taste the sweat on your grimy skin.

You have arrived now. The cauldron is large, and many strange runes are etched upon it that your broken mind cannot comprehend. Many figures are drawn on it, too, in various positions of torture, but your eyes are too unfocused to see. The odor of the concoction is putrid, but your nose has been long accustomed to the repugnant reek of graves. The fires, unyielding to your supplications, lash at you, trying to partake of your flesh, and you oblige. Rising to your feet, you clamber into the cauldron unceremoniously with a mighty splash. Then you howl your lungs out till they rupture.

An old woman with stygian eyes is stirring the cauldron. There are no whites to those eyes, and no mercy in her immovable, callous stare. She mixes strange herbs and sings in a deathly litany of sound. Then she begins to peel your skin from your body, inch by inch, reaping a shrill cry with each cut. She scalps you with relentless agility, and you cannot elude the grasp of her gnarled hands as you plead futilely, earning her rebukes.

When she is finished, she rips out your muscles, severing them from arm to leg dexterously and with deliberation. You curse yourself, turning your appeals to the heavens and the devil, but she seems both deaf and cruel as she smiles with the tenderness of a lover. The trees around the cauldron are now littered with slivers of your carved flesh as ravens squawk ominously overhead. Your severed mind is set above the cauldron to watch and relive the agony of your disembowelment while your bones are broiled and bleached.

This could have been a day or a week, for the endless, languishing torture transcends all the dimensions of hell. But then she comes again to the cauldron and seeks your bones. She binds them back together with her incantations, and the skeleton becomes whole again. Then she clothes it afresh with blood and vessels, and it shines raw in the morose light. Then the flesh comes anew, fresh and sinewy. Then the new, pristine skin. And when you are returned, reassembled in your previous likeness, you weep with immeasurable relief, then fall into oblivion.

YOU ARE STRUGGLING for your life against a giant serpent, its fangs dripping poison. You strive to prove your temerity and the mettle of your spirit. You do not wish to die again and decompose into the darkness of the demonic hells. You wield your mind, your soul, your essence, and engage with the serpent for your right to exist. You do not plead or cajole, for you know the reward of both shall be the cruelest death imaginable. You win and she accepts. She nods and you fall into the abyss.

You are alive and in a beautiful glade. The sunlight is warm upon your unmarred skin. The music of the birds fills your buzzing ears with joy, and your heart is light like a feather. You are hanging from a yew tree by a rope suspended precariously above the ground. You struggle and the rope tightens, and yet you cannot die. Your life is gently squeezed out of you, and your body is alight with ecstasy and pain. You convulse and tremble, and each tremor sends your mind into further chaotic realms of consciousness. You have broken the doors of death and stand in its pathway between both worlds, each pulling harder with opposing force, fragmenting your mind.

You are aware and alive and your eyes see for the first time; the tree's veins and the breathing of its leaves, the sound of the light falling upon your face, and the names of the runes it was fashioned with. The speech of the wind is revealed to you, as well as the wrathful pride of earth that is beckoning for you to fall into its embrace. Days go by, and you understand the patterns of matter and thought and discover the will that forges existence and the secret codes of magic that peel away the dead layers of dimensions.

Your mind threatens to cave in and divulge its craving for death, and it is denied it again. It is chastised and taunted, stretched as far as the stars till it is gossamer thin. Then it detaches itself entirely from the reality of earth, set free to roam astride the solar flare. You are singing the music of death and staring into the eyes of the deathly warden, withheld from his clutches, and all the layers of space and time converge on you, and your mind is sliced away.

Nothing exists outside of the thought of the divine. Outside of the confines of space and time reigns the eternal ruler upon his throne. We are breathing inside the womb of existence, and we are contained in its material grasp of thought made reality. And that reality is pure illusion, restored through will. Whoever wields the will is master of creation.

There is no such thing as the mind, for it is merely constructed of thought and memory and ideology. Combined, we are walking echoes mirroring each other, decaying organisms that thrive to die, our uniqueness lost in our ultimate weakness. You fall from the tree supine, and you look up at the revealed skies as you grasp the runes that have been offered to you.

Leaning against a tree resting, your eyes filled with the magnitude of the wonders of nature, you understand the patterns of the ants and the dances of the bees before you. But you are not resting; the spear at your side has pinned you to the tree, and your torn innards are quivering, though you have now forgotten the meaning of pain. Your blood runs freely, and you offer it to the ground as a sacrificial libation to the watchful spirits. Your heat you donate back to the tree, a token of grief for the spear that has pierced it.

You are patient for the process of the slow death, and your ragged breath becomes a meditation. You cede to the pain as if it were the embrace of a fiery lover, savoring its scorching lashes, its relentlessness. You admire its poignancy and its role in creation, acknowledging its purpose in the scheme of things as you exhale your life force, the rigidity of death dethroning you from life. Night falls, and your vision grows dark till you can no longer see. Then blackness envelops you tightly, pressing against your eyes, and you fall away again.

You are kneeling reverently, naked beside the river, contemplating its continuity and grace. Then a mighty weariness around your neck grips you and you realize there is a millstone around it. You nod and rise to your feet, swaying slightly, and without a second thought or regret cast yourself in. There is no interlude to the plunge but the whistling of the wind and the coldness of the whipping waters. You are stripped of breath, hurled down to depths unknown. You are long dead before you hit the bottom, and you are no longer bound to the body of mortality you grew accustomed to. You ponder in that darkness like a child in the womb, ensconced in the bosom of the river. You have seen the earth give in to time, but the water endures in its course towards the sea, forever echoing the primordial music of infinity.

———∞∞∞———

OSWALD WAS AWAKE again, and this time he recognized the habitual noises and odors of the earth. For a moment he braced himself, waiting for the insatiable pain to seize him. But nothing happened. He was himself, but not. He was Oswald by name, but the memory of what he used to be was a long dead echo. His old self seemed transient, feeble, as if it were a shadow from a former lifetime, callow and unworthy of his current thoughts and precise machinations. He stirred now, sighing as he lifted himself to his feet, breathing in deeply.

It was noon and the sun was at its zenith, beaming from the skies like a beacon. Oswald smiled with assurance. His hair had grown long behind him, and his ashen grey beard now fell unkempt to his belt. He was clothed in long robes of the palest blue girt with a simple leather belt which held a long sheathe. He removed the blade from it curiously, examining it carefully, observing the runes and the fine filigree patterns on the hilt. Then he noticed by his feet a long gnarled staff. It was black, knotted, and crudely shaped, like a spindle whorl bound with several gnarled boughs. He understood what it meant instantly, and as he grasped it in his right hand, he felt the power surge from his body into it and awaken the spirit within. It knew him and his name, and responded to him with the coldness of a dormant fiend. Only then did he notice that his hands were tattooed with an interlacing pattern. Rolling back his sleeves, he saw that the design climbed up his arms. That he also understood.

The cairn stood as it had before, unmoved by the events that had befallen Oswald. He approached it with quiet reverence, seeing it with the fresh eyes of wisdom as a mere resting place for the mortal body. With a whisper he struck the cairn with his staff. White fire blossomed around it in a circle in the broad daylight. Now whoever approached it would be dissuaded from their purpose, for the fires would leap into the shape of armed men and burn whoever tried to disturb the stones. He bowed low before the cairn, then turned his back on the clearing and made his way out of the woods.

He was Oswald by name only, and even to that name he no longer belonged. He had died many deaths and come back again, purged from life and its futility through the perverse arts of initiation. He was truly reborn and truly awake. He was what they would name a wizard or shaman, something of the old world. He laughed softly to himself, thinking over his previous life, feeling nothing but pity for the vapid existence of mortals. And he knew what he needed to do.

He hummed a tune as he walked. Indeed, he was ready for the game ahead . . .

TAMARA LAKOMY is an archaeologist specializing in the occult, shamanistic practices of indigenous people. She runs a foundation operating in East Africa that specializes in the cultural preservation of indigenous tribes and women's rights and education, and she also advises East African governments. Additionally, she is a cofounder and pioneer of Blueprints.org, a global think tank providing sustainable solutions to challenged regions. Lakomy is a priestess in training, having embraced the faith of the Mother Goddess, and is a great animal lover, saving stray and neglected animals in her native country since she was young. She is of Berber (Amazigh) and Slavic descent.